CARTOON NETWORK

ADVENTURE TIME

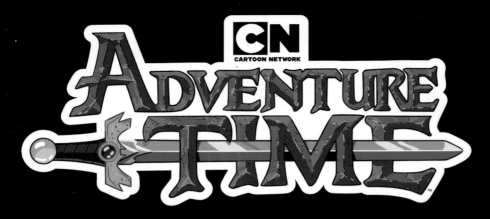

SUGARY SHORTS
VOLUME 5

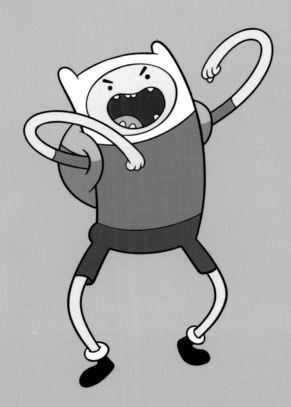

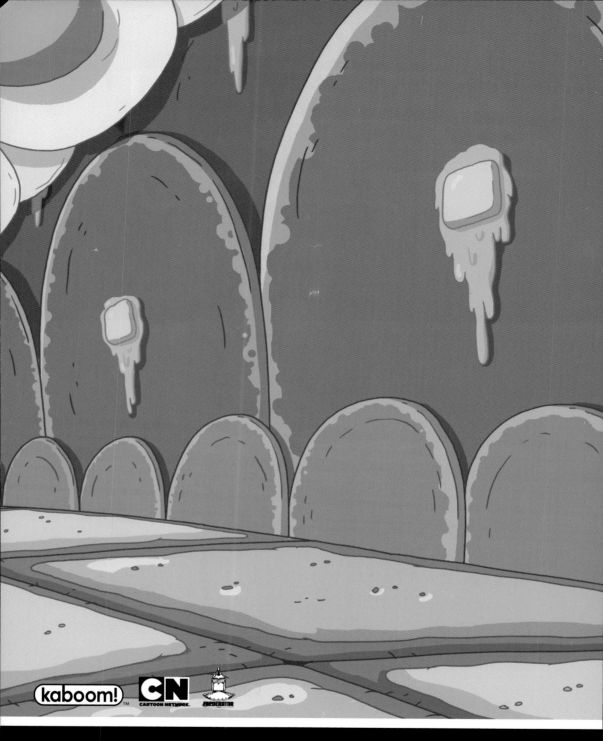

ROSS RICHIE CEO & Founder • JOY HUFFMAN CFO • MATT GAGNON Editor-in-Chief • FILIP SABLIK President, Publishing & Marketing • STEPHEN CHRISTY President, Development • LANCE KREITER Vice President, Licensing & Merchandising
PHIL BARBARO Vice President, Finance & Human Resources • ARUNE SINGH Vice President, Marketing • BRYCE CARLSON Vice President, Editorial & Creative Strategy • SCOTT NEWMAN Manager, Production Design • KATE HENNING Manager, Operations
SPENCER SIMPSON Manager, Sales • SIERRA HAHN Executive Editor • JEANINE SCHAEFER Executive Editor • DAFNA PLEBAN Senior Editor • SHANNON WATTERS Senior Editor • ERIC HARBURN Senior Editor
WHITNEY LEOPARD Editor • CAMERON CHITTOCK Editor • CHRIS ROSA Editor • MATTHEW LEVINE Editor • SOPHIE PHILIPS-ROBERTS Assistant Editor • GAVIN GRONENTHAL Assistant Editor • MICHAEL MOCCIO Assistant Editor
AMANDA LaFRANCO Executive Assistant • JILLIAN CRAB Design Coordinator • MICHELLE ANKLEY Design Coordinator • KARA LEOPARD Production Designer • MARIE KRUPINA Production Designer • GRACE PARK Production Design Assistant
CHELSEA ROBERTS Production Design Assistant • SAMANTHA KNAPP Production Design Assistant • ELIZABETH LOUGHRIDGE Accounting Coordinator • STEPHANIE HOCUTT Social Media Coordinator • JOSÉ MEZA Event Coordinator
HOLLY AITCHISON Operations Coordinator • MEGAN CHRISTOPHER Operations Assistant • RODRIGO HERNANDEZ Mailroom Assistant • MORGAN PERRY Direct Market Representative • CAT O'GRADY Marketing Assistant • BREANNA SARPY Executive Assistant

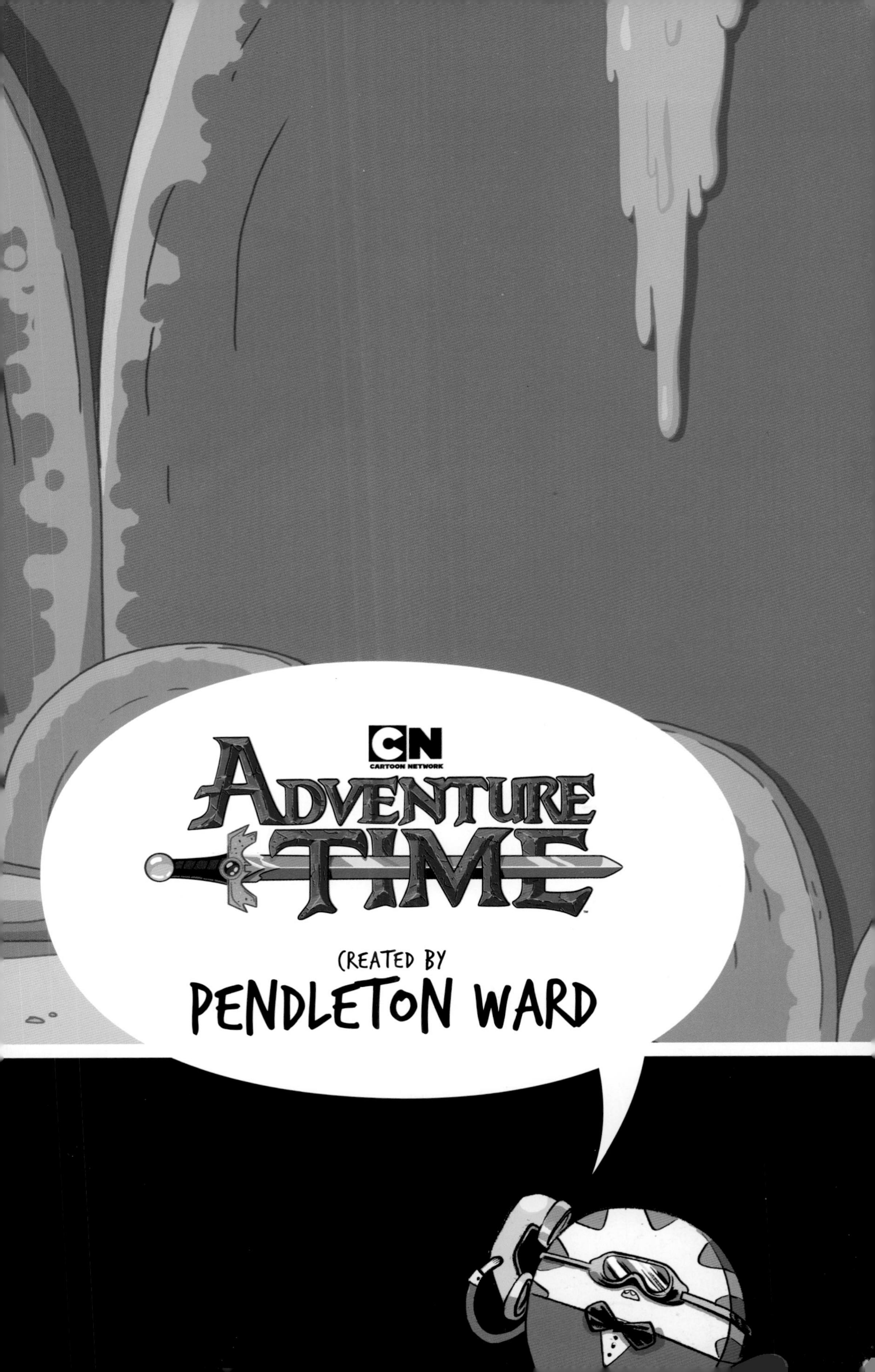
CN
CARTOON NETWORK
ADVENTURE TIME
CREATED BY
PENDLETON WARD

"GIVE US BACK BMO!"

Written and Illustrated by

JEREMY SORESE

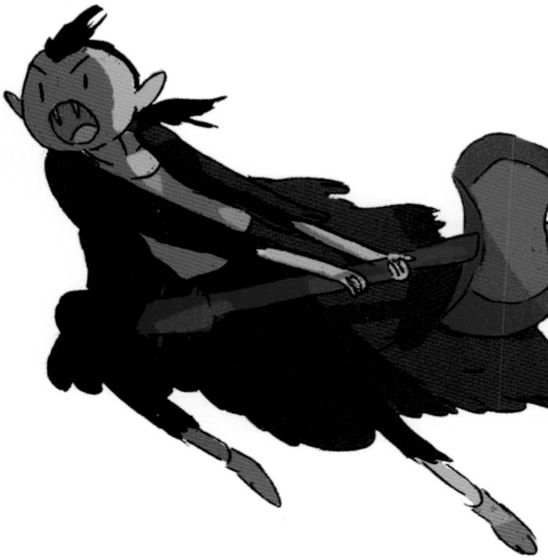

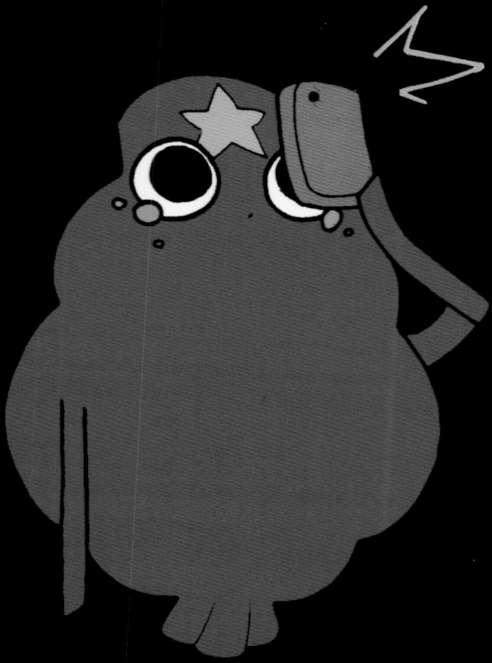

"THE MIND OF GUNTER"

Written and Illustrated by

MEREDITH McCLAREN

Tones by

AMANDA LAFRENAIS

"ADVENTURE TIME WITH BMO!"

Written and Illustrated by

MEREDITH McCLAREN

Cover by

JAMIE COE

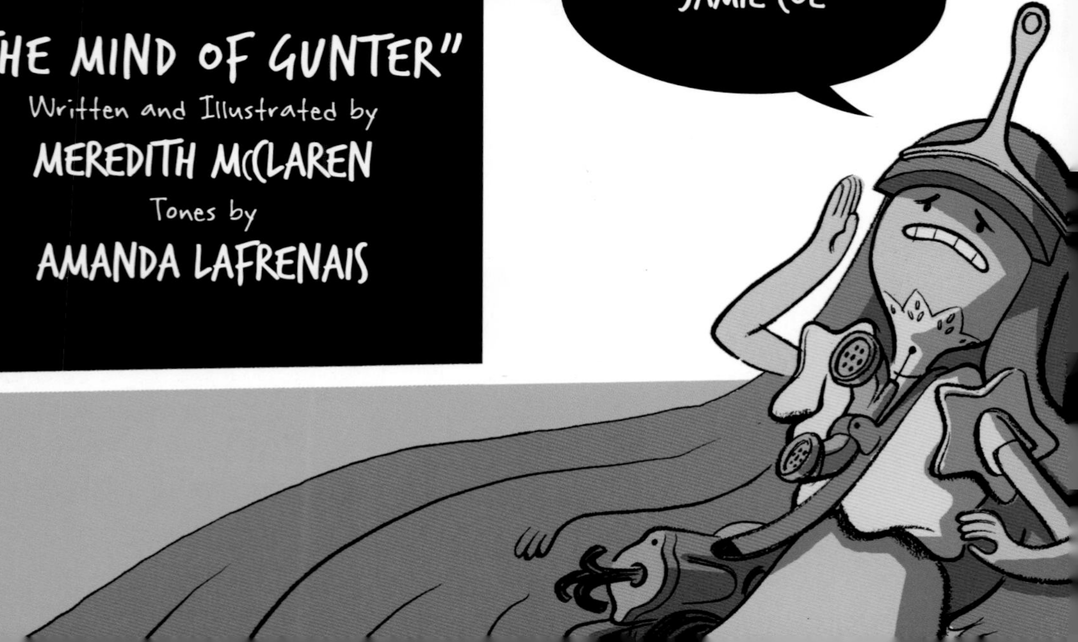

"LSP'S PURSE"
Written and Illustrated by
MEREDITH McCLAREN
Tones by
AMANDA LAFRENAIS

"FOREST PRINCESS GETS A PET"
Written and Illustrated by
MEREDITH McCLAREN

"THE MOON — ECLIPSE"
Written and Illustrated by
HANNA K

"BMO AND FLAN"
Written and Illustrated by
MEREDITH McCLAREN

Designer
CHELSEA ROBERTS

Assistant Editor
MICHAEL MOCCIO

Editor
WHITNEY LEOPARD

With Special Thanks to Marisa Marionakis, Janet No, Becky M. Yang, Conrad Montgomery, Kelly Crews, Scott Malchus, Adam Muto and the wonderful folks at Cartoon Network.

GIVE US BACK BMO!

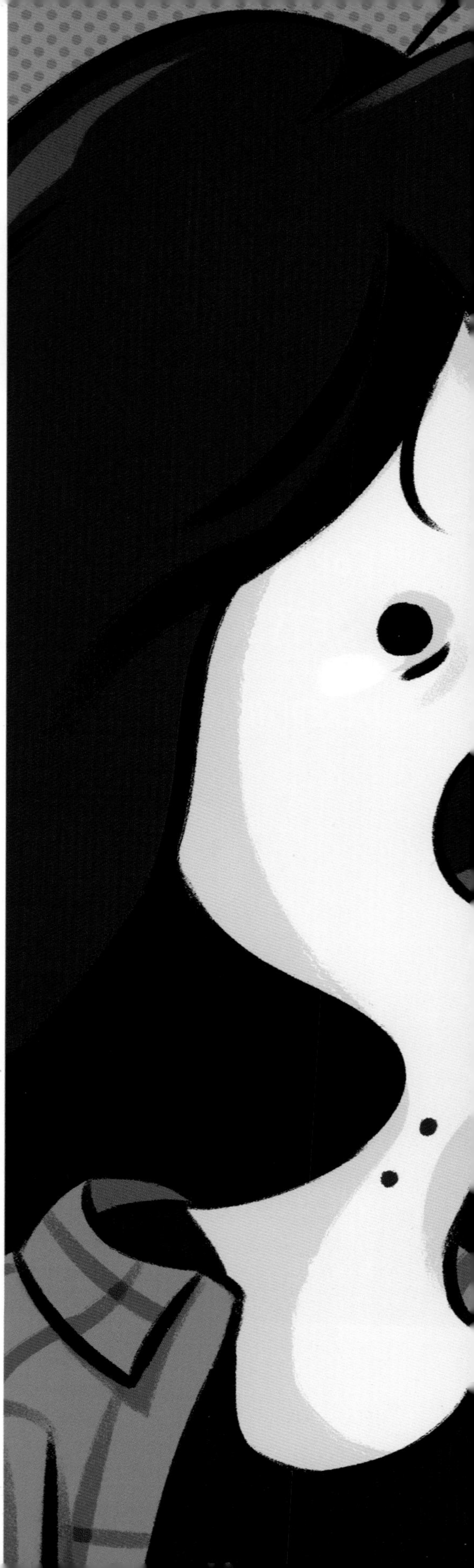

BRETT'S COLLECTOR'S EDITION ISSUE FIFTEEN COVER
JJ HARRISON

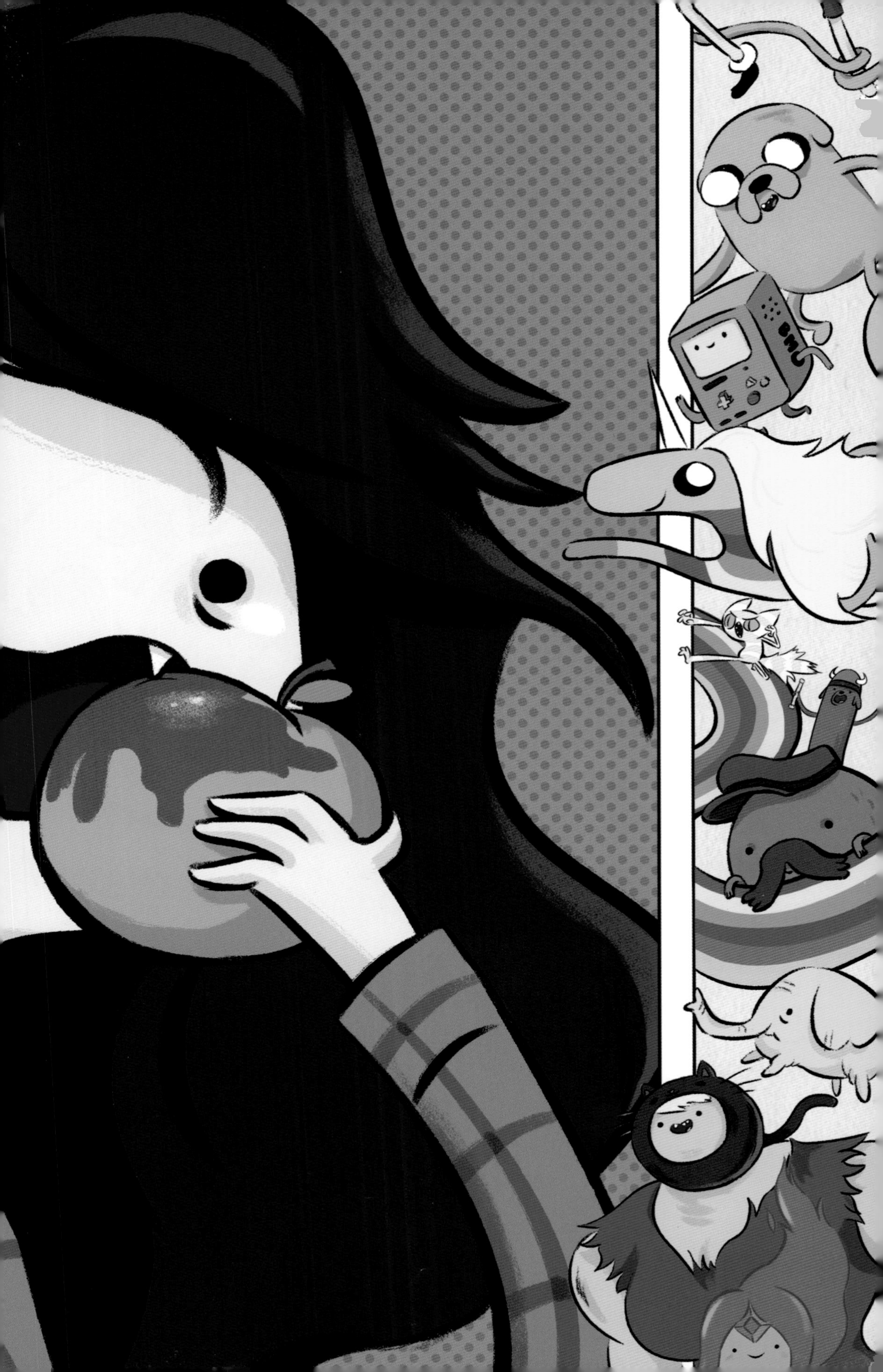

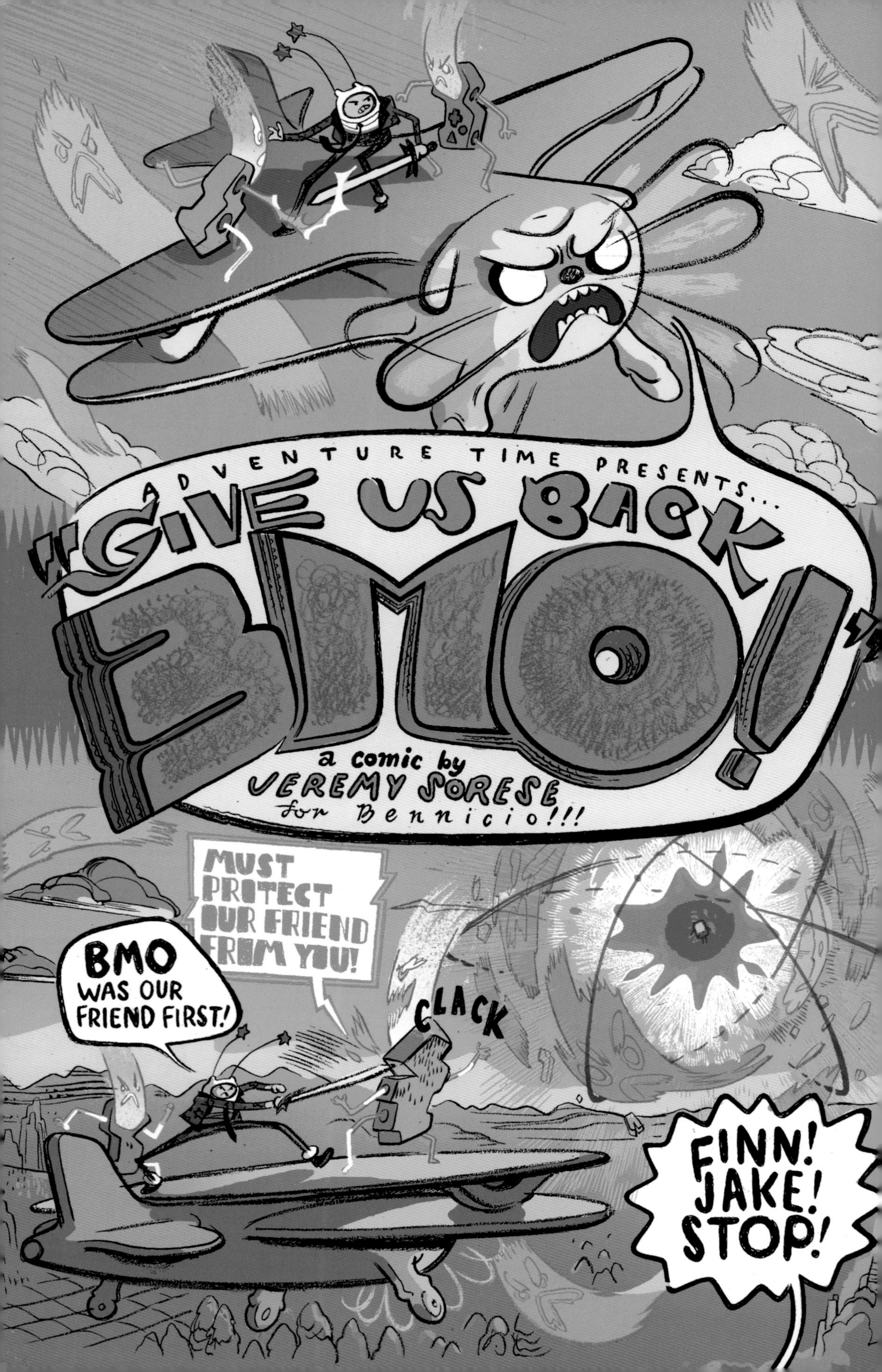
ADVENTURE TIME PRESENTS...
"GIVE US BACK BMO!"
a comic by JEREMY SORESE
for Bennicio!!!
MUST PROTECT OUR FRIEND FROM YOU!
BMO WAS OUR FRIEND FIRST!
CLACK
FINN! JAKE! STOP!

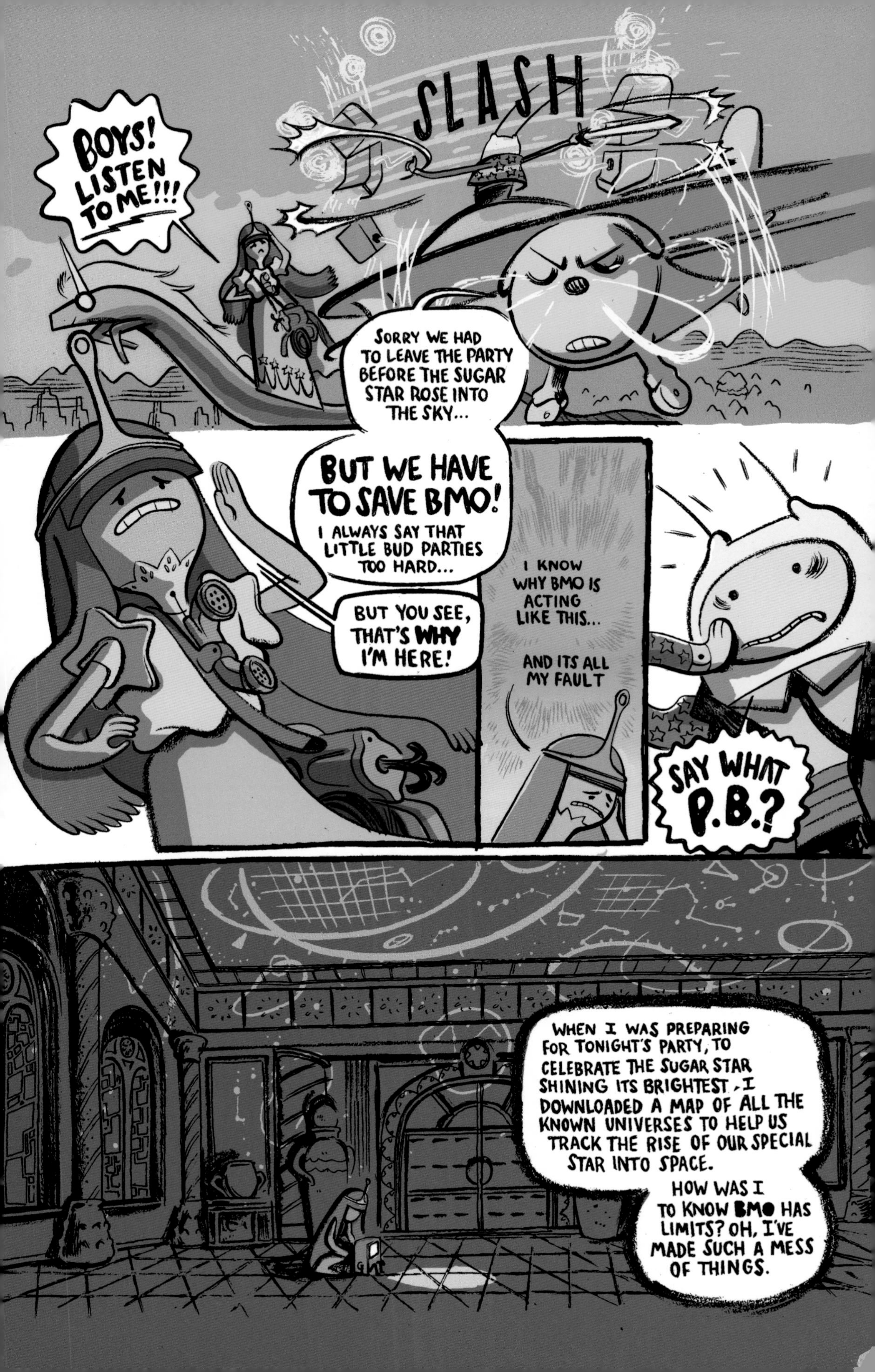

SLASH
BOYS! LISTEN TO ME!!!
SORRY WE HAD TO LEAVE THE PARTY BEFORE THE SUGAR STAR ROSE INTO THE SKY...
BUT WE HAVE TO SAVE BMO!
I ALWAYS SAY THAT LITTLE BUD PARTIES TOO HARD...
BUT YOU SEE, THAT'S WHY I'M HERE!
I KNOW WHY BMO IS ACTING LIKE THIS...
AND ITS ALL MY FAULT
SAY WHAT P.B.?
WHEN I WAS PREPARING FOR TONIGHT'S PARTY, TO CELEBRATE THE SUGAR STAR SHINING ITS BRIGHTEST, I DOWNLOADED A MAP OF ALL THE KNOWN UNIVERSES TO HELP US TRACK THE RISE OF OUR SPECIAL STAR INTO SPACE.
HOW WAS I TO KNOW BMO HAS LIMITS? OH, I'VE MADE SUCH A MESS OF THINGS.

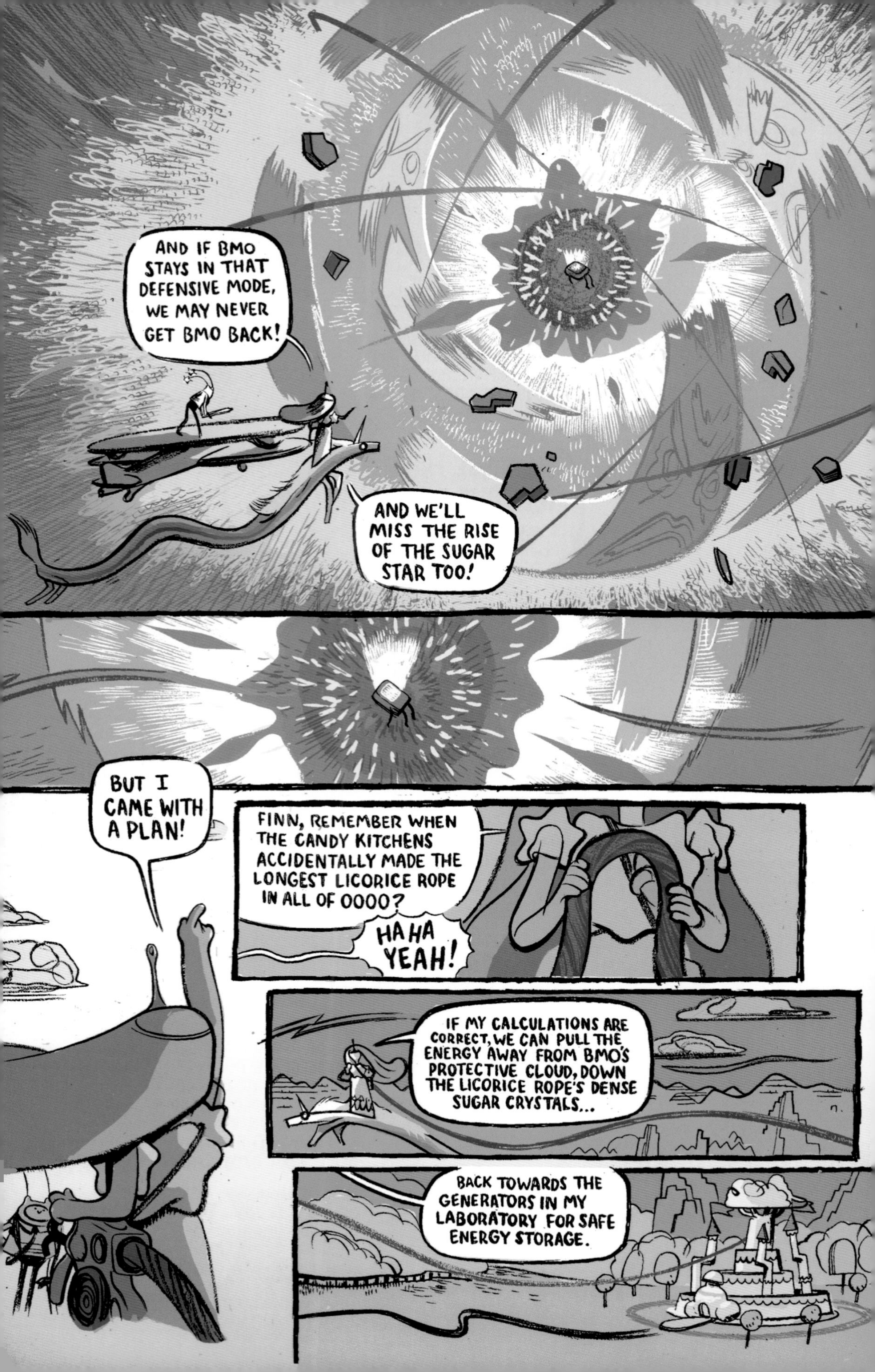

AND IF BMO STAYS IN THAT DEFENSIVE MODE, WE MAY NEVER GET BMO BACK!
AND WE'LL MISS THE RISE OF THE SUGAR STAR TOO!
BUT I CAME WITH A PLAN!
FINN, REMEMBER WHEN THE CANDY KITCHENS ACCIDENTALLY MADE THE LONGEST LICORICE ROPE IN ALL OF OOOO?
HA HA YEAH!
IF MY CALCULATIONS ARE CORRECT, WE CAN PULL THE ENERGY AWAY FROM BMO'S PROTECTIVE CLOUD, DOWN THE LICORICE ROPE'S DENSE SUGAR CRYSTALS...
BACK TOWARDS THE GENERATORS IN MY LABORATORY FOR SAFE ENERGY STORAGE.

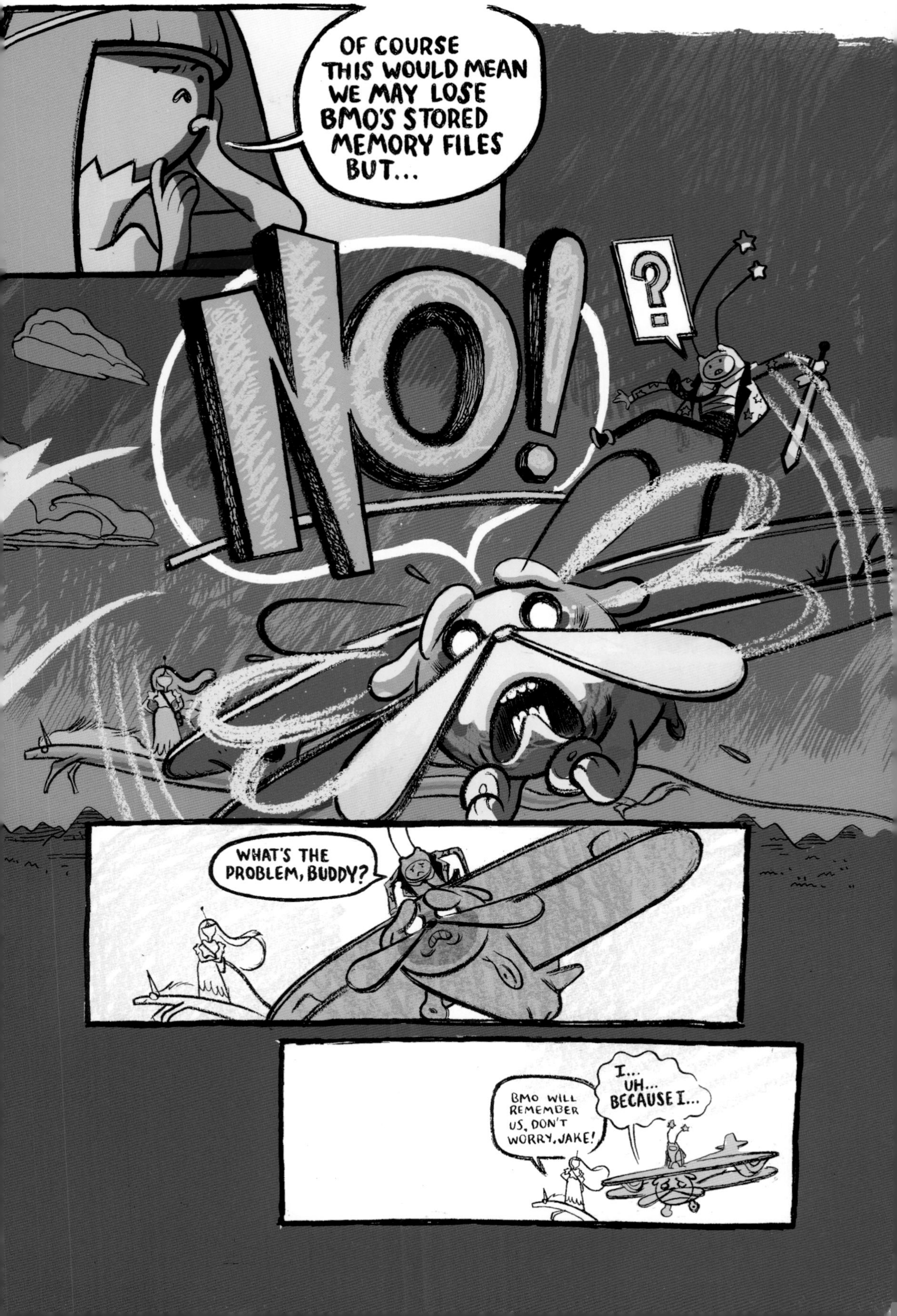
OF COURSE THIS WOULD MEAN WE MAY LOSE BMO'S STORED MEMORY FILES BUT...
NO!
?
WHAT'S THE PROBLEM, BUDDY?
BMO WILL REMEMBER US, DON'T WORRY, JAKE!
I... UH... BECAUSE I...

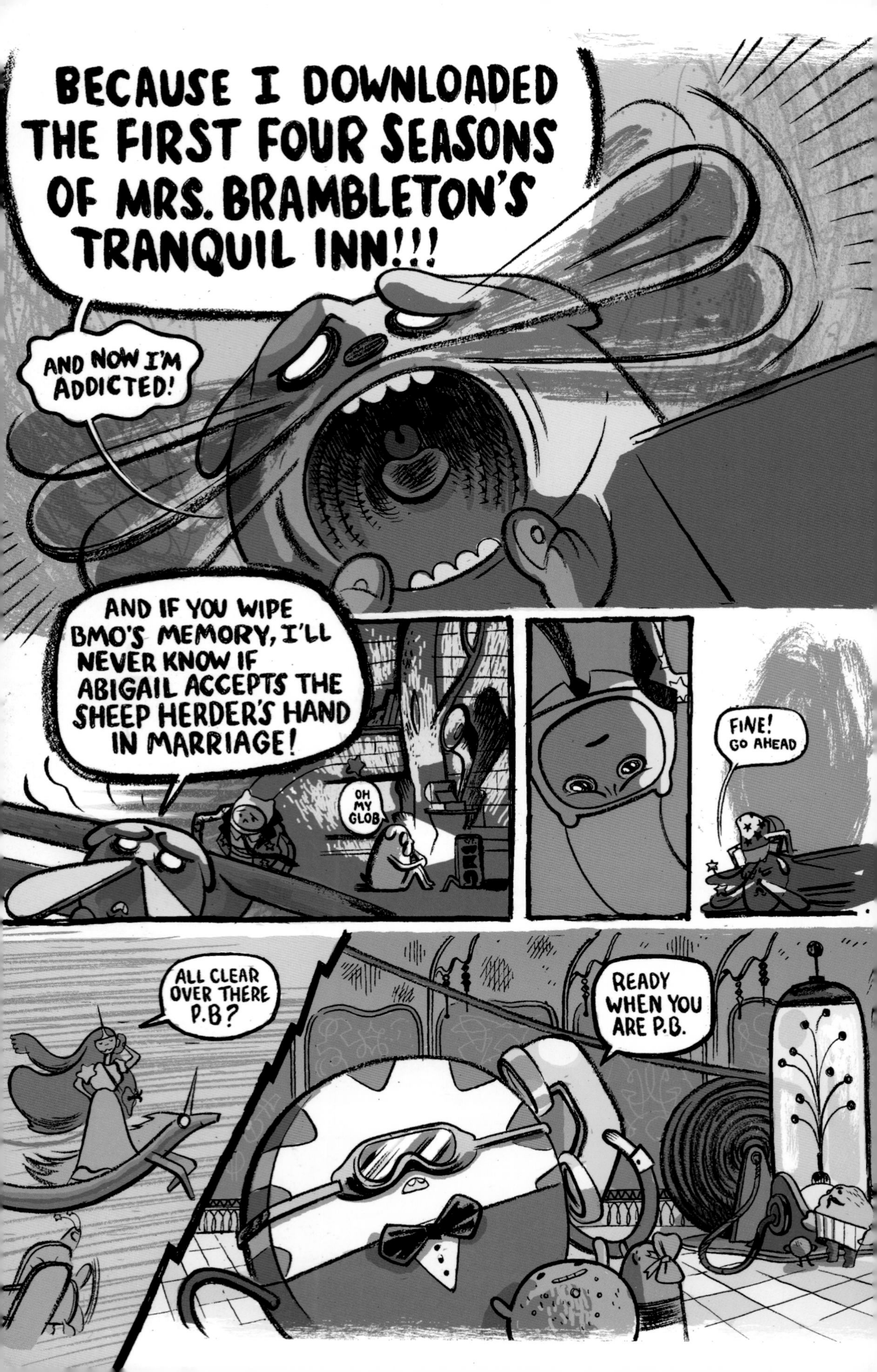
BECAUSE I DOWNLOADED THE FIRST FOUR SEASONS OF MRS. BRAMBLETON'S TRANQUIL INN!!!
AND NOW I'M ADDICTED!
AND IF YOU WIPE BMO'S MEMORY, I'LL NEVER KNOW IF ABIGAIL ACCEPTS THE SHEEP HERDER'S HAND IN MARRIAGE!
OH MY GLOB
FINE! GO AHEAD
ALL CLEAR OVER THERE P.B?
READY WHEN YOU ARE P.B.

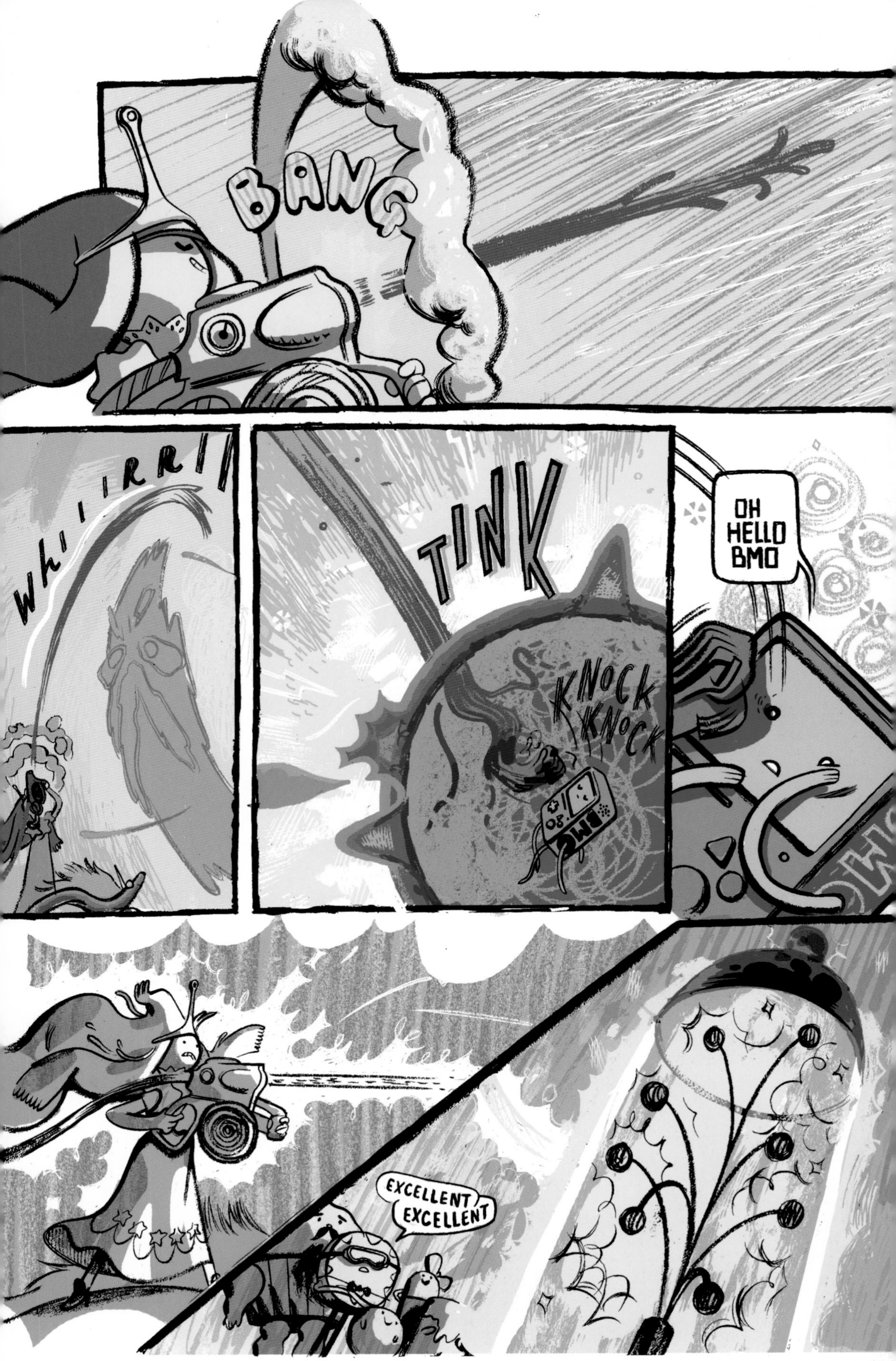

BANG
WHIIIRRR!!
TINK
KNOCK KNOCK
OH HELLO BMO
EXCELLENT, EXCELLENT

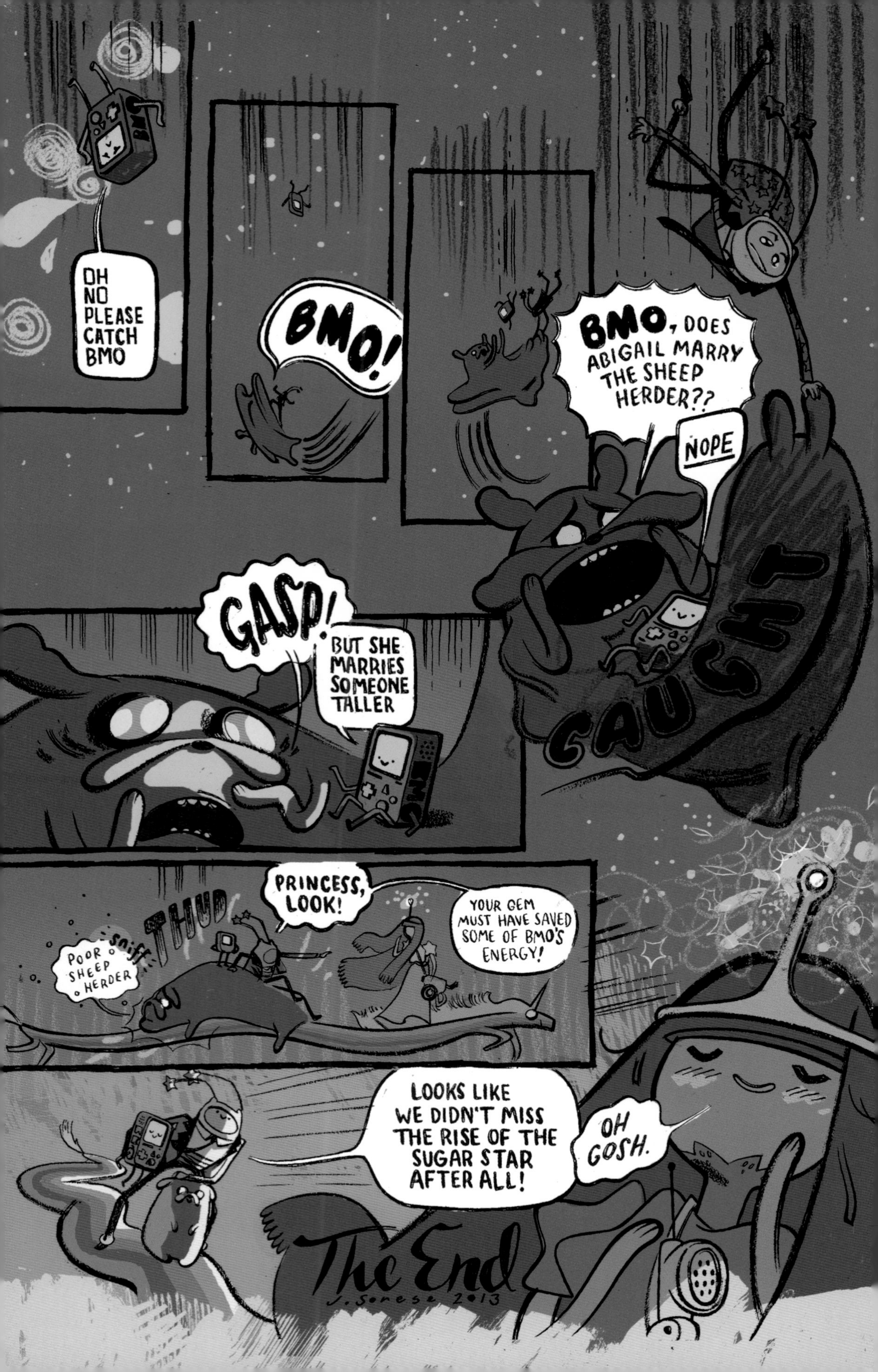
OH NO PLEASE CATCH BMO
BMO!
BMO, DOES ABIGAIL MARRY THE SHEEP HERDER??
NOPE
CAUGHT
GASP!
BUT SHE MARRIES SOMEONE TALLER
THUD
sniff
POOR SHEEP HERDER
PRINCESS, LOOK!
YOUR GEM MUST HAVE SAVED SOME OF BMO'S ENERGY!
LOOKS LIKE WE DIDN'T MISS THE RISE OF THE SUGAR STAR AFTER ALL!
OH GOSH.
The End
J. Sorese 2013

ADVENTURE TIME
WITH BMO

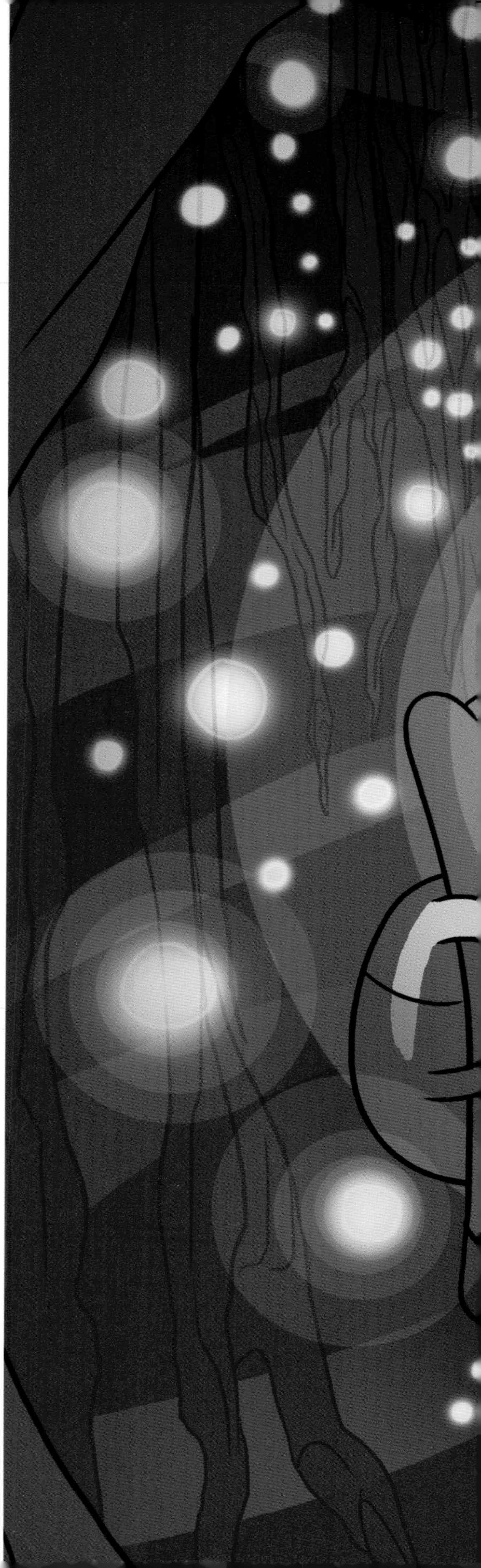

ADVENTURE TIME PLAYING WITH FIRE COVER
STEPHANIE GONZAGA
COLORS BY KASSANDRA HELLER

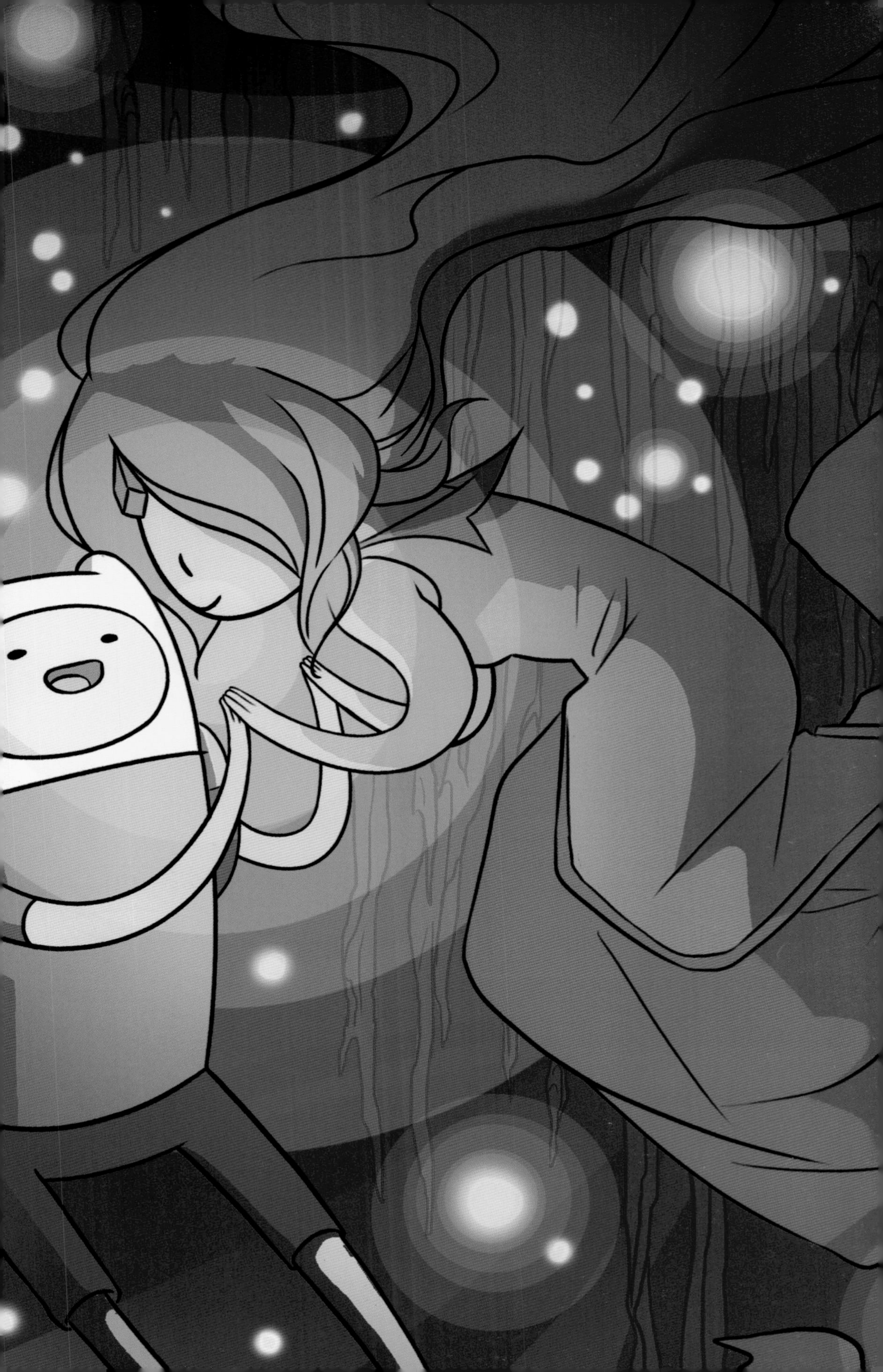

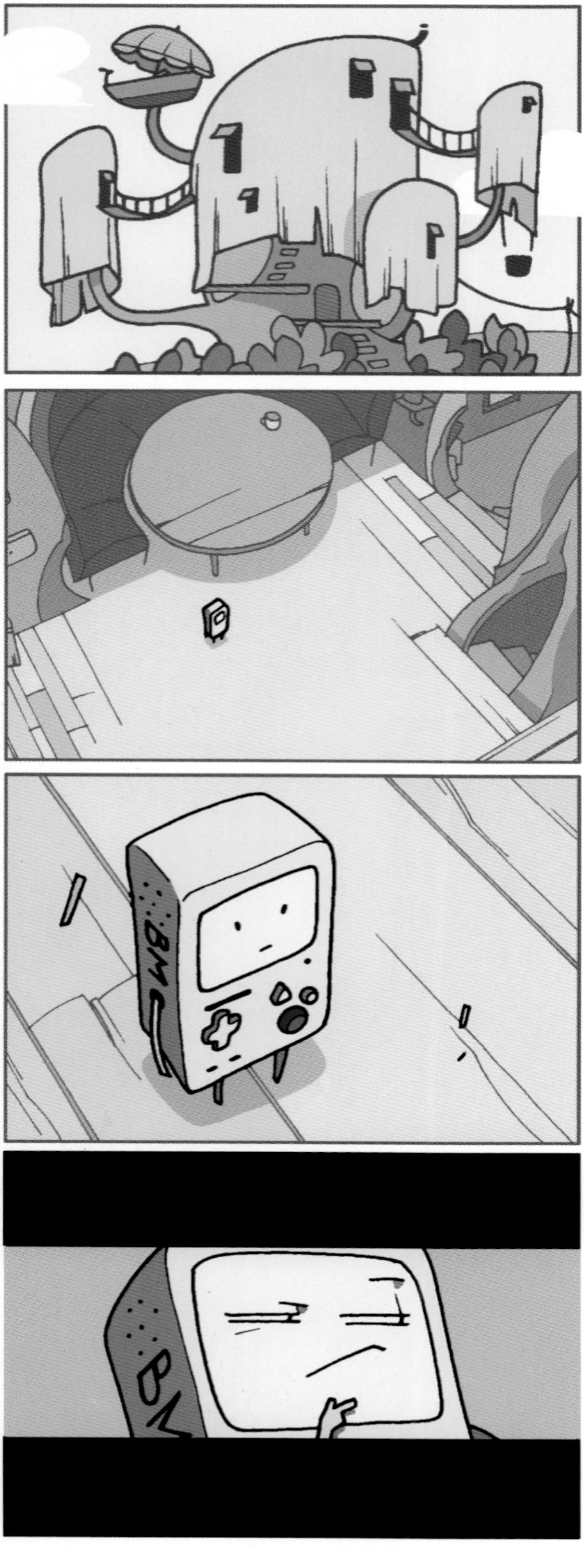
BMO

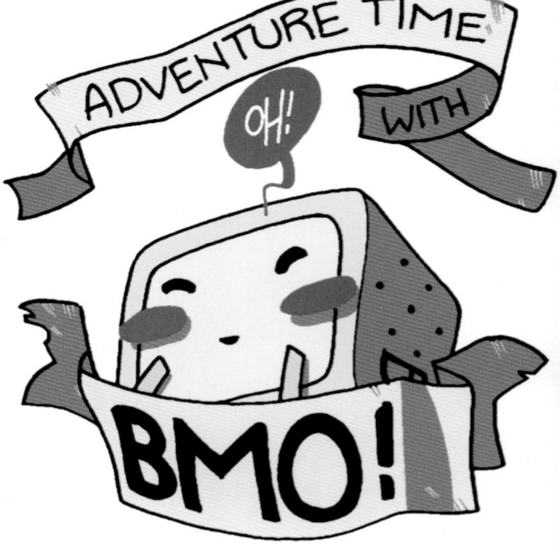
ADVENTURE TIME
OH!
WITH
BMO!

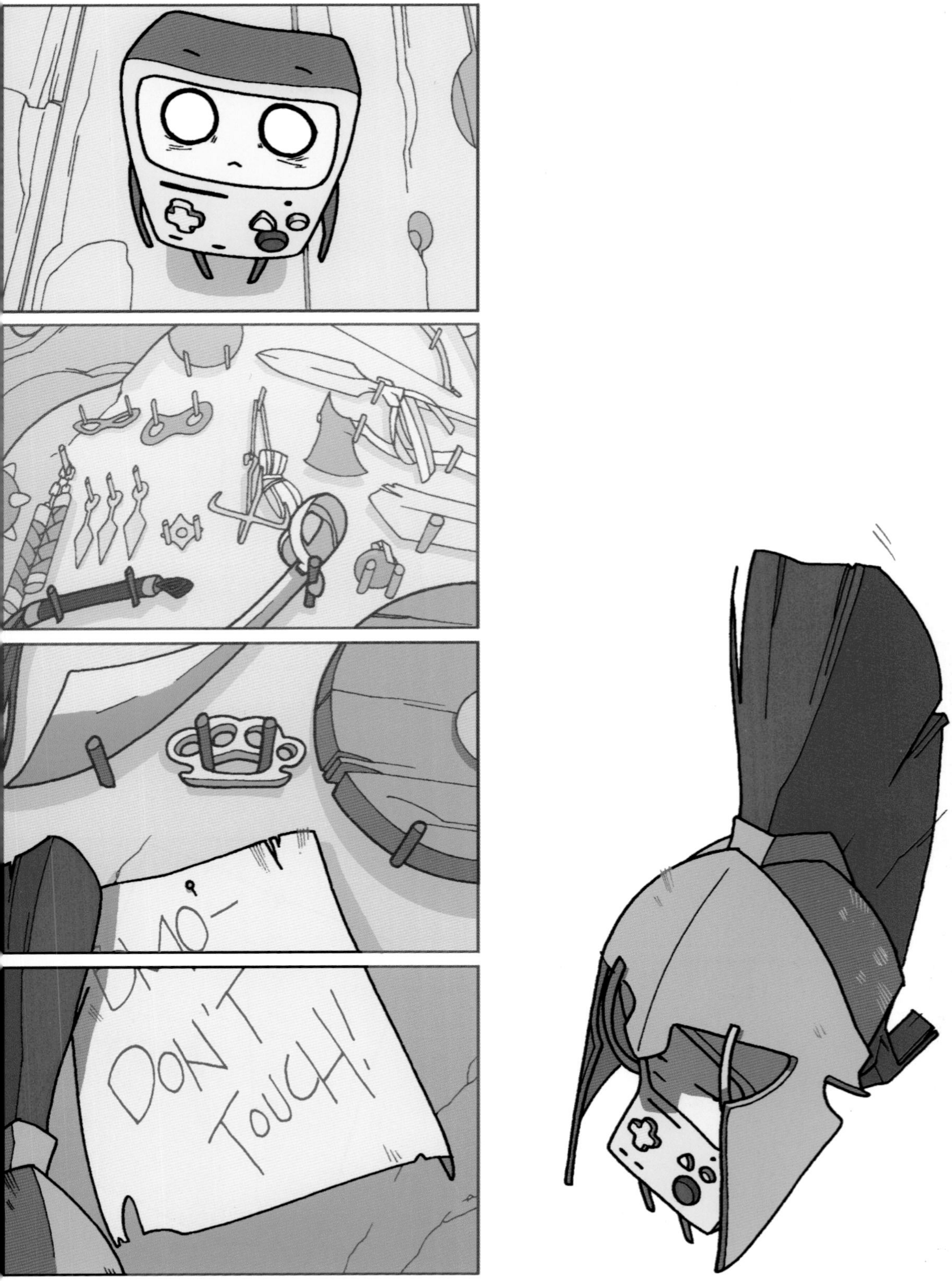
DON'T TOUCH!

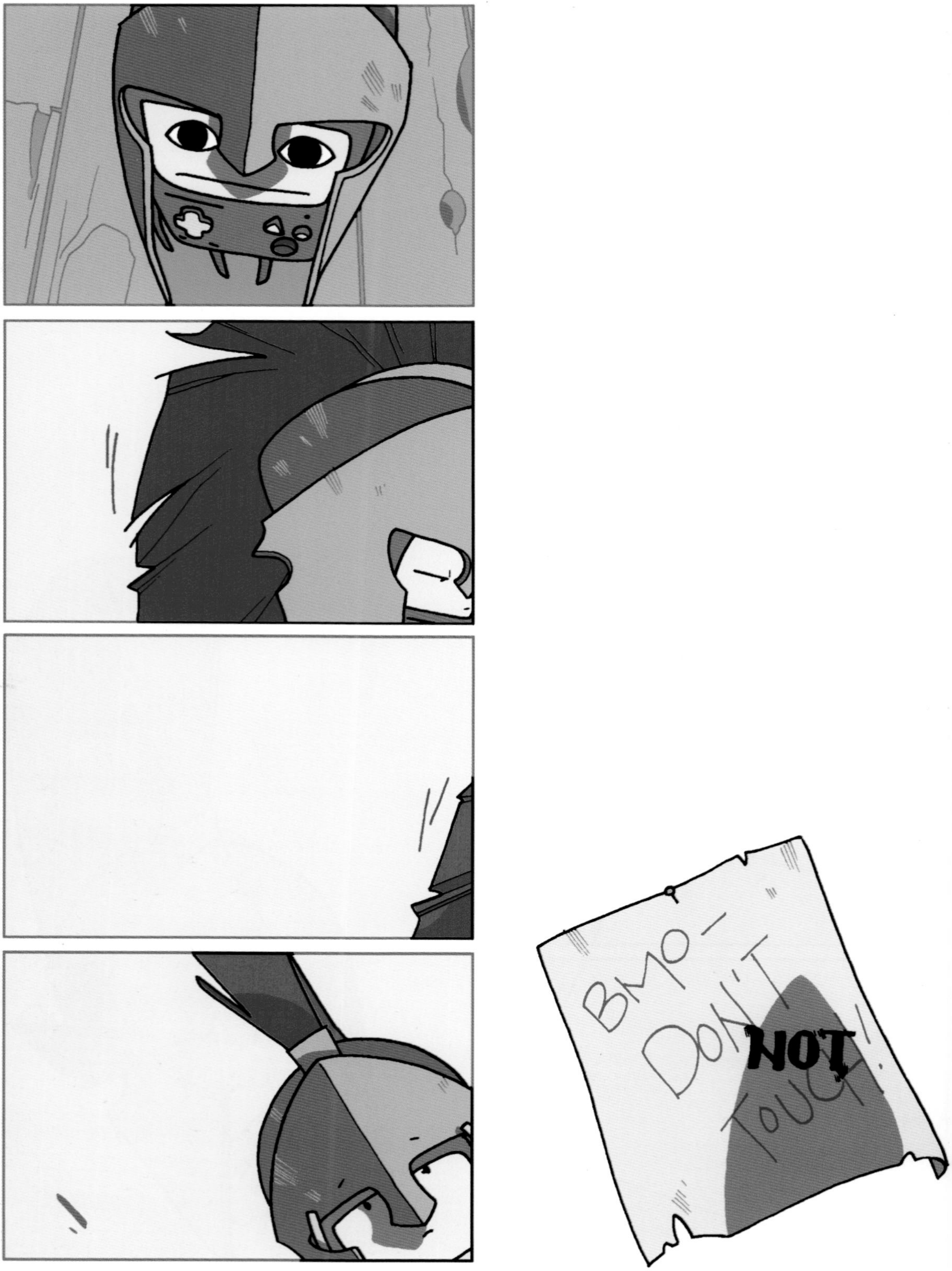
BMO—
DON'T
NOT
TOUCH!

THUNK!

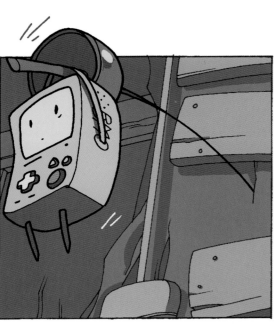

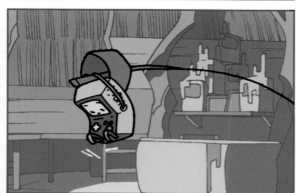

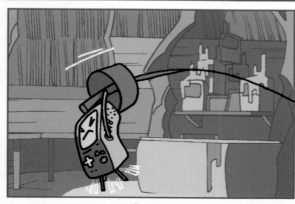

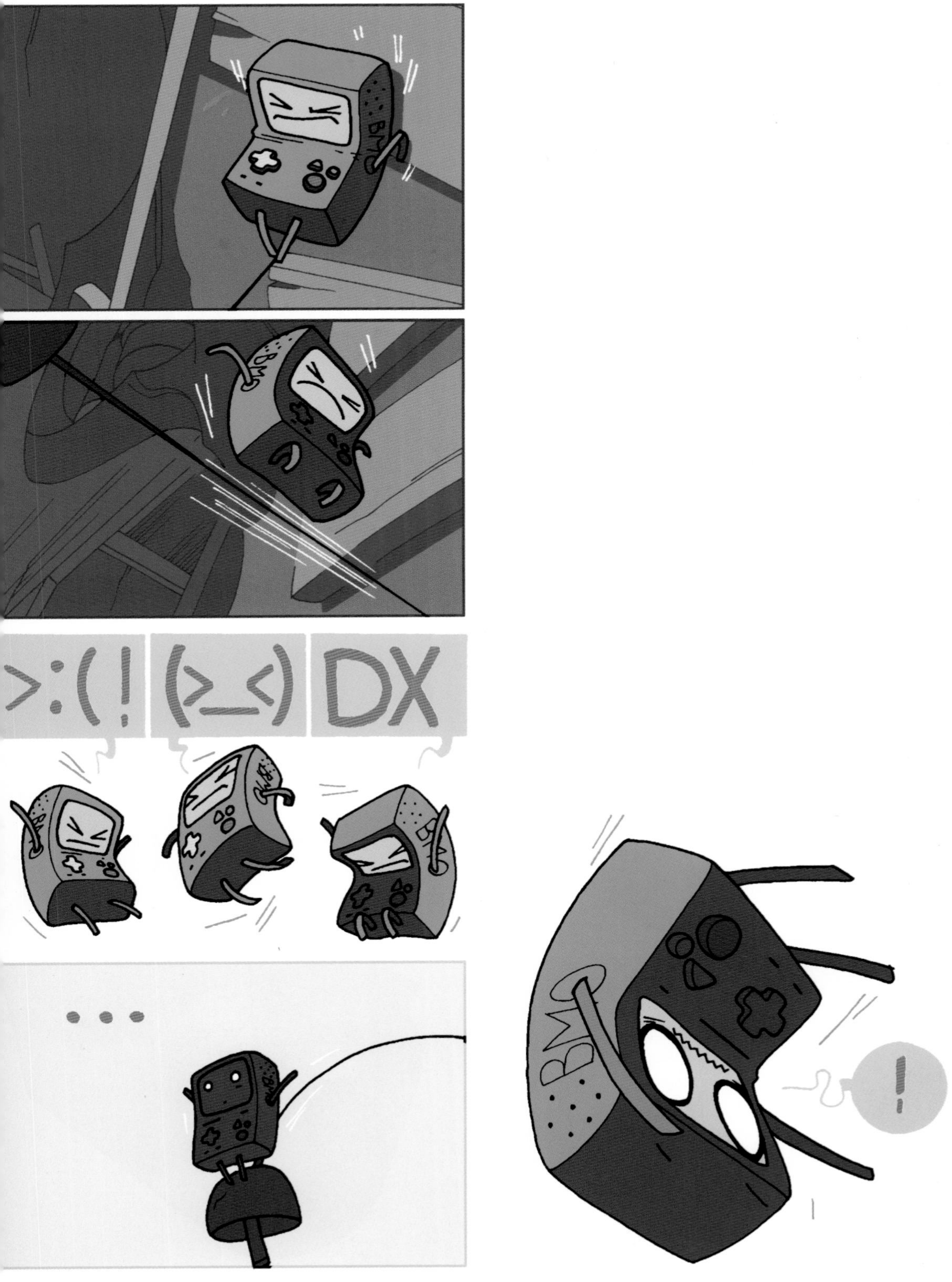

>:(!
(>_<)
DX
...
!

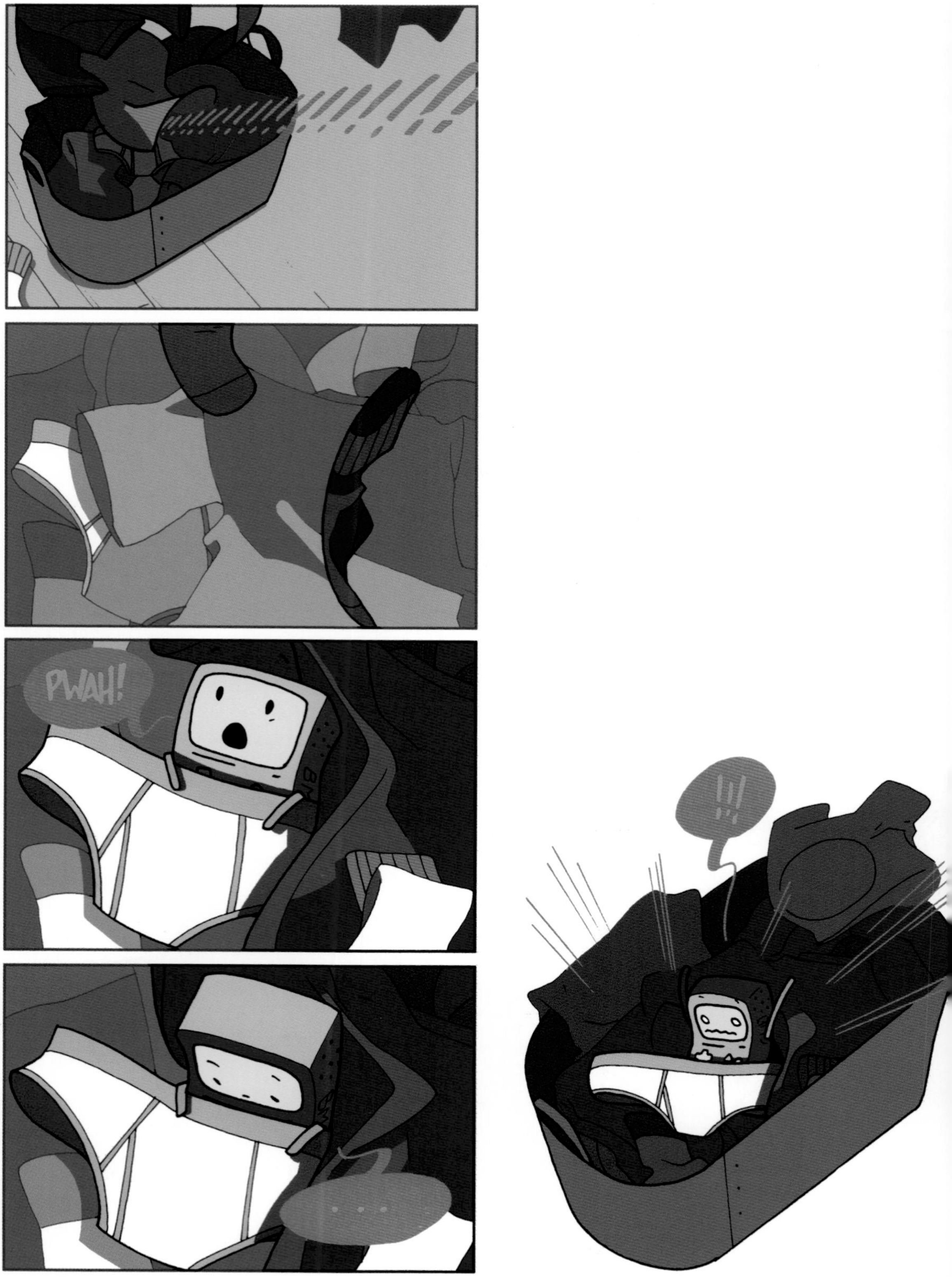
PWAH!
....
!!!

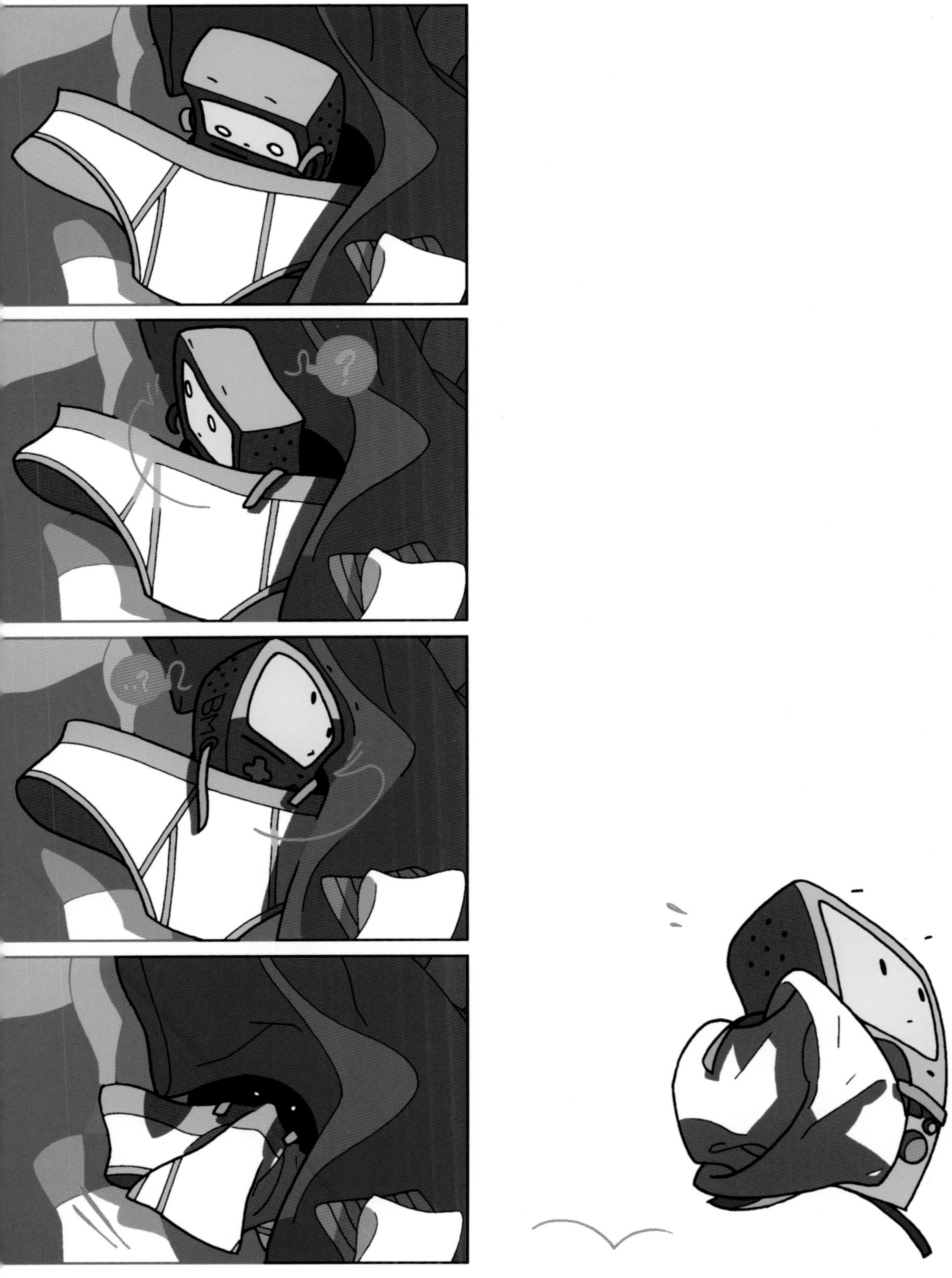

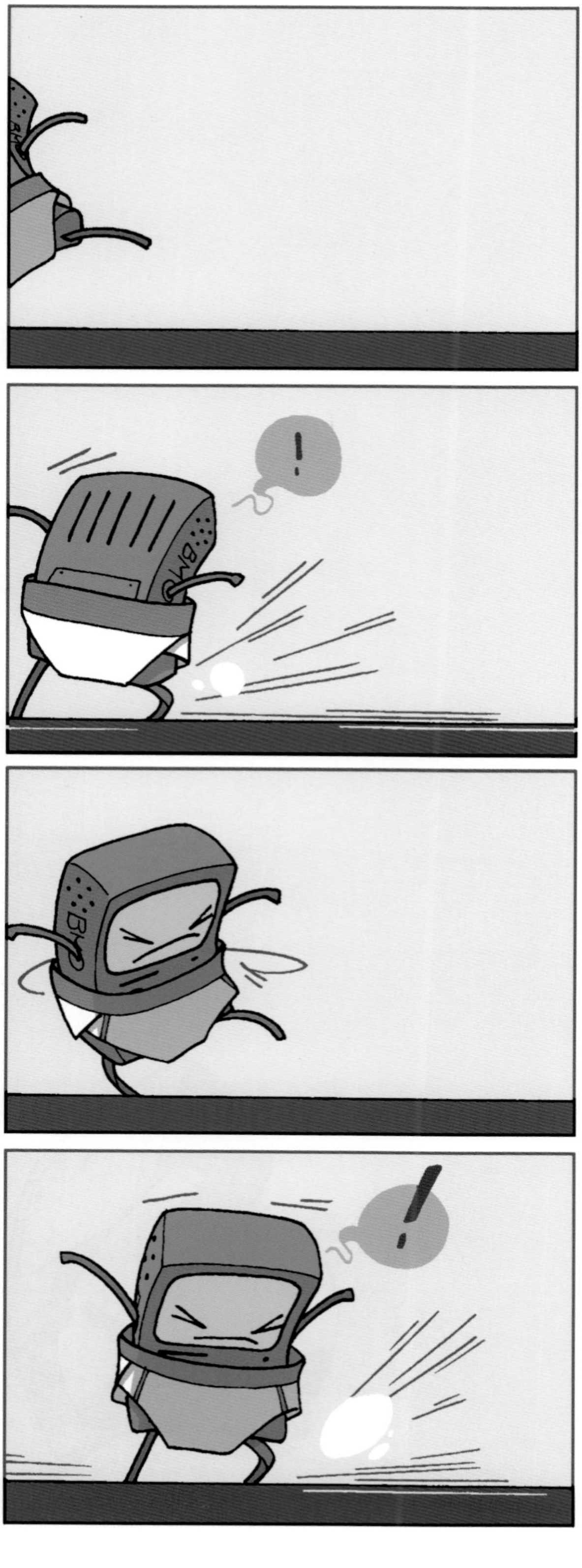
!
!

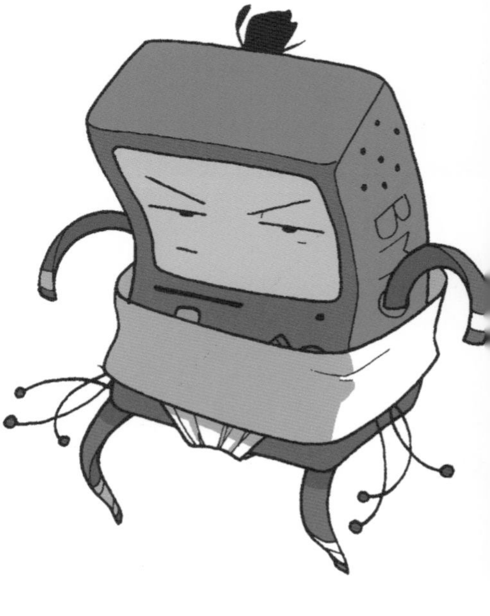

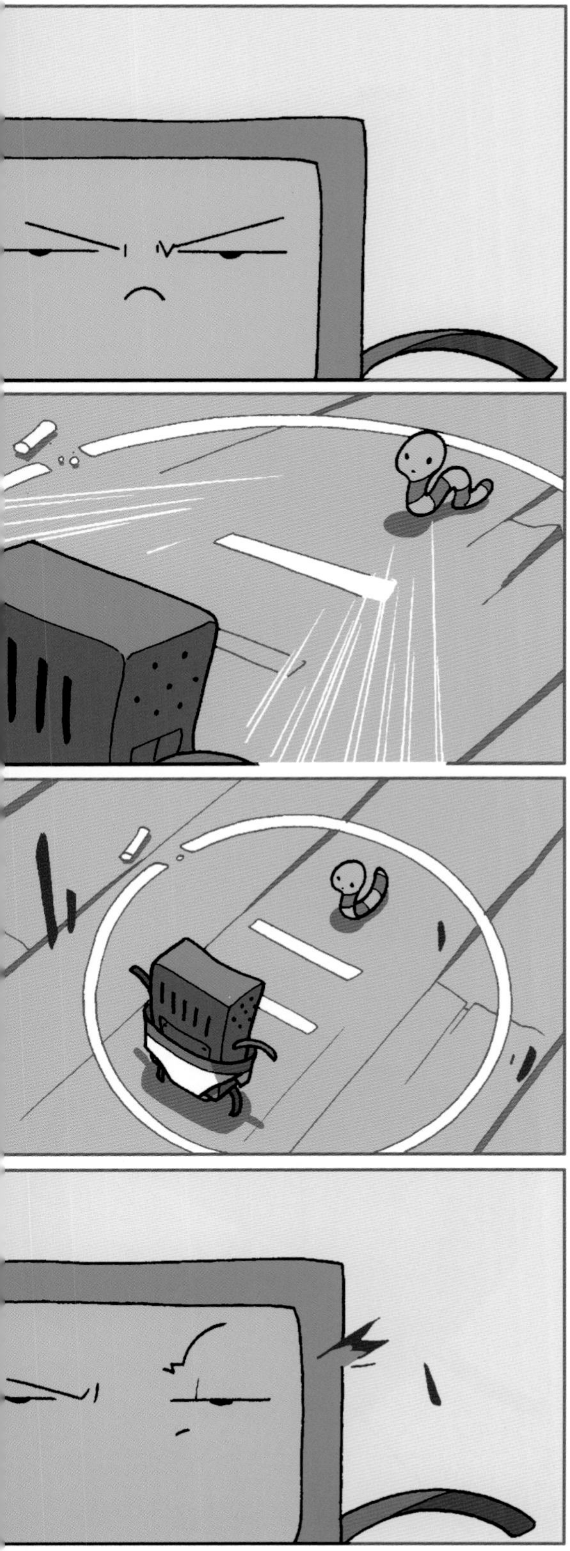

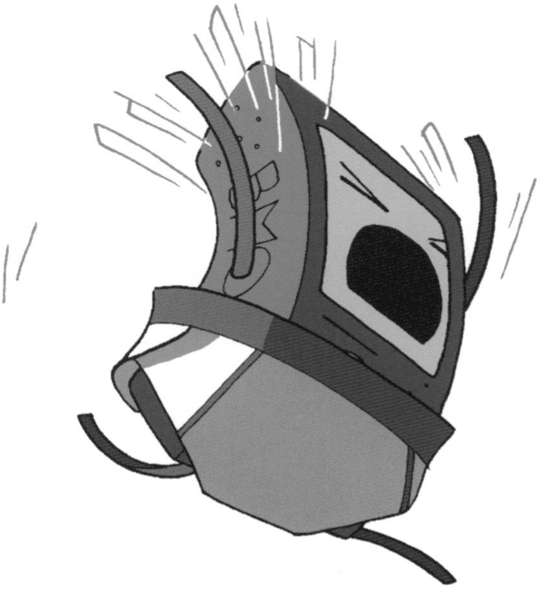

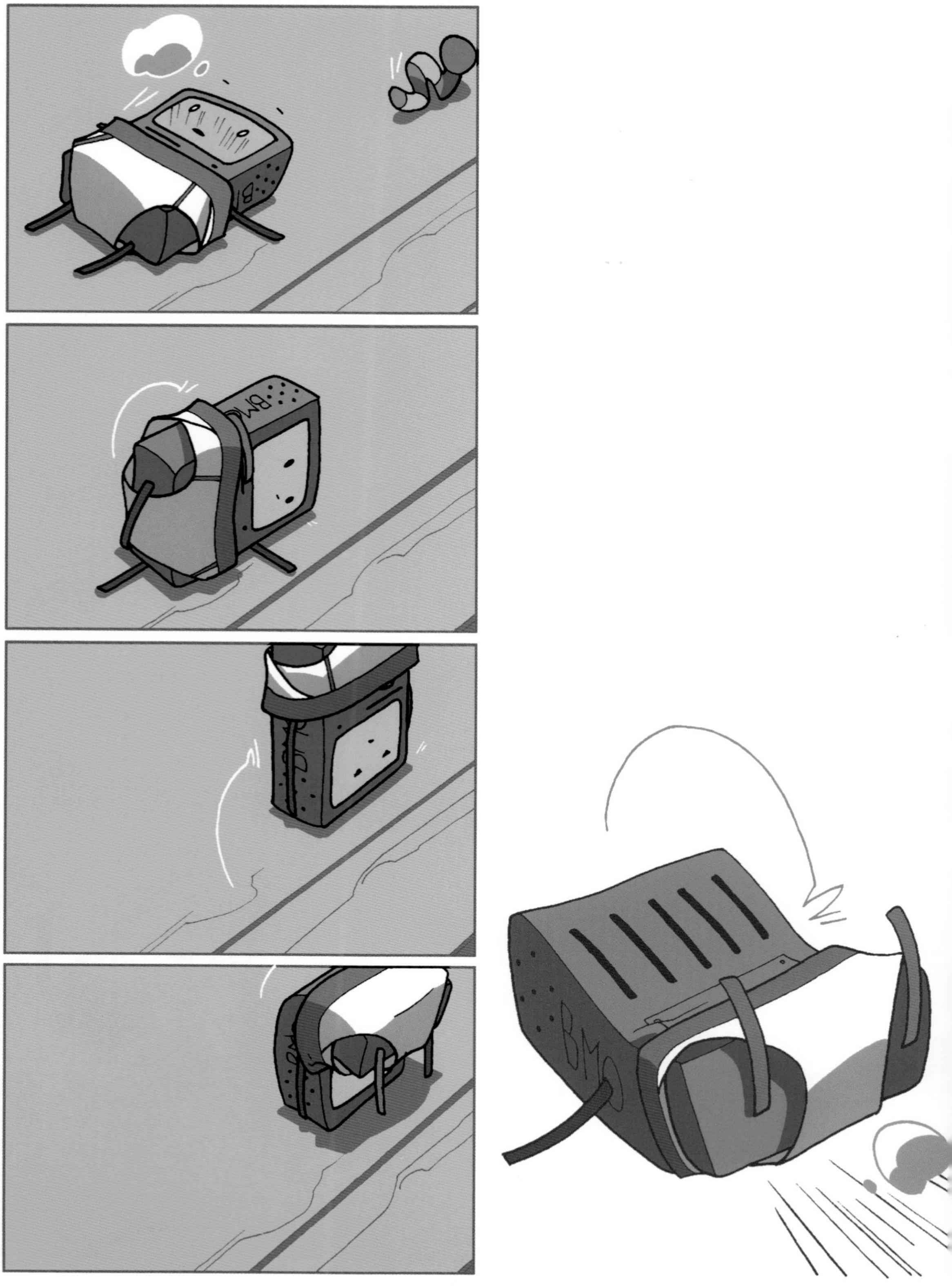
BMO

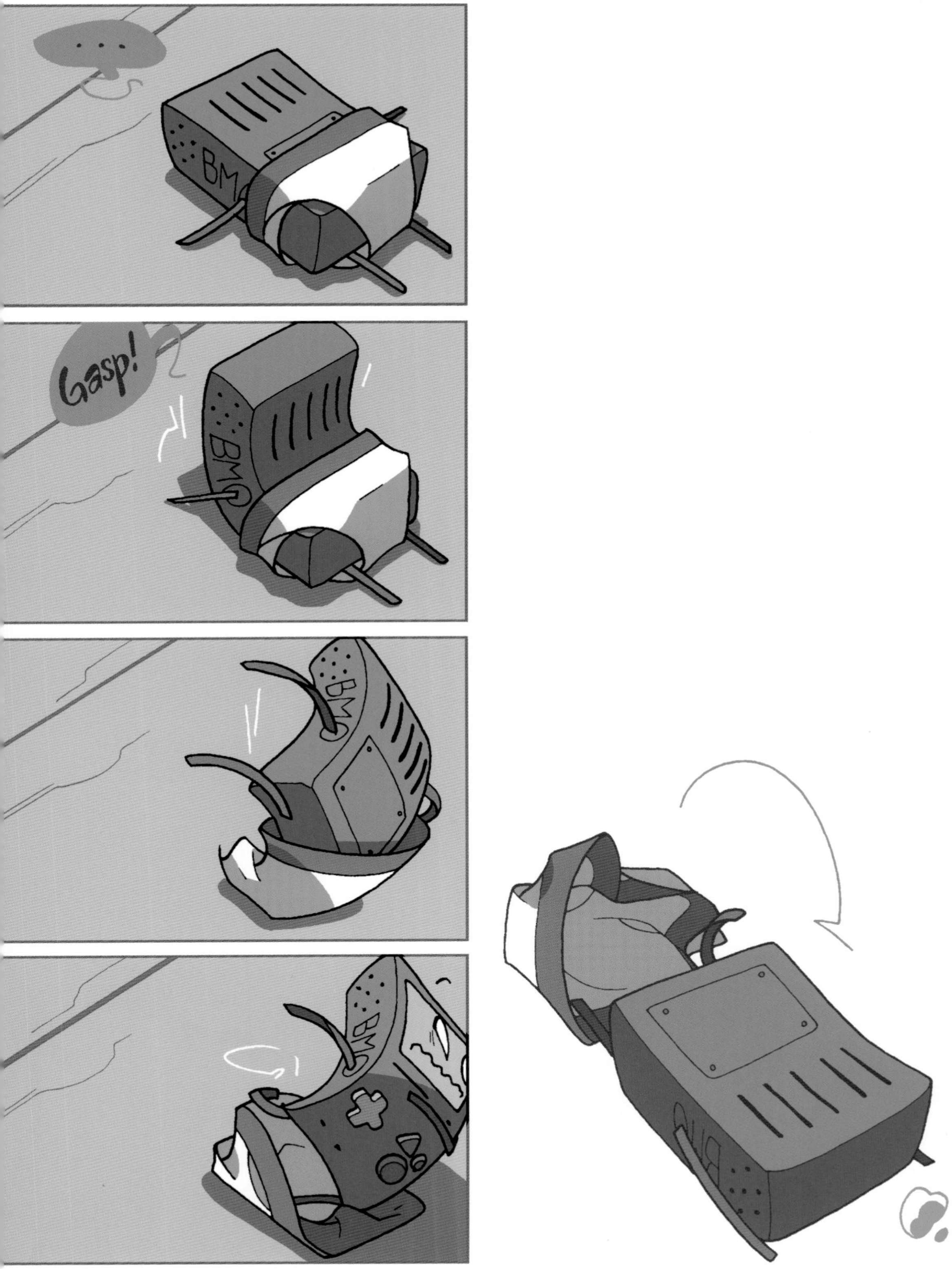
. . . .
Gasp!

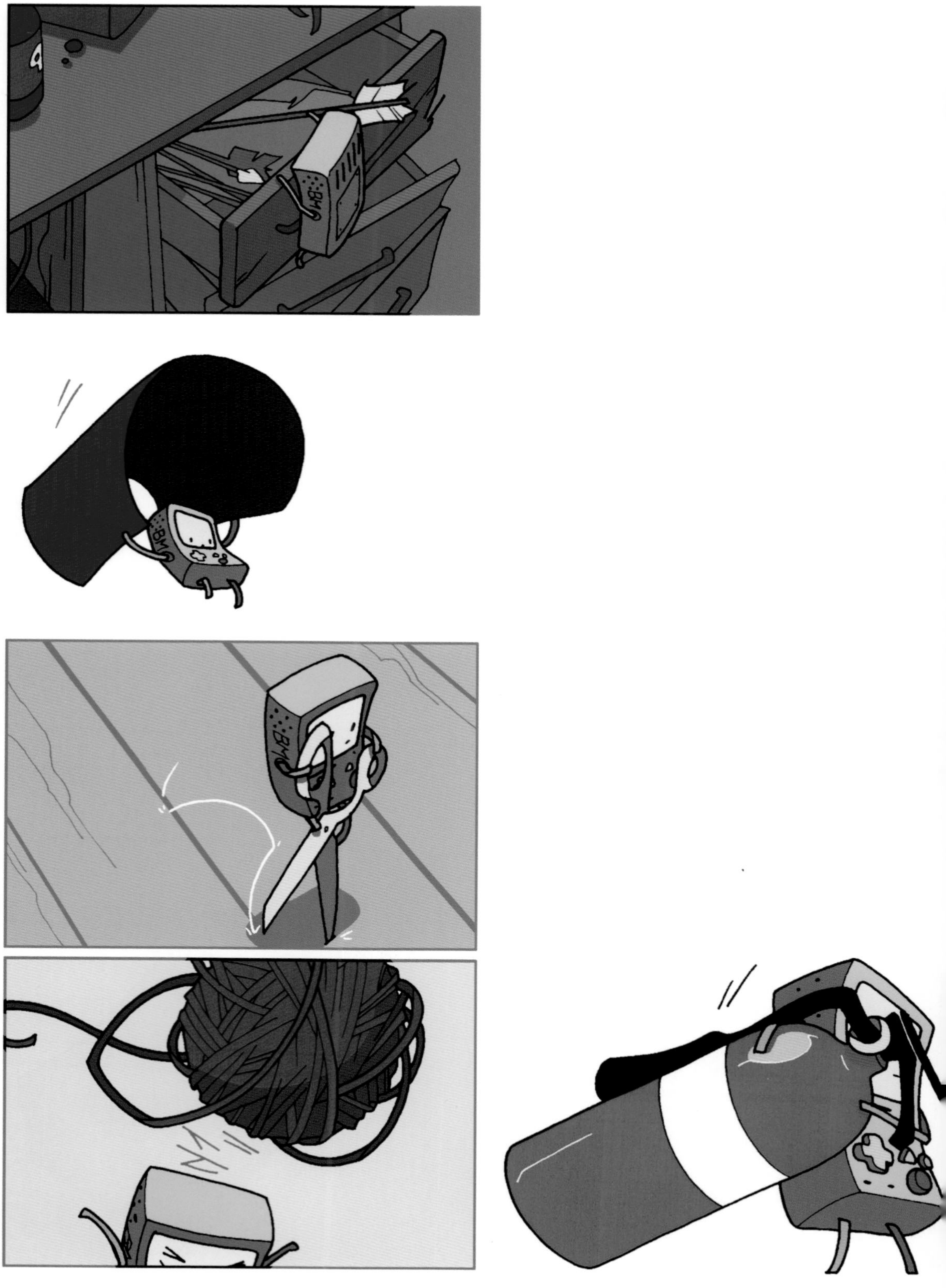

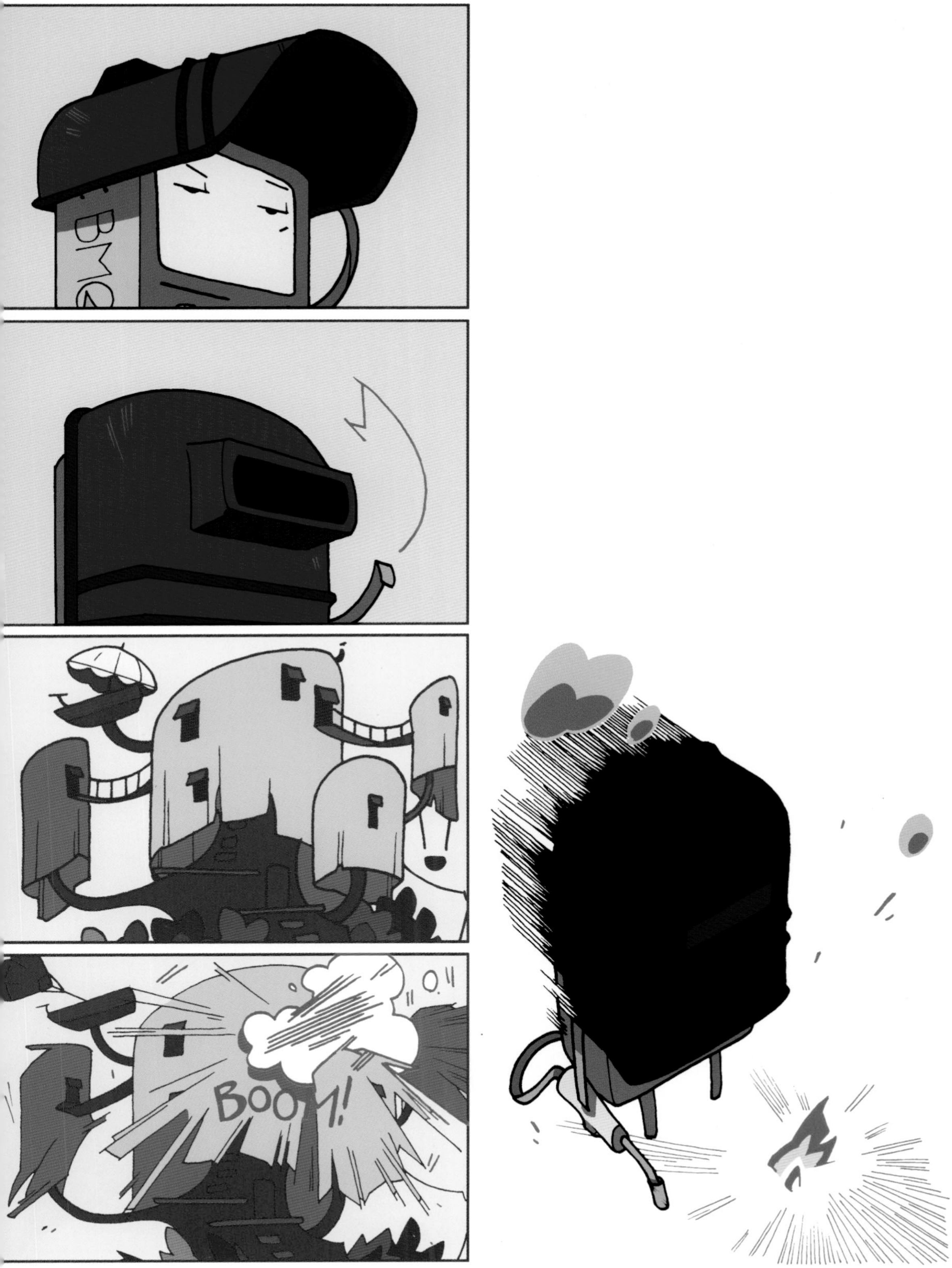
BOOM!

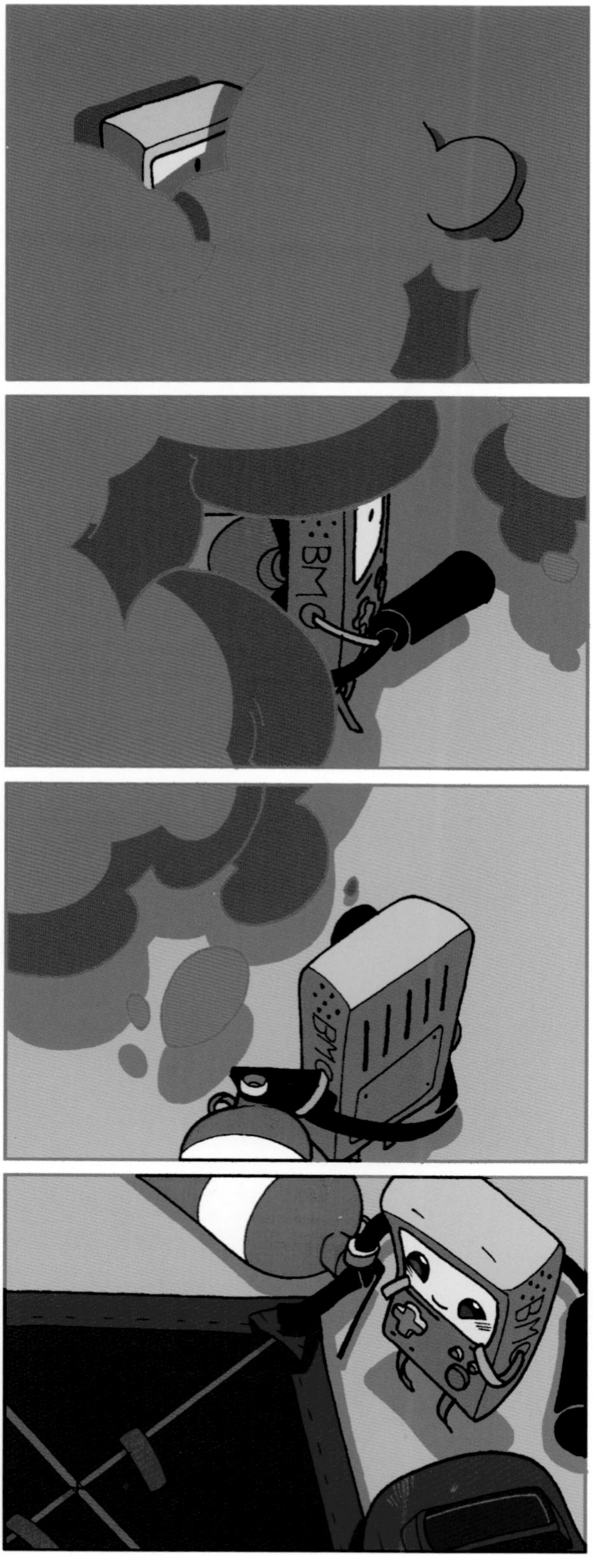
BMO

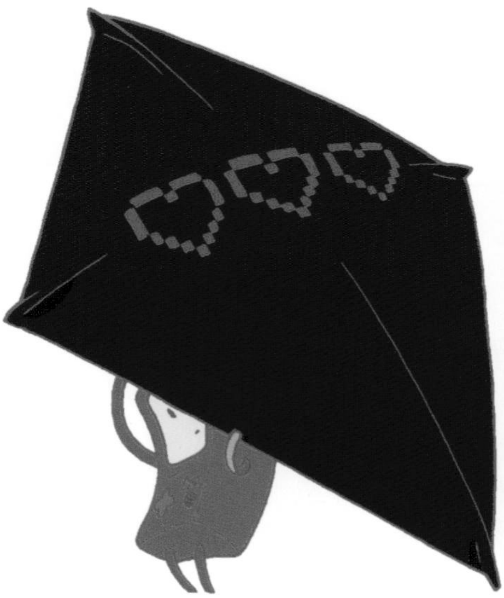

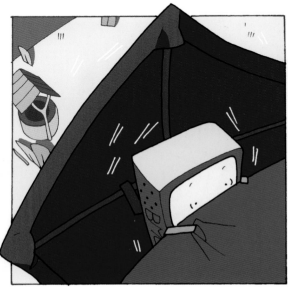

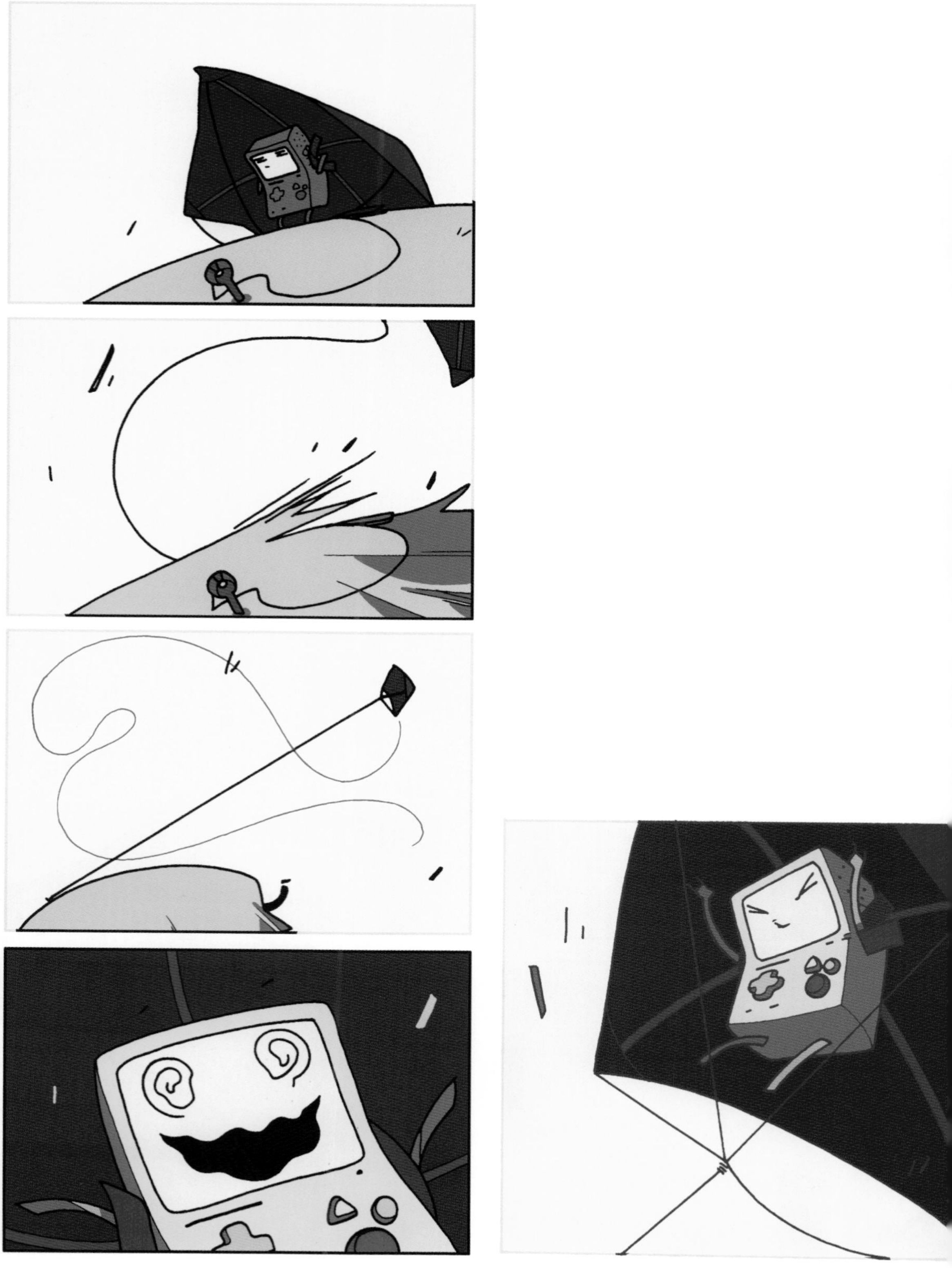

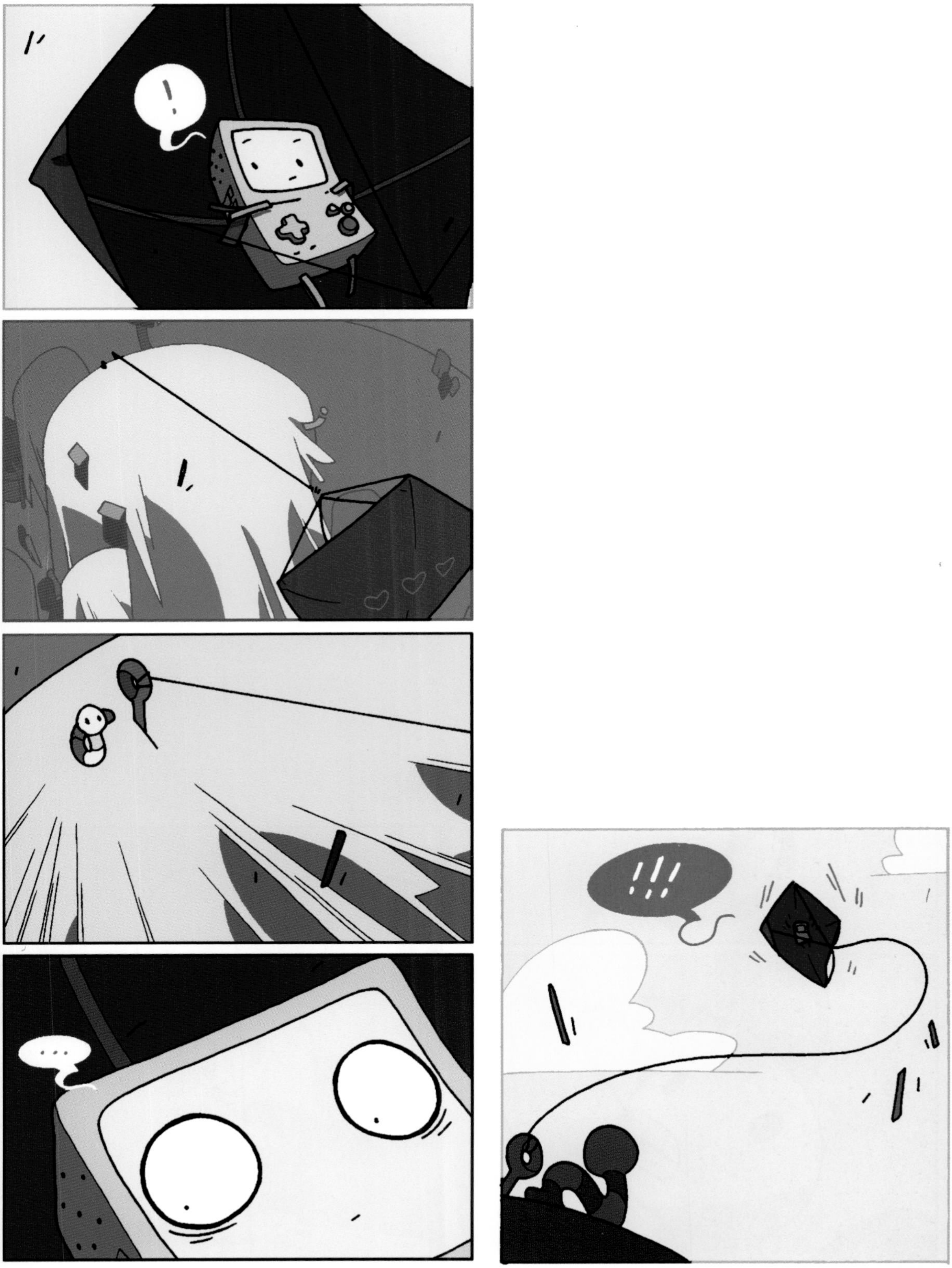
!
...
!!!

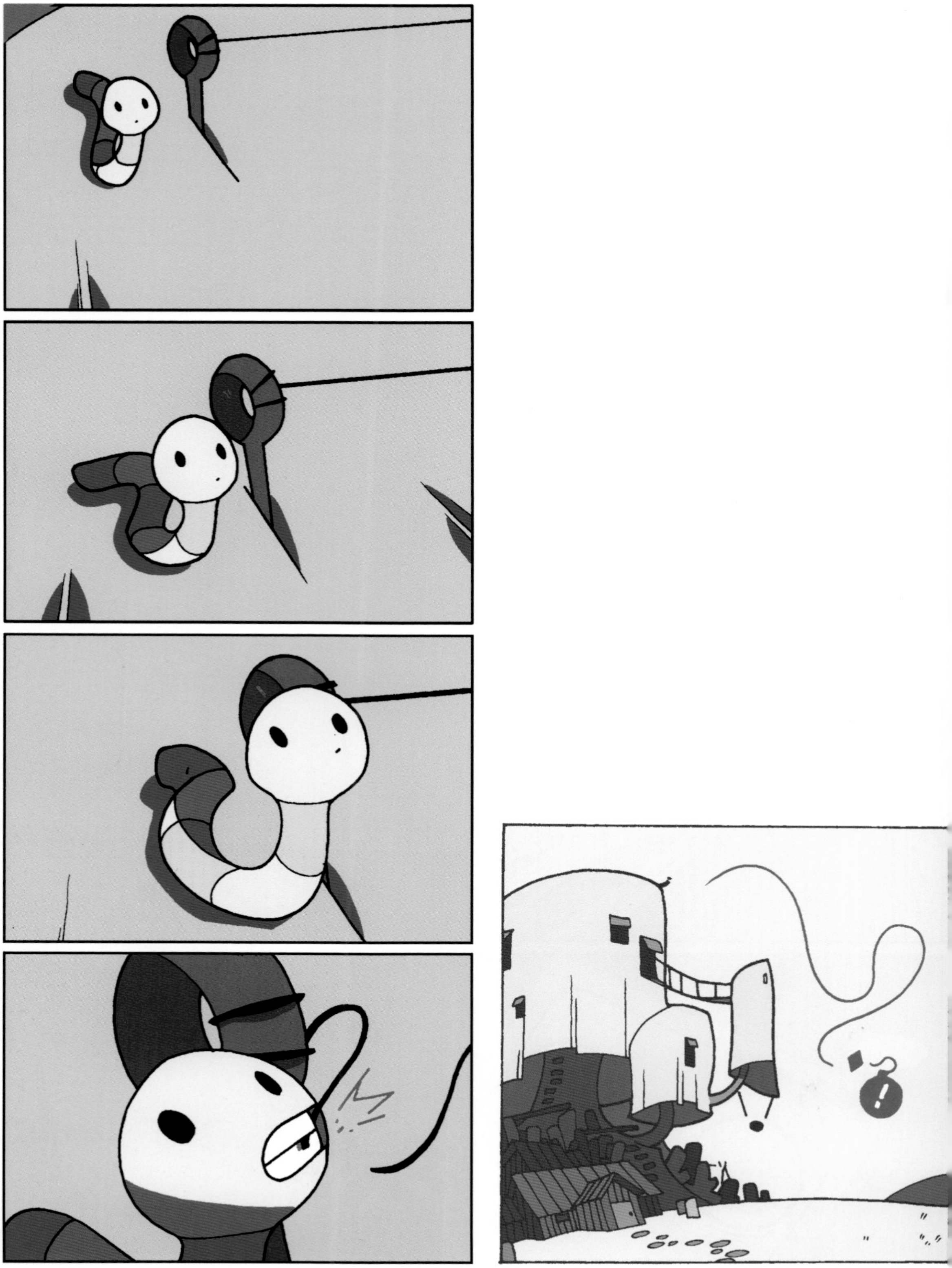

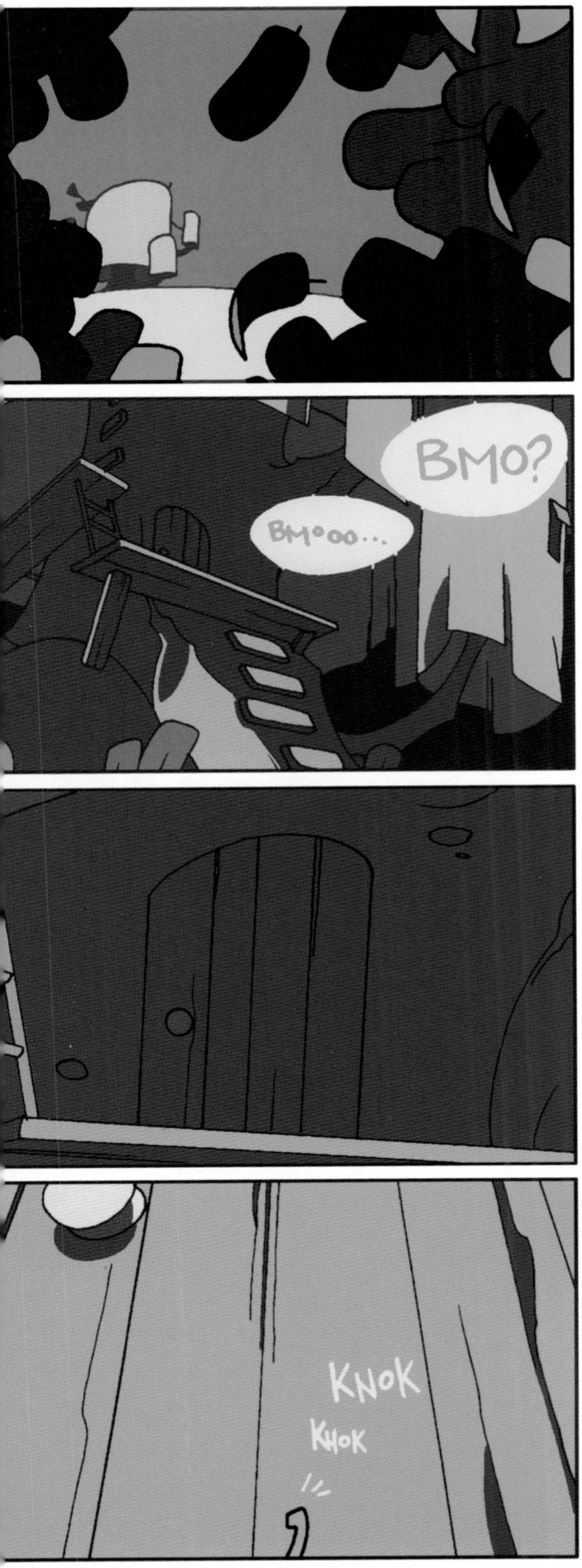
BMO?
BMOoo...
KNOK
KNOK
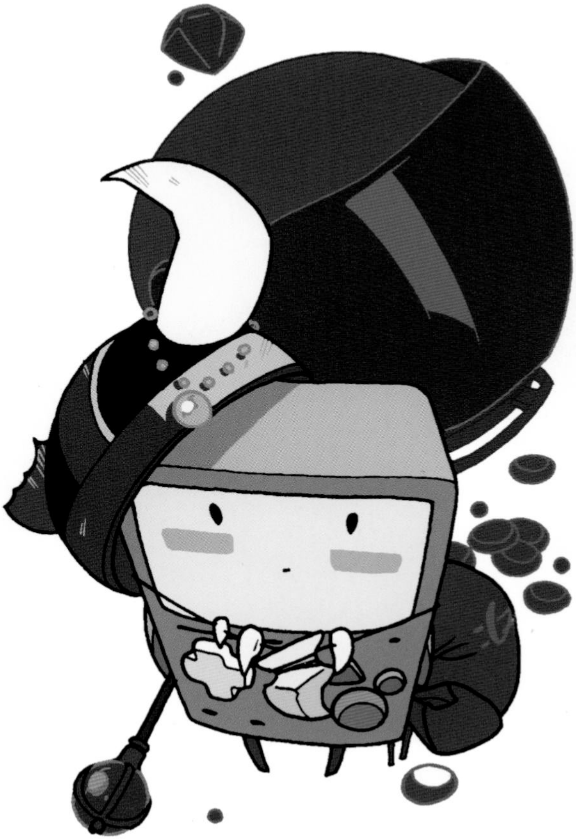

THE MIND OF GUNTER

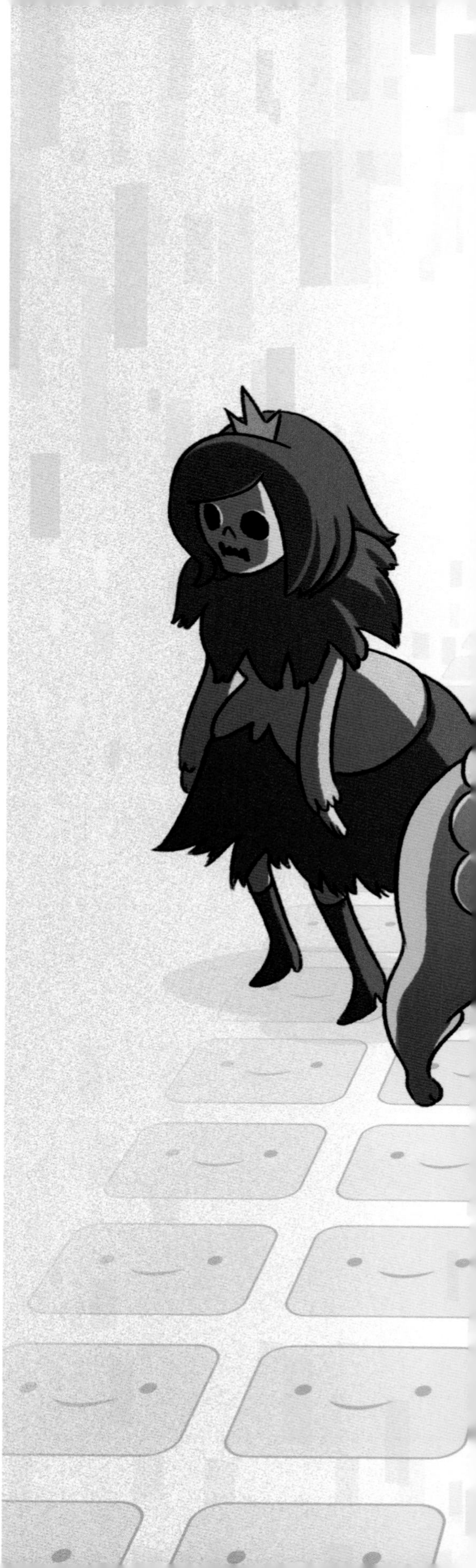

ADVENTURE TIME PIXEL PRINCESSES COVER
STEPHANIE GONZAGA

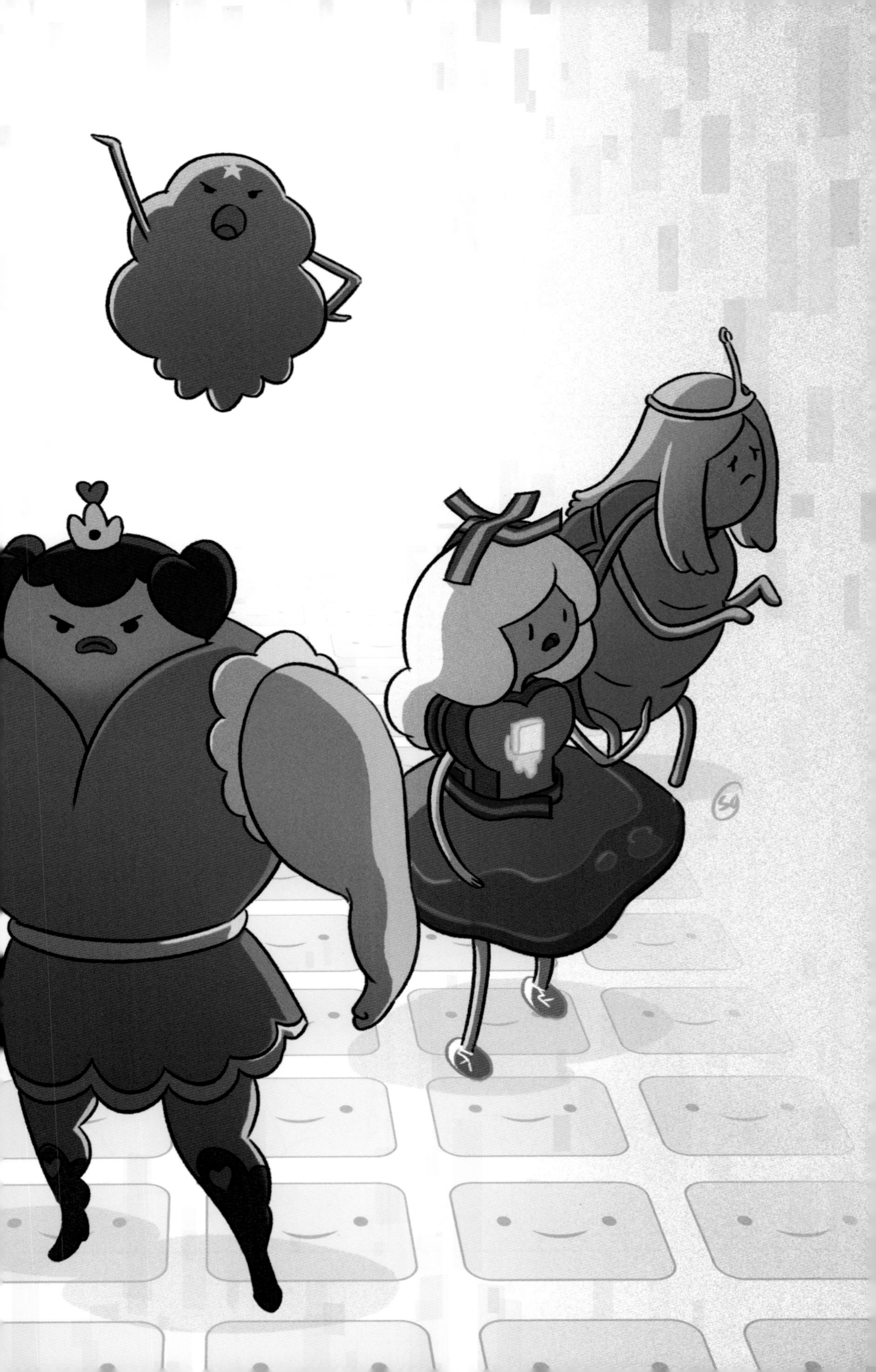

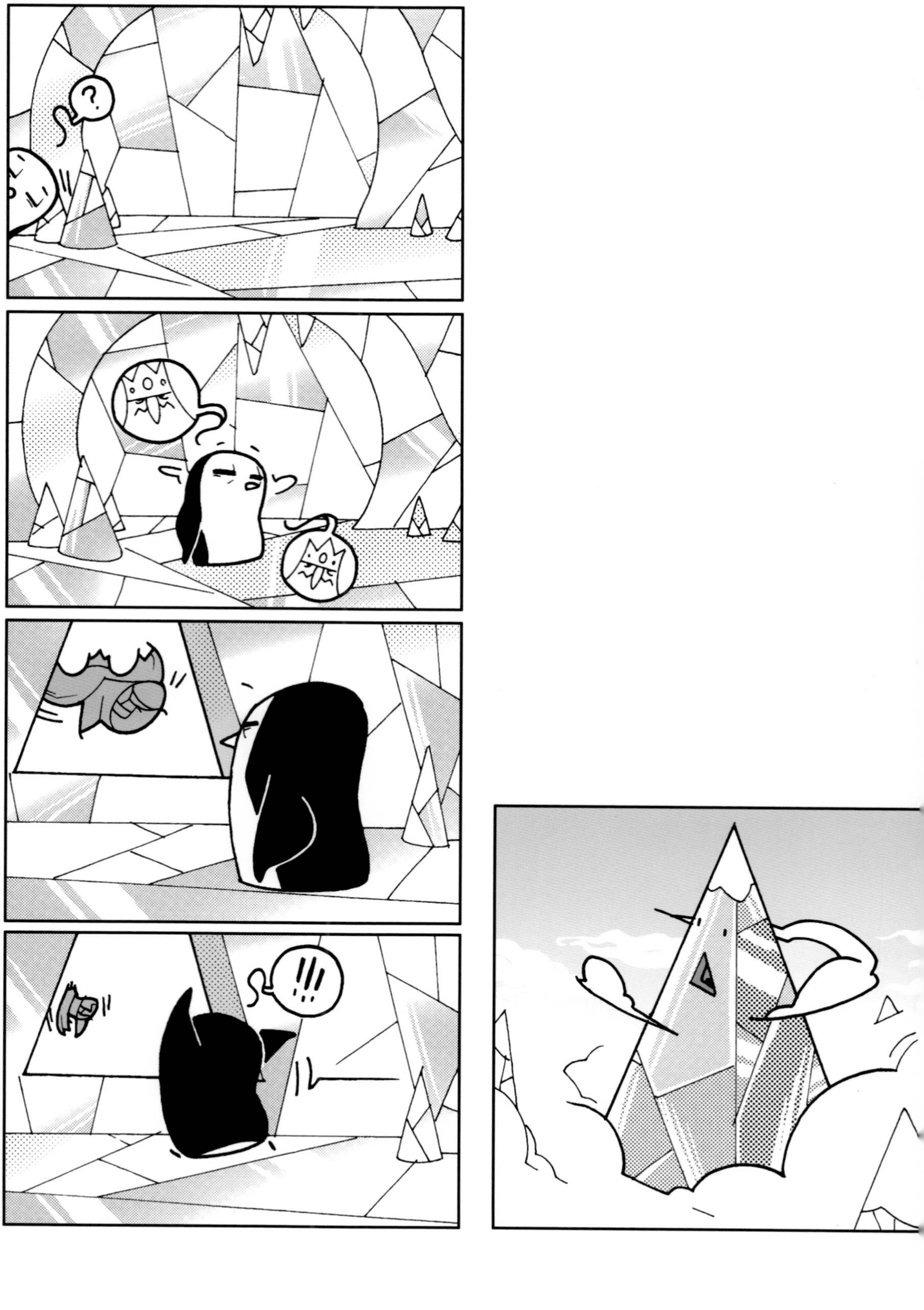
?
!!!

BREAKING STUFF
ICE KING
EVIL
CRAZY BEATS

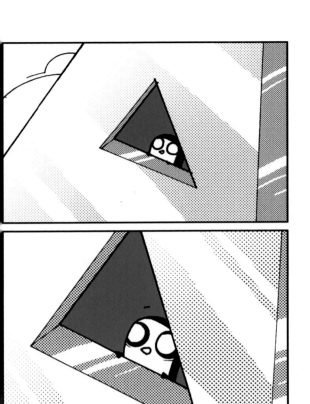

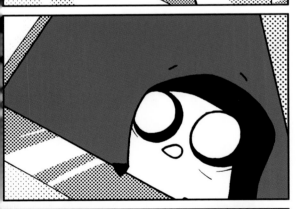

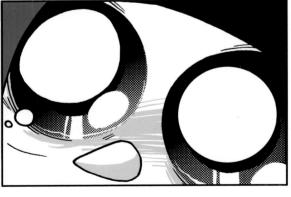

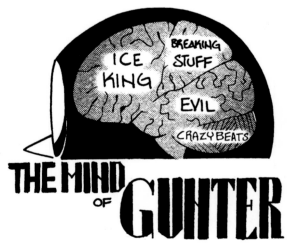

THE MIND OF GUNTER

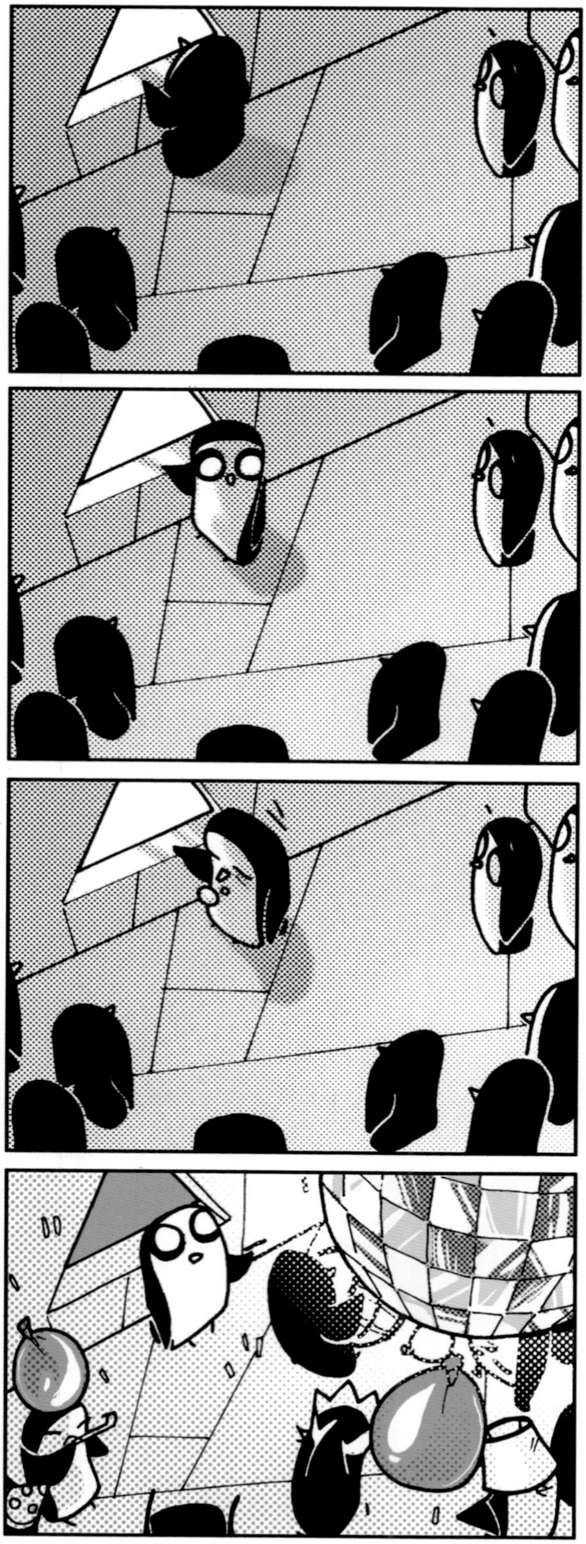

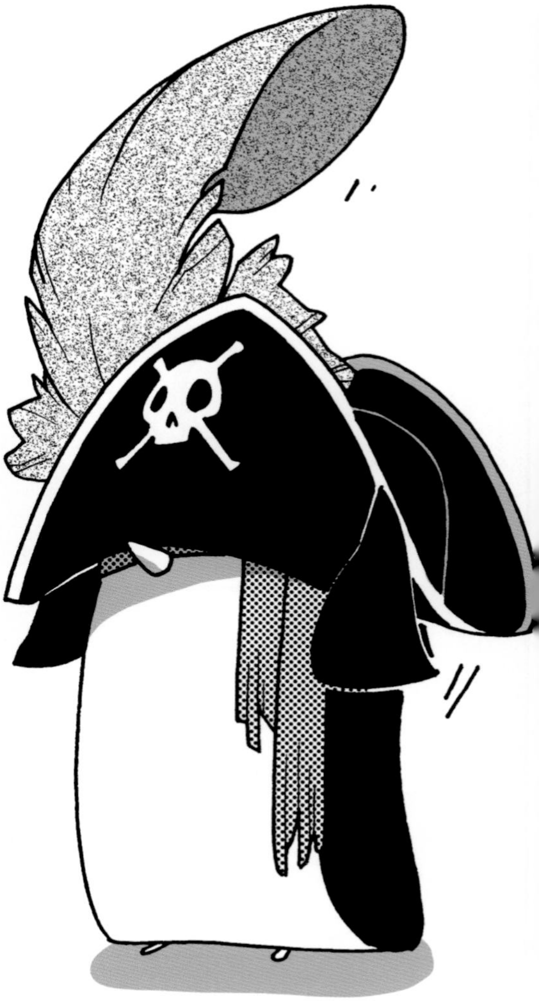

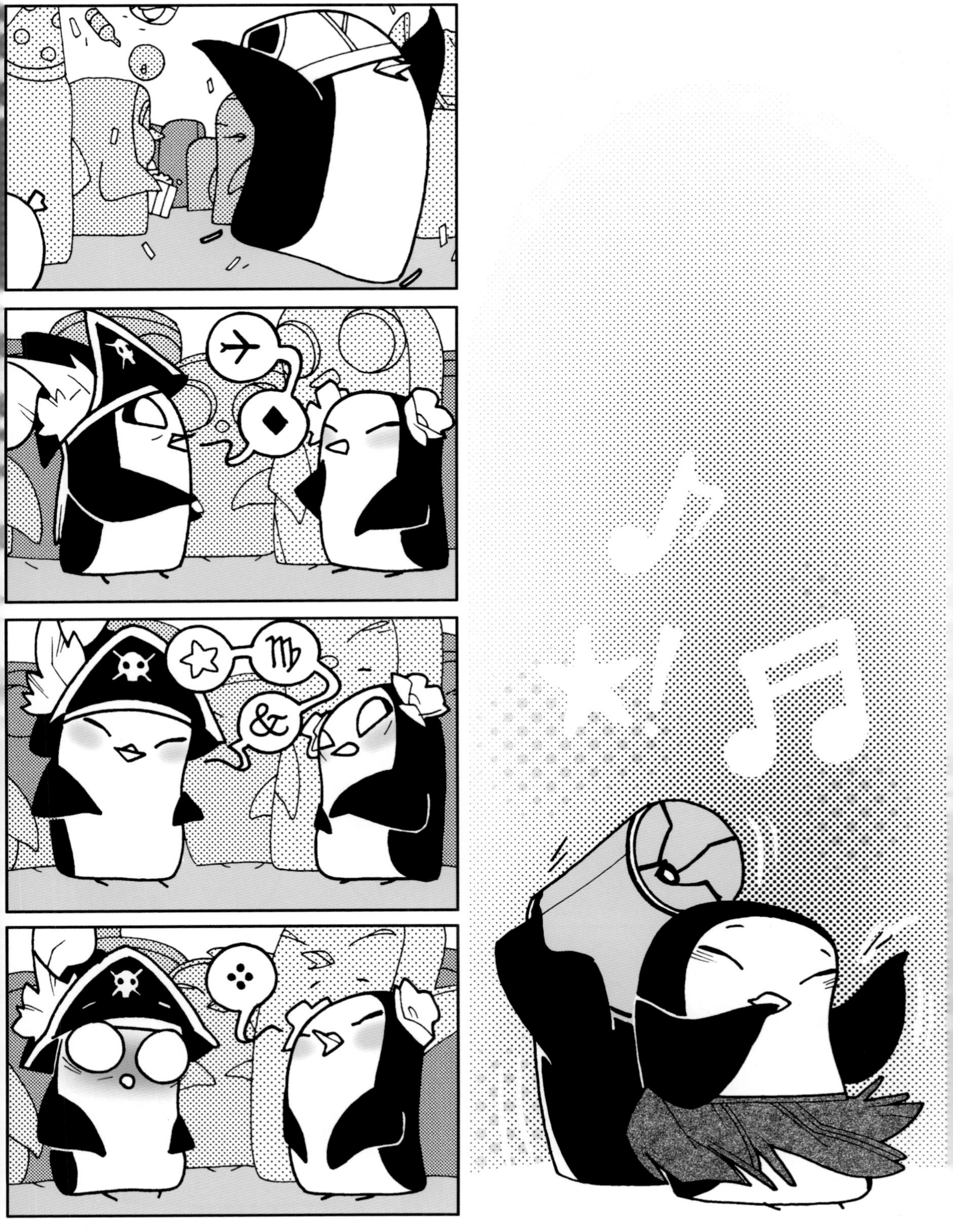

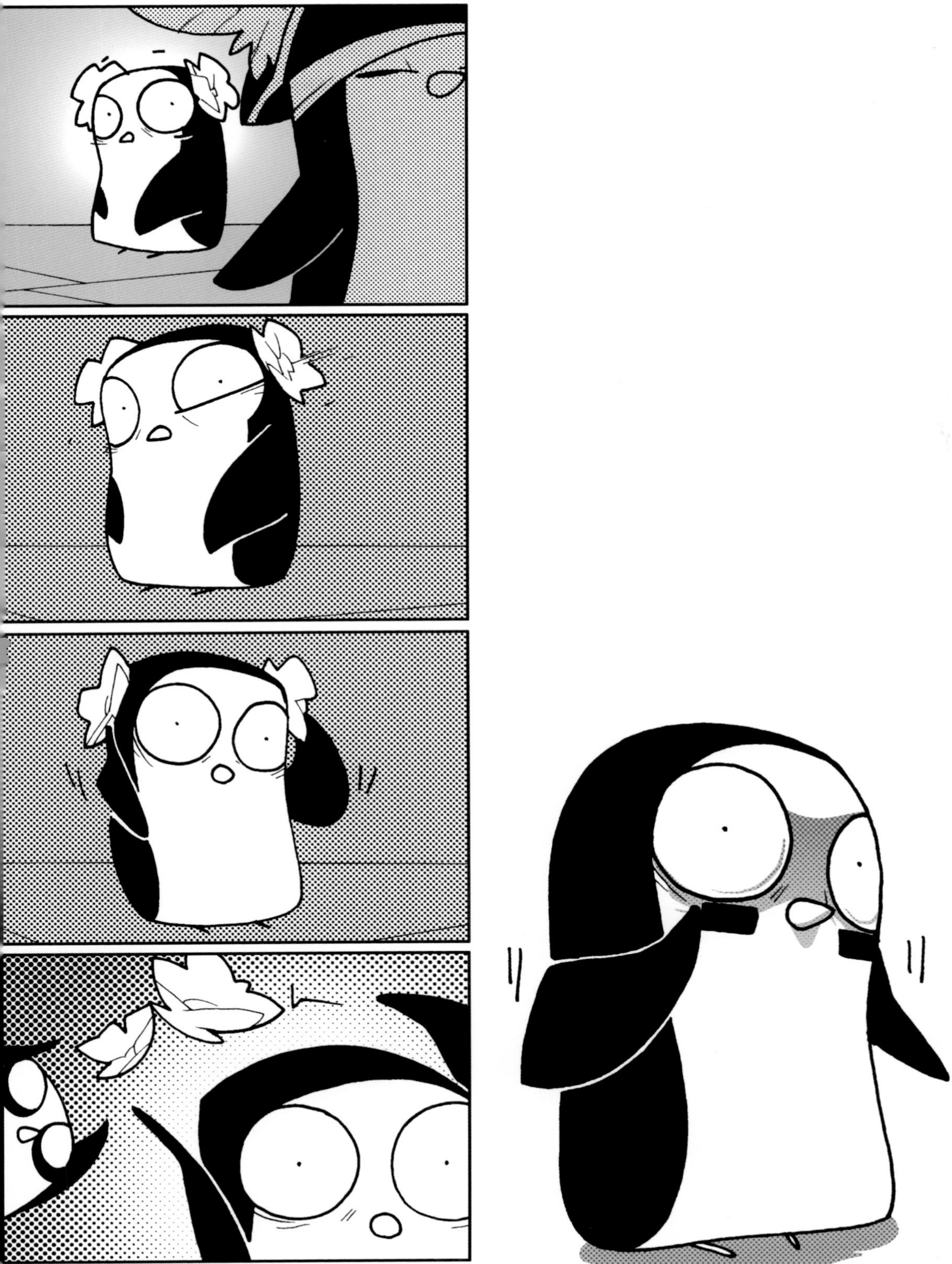

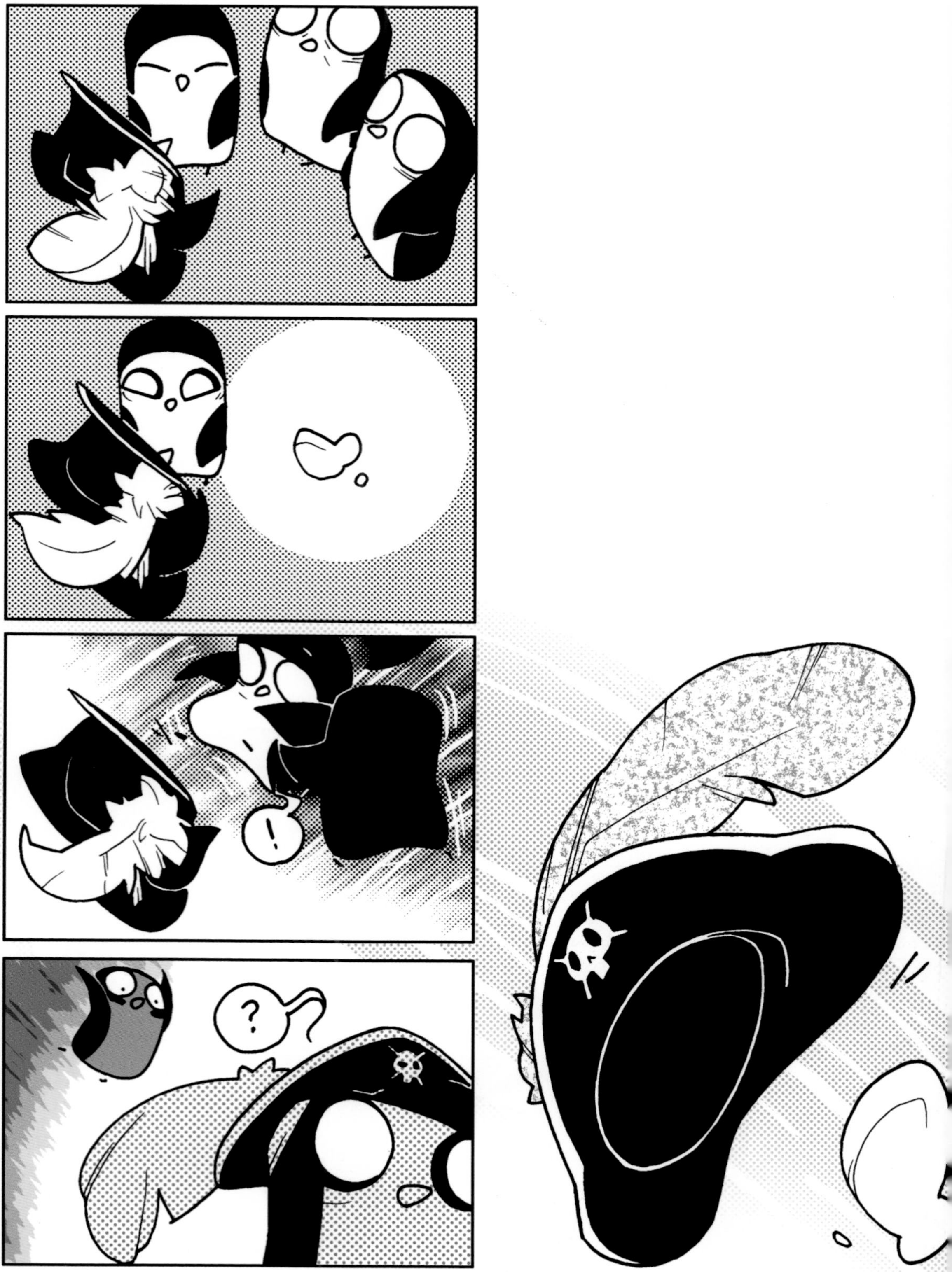
!
?

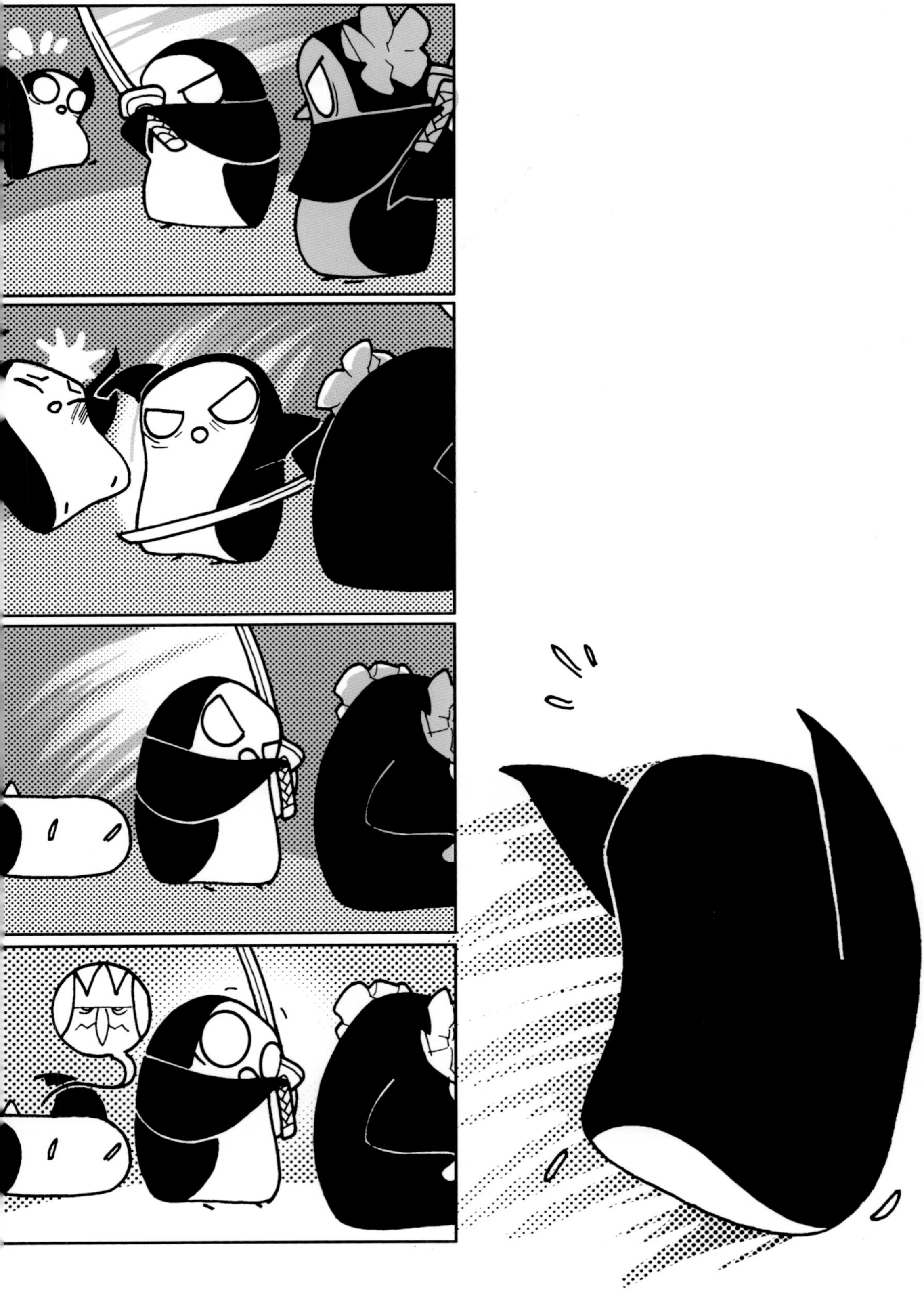

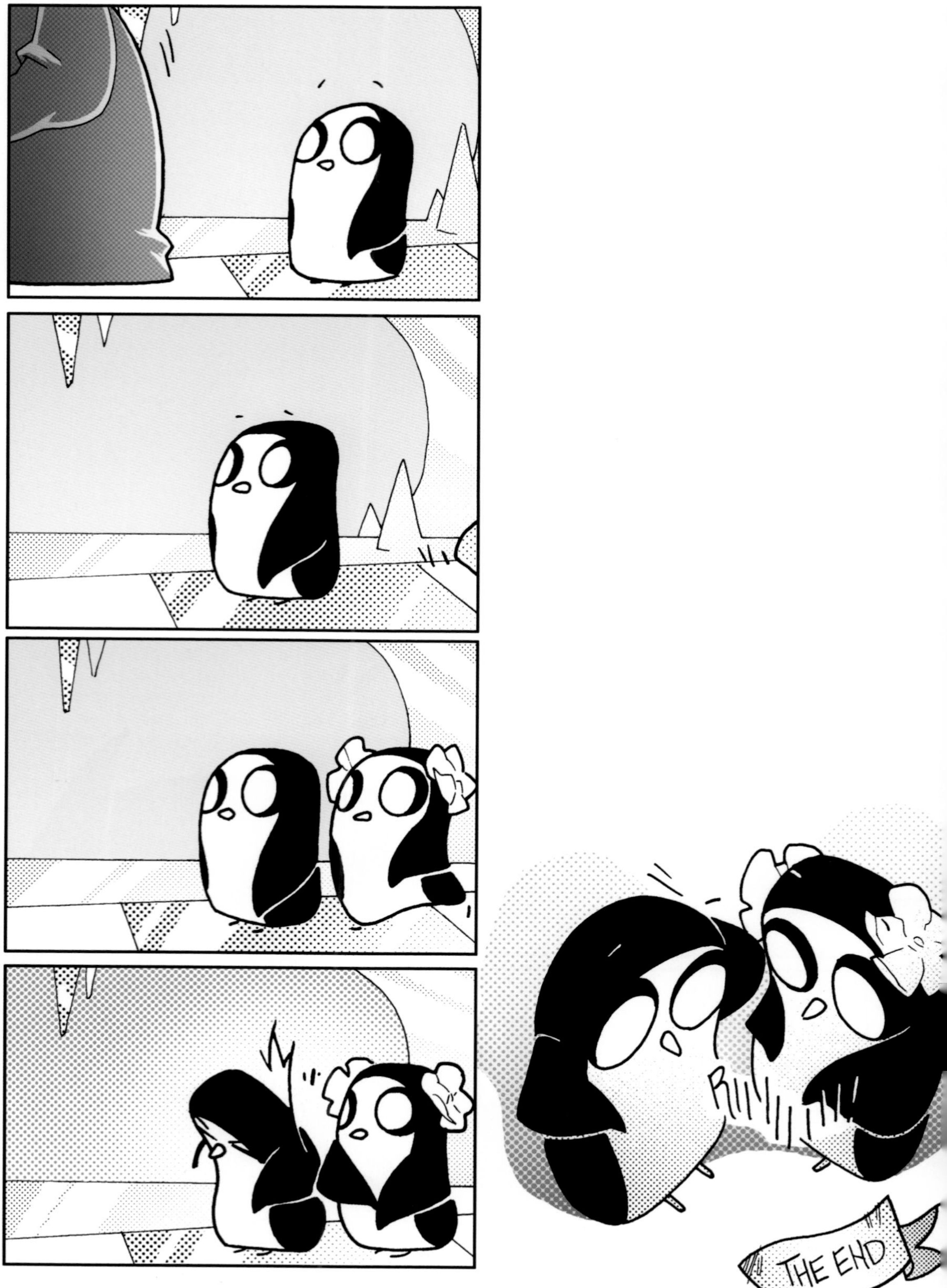
THE END

LSP'S PURSE

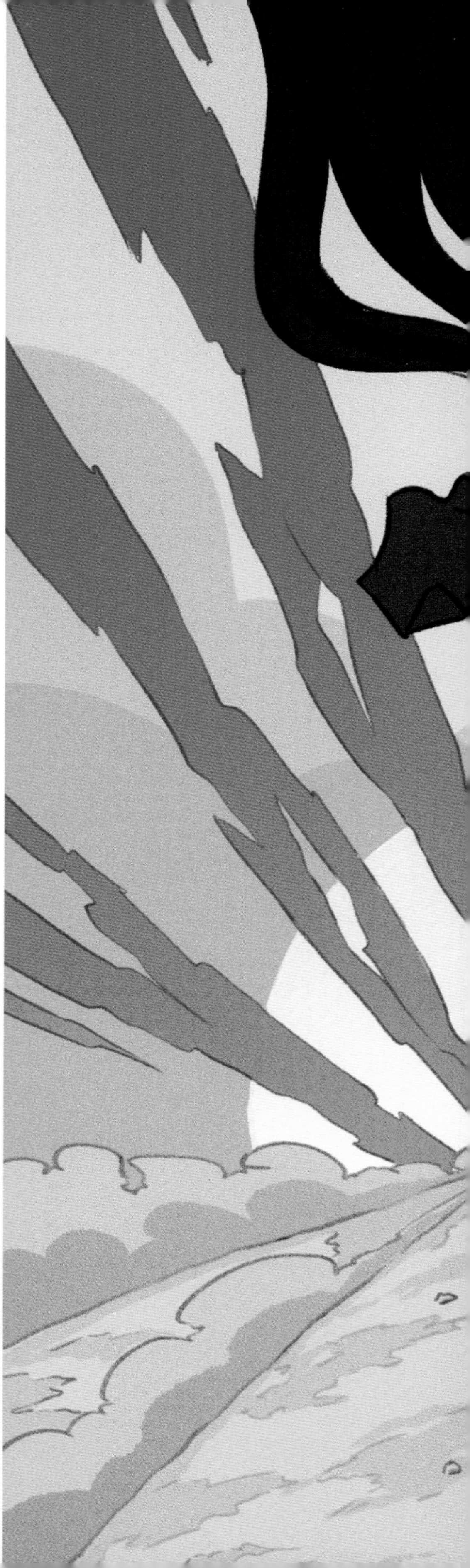

ADVENTURE TIME SEEING RED COVER
STEPHANIE GONZAGA

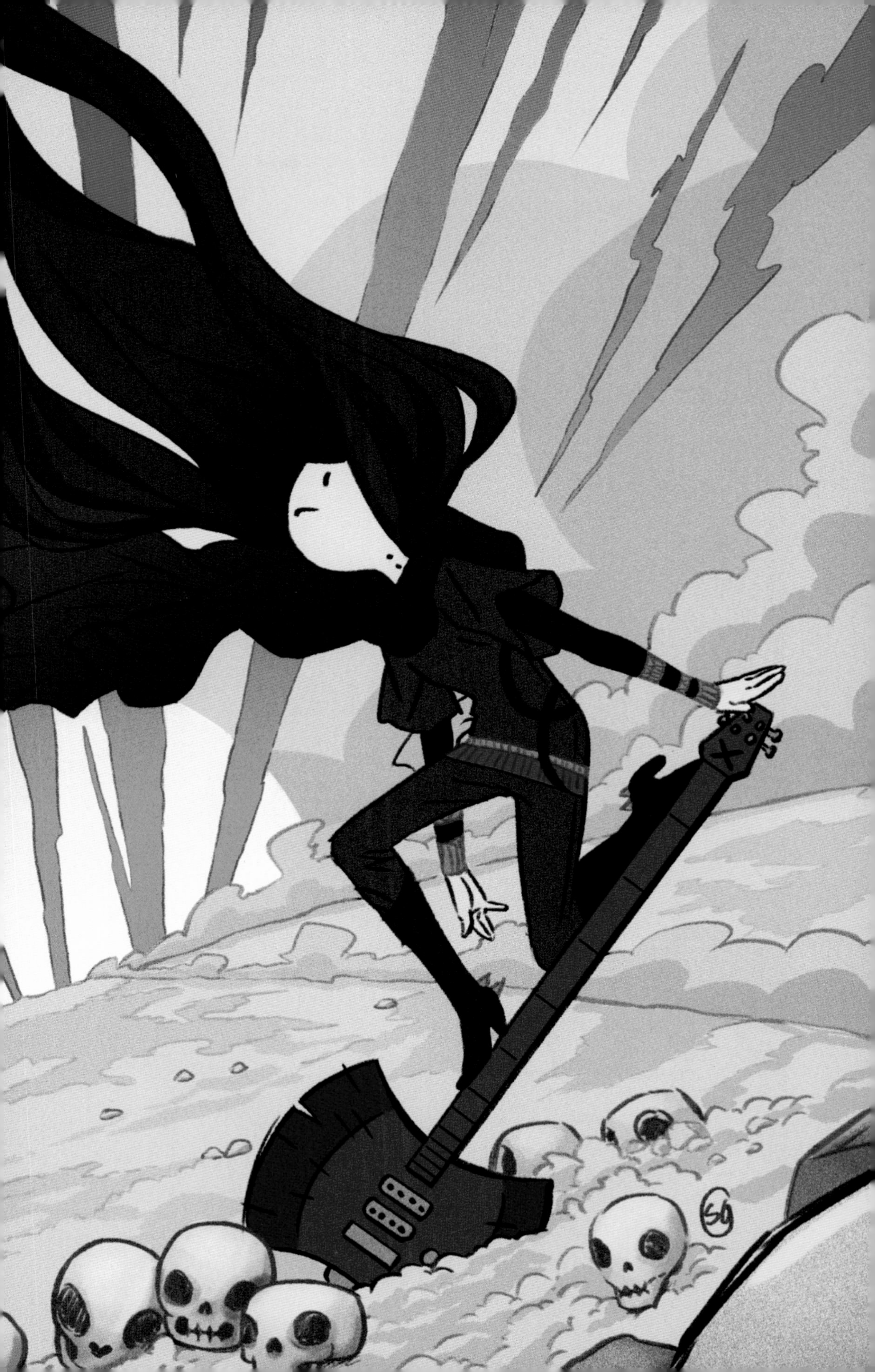

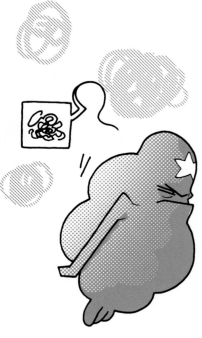

PURSES
HELP. ME.

LSP
GONE QUESTIN'

WHAT? LIKE IT'S HARD?

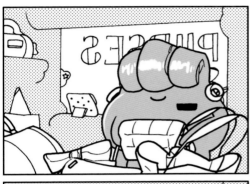

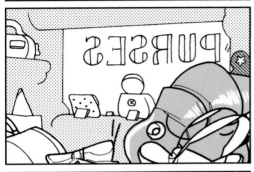

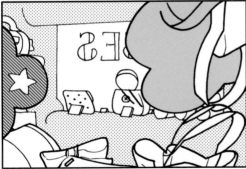

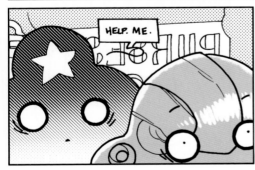

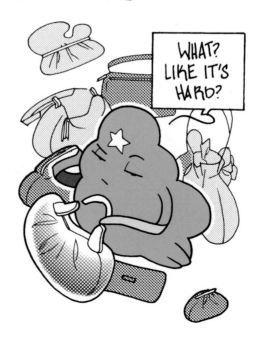

WHAT KIND OF PURSE WOULD YOU LIKE—

THE
BEST
ONE

ELSEWHERE
...

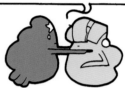

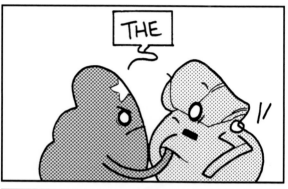

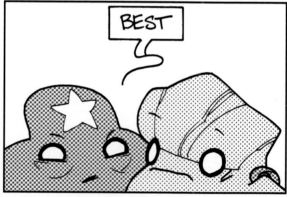

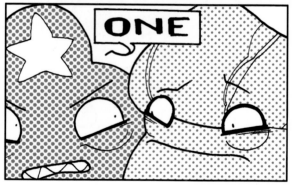

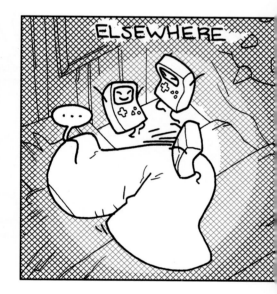

no.
NO.
NO!
NONE OF THESE PURSES HAVE WHAT I WANT!!!

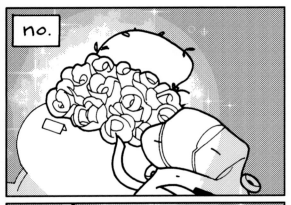

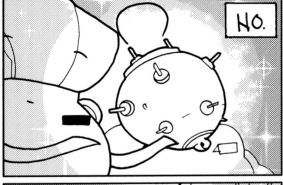

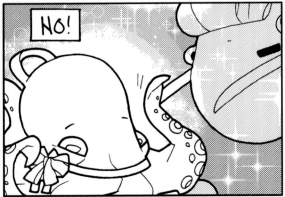

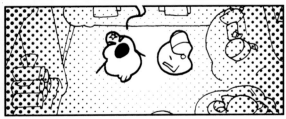

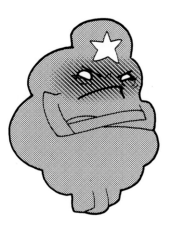

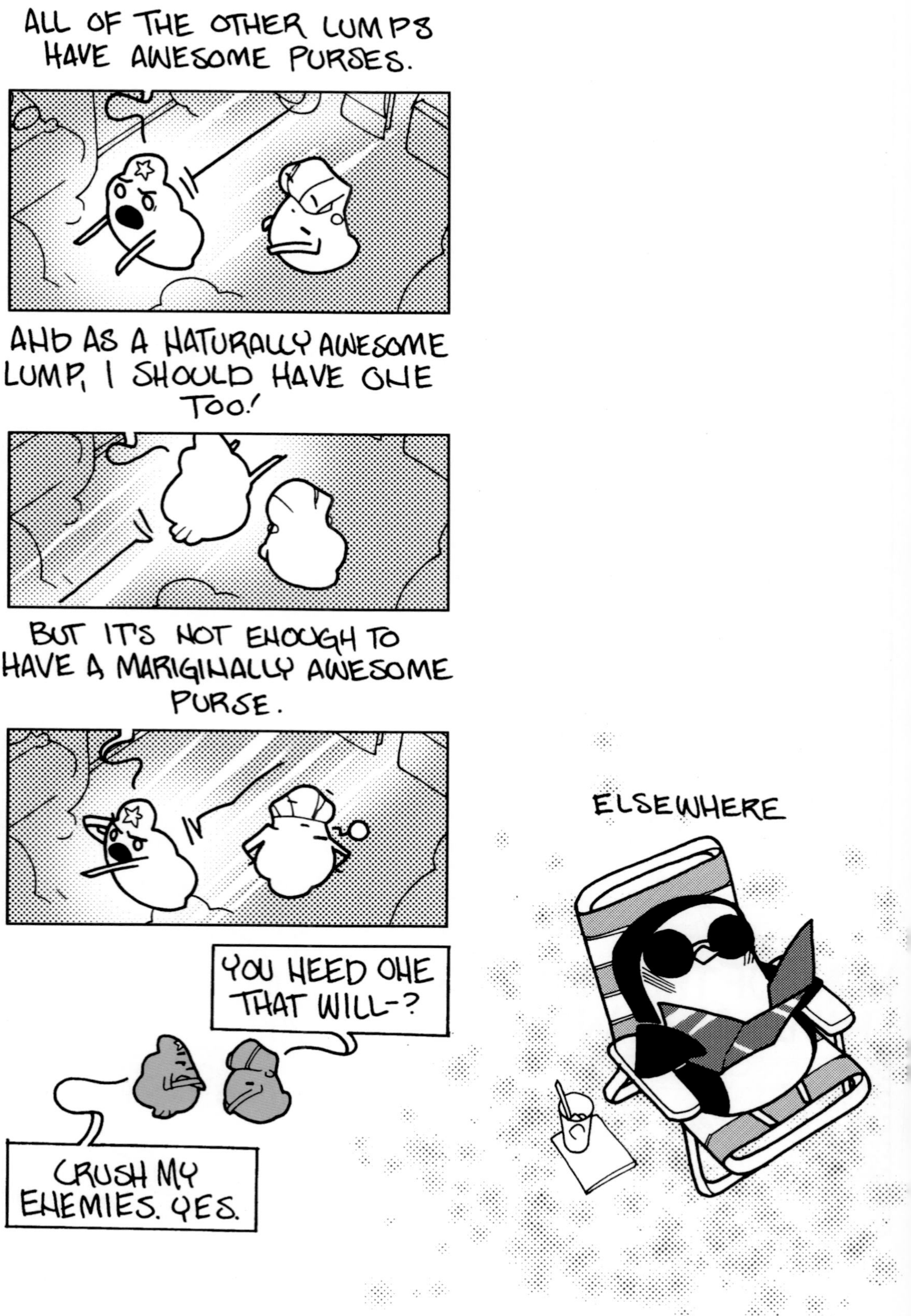
ALL OF THE OTHER LUMPS HAVE AWESOME PURSES.
AND AS A NATURALLY AWESOME LUMP, I SHOULD HAVE ONE TOO!
BUT IT'S NOT ENOUGH TO HAVE A MARIGINALLY AWESOME PURSE.
YOU NEED ONE THAT WILL-?
CRUSH MY ENEMIES. YES.
ELSEWHERE

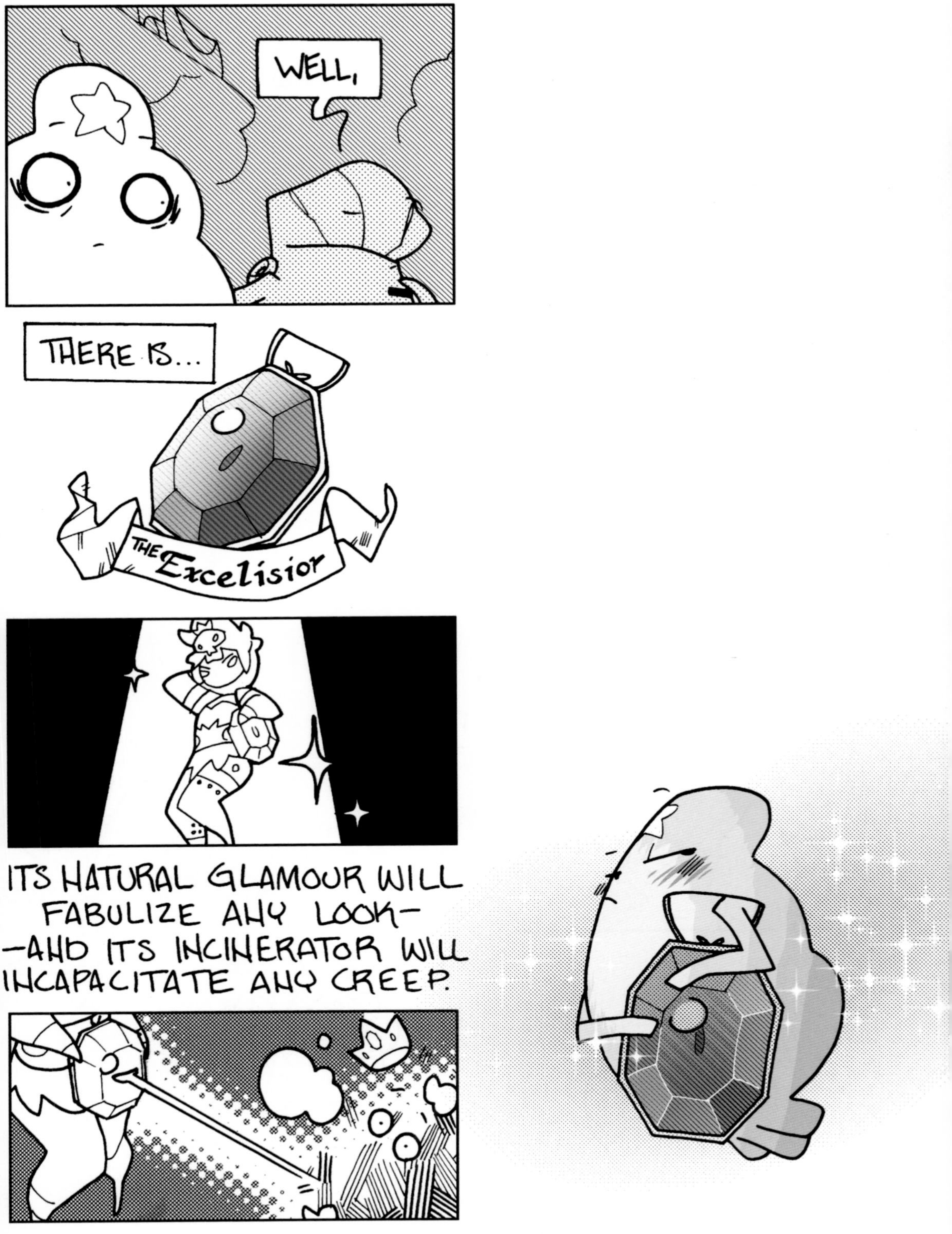
WELL,
THERE IS...
THE Excelisior
ITS NATURAL GLAMOUR WILL FABULIZE ANY LOOK—
—AND ITS INCINERATOR WILL INCAPACITATE ANY CREEP.

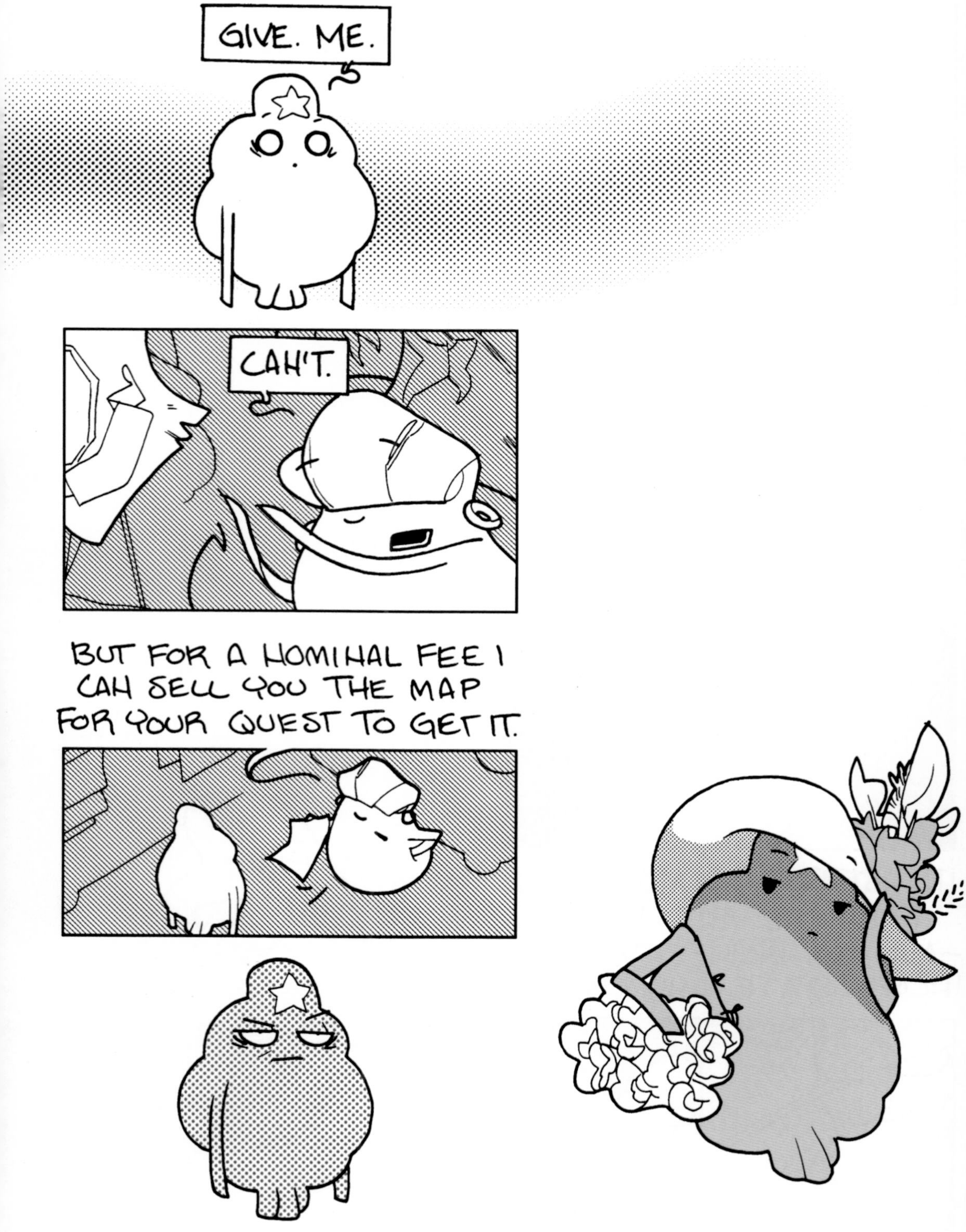
GIVE. ME.
CAN'T.
BUT FOR A NOMINAL FEE I CAN SELL YOU THE MAP FOR YOUR QUEST TO GET IT.

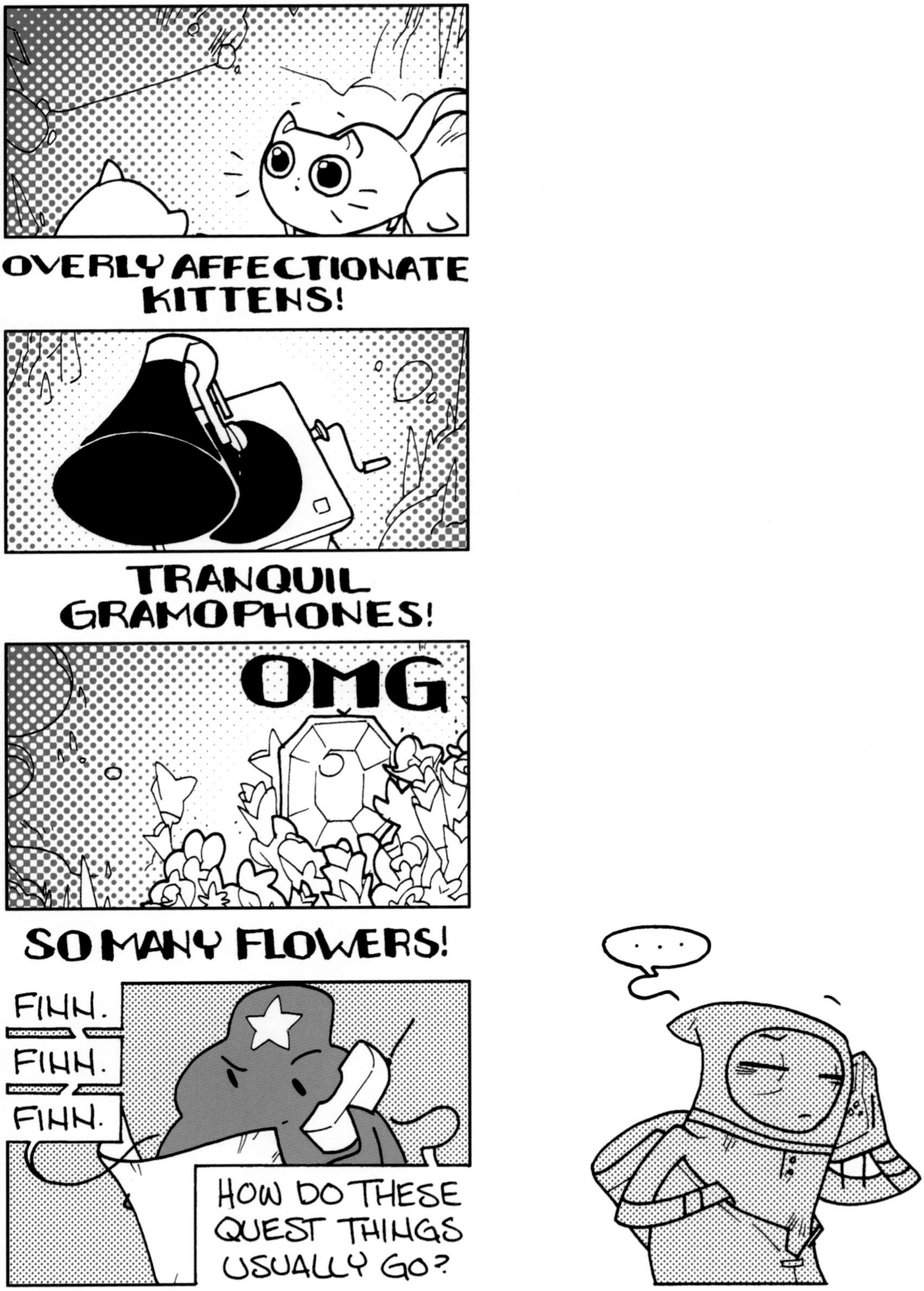
OVERLY AFFECTIONATE KITTENS!
TRANQUIL GRAMOPHONES!
OMG
SO MANY FLOWERS!
FINN.
FINN.
FINN.
HOW DO THESE QUEST THINGS USUALLY GO?
. . .

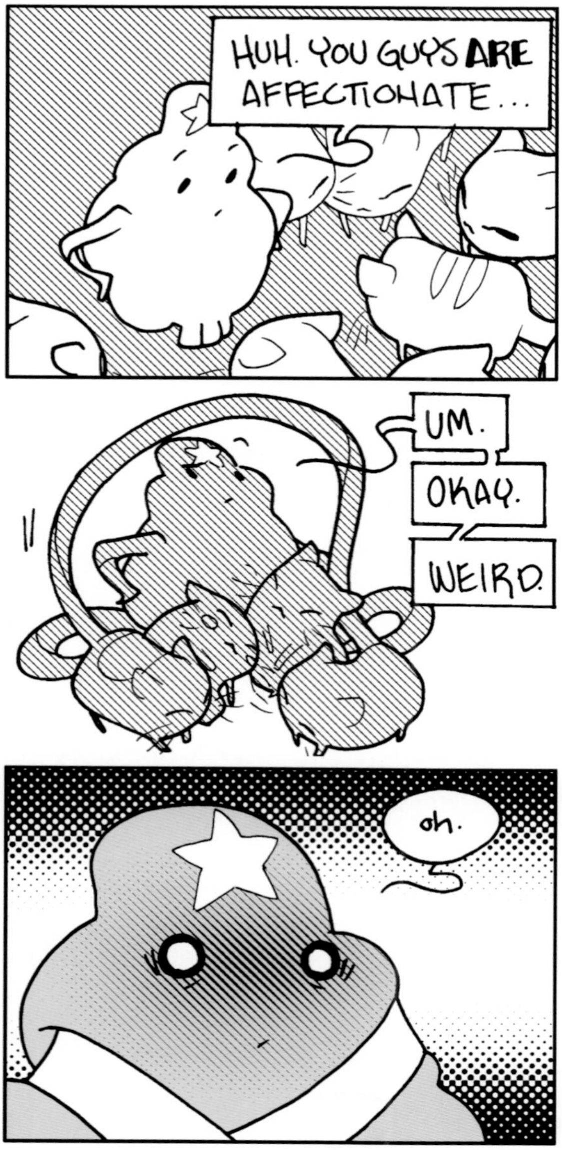
HUH. YOU GUYS ARE AFFECTIONATE...
UM.
OKAY.
WEIRD.
oh.

I THINK THIS QUEST HAS BEEN MISREPRESENTED.

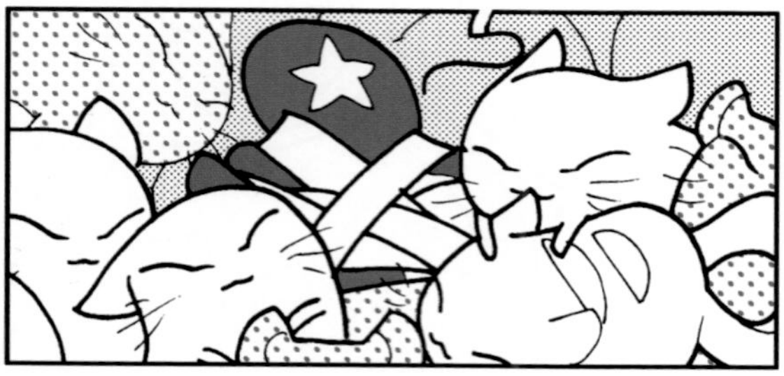

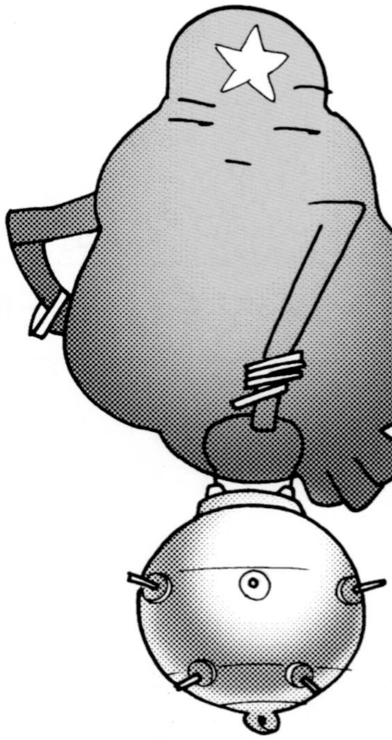

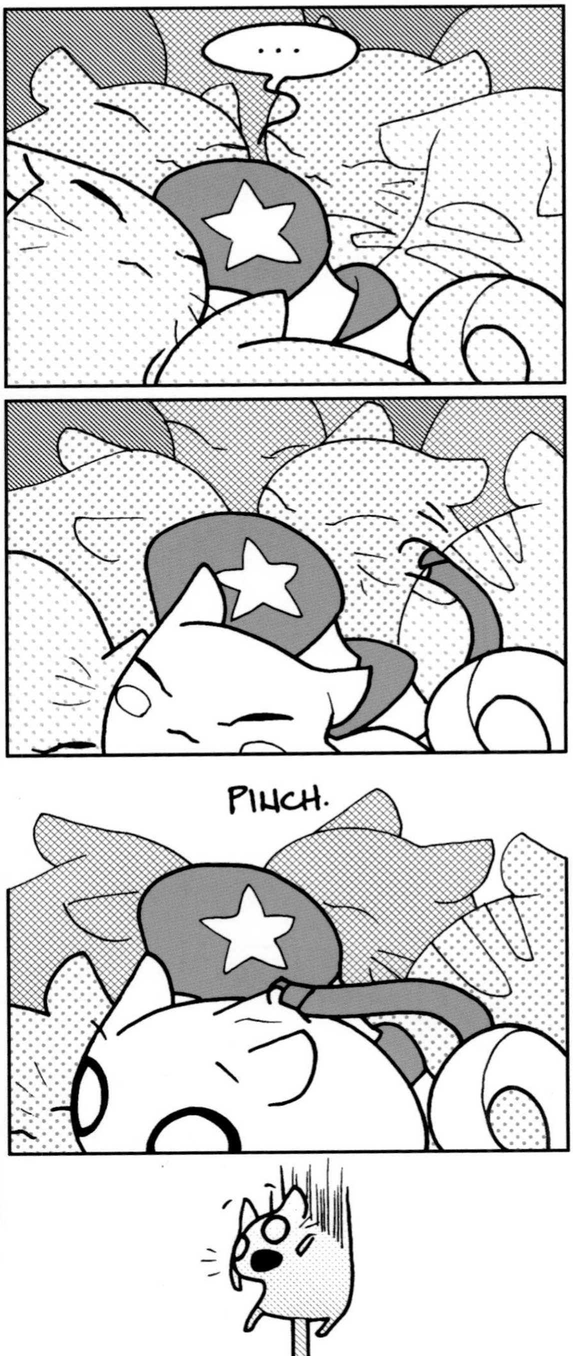
. . . .
PINCH.

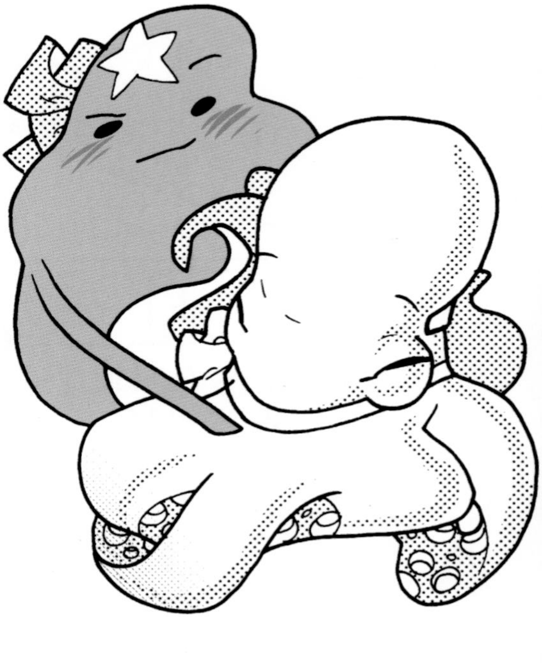

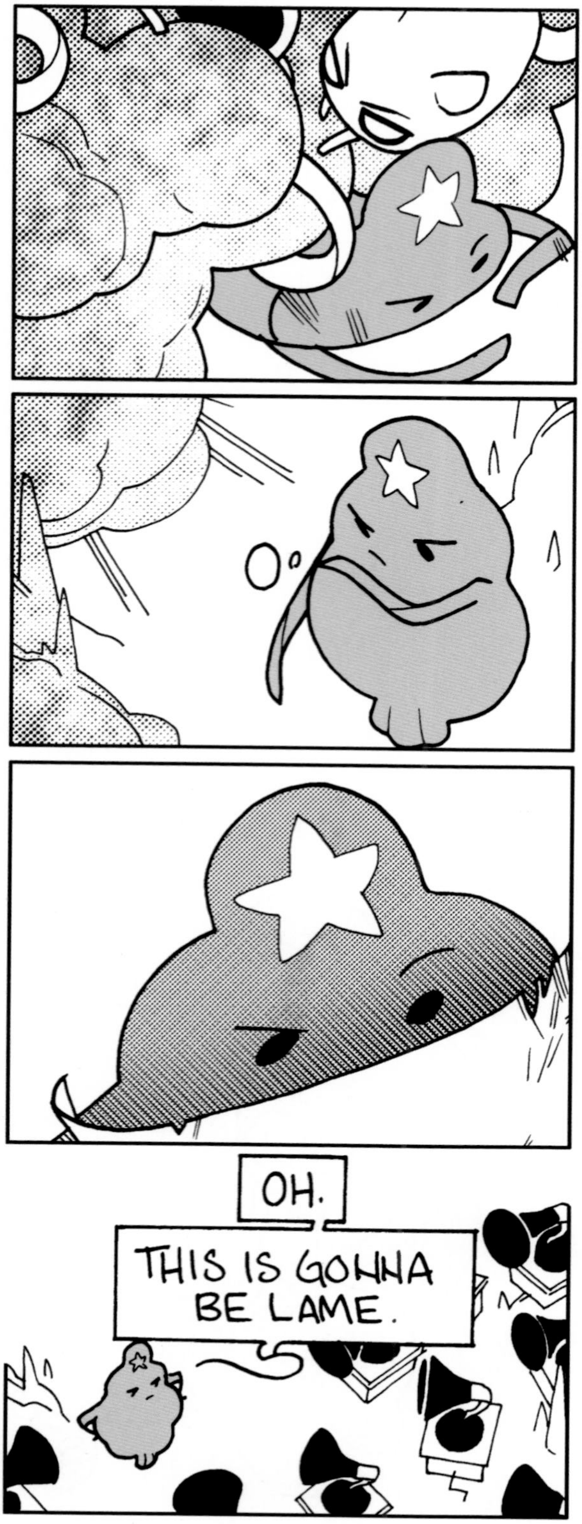
OH.
THIS IS GONNA BE LAME.

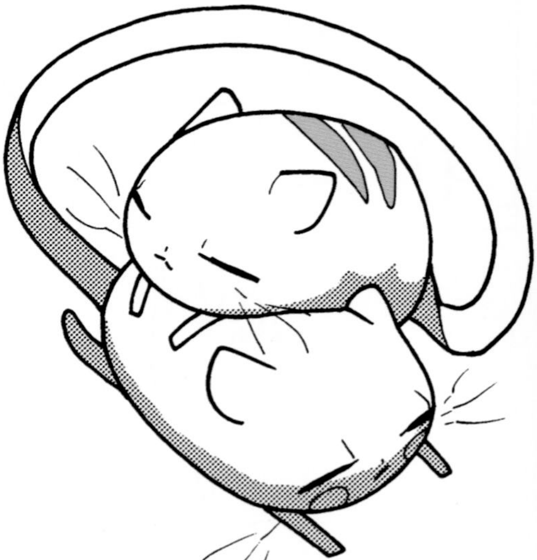

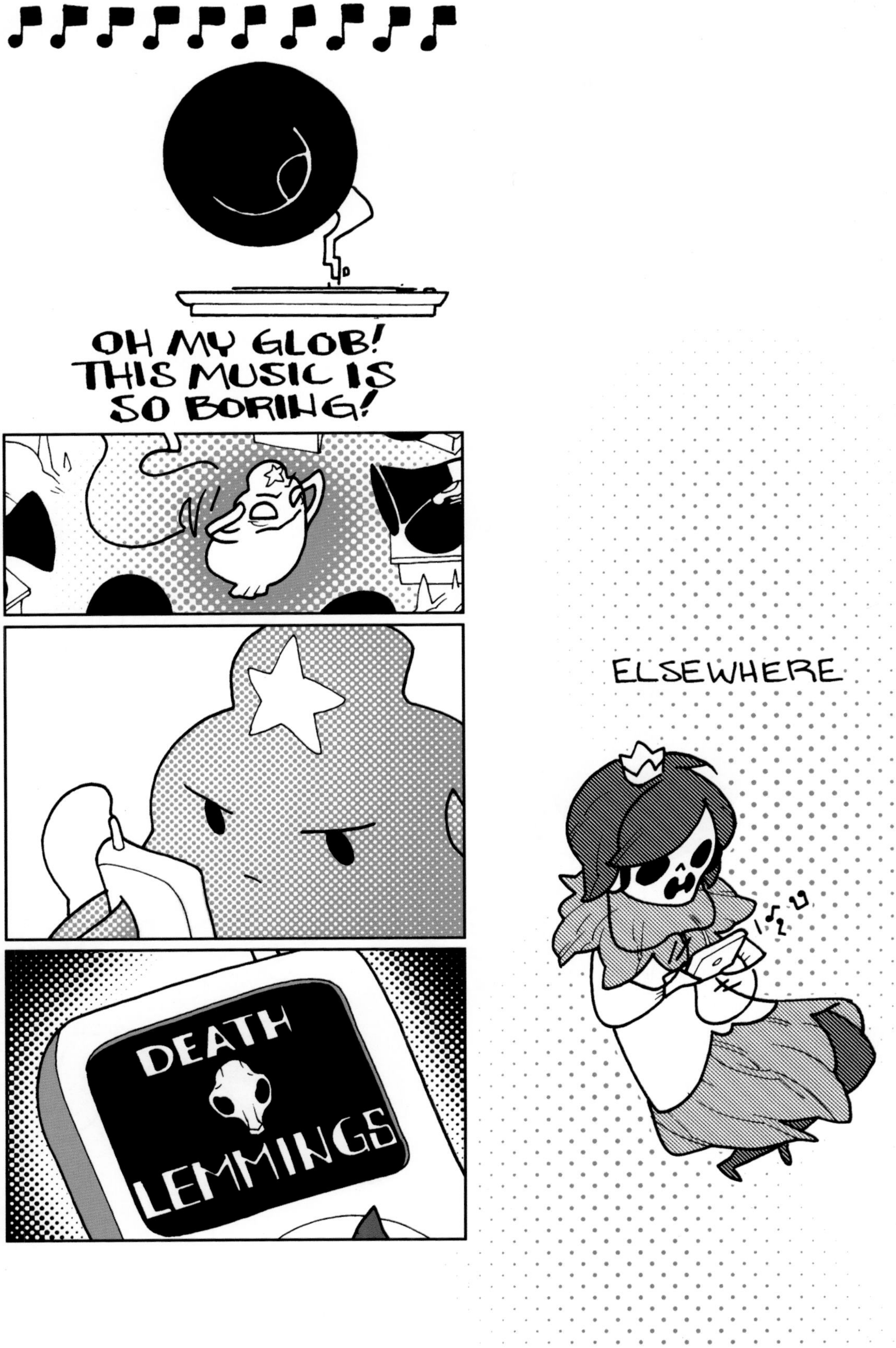
OH MY GLOB! THIS MUSIC IS SO BORING!
DEATH LEMMINGS
ELSEWHERE

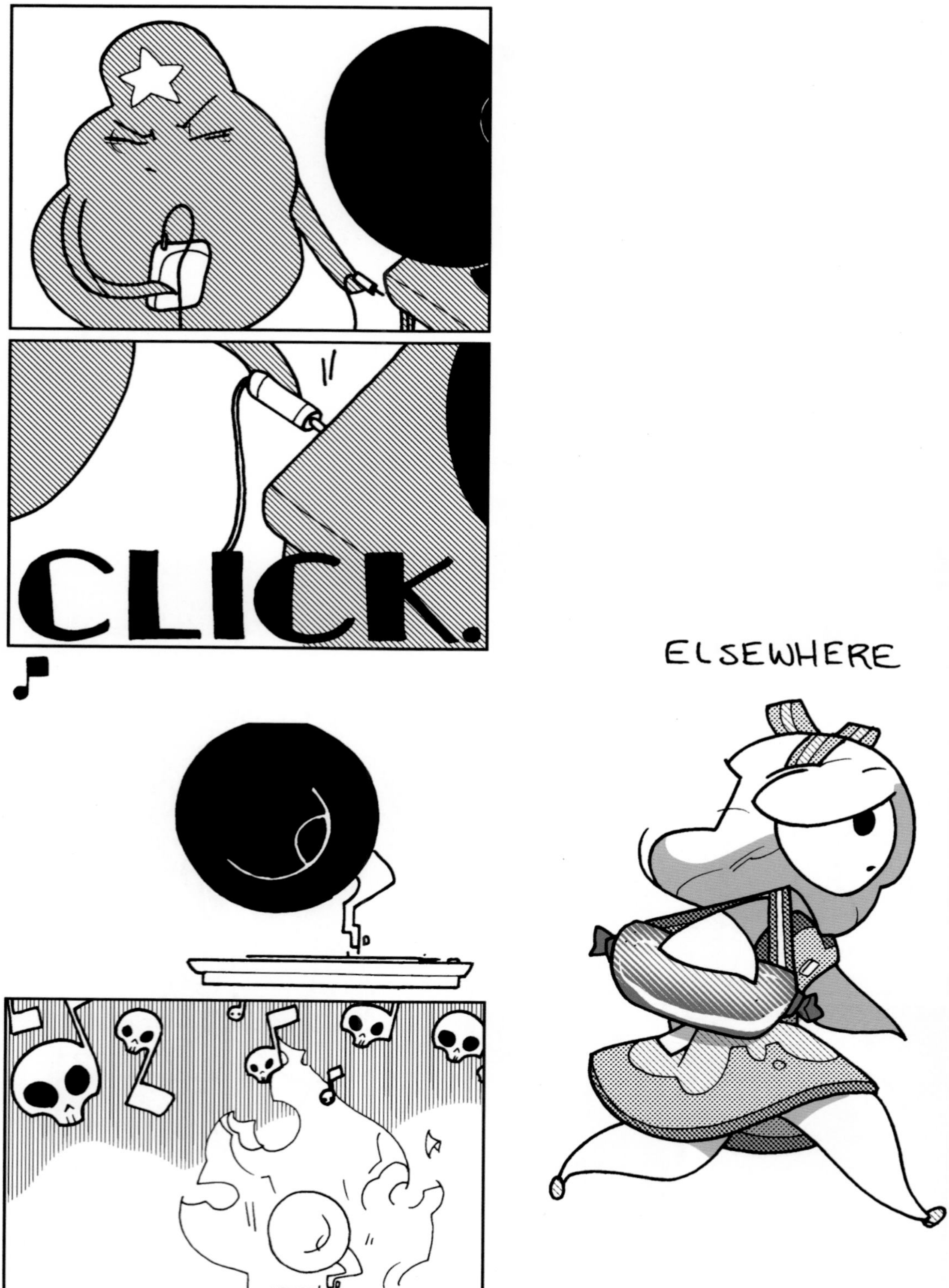
CLICK.
ELSEWHERE

ELSEWHERE

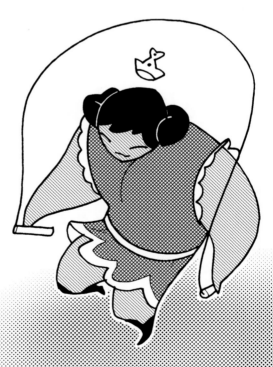

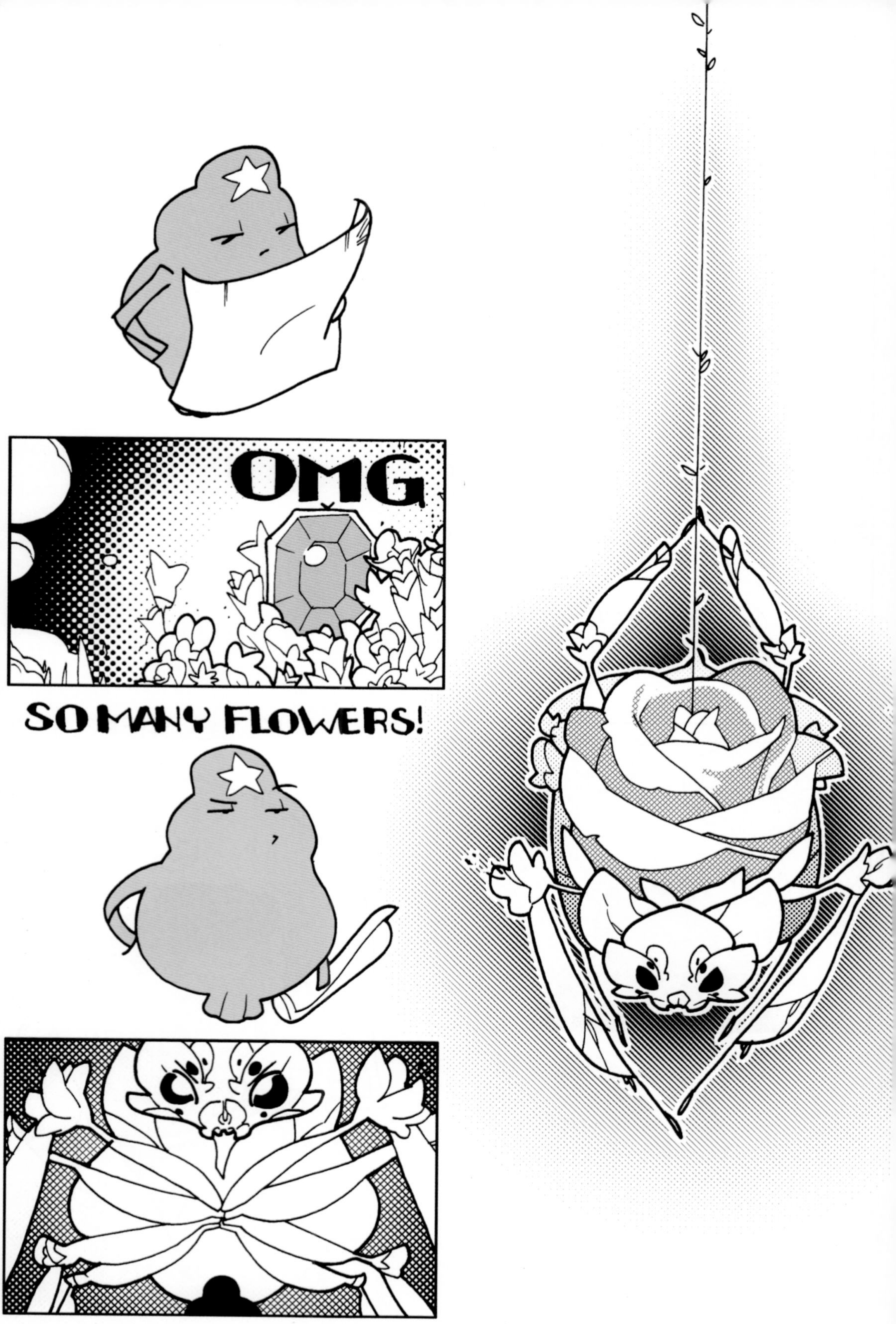
OMG
SO MANY FLOWERS!

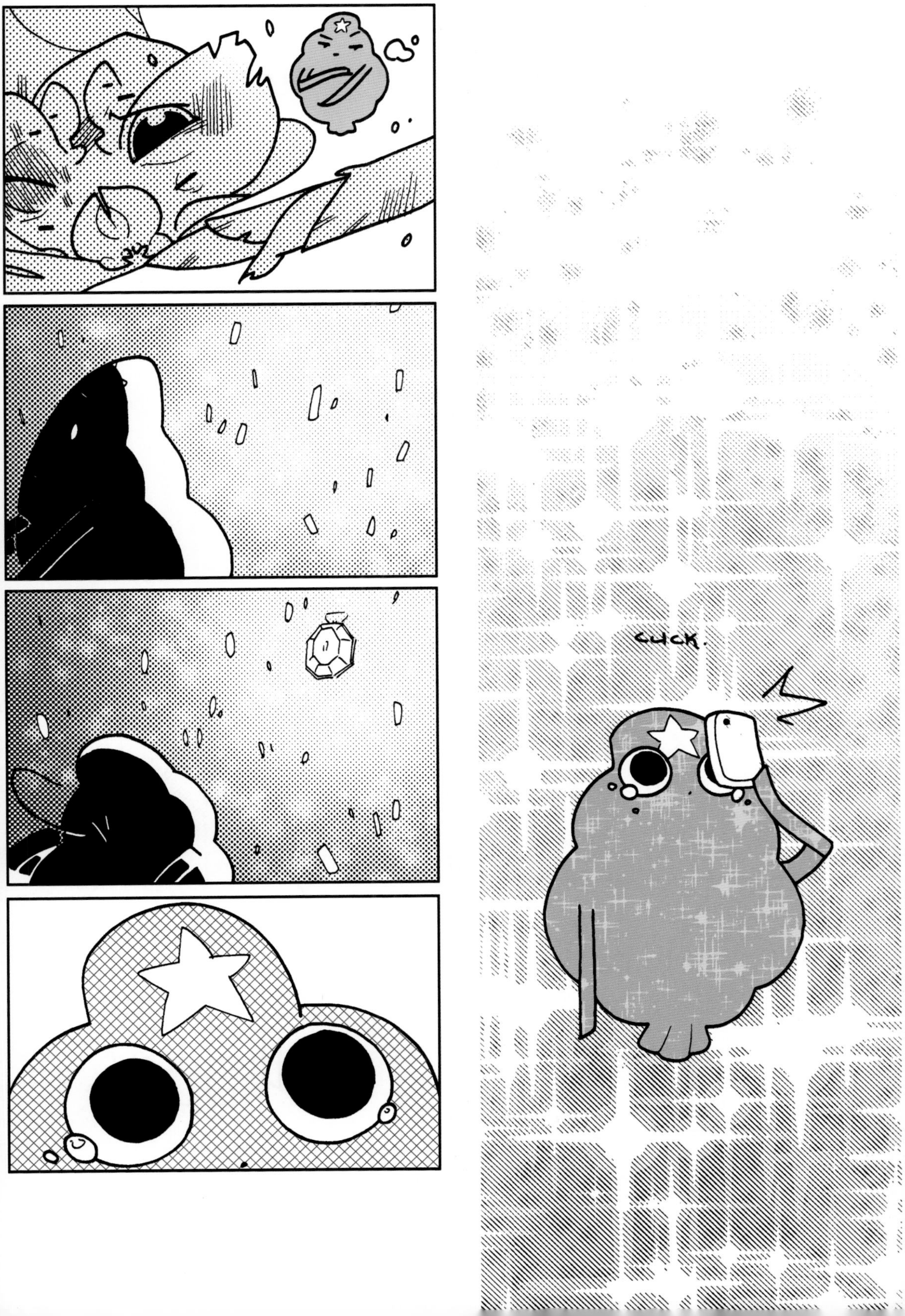
CLICK.

YOU HAVE PROVEN YOURSELF WORTHY OF THE ULTIMATE TRUTH.

THIS IS HOT A QUEST FOR MERE WORLDLY POSSESSIONS! THIS IS A QUEST FOR YOUR INNER WORTH!

YOU'RE NOT A PURSE ARE YOU?

HOT AS SUCH. NO.

LISTEN, SHINY, I DID NOT COME ALL THIS WAY JUST TO HEAR YOU TALK! I WANT MY PURSE. I EARNED MY PURSE. GIVE ME THE GLOBBIN' PURSE!

BUT.

BUT.

YOU DON'T NEED THE PURSE. THE FABULOUSNESS WAS INSIDE YOU ALL ALONG!

I ALREADY KNEW THAT.

ELSEWHERE

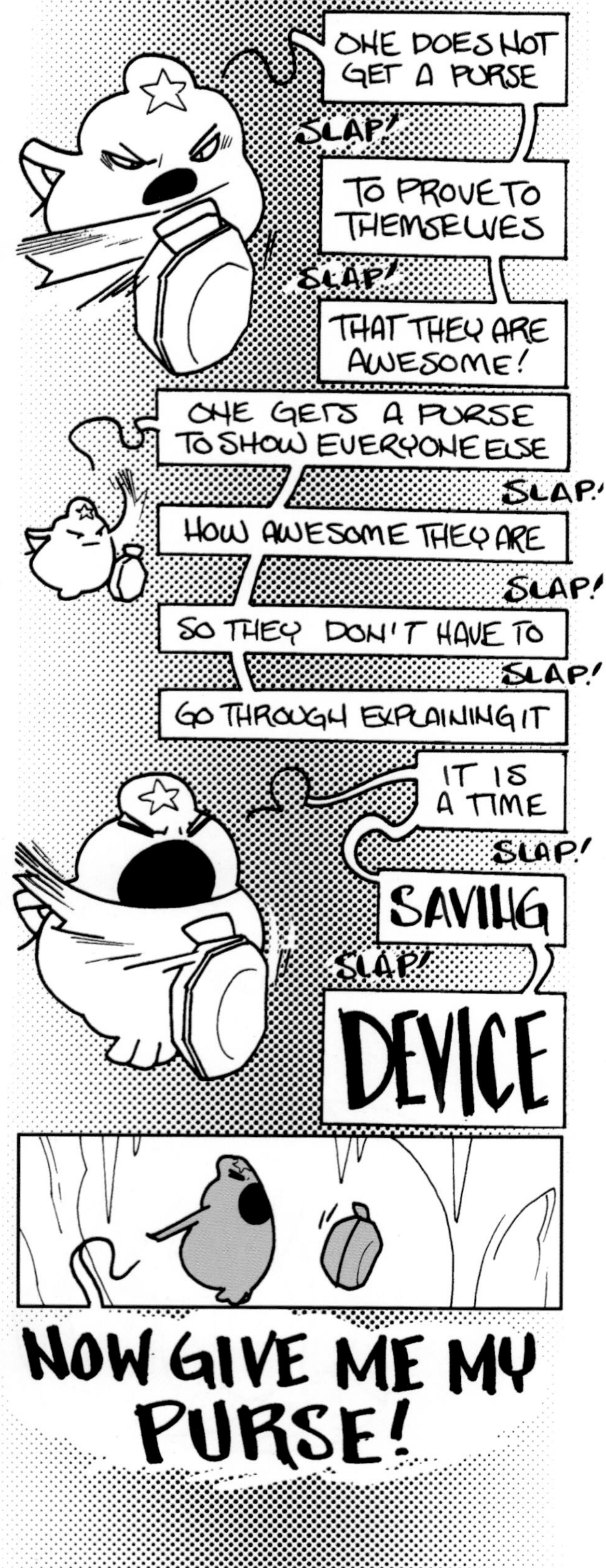
ONE DOES NOT GET A PURSE
SLAP!
TO PROVE TO THEMSELVES
SLAP!
THAT THEY ARE AWESOME!
ONE GETS A PURSE TO SHOW EVERYONE ELSE
SLAP!
HOW AWESOME THEY ARE
SLAP!
SO THEY DON'T HAVE TO
SLAP!
GO THROUGH EXPLAINING IT
IT IS A TIME
SLAP!
SAVING
SLAP!
DEVICE
NOW GIVE ME MY PURSE!

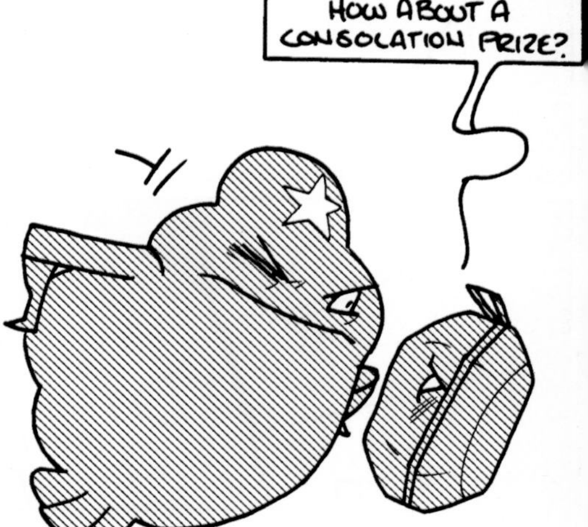
HOW ABOUT A CONSOLATION PRIZE?

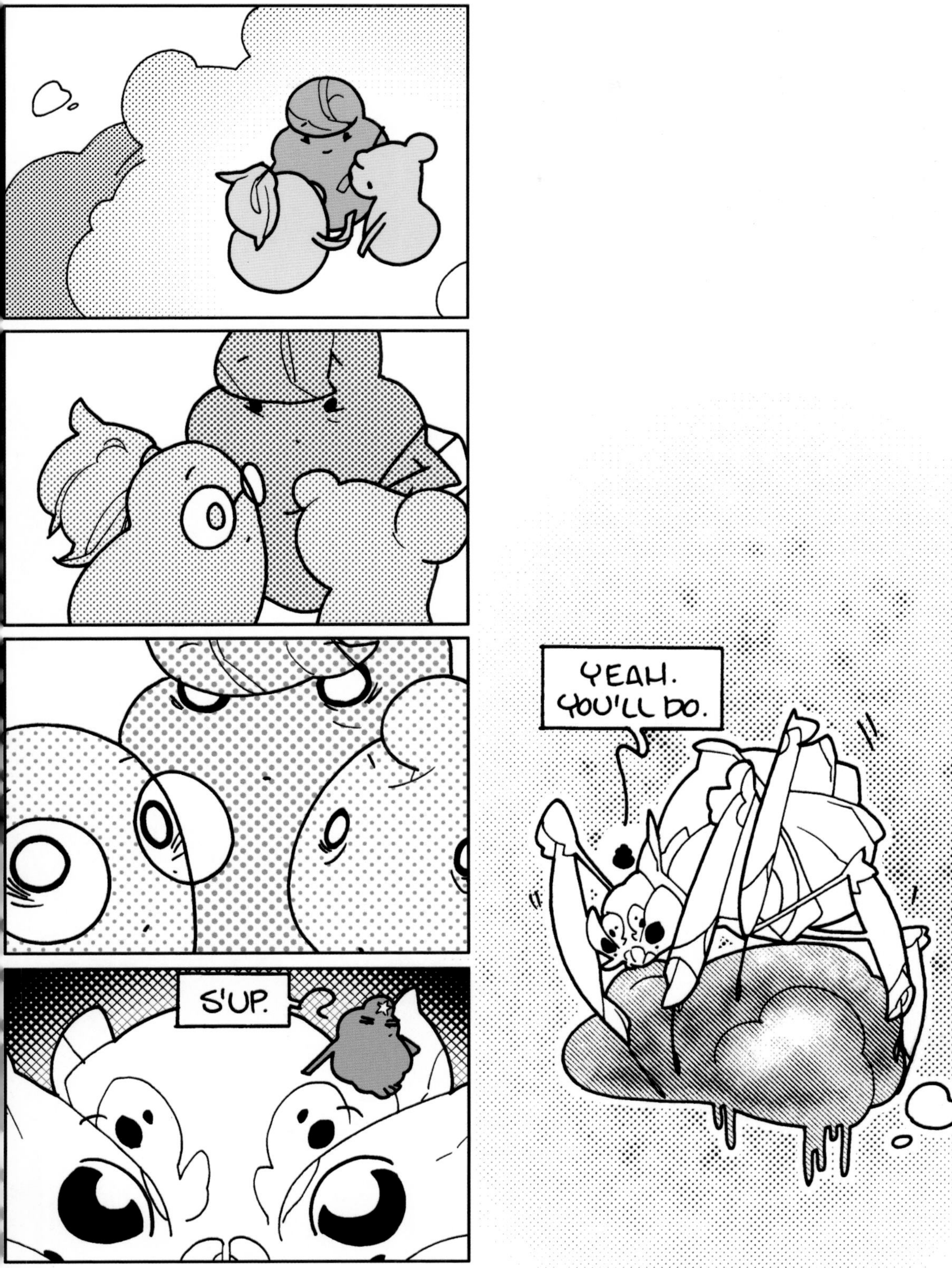
S'UP.
YEAH.
YOU'LL DO.

END.

FOREST PRINCESS GETS A PET

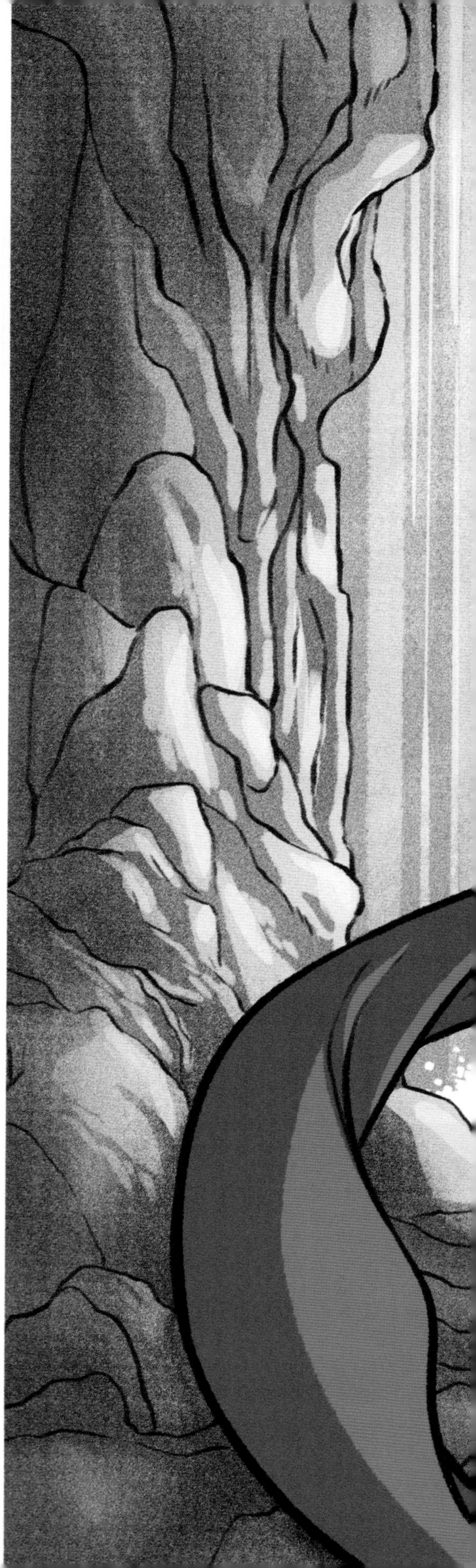

ADVENTURE TIME: BITTER SWEETS COVER
STEPHANIE GONZAGA

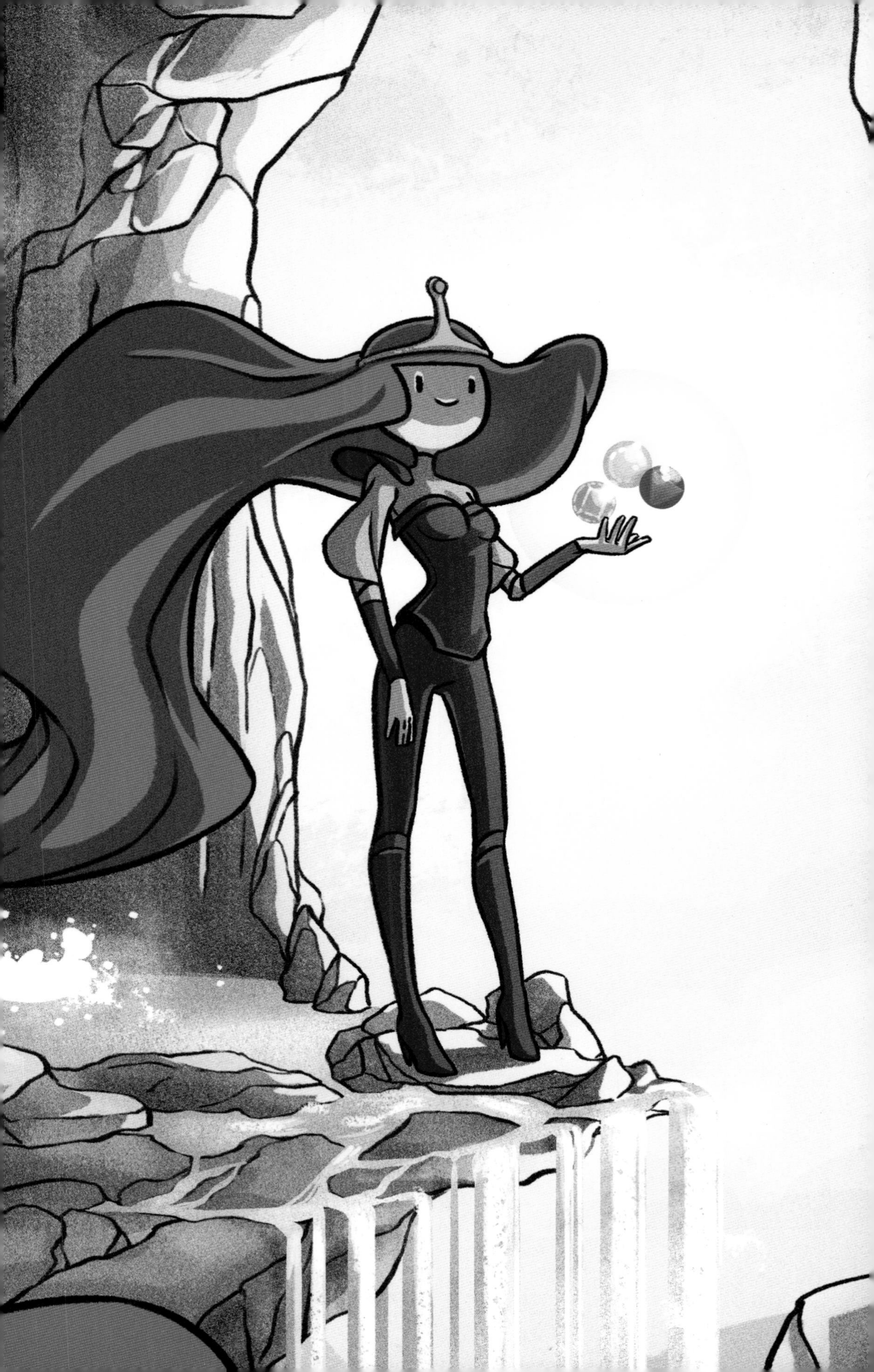

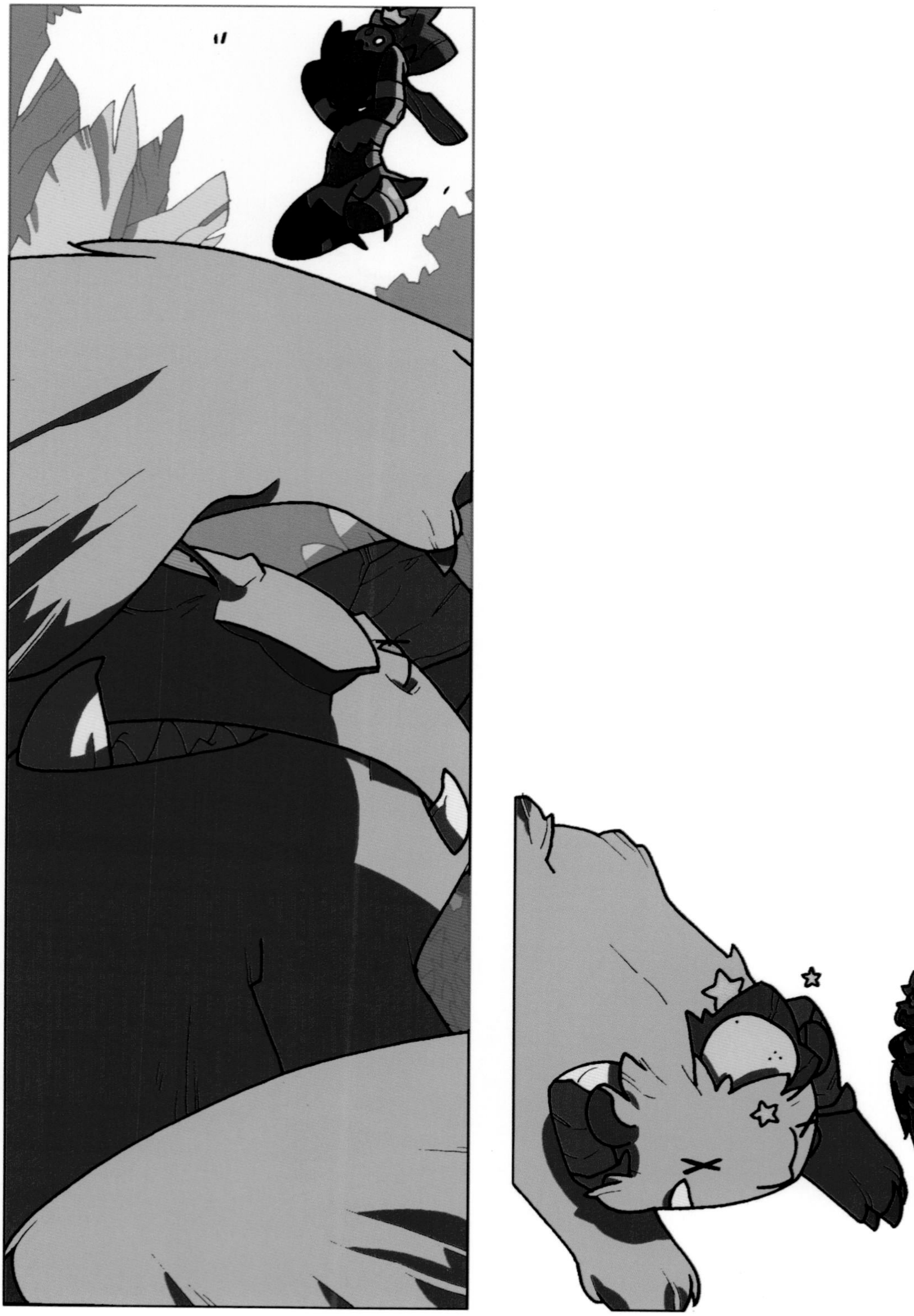

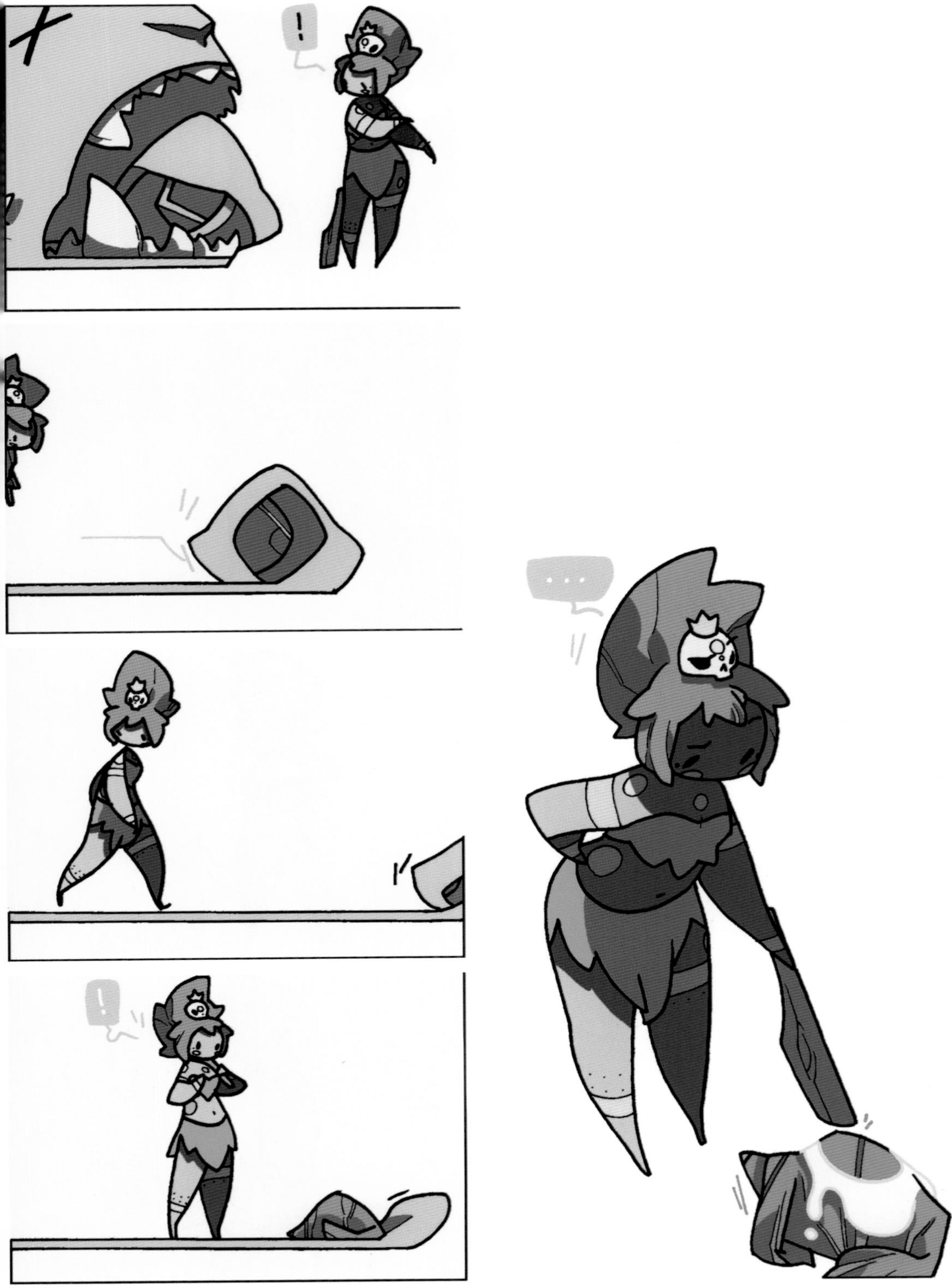
!
!
...

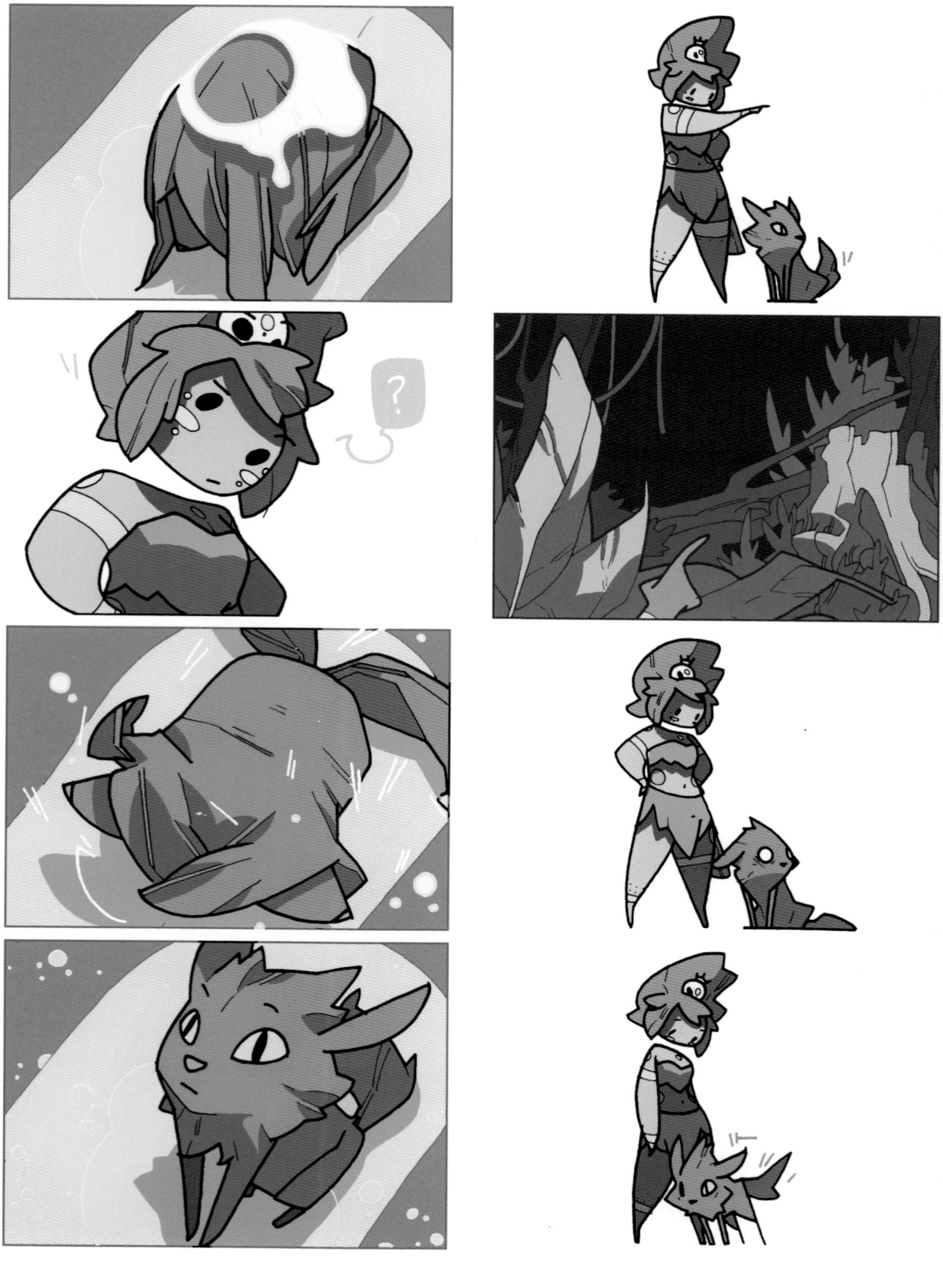
?

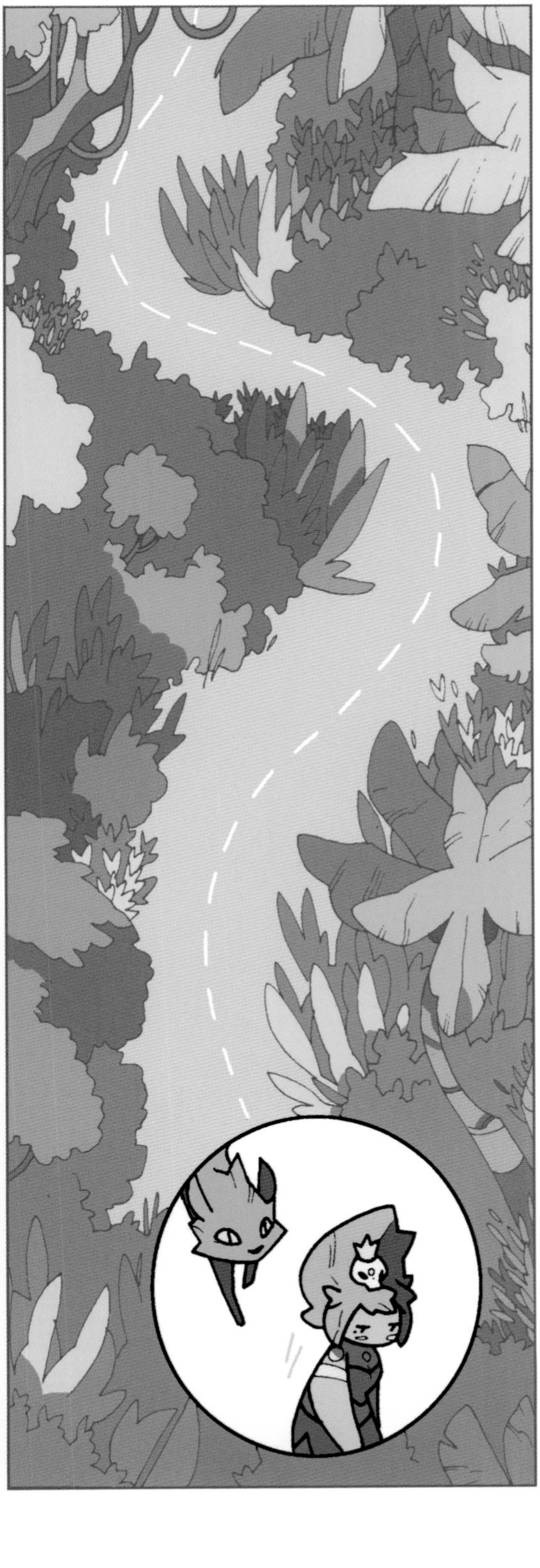
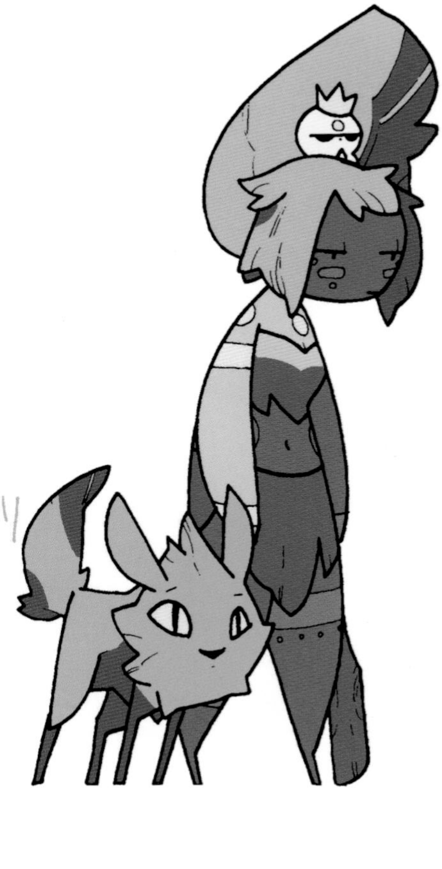

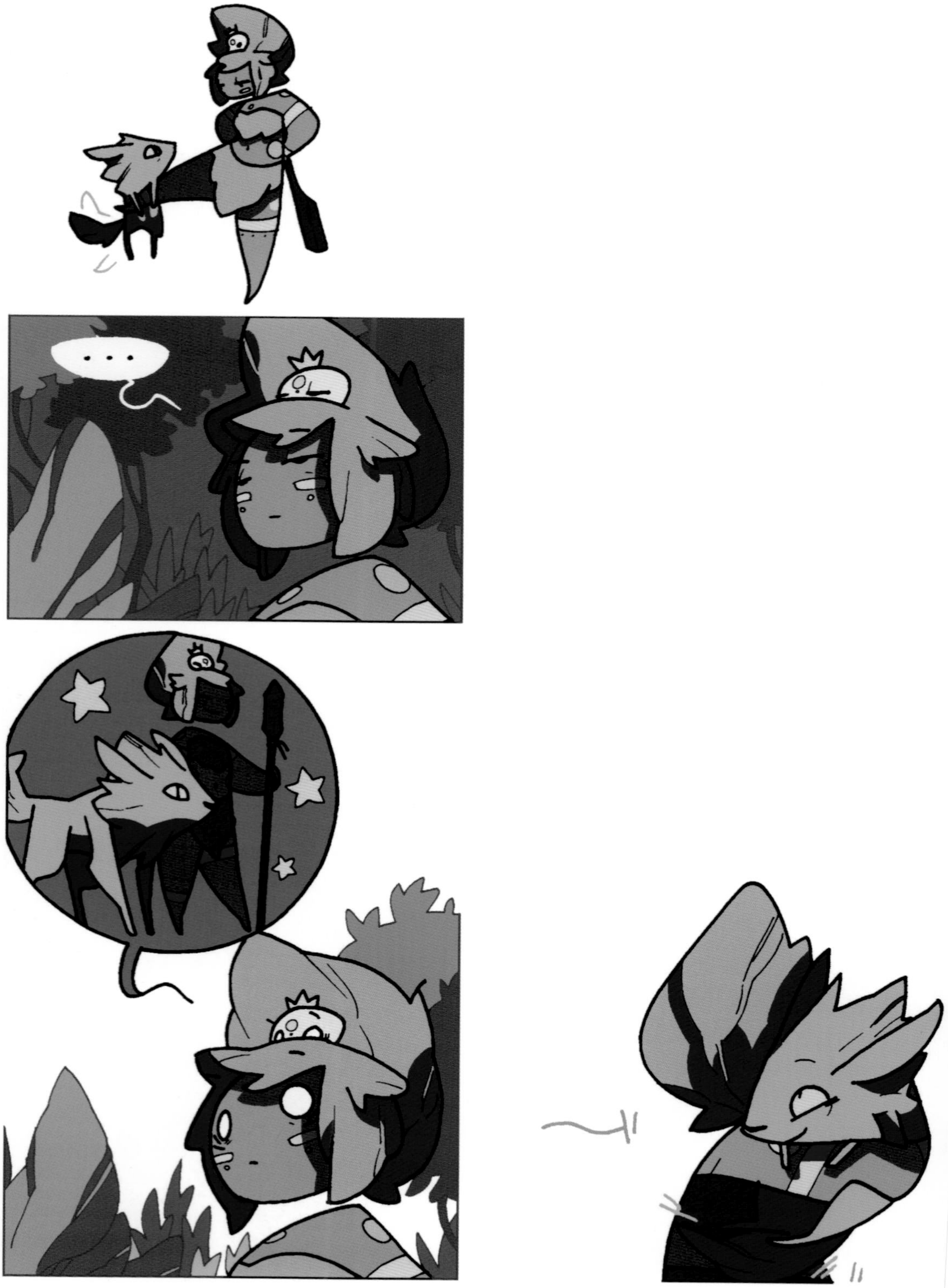
...

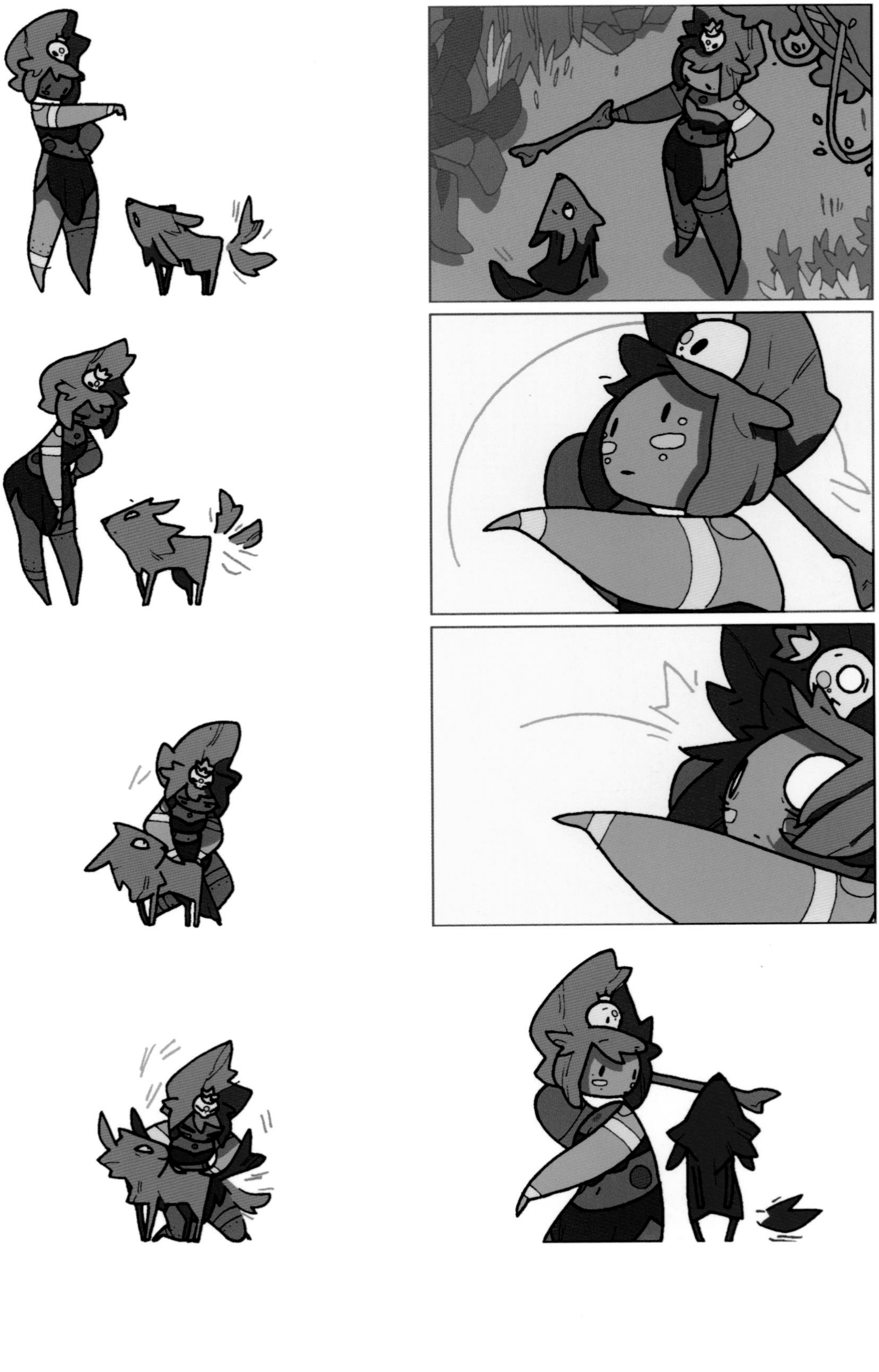

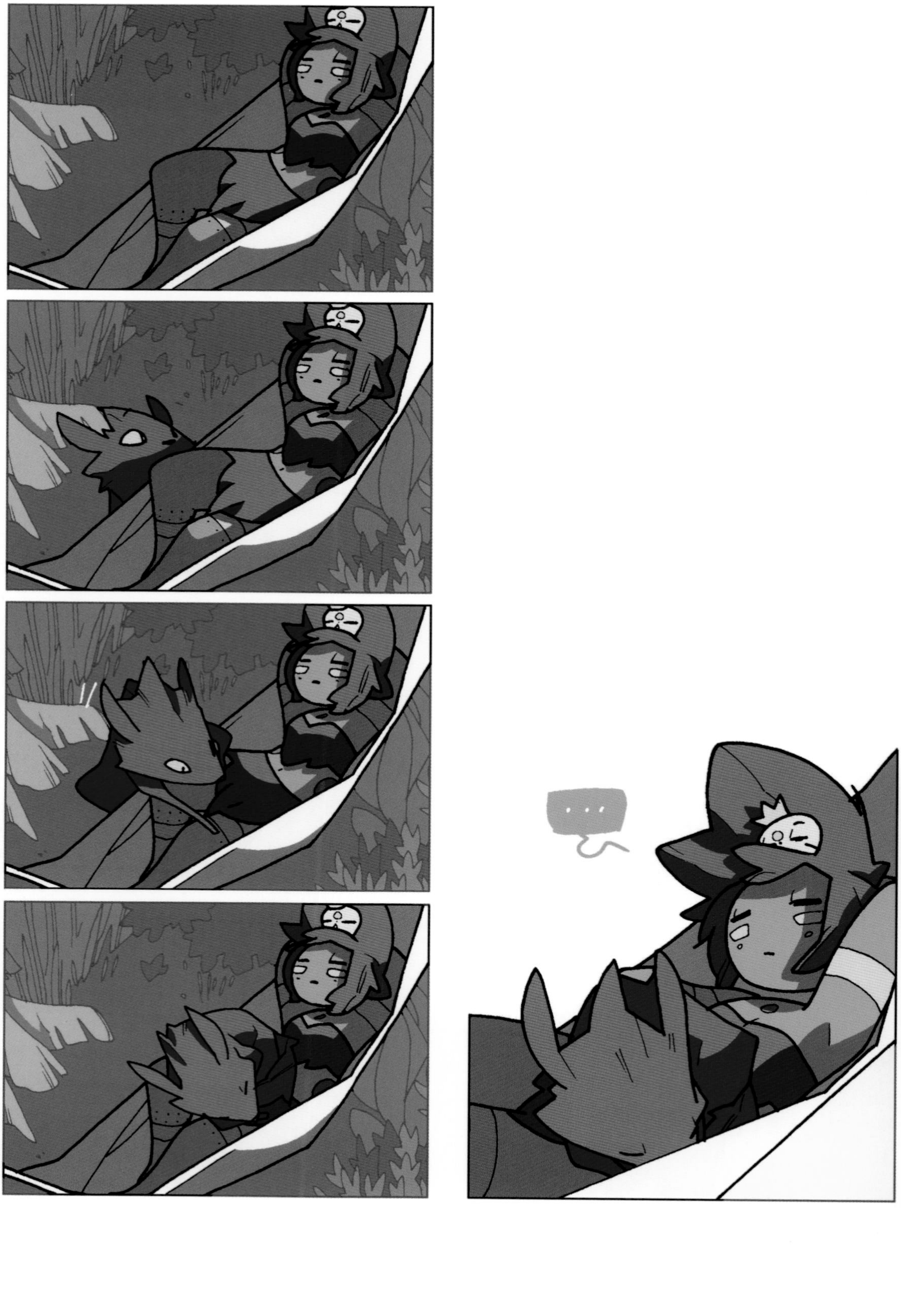
...

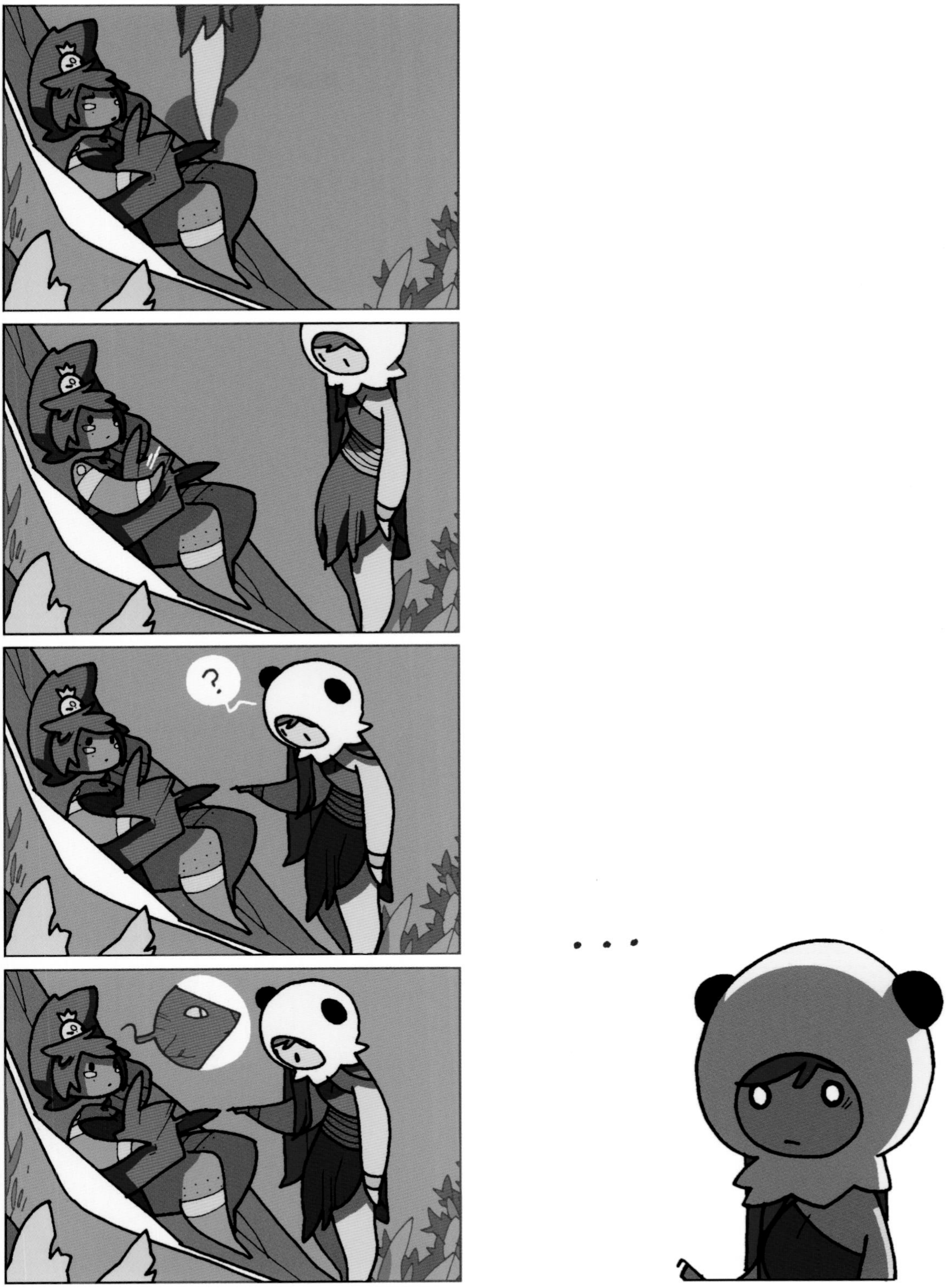
?
. . .

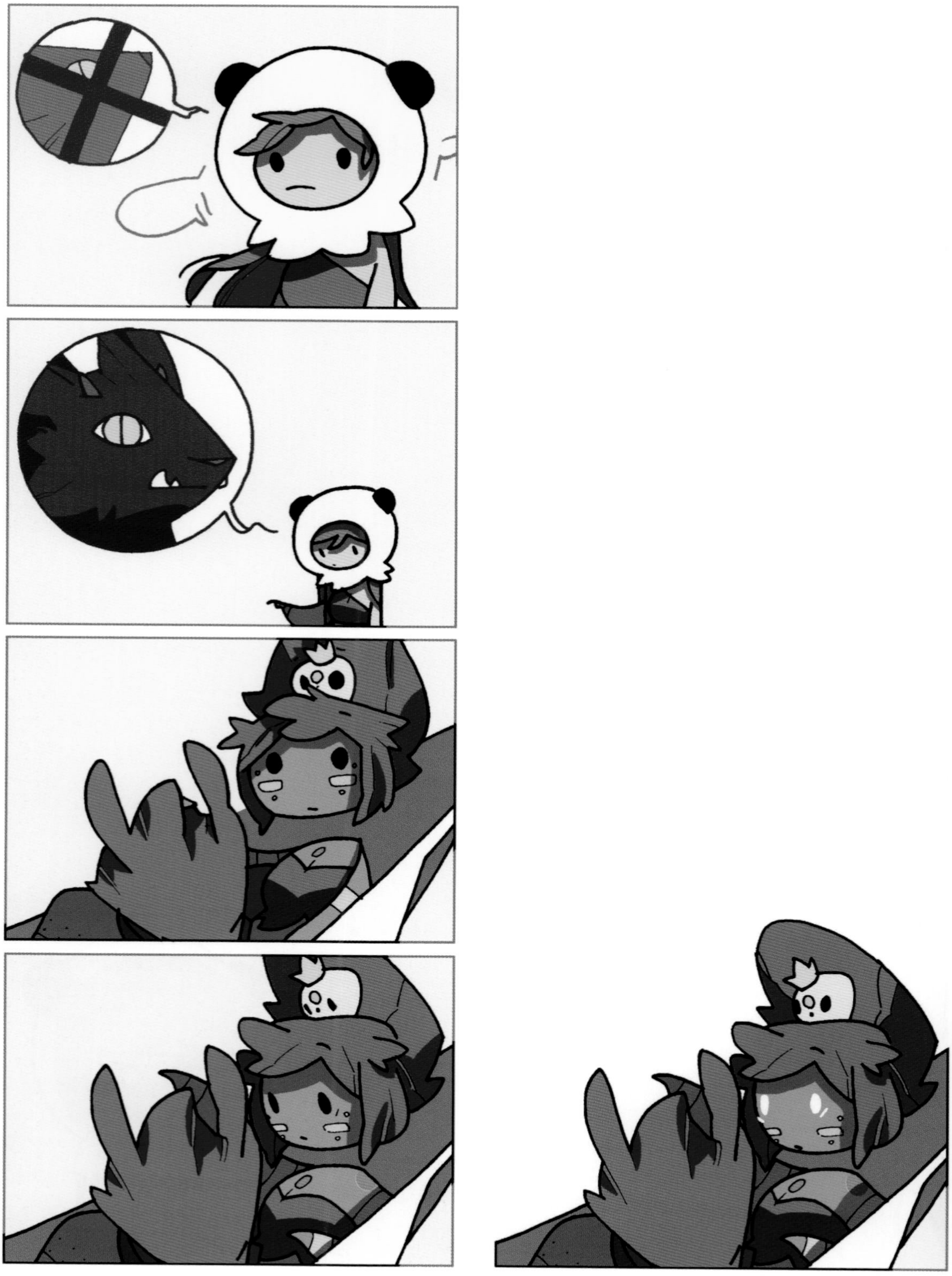

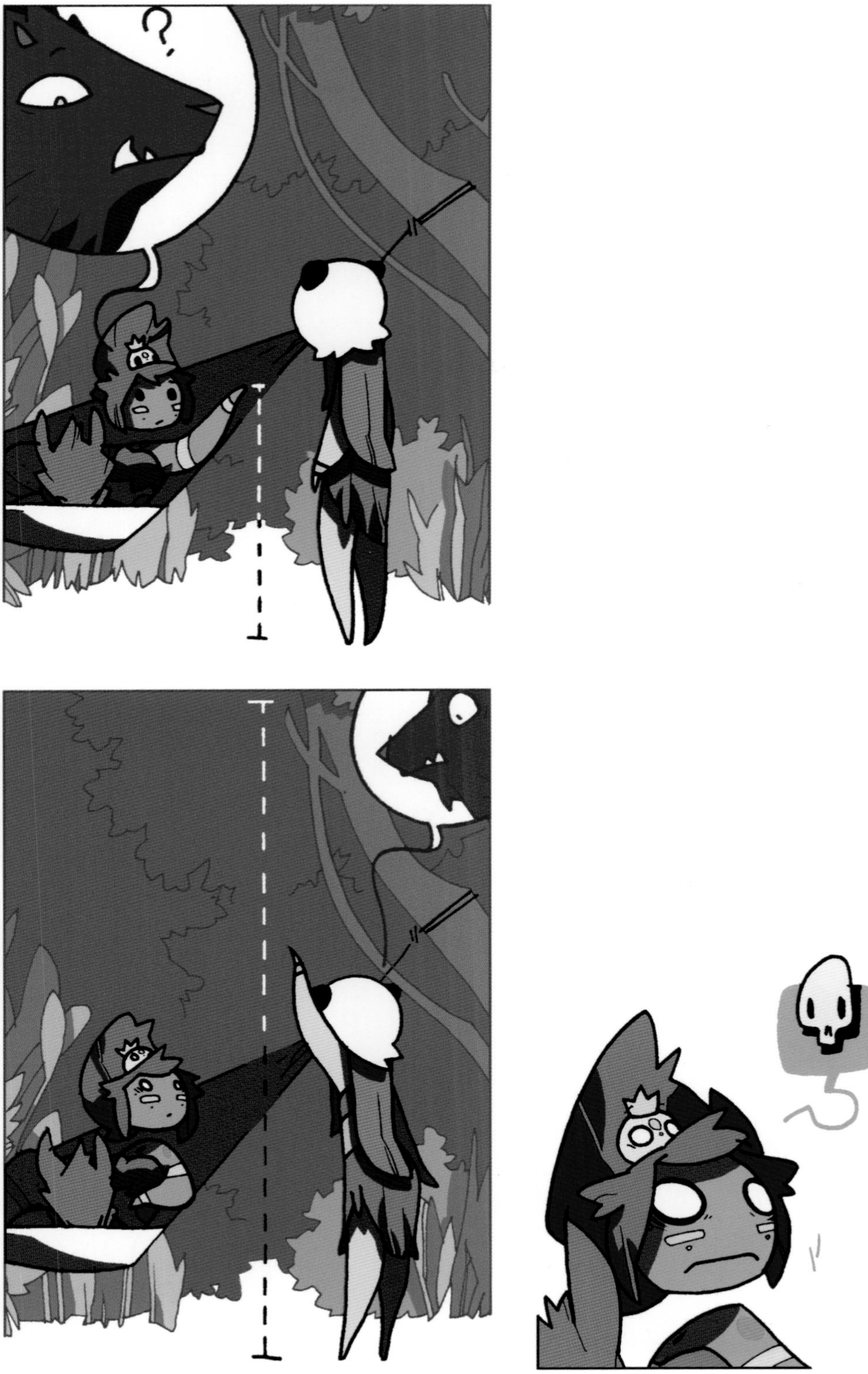
?

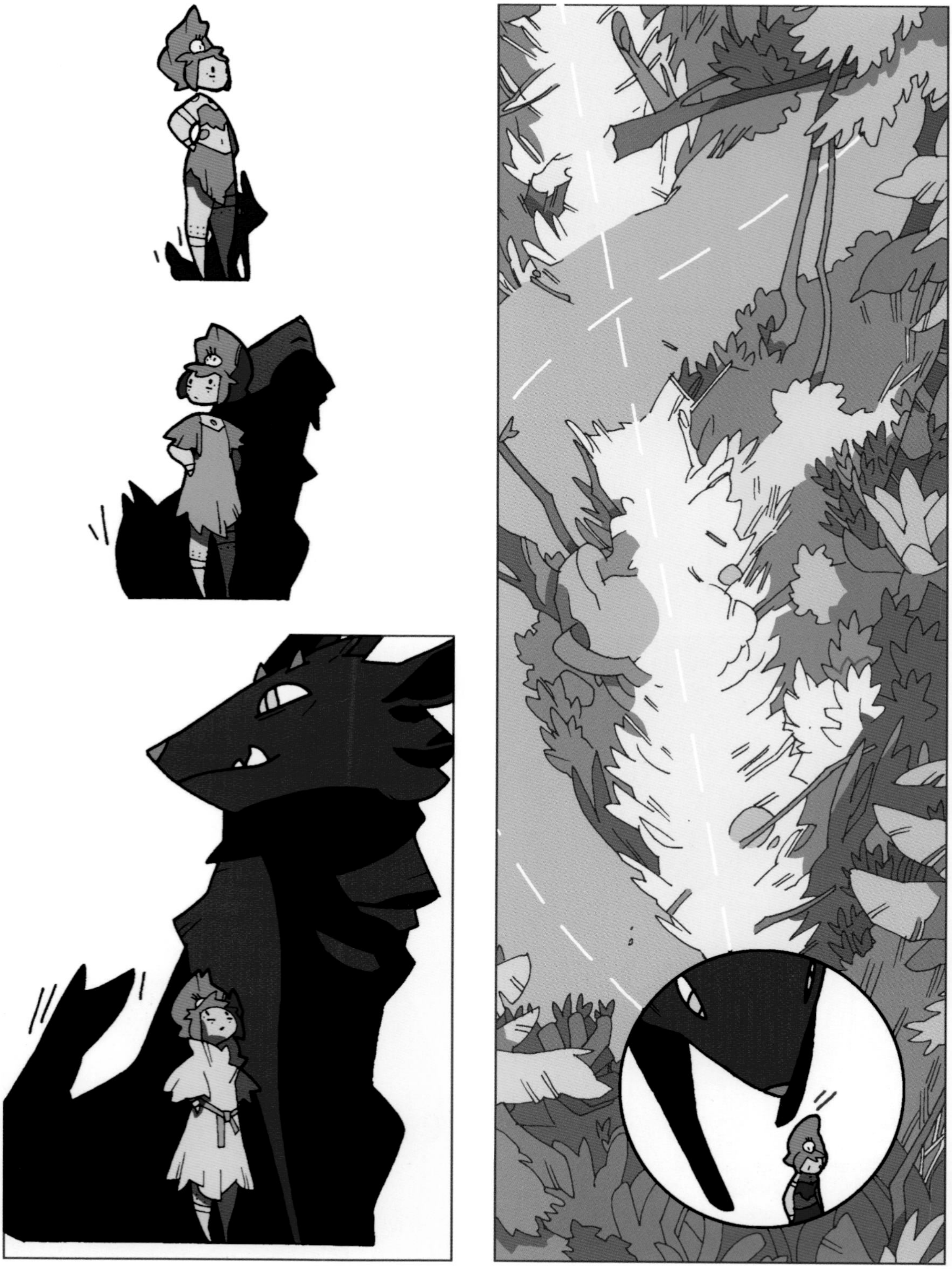

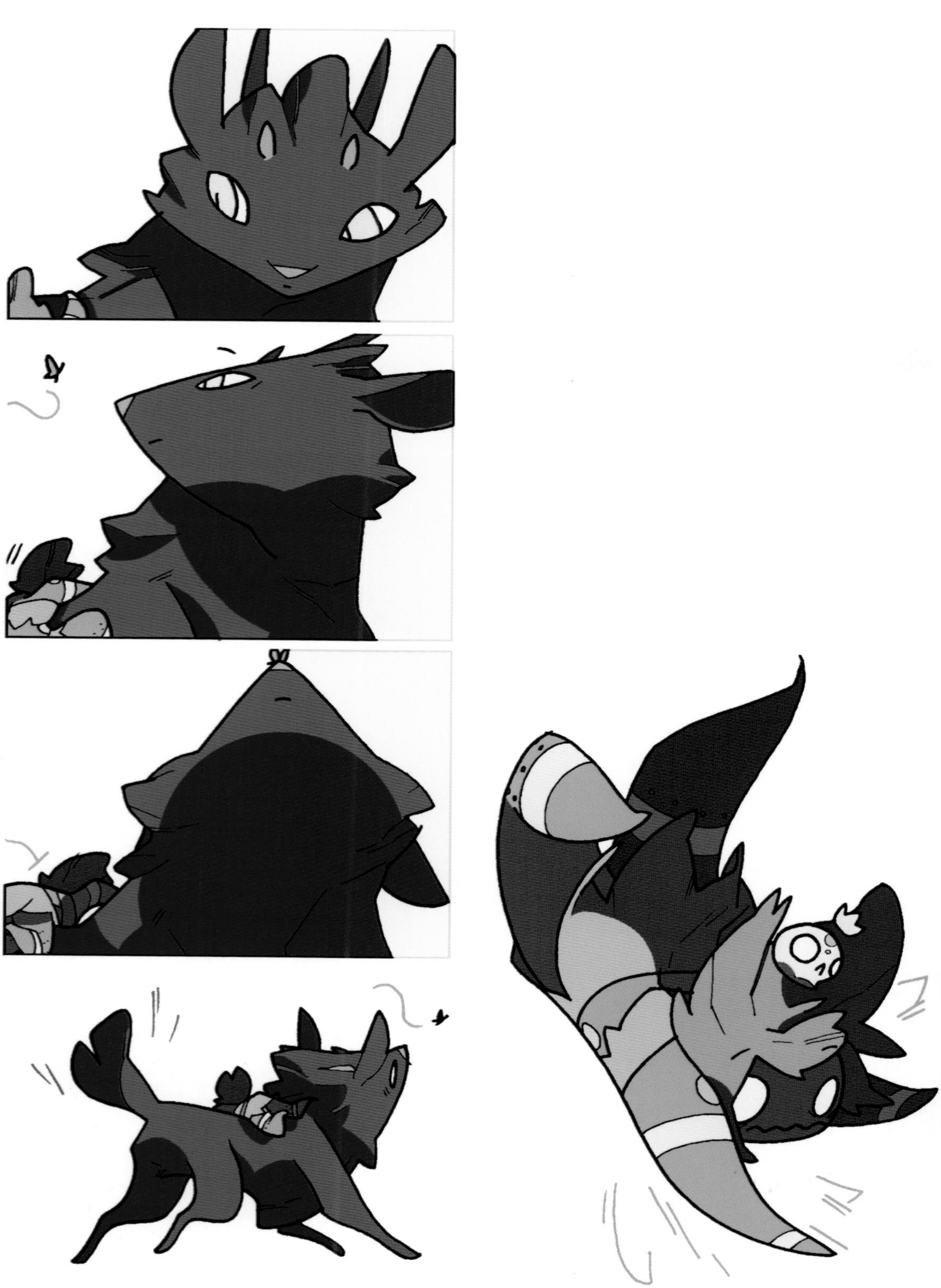

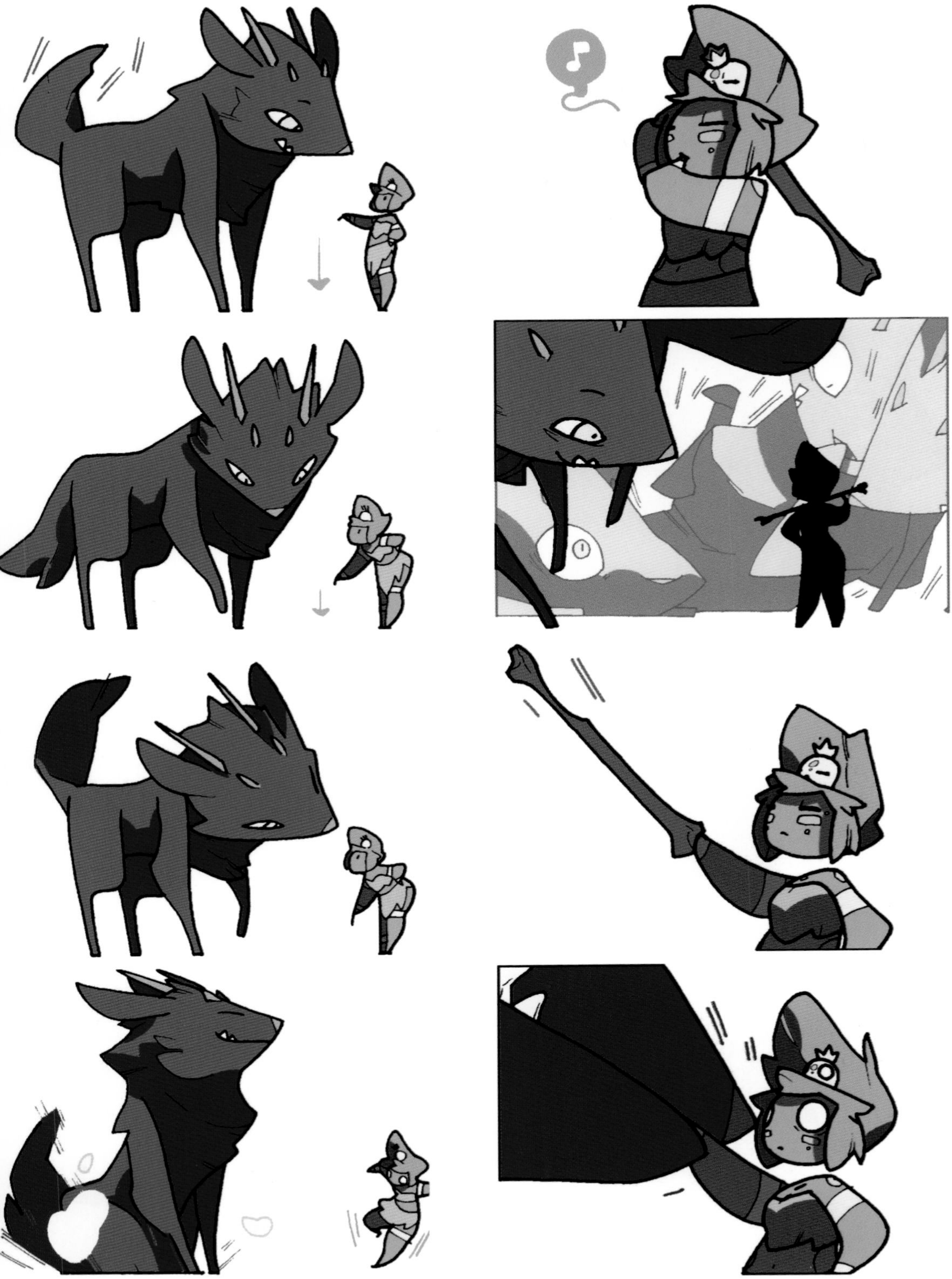

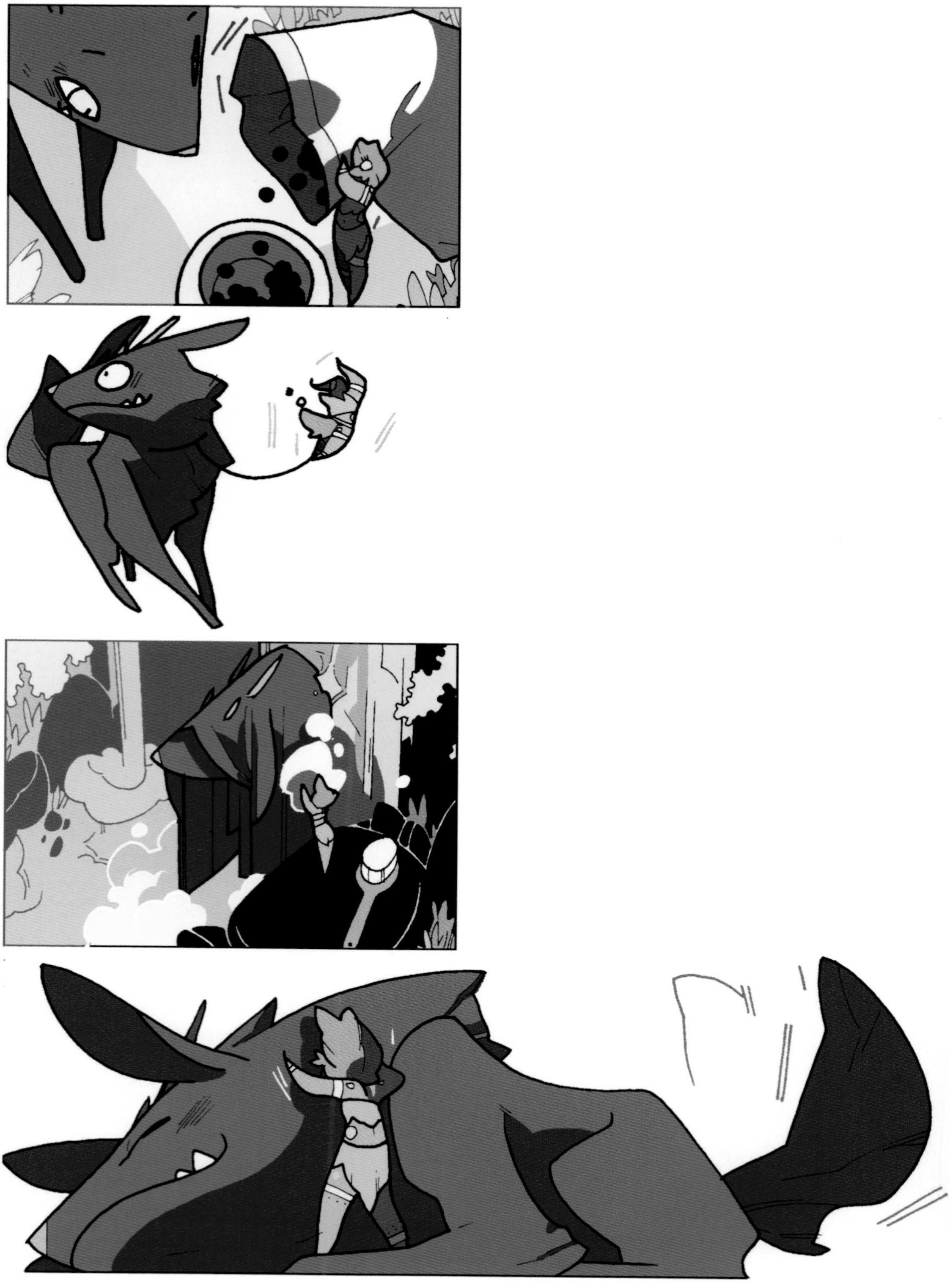

Z

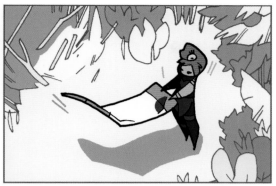

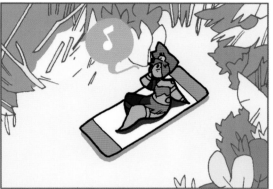

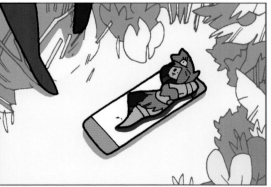

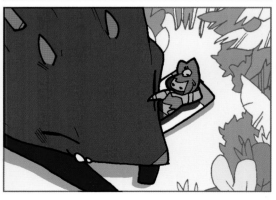

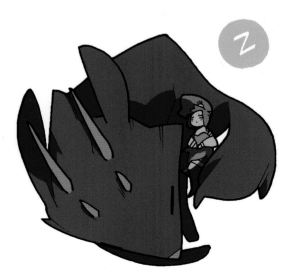

THE MOON — ECLIPSE

2015 SPOOOKTACULAR ISSUE ONE INCENTIVE COVER
EMILY PARTRIDGE

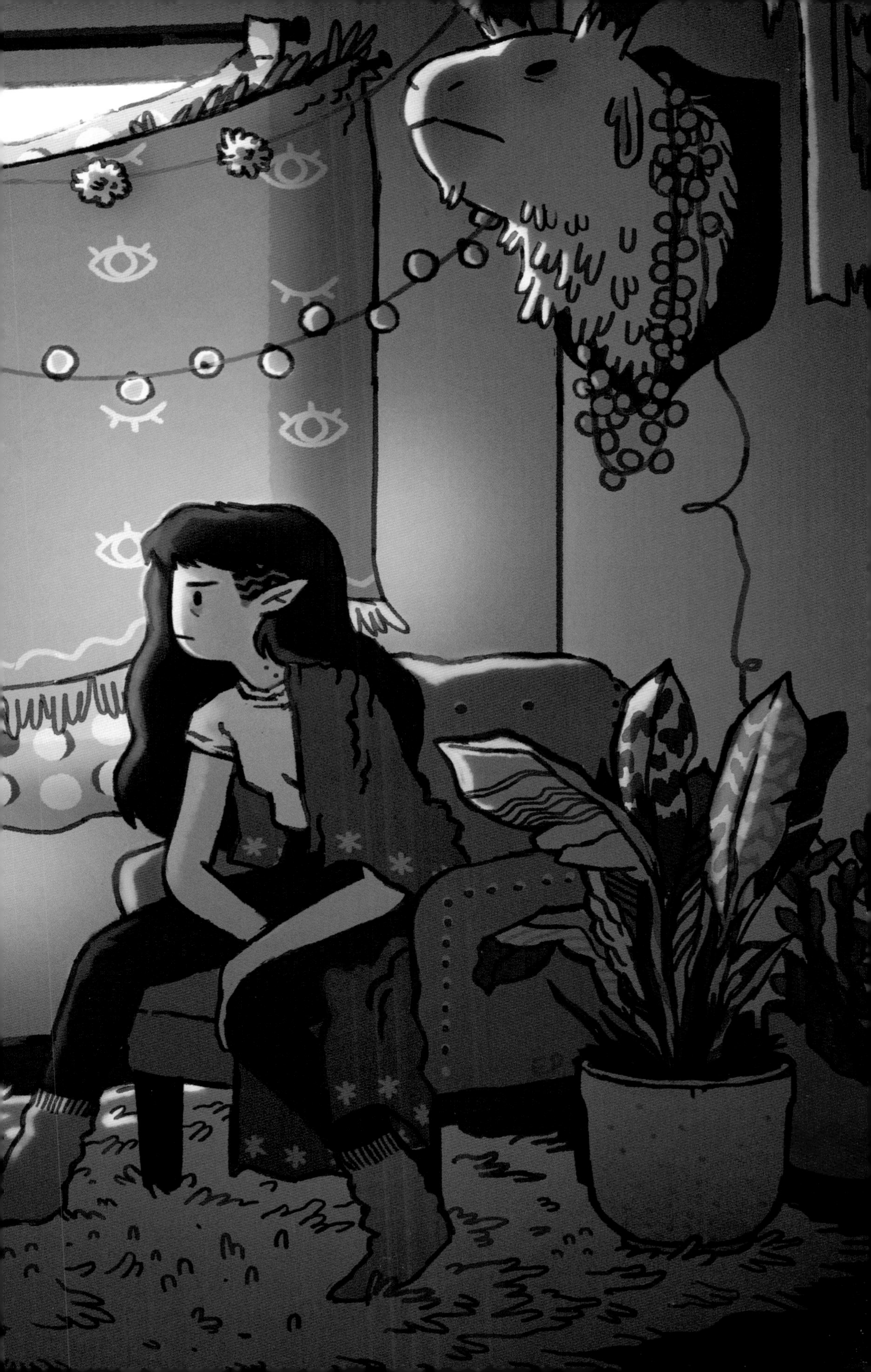

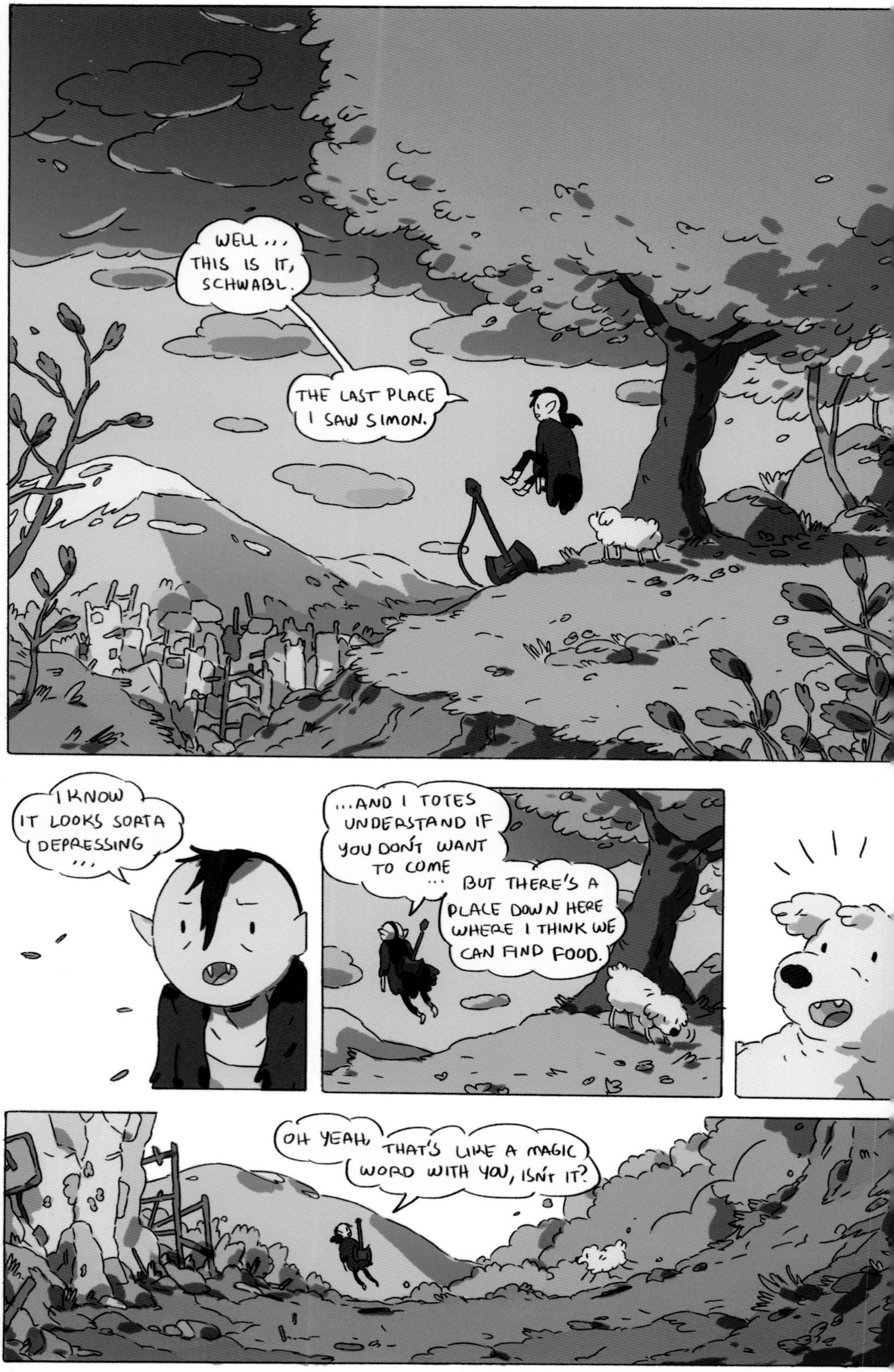
WELL... THIS IS IT, SCHWABL.
THE LAST PLACE I SAW SIMON.
I KNOW IT LOOKS SORTA DEPRESSING ...
...AND I TOTES UNDERSTAND IF YOU DON'T WANT TO COME ...
BUT THERE'S A PLACE DOWN HERE WHERE I THINK WE CAN FIND FOOD.
OH YEAH,
THAT'S LIKE A MAGIC WORD WITH YOU, ISN'T IT?

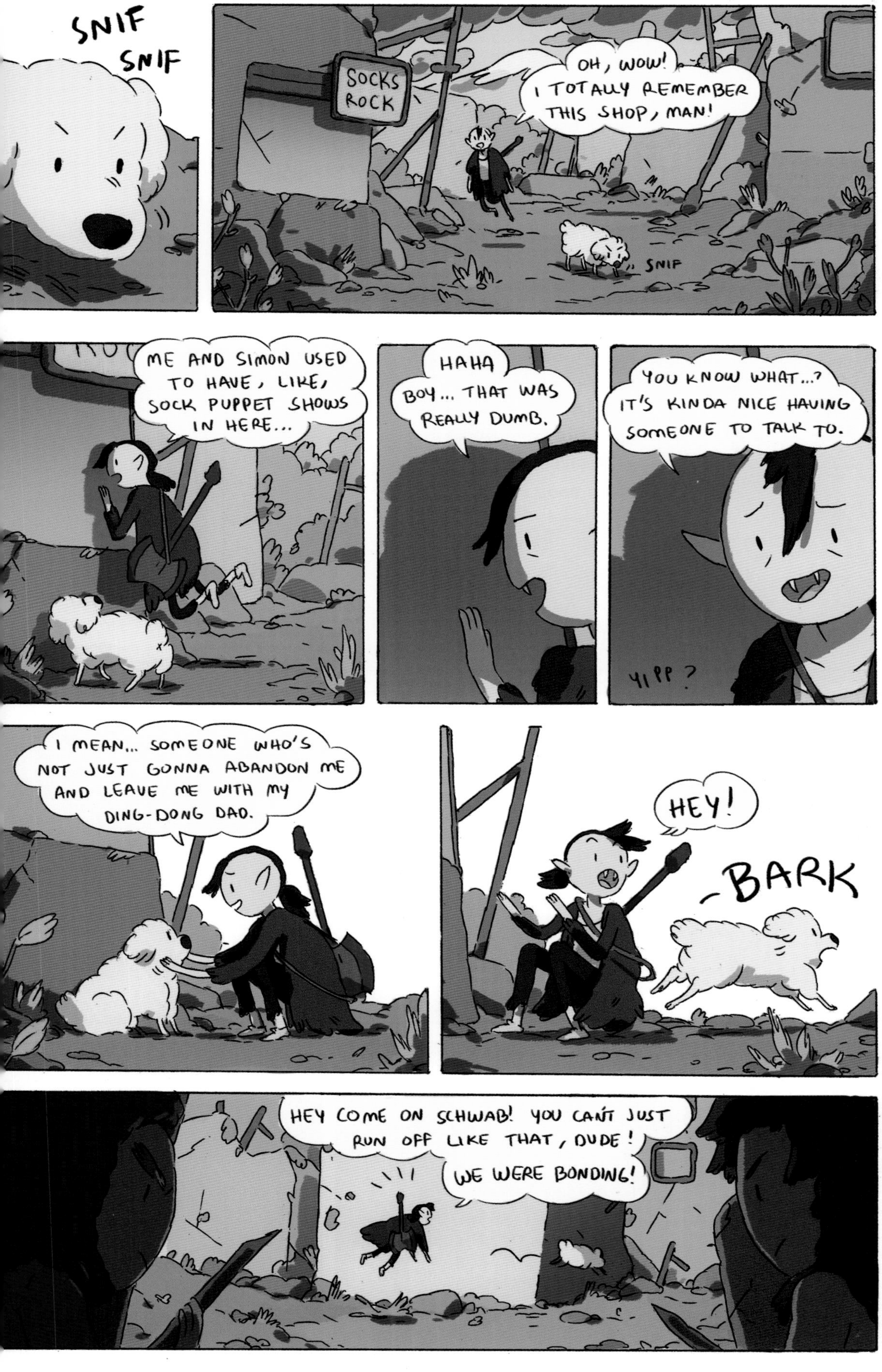
SNIF
SNIF
SOCKS ROCK
OH, WOW! I TOTALLY REMEMBER THIS SHOP, MAN!
SNIF
ME AND SIMON USED TO HAVE, LIKE, SOCK PUPPET SHOWS IN HERE...
HAHA
BOY... THAT WAS REALLY DUMB.
YOU KNOW WHAT...? IT'S KINDA NICE HAVING SOMEONE TO TALK TO.
YIPP?
I MEAN... SOMEONE WHO'S NOT JUST GONNA ABANDON ME AND LEAVE ME WITH MY DING-DONG DAD.
HEY!
BARK
HEY COME ON SCHWAB! YOU CAN'T JUST RUN OFF LIKE THAT, DUDE!
WE WERE BONDING!

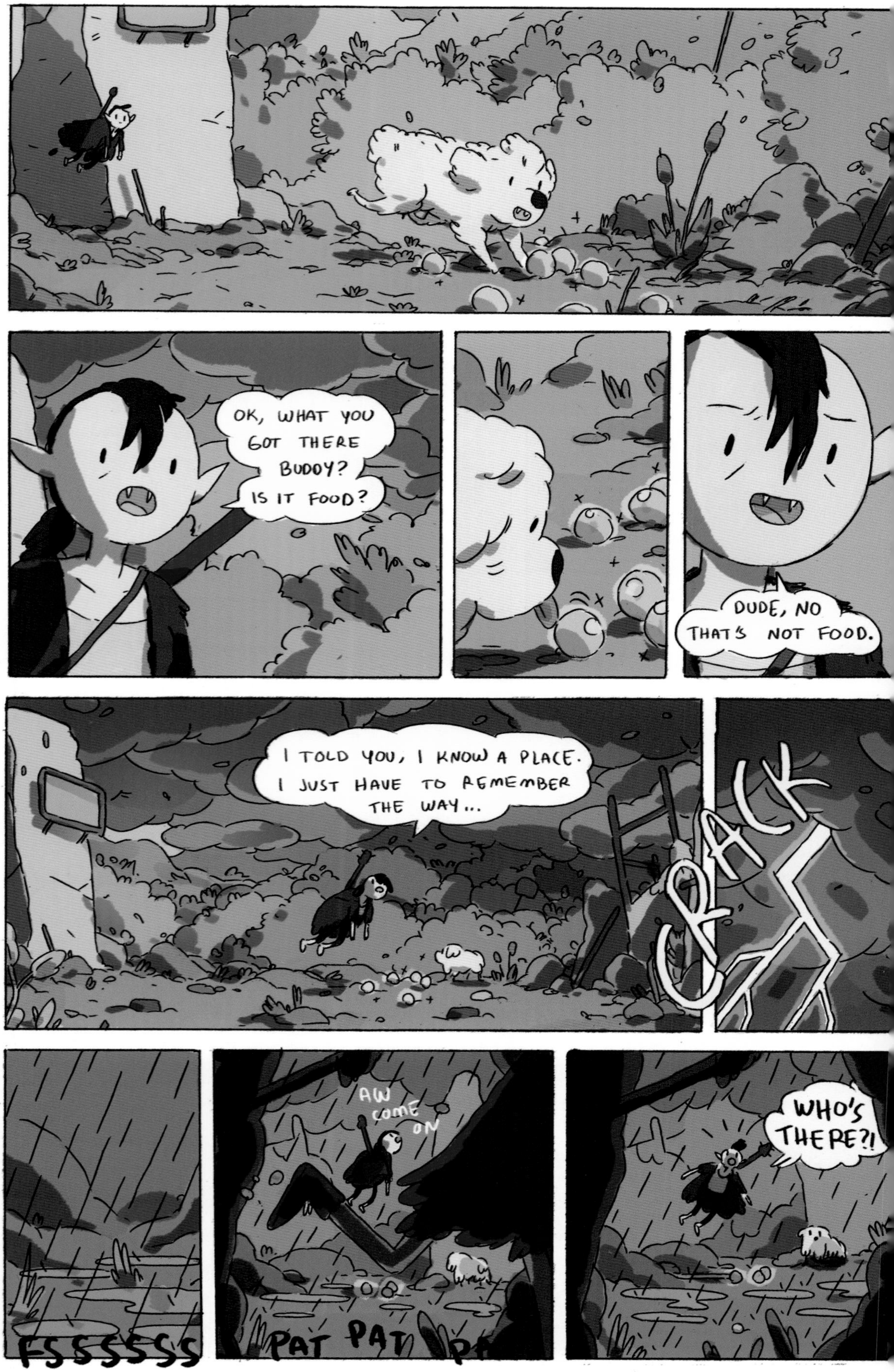
OK, WHAT YOU GOT THERE BUDDY? IS IT FOOD?
DUDE, NO THAT'S NOT FOOD.
I TOLD YOU, I KNOW A PLACE. I JUST HAVE TO REMEMBER THE WAY...
CRACK
FSSSSSS
AW COME ON
PAT PAT
WHO'S THERE?!

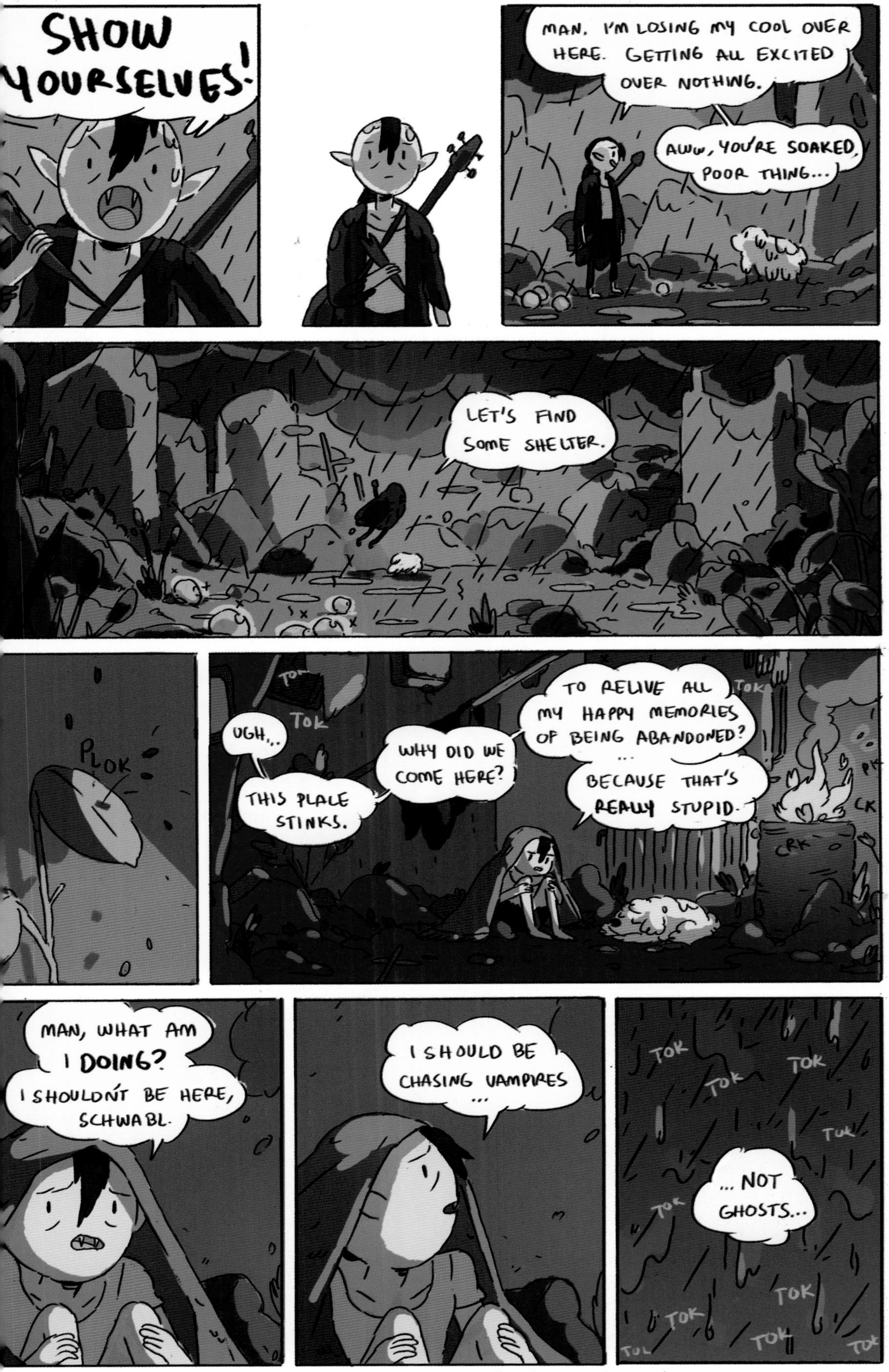
SHOW YOURSELVES!
MAN. I'M LOSING MY COOL OVER HERE. GETTING ALL EXCITED OVER NOTHING.
AWW, YOU'RE SOAKED, POOR THING...
LET'S FIND SOME SHELTER.
PLOK
TOK
TOK
UGH...
THIS PLACE STINKS.
WHY DID WE COME HERE?
TO RELIVE ALL MY HAPPY MEMORIES OF BEING ABANDONED?
...
BECAUSE THAT'S REALLY STUPID.
TOK
CRK
CK
MAN, WHAT AM I DOING?
I SHOULDN'T BE HERE, SCHWABL.
I SHOULD BE CHASING VAMPIRES
...
TOK
TOK
TOK
TOK
TOK
...NOT GHOSTS...
TOK
TOK
TOK
TOK
TOK

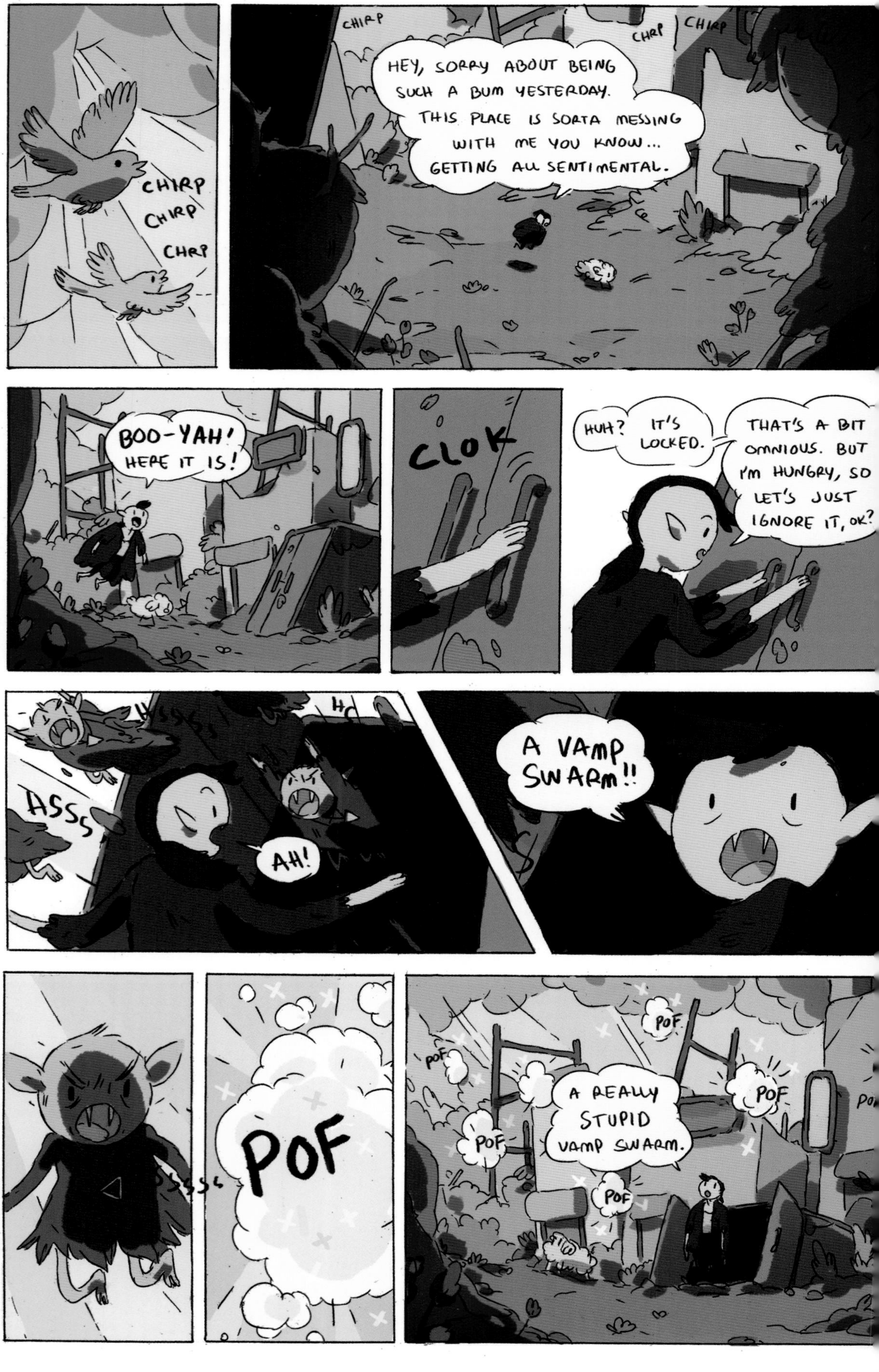
CHIRP
CHIRP
CHRP
CHIRP
CHRP
CHIRP
HEY, SORRY ABOUT BEING SUCH A BUM YESTERDAY. THIS PLACE IS SORTA MESSING WITH ME YOU KNOW... GETTING ALL SENTIMENTAL.
BOO-YAH! HERE IT IS!
CLOK
HUH? IT'S LOCKED.
THAT'S A BIT OMNIOUS. BUT I'M HUNGRY, SO LET'S JUST IGNORE IT, OK?
HSSSS
ASSS
AH!
A VAMP SWARM!!
POF
POF
POF
POF
A REALLY STUPID VAMP SWARM.
POF
POF

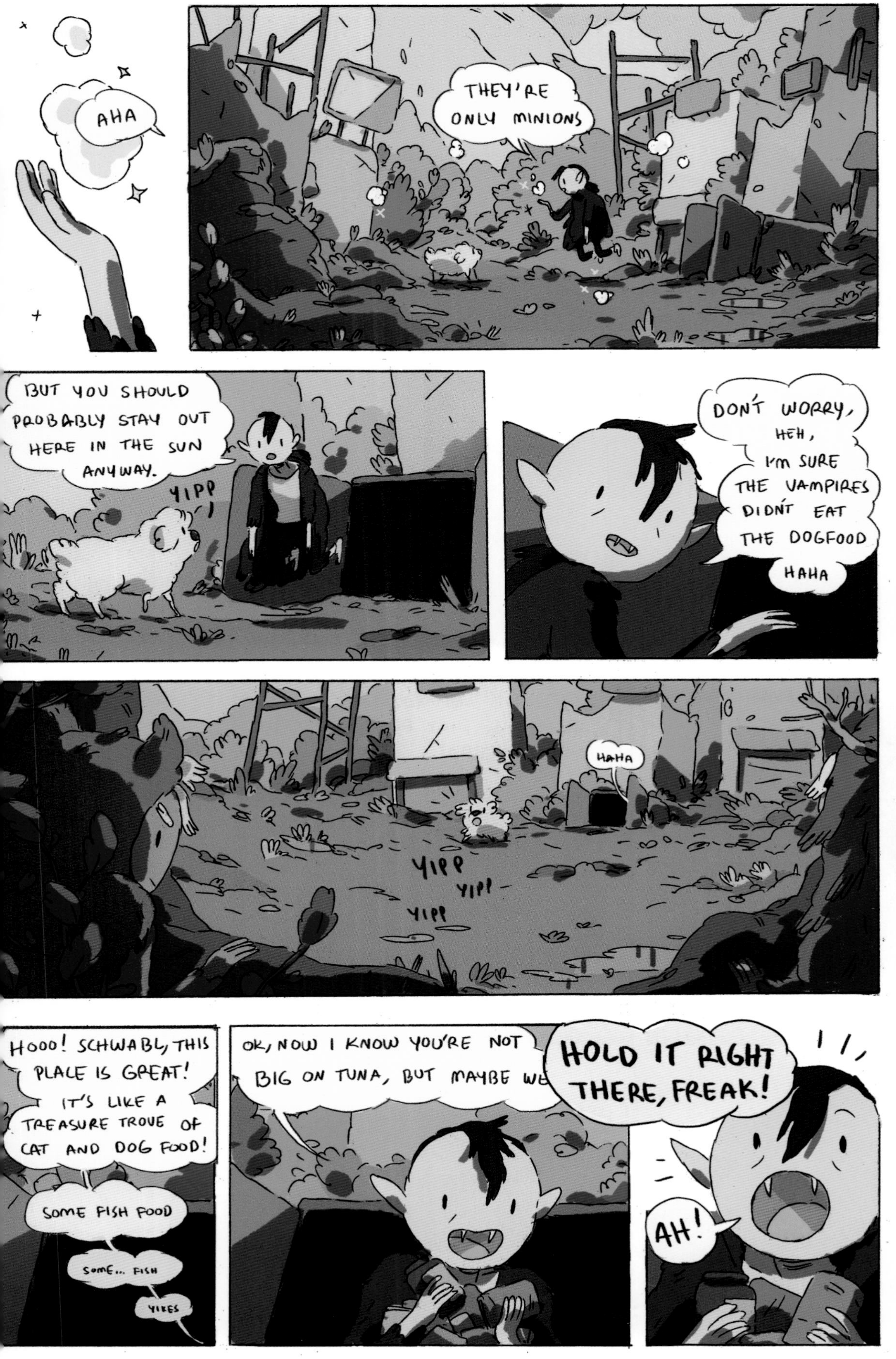
AHA
THEY'RE ONLY MINIONS
BUT YOU SHOULD PROBABLY STAY OUT HERE IN THE SUN ANYWAY.
YIPP
DON'T WORRY, HEH, I'M SURE THE VAMPIRES DIDN'T EAT THE DOGFOOD
HAHA
HAHA
YIPP
YIPP
YIPP
HOOO! SCHWABL, THIS PLACE IS GREAT! IT'S LIKE A TREASURE TROVE OF CAT AND DOG FOOD!
SOME FISH FOOD
SOME... FISH
YIKES
OK, NOW I KNOW YOU'RE NOT BIG ON TUNA, BUT MAYBE WE
HOLD IT RIGHT THERE, FREAK!
AH!

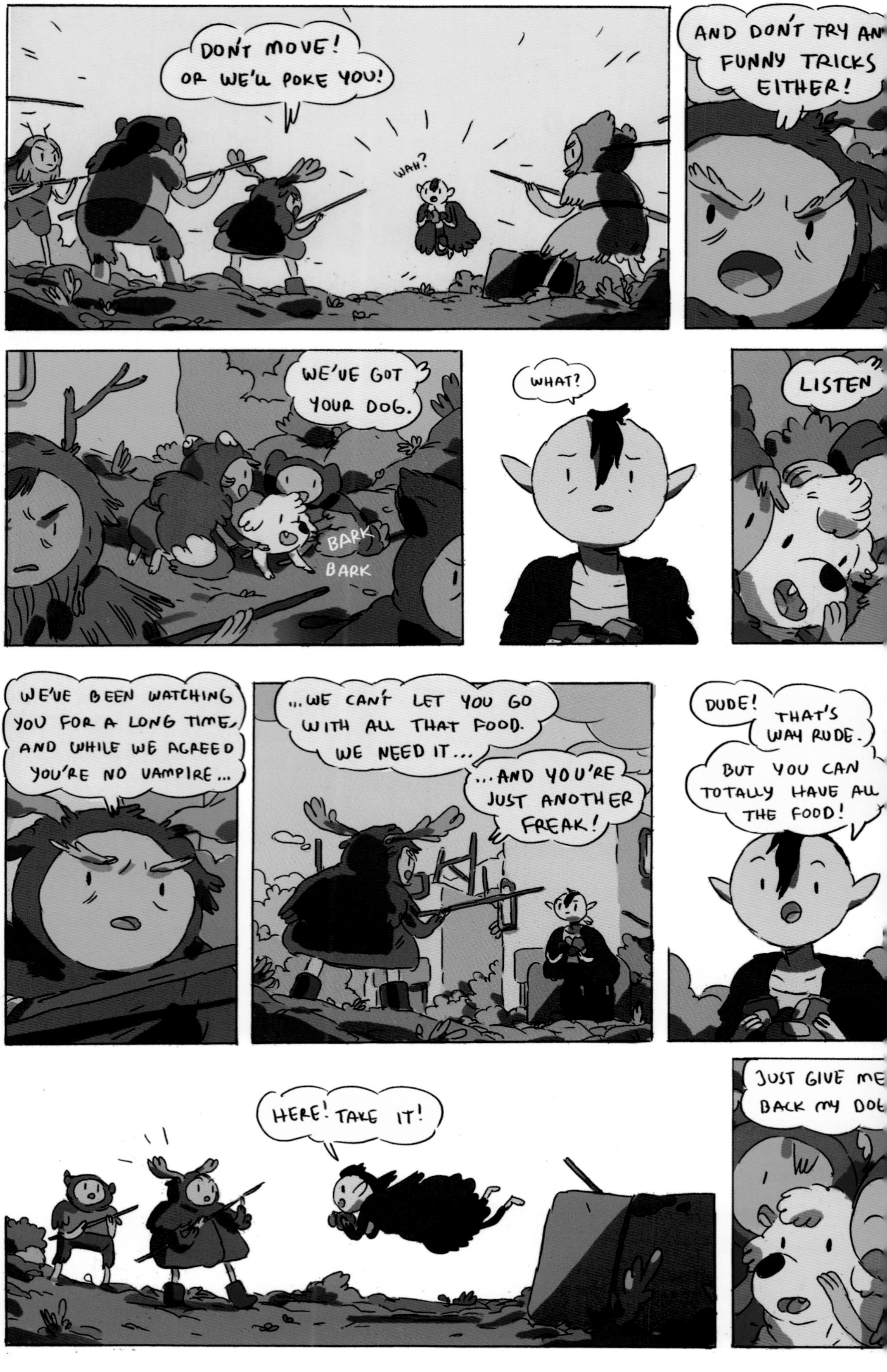

DON'T MOVE! OR WE'LL POKE YOU!
WAH?
AND DON'T TRY AN FUNNY TRICKS EITHER!
WE'VE GOT YOUR DOG.
BARK
BARK
WHAT?
LISTEN
WE'VE BEEN WATCHING YOU FOR A LONG TIME, AND WHILE WE AGREED YOU'RE NO VAMPIRE...
...WE CAN'T LET YOU GO WITH ALL THAT FOOD. WE NEED IT...
...AND YOU'RE JUST ANOTHER FREAK!
DUDE!
THAT'S WAY RUDE.
BUT YOU CAN TOTALLY HAVE ALL THE FOOD!
HERE! TAKE IT!
JUST GIVE ME BACK MY DOG

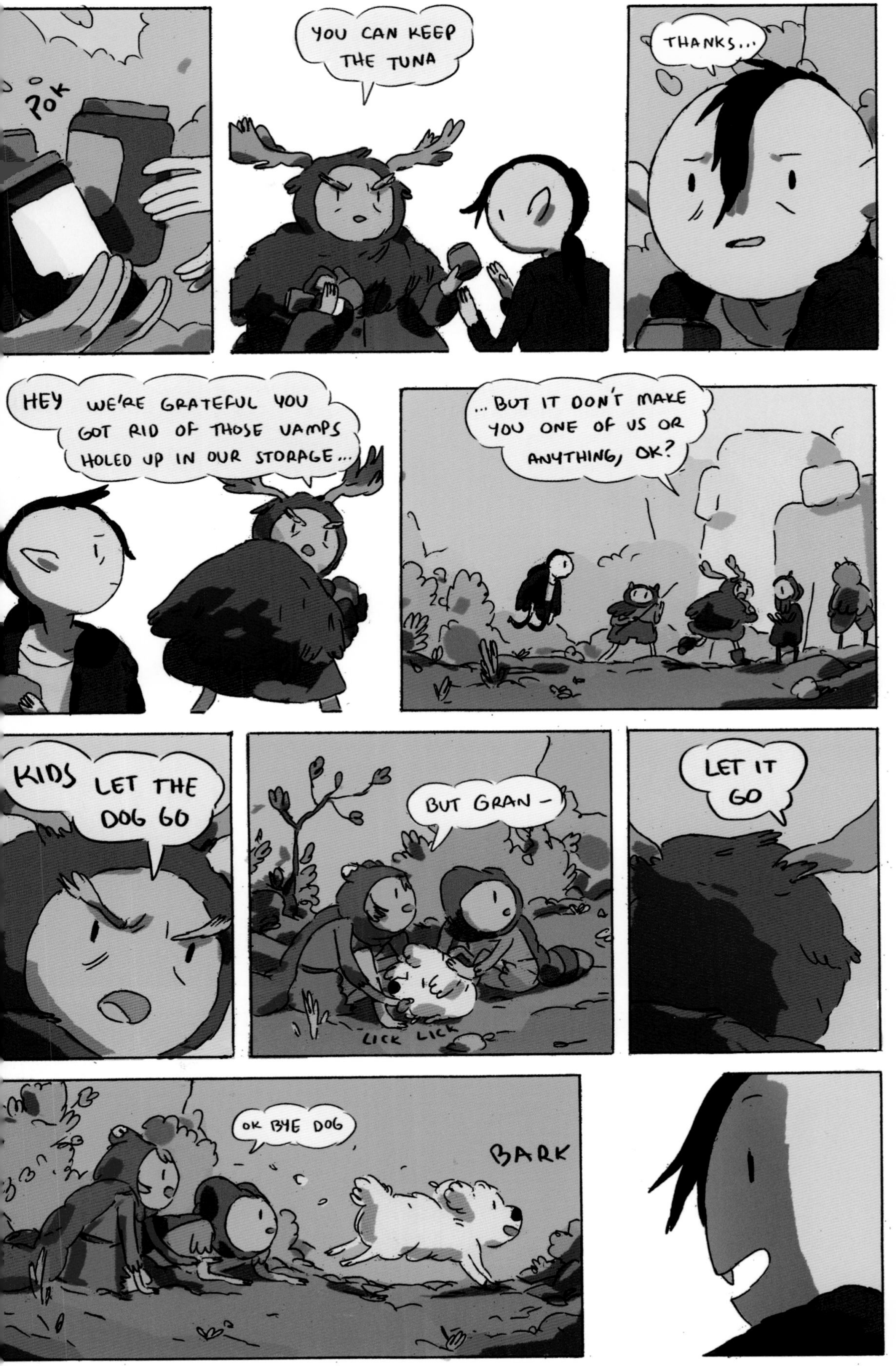
POK
YOU CAN KEEP THE TUNA
THANKS...
HEY
WE'RE GRATEFUL YOU GOT RID OF THOSE VAMPS HOLED UP IN OUR STORAGE...
...BUT IT DON'T MAKE YOU ONE OF US OR ANYTHING, OK?
KIDS
LET THE DOG GO
BUT GRAN -
LET IT GO
OK BYE DOG
BARK

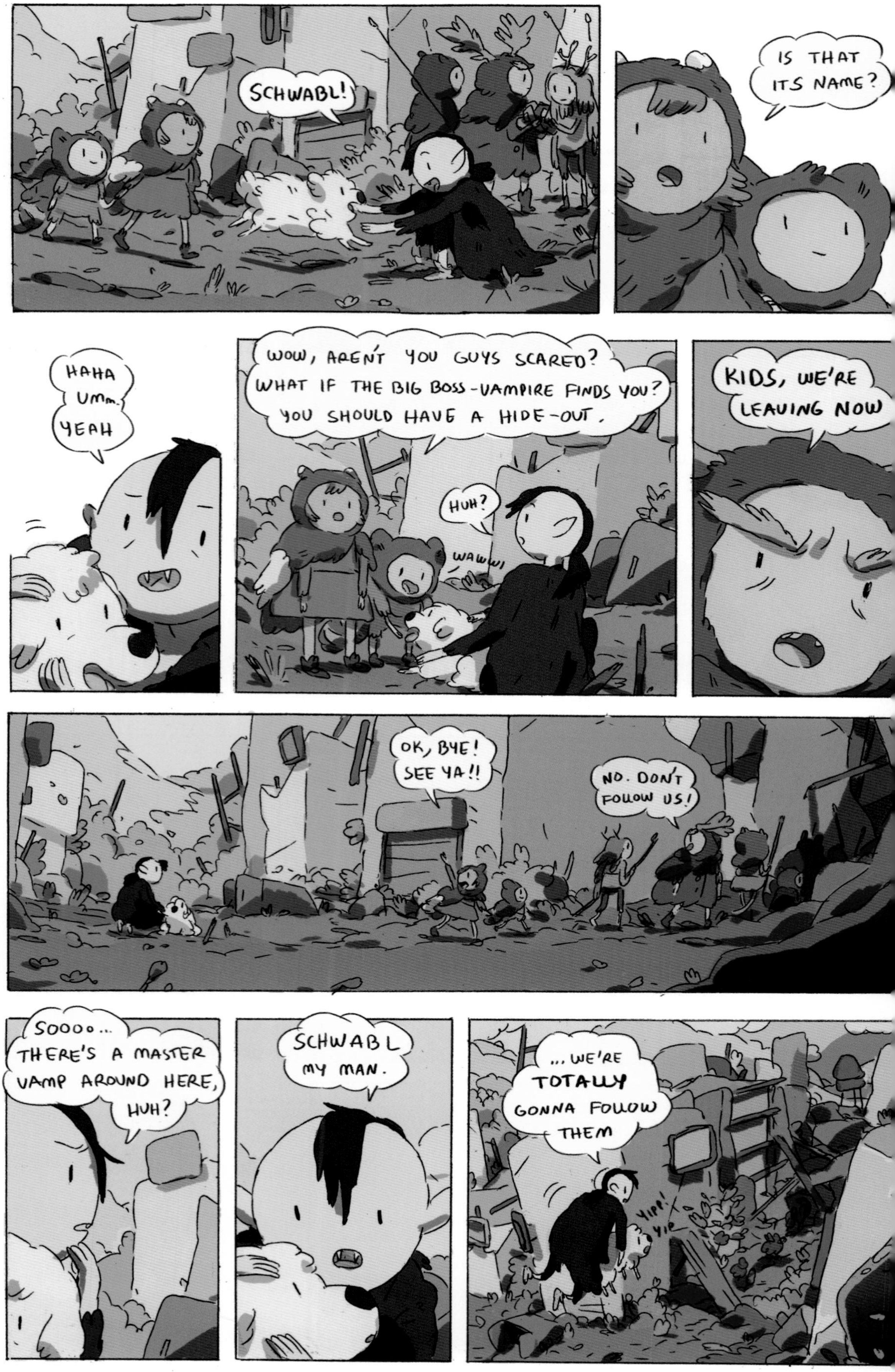
SCHWABL!
IS THAT ITS NAME?
HAHA UMM... YEAH
WOW, AREN'T YOU GUYS SCARED? WHAT IF THE BIG BOSS-VAMPIRE FINDS YOU? YOU SHOULD HAVE A HIDE-OUT.
HUH?
WAWW!
KIDS, WE'RE LEAVING NOW
OK, BYE! SEE YA!!
NO. DON'T FOLLOW US!
SOOOO... THERE'S A MASTER VAMP AROUND HERE, HUH?
SCHWABL MY MAN.
...WE'RE TOTALLY GONNA FOLLOW THEM
YIPP! YIP

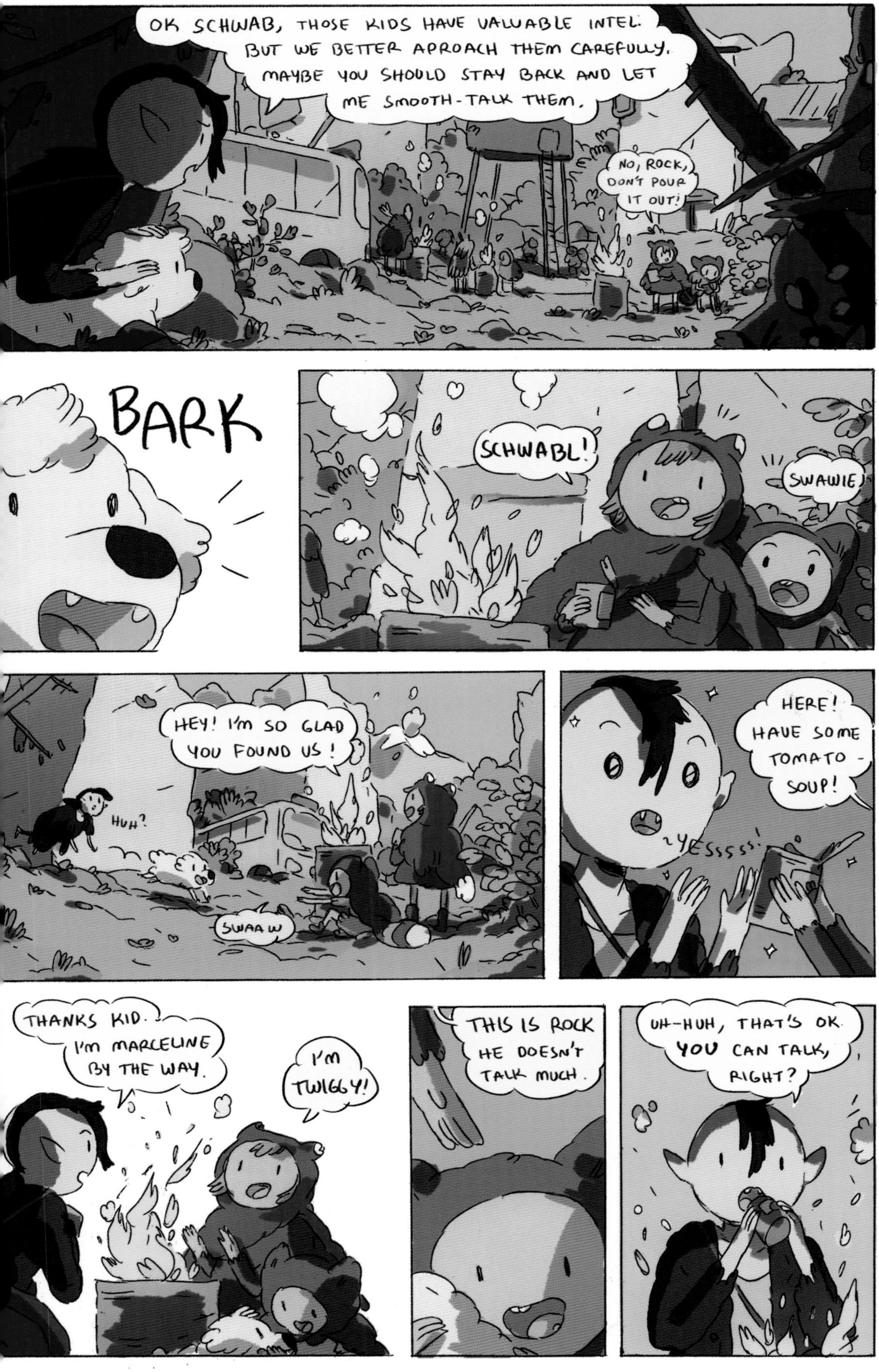
OK SCHWAB, THOSE KIDS HAVE VALUABLE INTEL. BUT WE BETTER APROACH THEM CAREFULLY. MAYBE YOU SHOULD STAY BACK AND LET ME SMOOTH-TALK THEM.
NO, ROCK, DON'T POUR IT OUT!
BARK
SCHWABL!
SWAWIE!
HEY! I'M SO GLAD YOU FOUND US!
HUH?
SWAAW
HERE! HAVE SOME TOMATO-SOUP!
YESSSSS!
THANKS KID. I'M MARCELINE BY THE WAY.
I'M TWIGGY!
THIS IS ROCK HE DOESN'T TALK MUCH.
UH-HUH, THAT'S OK. YOU CAN TALK, RIGHT?

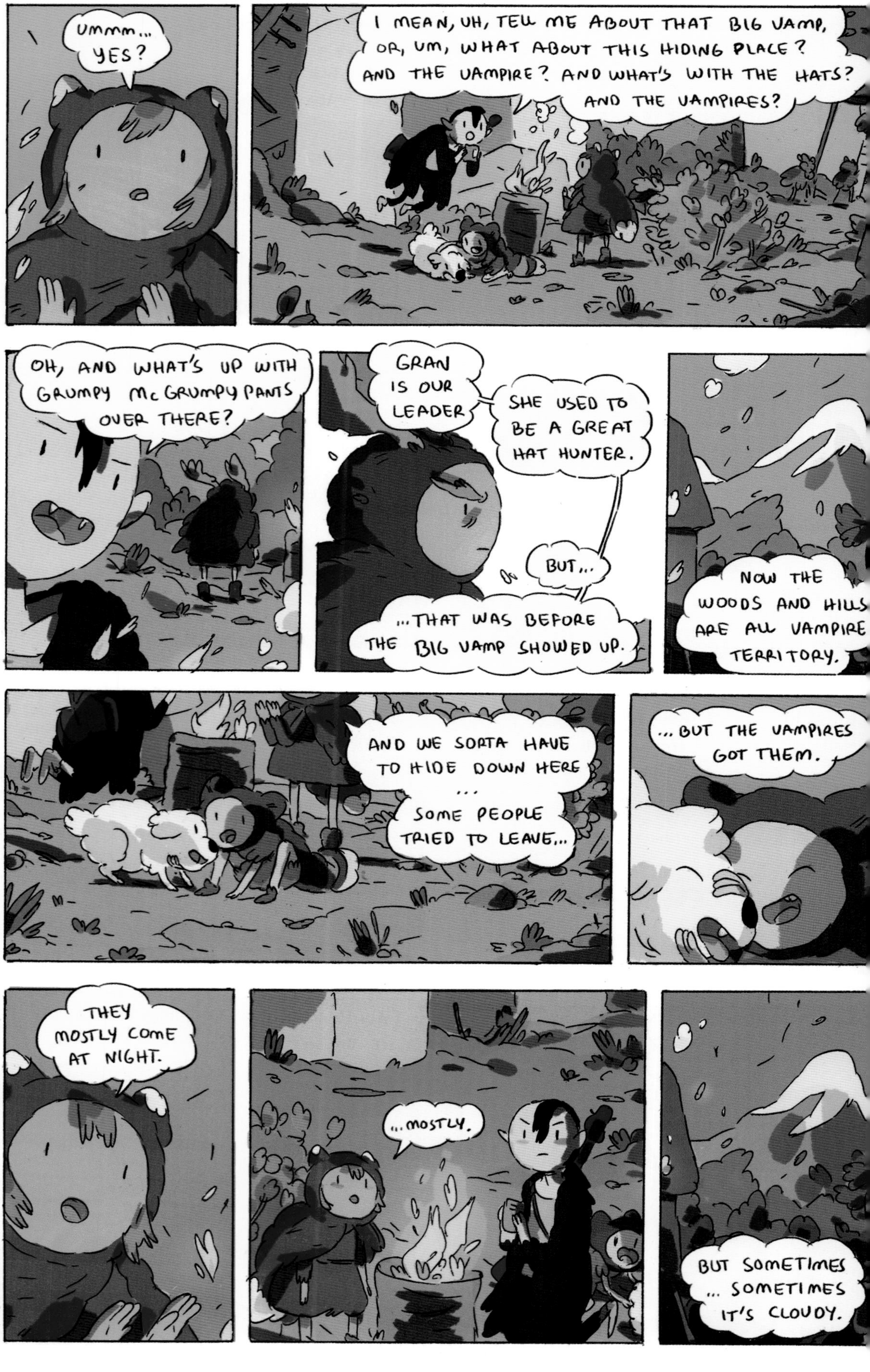
UMMM... YES?
I MEAN, UH, TELL ME ABOUT THAT BIG VAMP, OR, UM, WHAT ABOUT THIS HIDING PLACE? AND THE VAMPIRE?
AND WHAT'S WITH THE HATS? AND THE VAMPIRES?
OH, AND WHAT'S UP WITH GRUMPY McGRUMPYPANTS OVER THERE?
GRAN IS OUR LEADER
SHE USED TO BE A GREAT HAT HUNTER.
BUT...
...THAT WAS BEFORE THE BIG VAMP SHOWED UP.
NOW THE WOODS AND HILLS ARE ALL VAMPIRE TERRITORY.
AND WE SORTA HAVE TO HIDE DOWN HERE ... SOME PEOPLE TRIED TO LEAVE...
...BUT THE VAMPIRES GOT THEM.
THEY MOSTLY COME AT NIGHT.
...MOSTLY.
BUT SOMETIMES ... SOMETIMES IT'S CLOUDY.

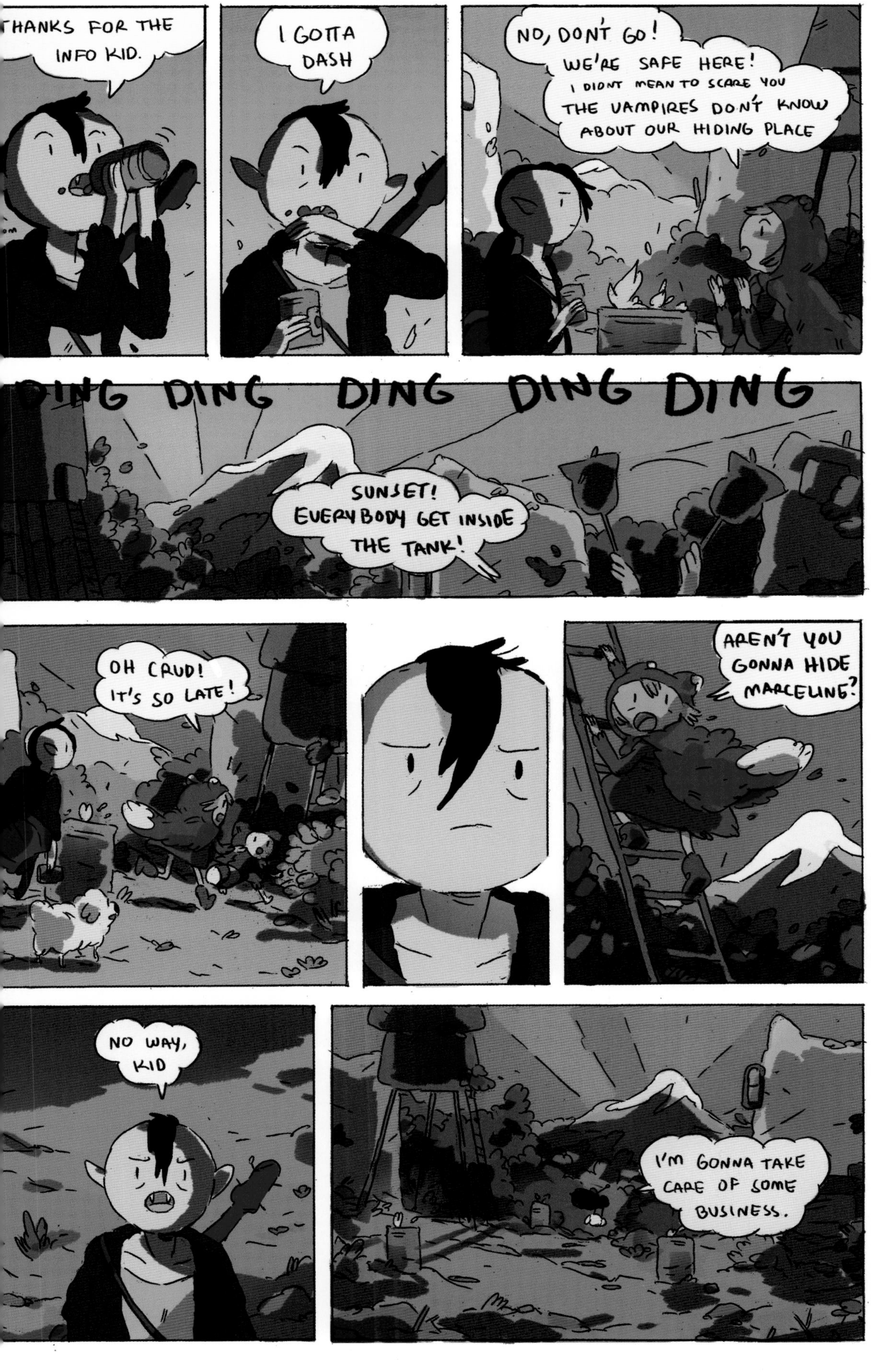
THANKS FOR THE INFO KID.
I GOTTA DASH
NO, DON'T GO! WE'RE SAFE HERE! I DIDNT MEAN TO SCARE YOU THE VAMPIRES DON'T KNOW ABOUT OUR HIDING PLACE
DING DING DING DING DING
SUNSET! EVERYBODY GET INSIDE THE TANK!
OH CRUD! IT'S SO LATE!
AREN'T YOU GONNA HIDE MARCELINE?
NO WAY, KID
I'M GONNA TAKE CARE OF SOME BUSINESS.

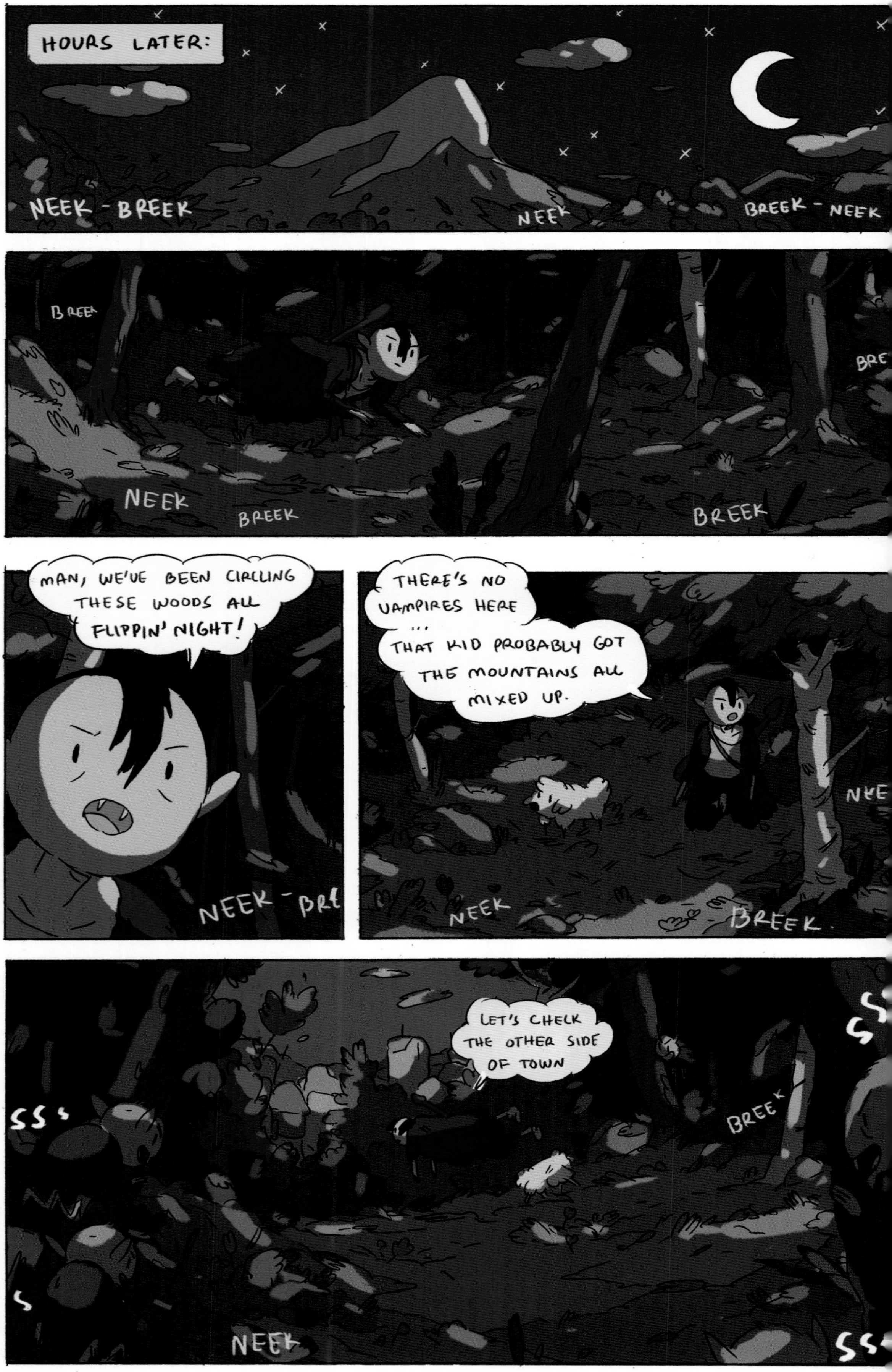
HOURS LATER:
NEEK - BREEK
NEEK
BREEK - NEEK
BREEK
BRE
NEEK
BREEK
BREEK
MAN, WE'VE BEEN CIRCLING THESE WOODS ALL FLIPPIN' NIGHT!
NEEK - BRE
THERE'S NO VAMPIRES HERE ... THAT KID PROBABLY GOT THE MOUNTAINS ALL MIXED UP.
NEE
NEEK
BREEK.
LET'S CHECK THE OTHER SIDE OF TOWN
BREEK
NEEK

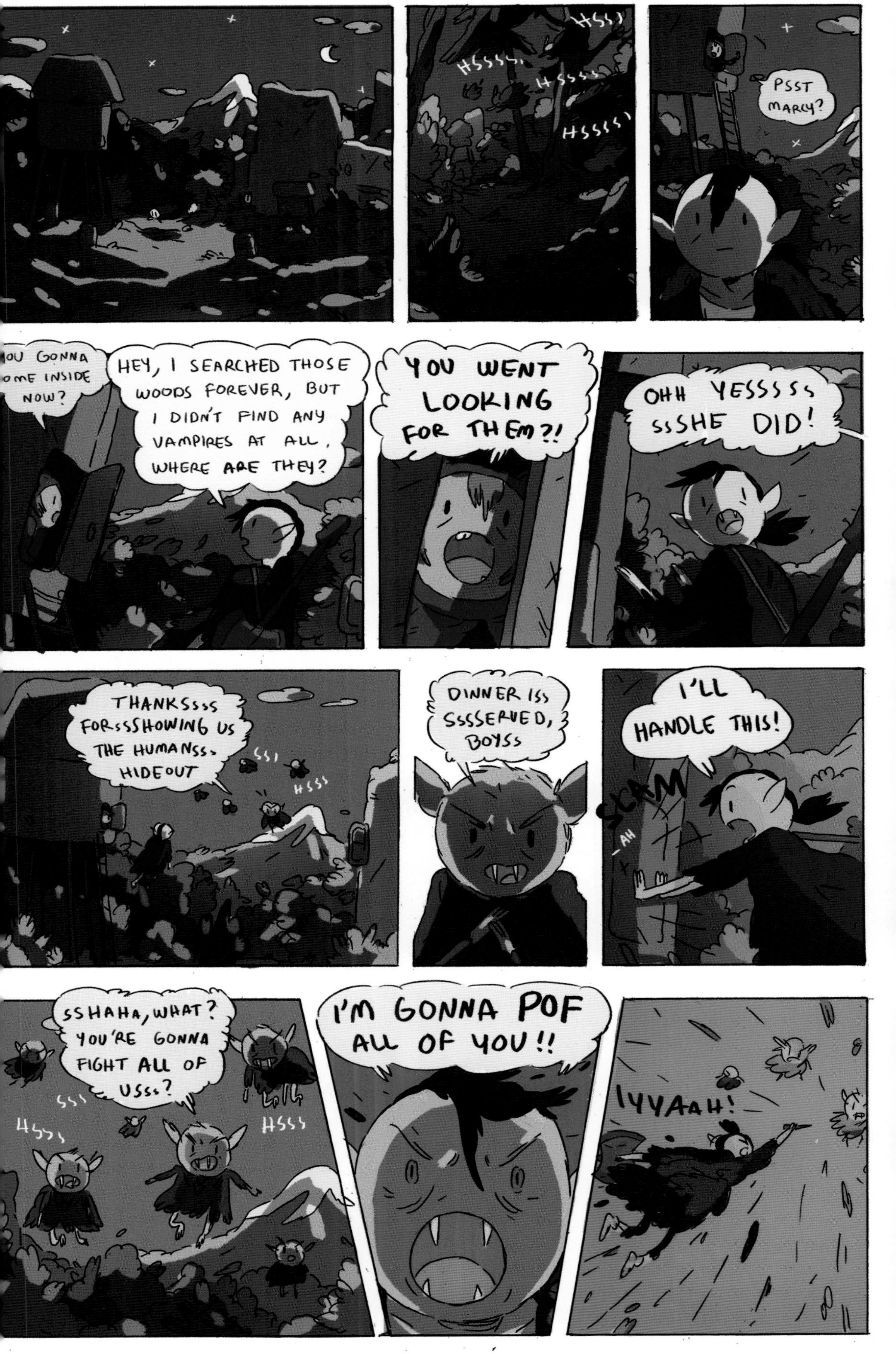
HSSS
HSSSS
HSSSS
HSSSS
PSST MARCY?
YOU GONNA COME INSIDE NOW?
HEY, I SEARCHED THOSE WOODS FOREVER, BUT I DIDN'T FIND ANY VAMPIRES AT ALL. WHERE ARE THEY?
YOU WENT LOOKING FOR THEM?!
OHH YESSSSS SSSHE DID!
THANKSSSS FORSSSHOWING US THE HUMANSSS HIDEOUT
SSS
HSSS
DINNER ISS SSSSERVED, BOYSS
I'LL HANDLE THIS!
SLAM
AH
SSHAHA, WHAT? YOU'RE GONNA FIGHT ALL OF USSS?
SSS
HSSS
HSSS
I'M GONNA POF ALL OF YOU!!
IYYAAH!

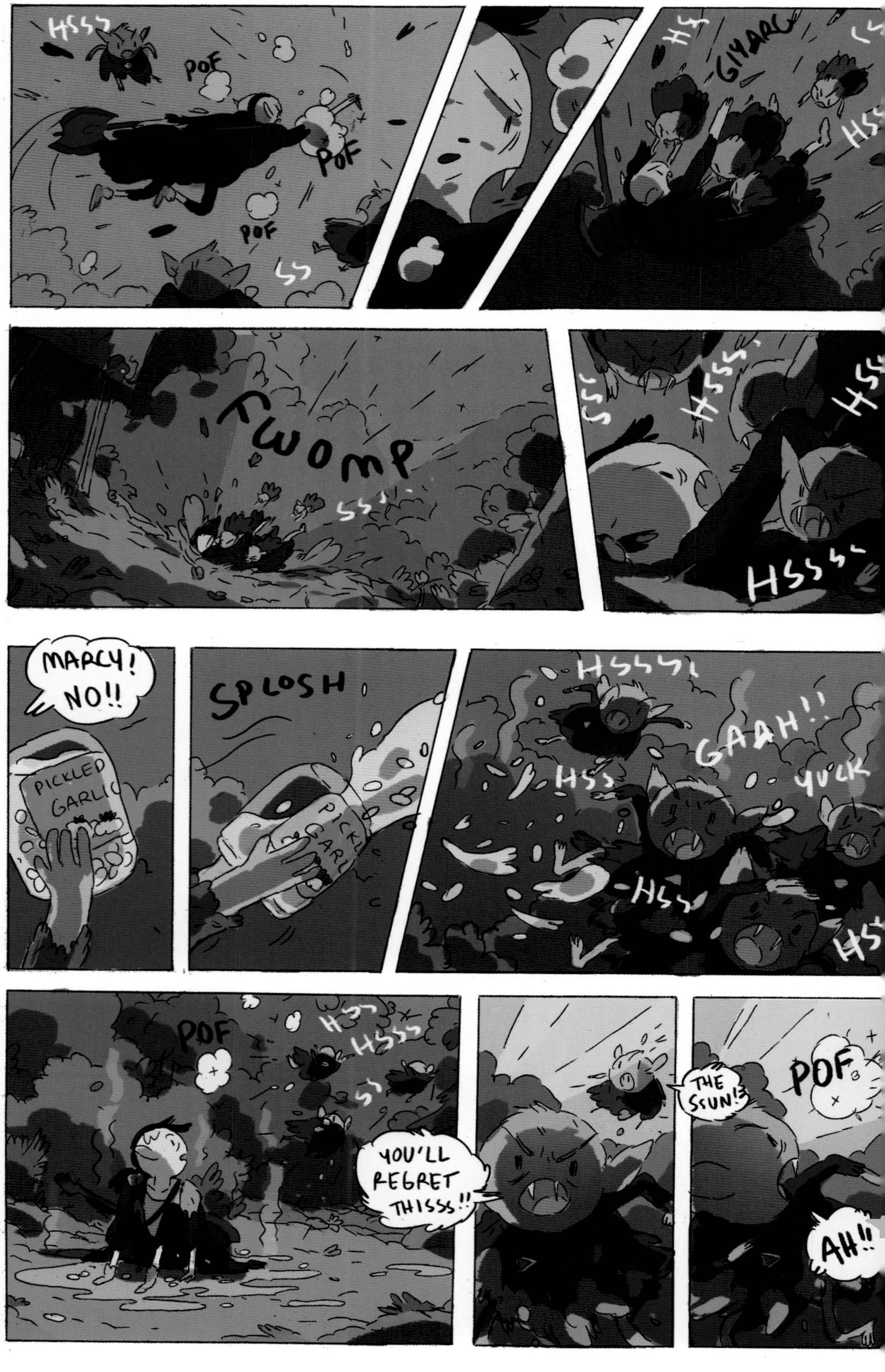
HSSS
POF
POF
POF
SS
HSS
GIYARG
HSS
FWOMP
SSS
HSSS
HSS
HSSS
MARCY! NO!!
PICKLED GARLIC
SPLOSH
HSSS
GAAH!!
HSS
YUCK
HSS
POF
HSS
HSSS
SS
YOU'LL REGRET THISSS!!
THE SSUN!
POF
AH!!

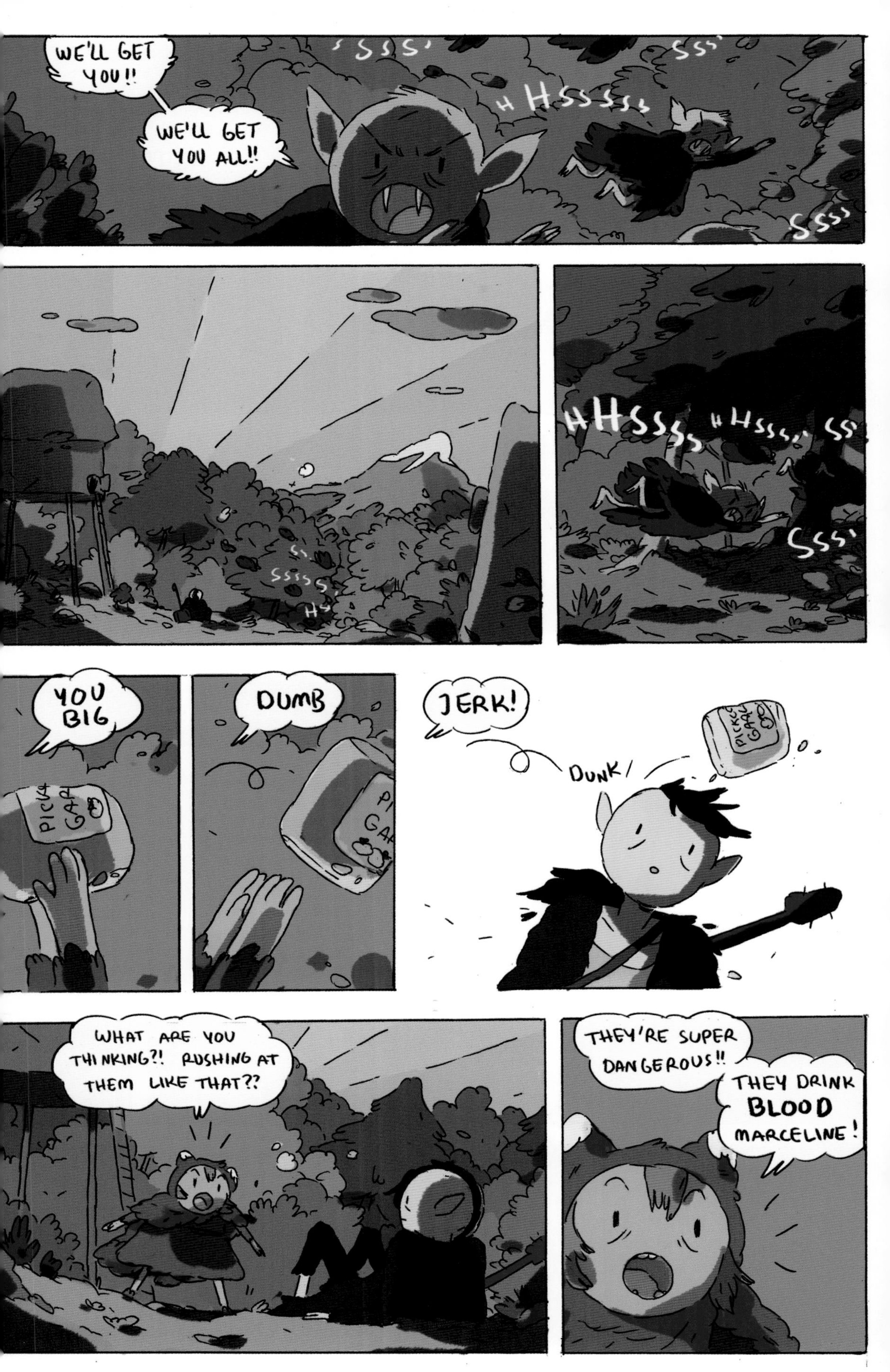

WE'LL GET YOU!!
WE'LL GET YOU ALL!!
SSS
HHSSSSS
SSS
SSS
SSSSS
HHSSSS
HHSSS
SS
SSS
YOU BIG
DUMB
JERK!
DUNK!
WHAT ARE YOU THINKING?! RUSHING AT THEM LIKE THAT??
THEY'RE SUPER DANGEROUS!!
THEY DRINK BLOOD MARCELINE!

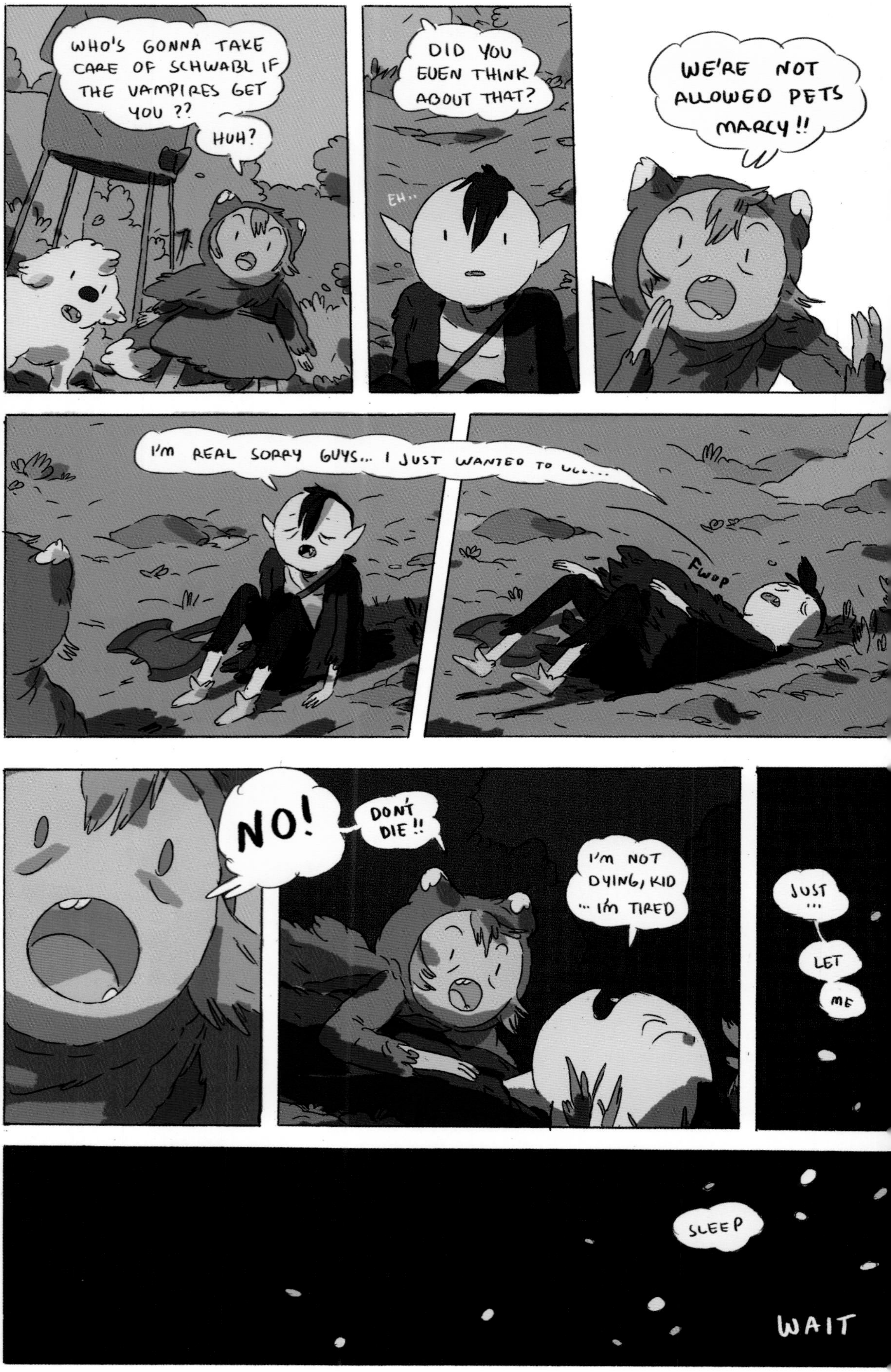
WHO'S GONNA TAKE CARE OF SCHWABL IF THE VAMPIRES GET YOU ??
HUH?
DID YOU EVEN THINK ABOUT THAT?
EH..
WE'RE NOT ALLOWED PETS MARCY !!
I'M REAL SORRY GUYS... I JUST WANTED TO ULL...
FWOP
NO!
DON'T DIE !!
I'M NOT DYING, KID ... I'M TIRED
JUST ...
LET
ME
SLEEP
WAIT

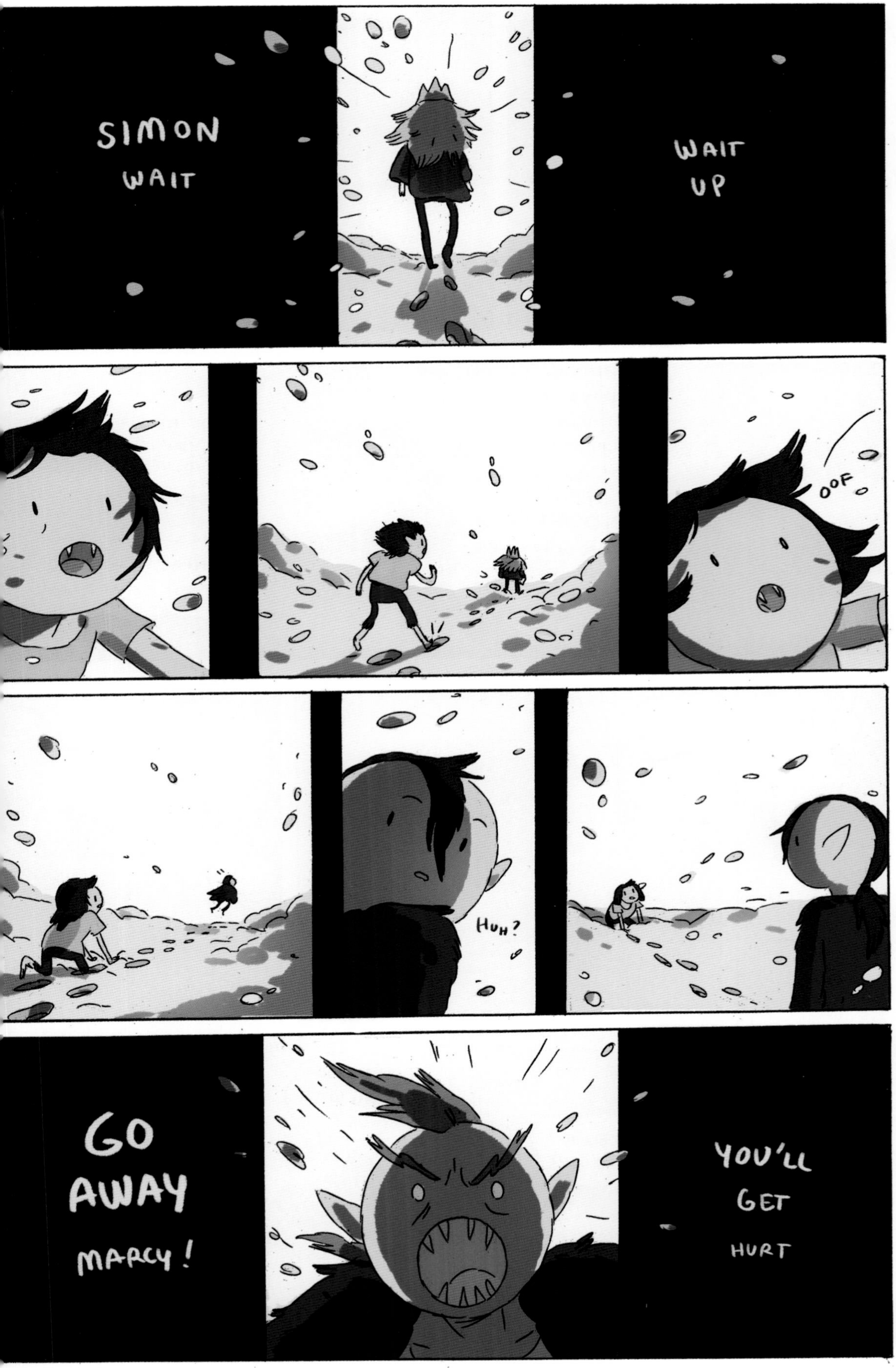
SIMON
WAIT
WAIT
UP
OOF
HUH?
GO
AWAY
MARCY!
YOU'LL
GET
HURT

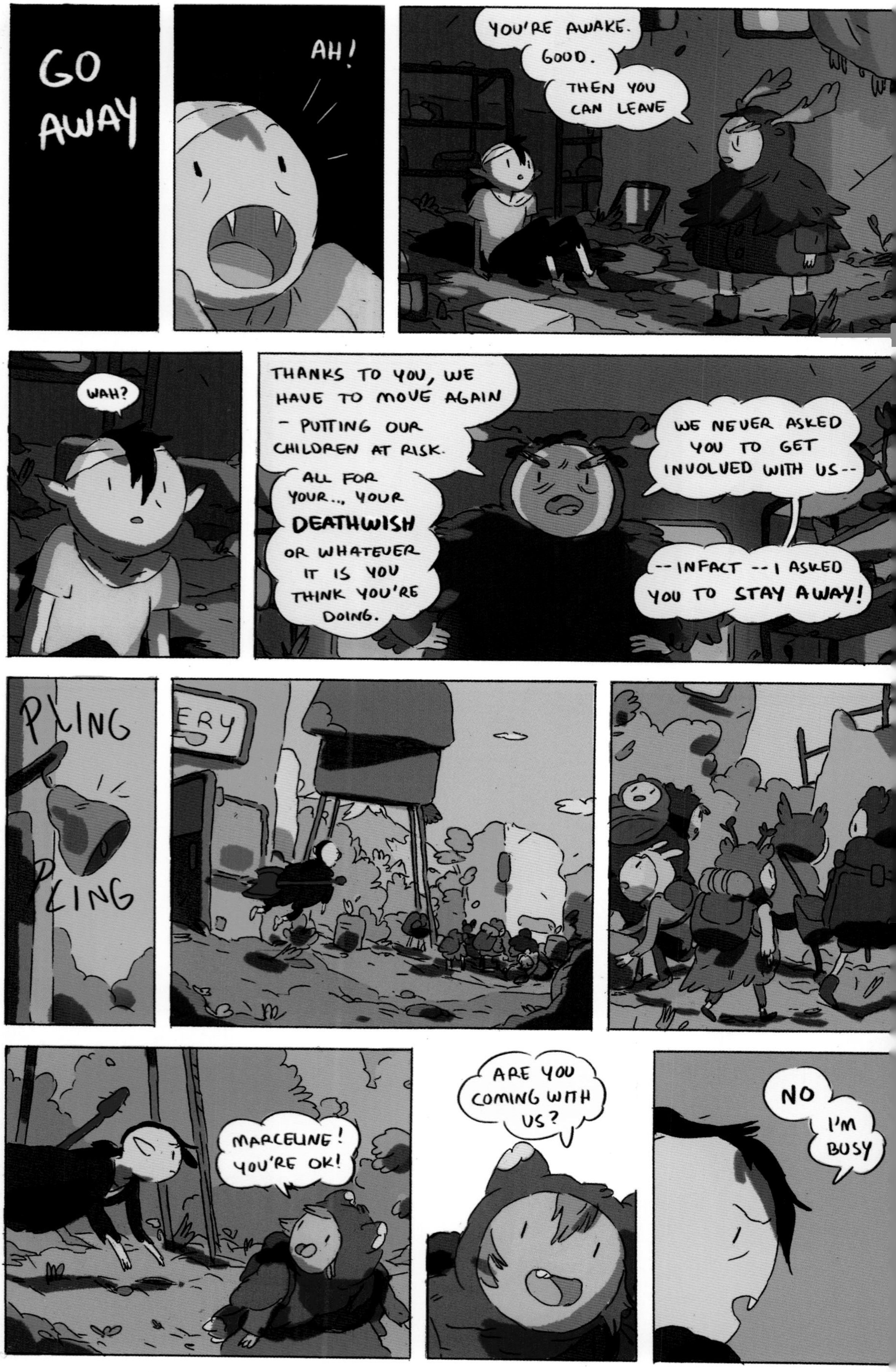
GO AWAY
AH!
YOU'RE AWAKE. GOOD.
THEN YOU CAN LEAVE
WAH?
THANKS TO YOU, WE HAVE TO MOVE AGAIN - PUTTING OUR CHILDREN AT RISK.
ALL FOR YOUR... YOUR DEATHWISH OR WHATEVER IT IS YOU THINK YOU'RE DOING.
WE NEVER ASKED YOU TO GET INVOLVED WITH US--
--INFACT --I ASKED YOU TO STAY AWAY!
PLING
PLING
ERY
MARCELINE! YOU'RE OK!
ARE YOU COMING WITH US?
NO
I'M BUSY

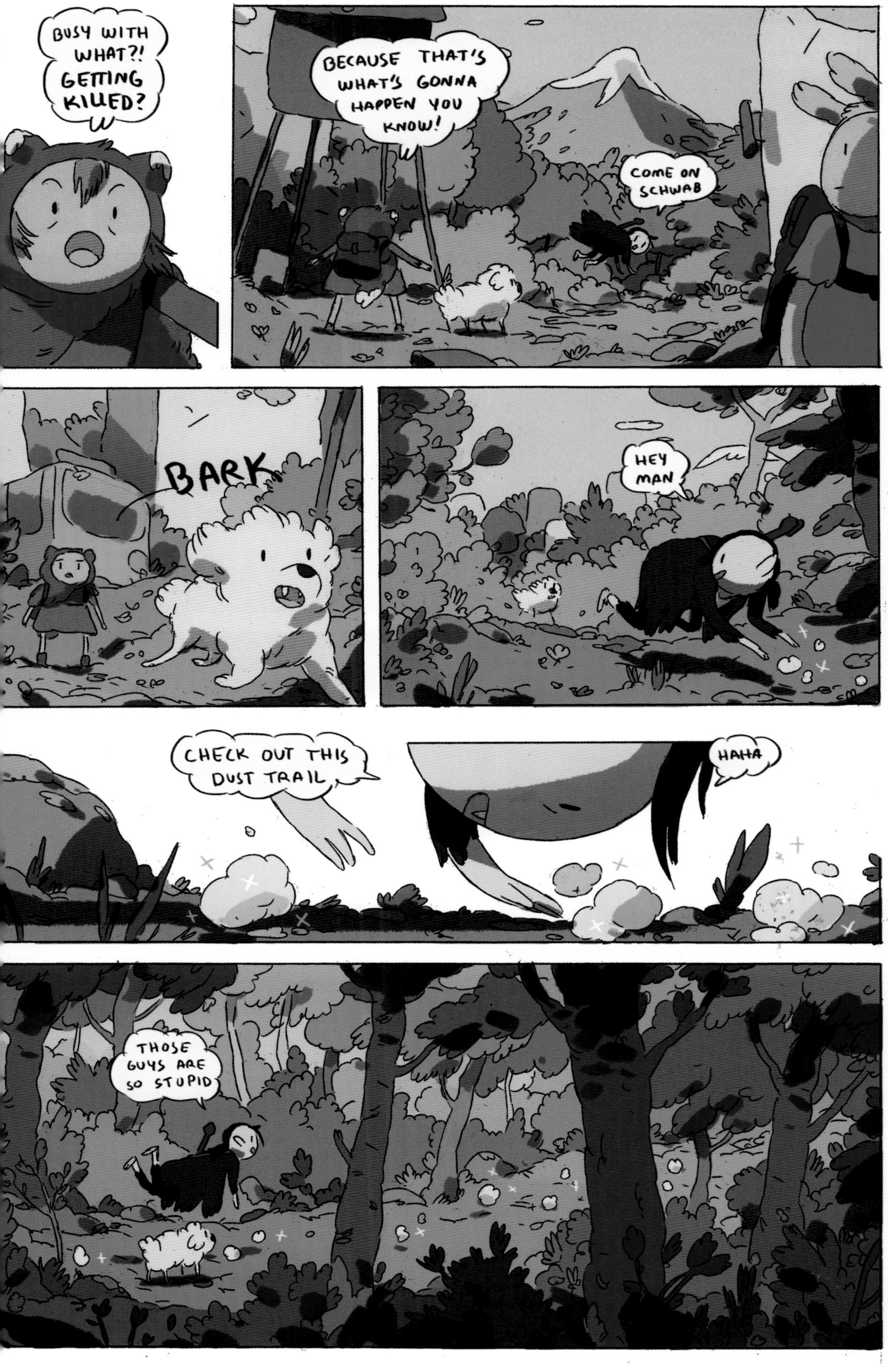
BUSY WITH WHAT?! GETTING KILLED?
BECAUSE THAT'S WHAT'S GONNA HAPPEN YOU KNOW!
COME ON SCHWAB
BARK
HEY MAN
CHECK OUT THIS DUST TRAIL
HAHA
THOSE GUYS ARE SO STUPID

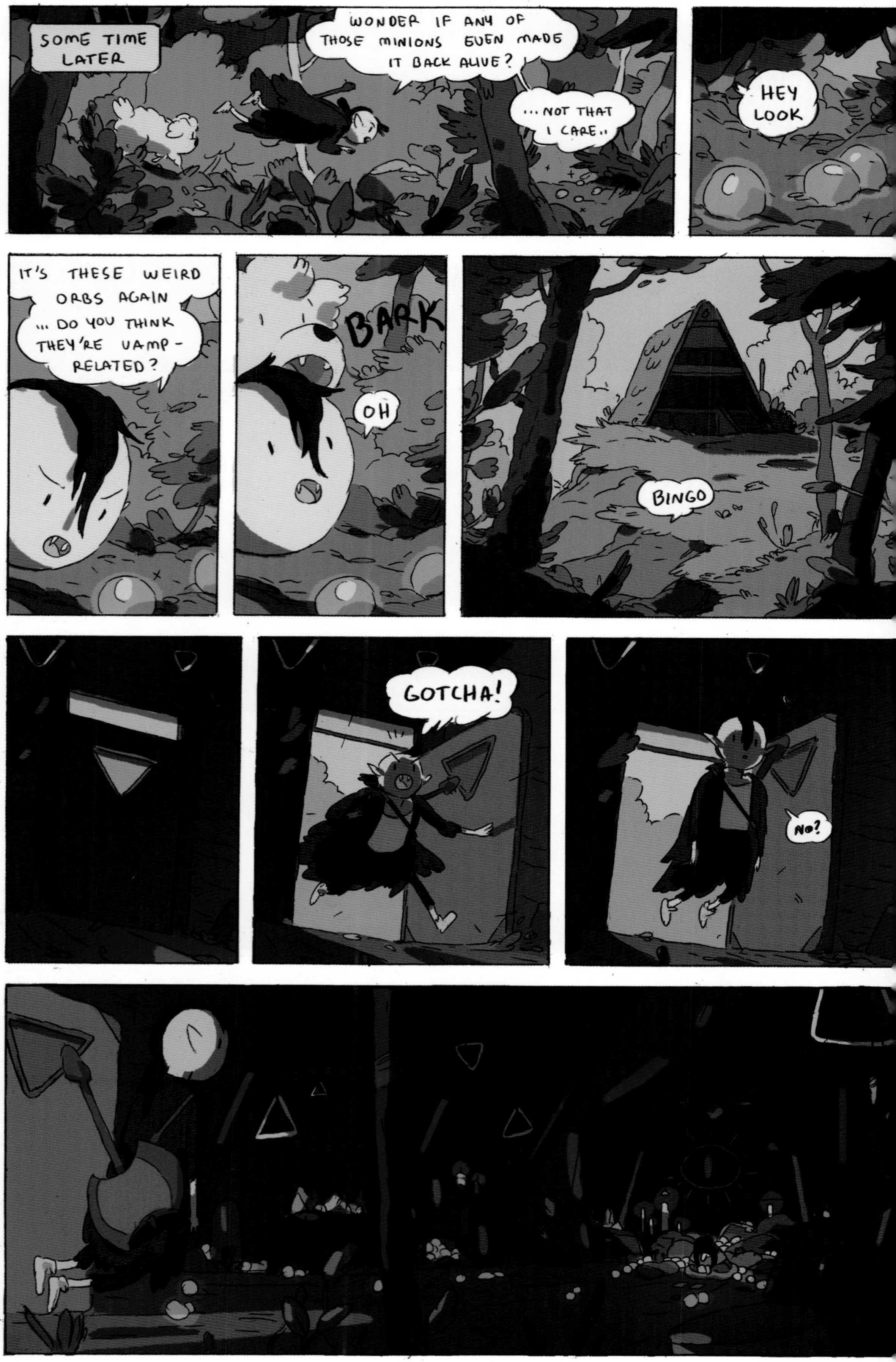
SOME TIME LATER
WONDER IF ANY OF THOSE MINIONS EVEN MADE IT BACK ALIVE?
... NOT THAT I CARE..
HEY LOOK
IT'S THESE WEIRD ORBS AGAIN ... DO YOU THINK THEY'RE VAMP-RELATED?
BARK
OH
BINGO
GOTCHA!
NO?

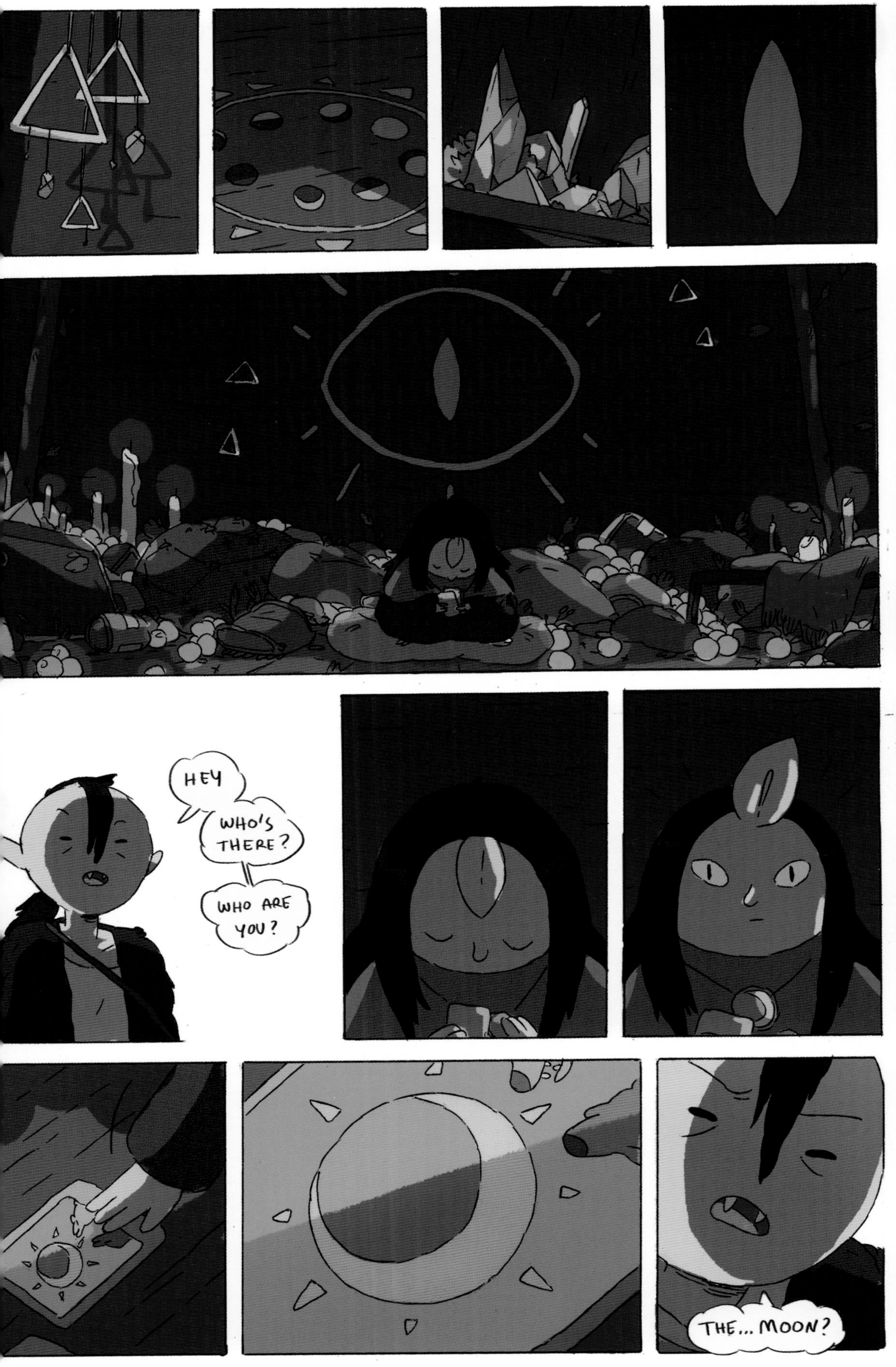
HEY
WHO'S THERE?
WHO ARE YOU?
THE... MOON?

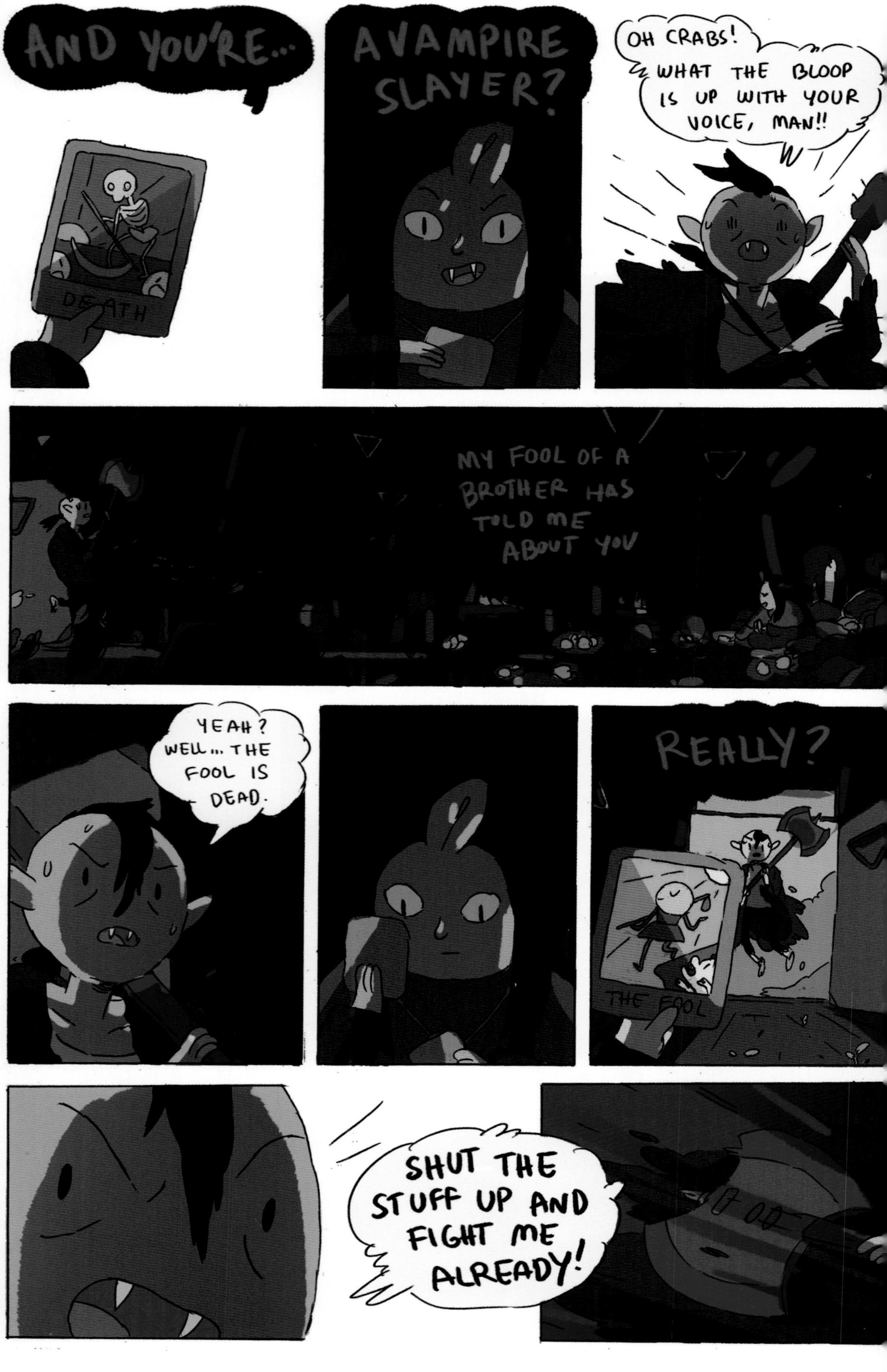
AND YOU'RE...
A VAMPIRE SLAYER?
DEATH
OH CRABS! WHAT THE BLOOP IS UP WITH YOUR VOICE, MAN!!
MY FOOL OF A BROTHER HAS TOLD ME ABOUT YOU
YEAH? WELL... THE FOOL IS DEAD.
REALLY?
THE FOOL
SHUT THE STUFF UP AND FIGHT ME ALREADY!

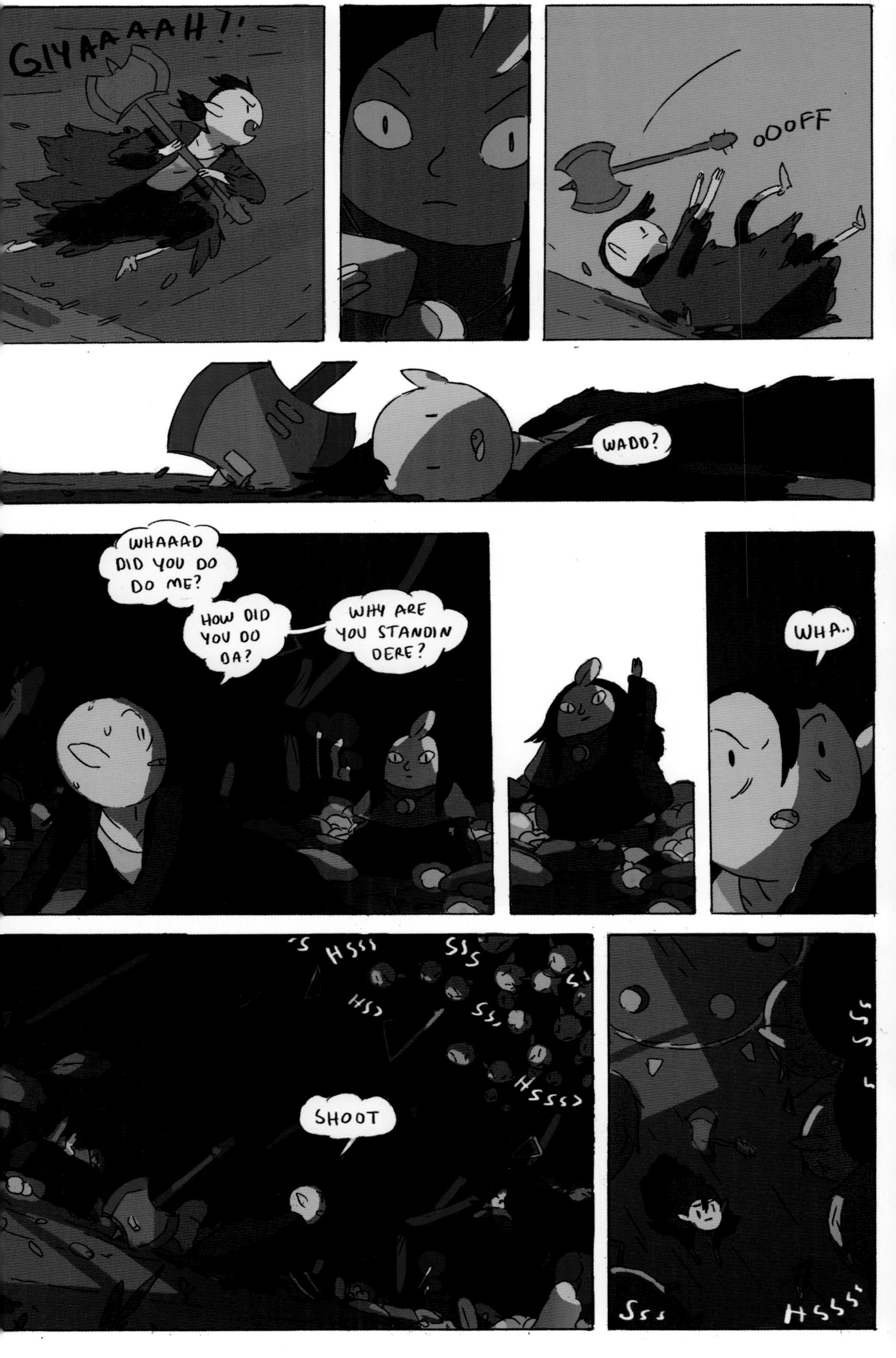
GIYAAAAH!!
oOOFF
WADO?
WHAAAD DID YOU DO DO ME?
HOW DID YOU DO DA?
WHY ARE YOU STANDIN DERE?
WHA..
HSSS
SSS
HSS
SSS
HSSSS
SHOOT
SSS
HSSS

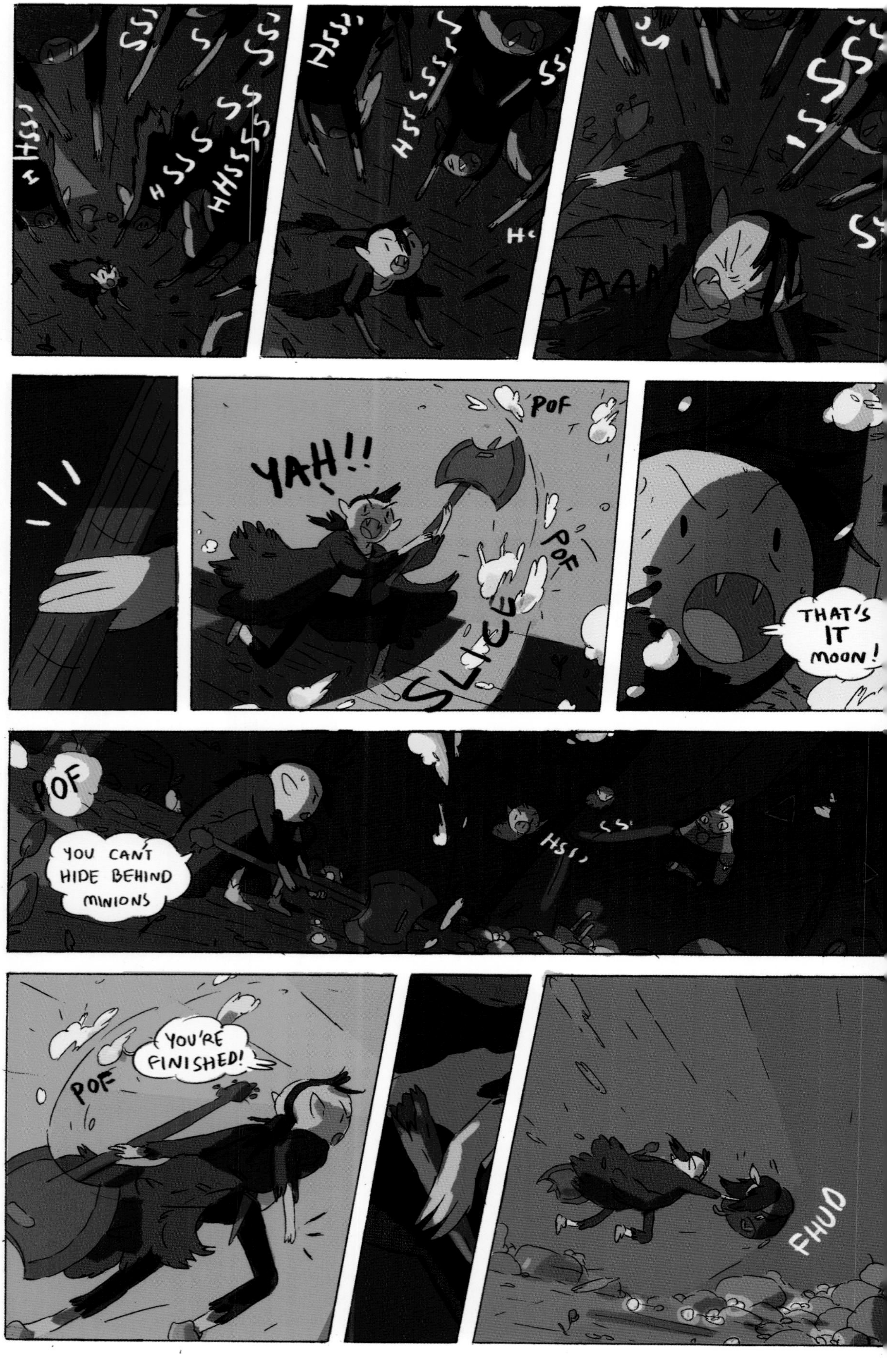

HSSS
HSSS
HSSSSS
HSSS
HSSSSSS
AAAA
YAH!!
POF
POF
SLICE
THAT'S IT MOON!
POF
YOU CAN'T HIDE BEHIND MINIONS
HSSS
YOU'RE FINISHED!
POF
FHUD

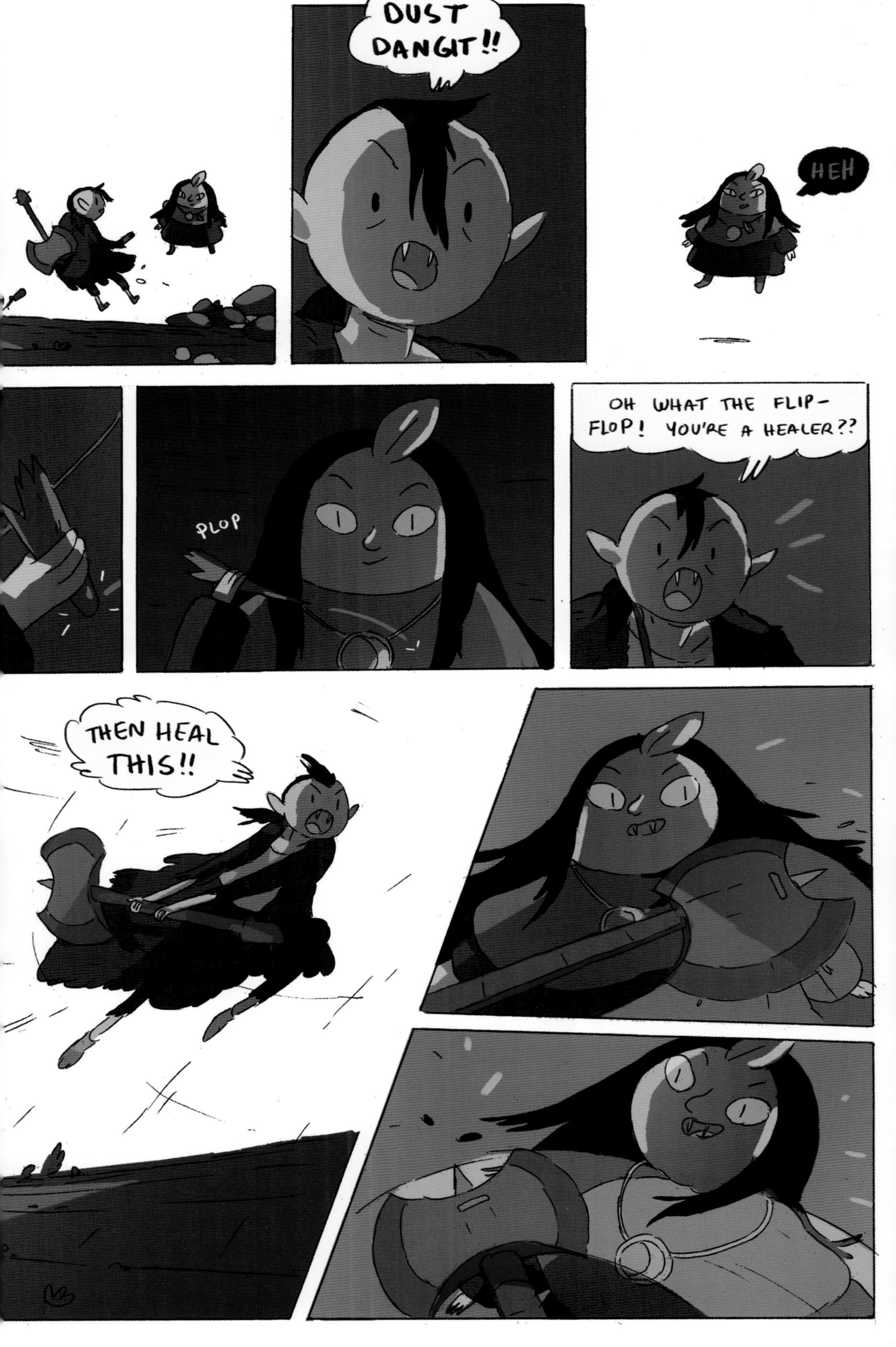

DUST DANGIT!!
HEH
PLOP
OH WHAT THE FLIP-FLOP! YOU'RE A HEALER??
THEN HEAL THIS!!

YOU WERE RIGHT KID..

OH, COME ON!!

..I FIGHT LIKE A DUMB JERK

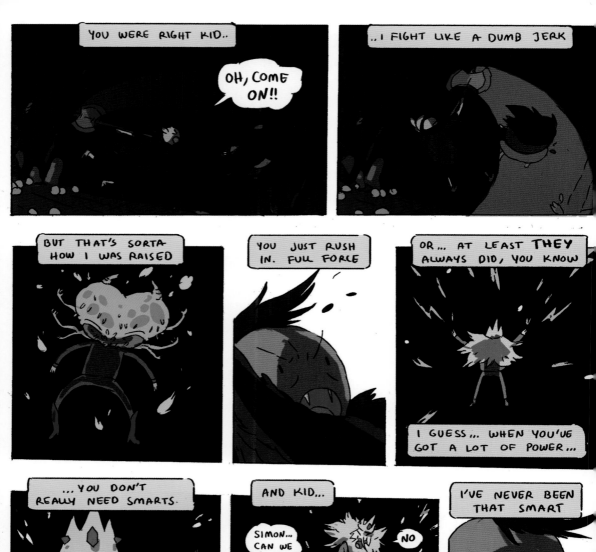

BUT THAT'S SORTA HOW I WAS RAISED

YOU JUST RUSH IN. FULL FORCE

OR... AT LEAST THEY ALWAYS DID, YOU KNOW

I GUESS... WHEN YOU'VE GOT A LOT OF POWER...

...YOU DON'T REALLY NEED SMARTS.

GUNTER! NO!

AND KID...

SIMON... CAN WE GO?

NO

I'VE NEVER BEEN THAT SMART

-SO I RUSH IN

...BUT I GUESS I'M TOO WEAK...

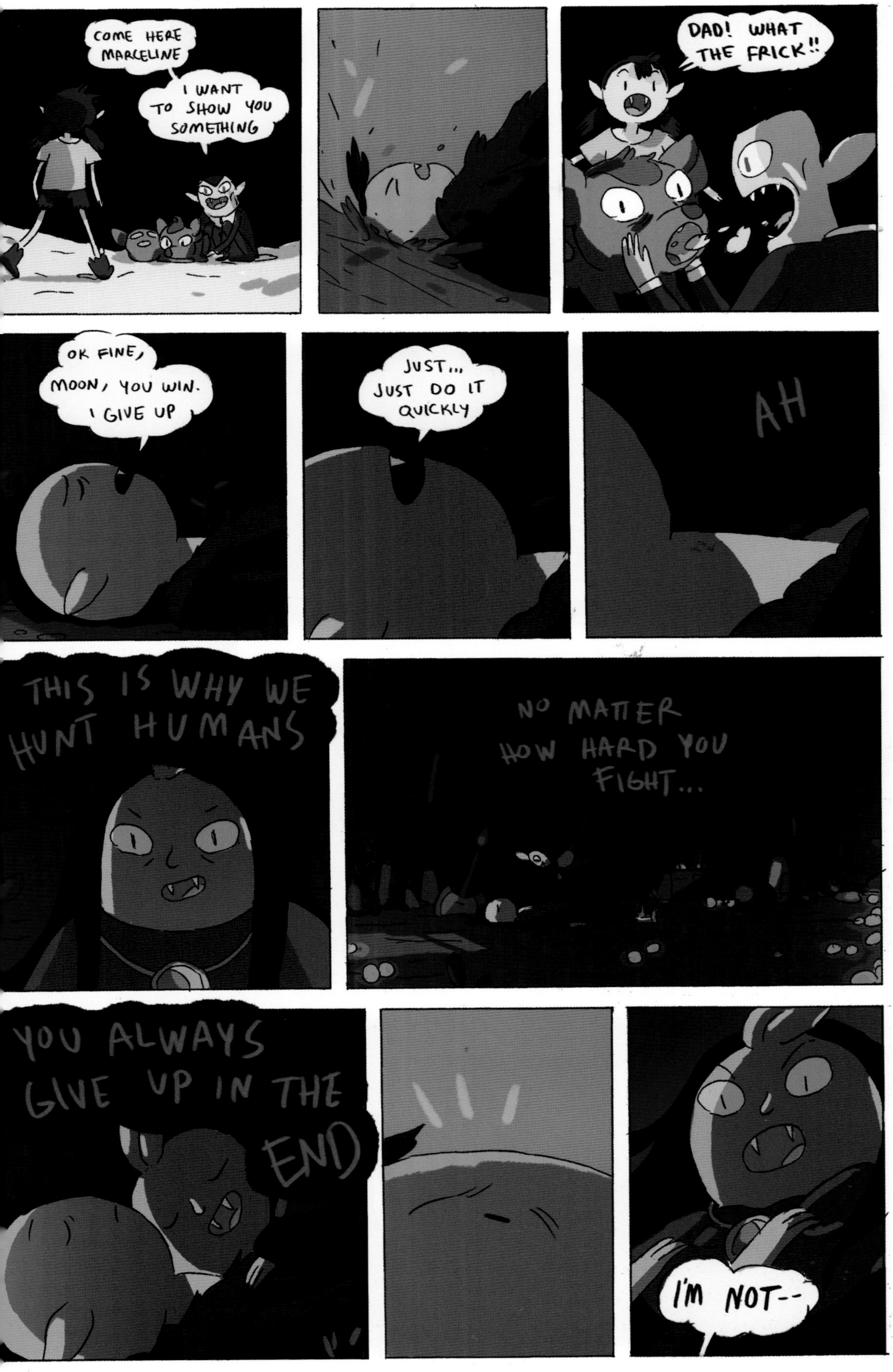
COME HERE MARCELINE
I WANT TO SHOW YOU SOMETHING
DAD! WHAT THE FRICK!!
OK FINE, MOON, YOU WIN. I GIVE UP
JUST... JUST DO IT QUICKLY
AH
THIS IS WHY WE HUNT HUMANS
NO MATTER HOW HARD YOU FIGHT...
YOU ALWAYS GIVE UP IN THE END
I'M NOT--

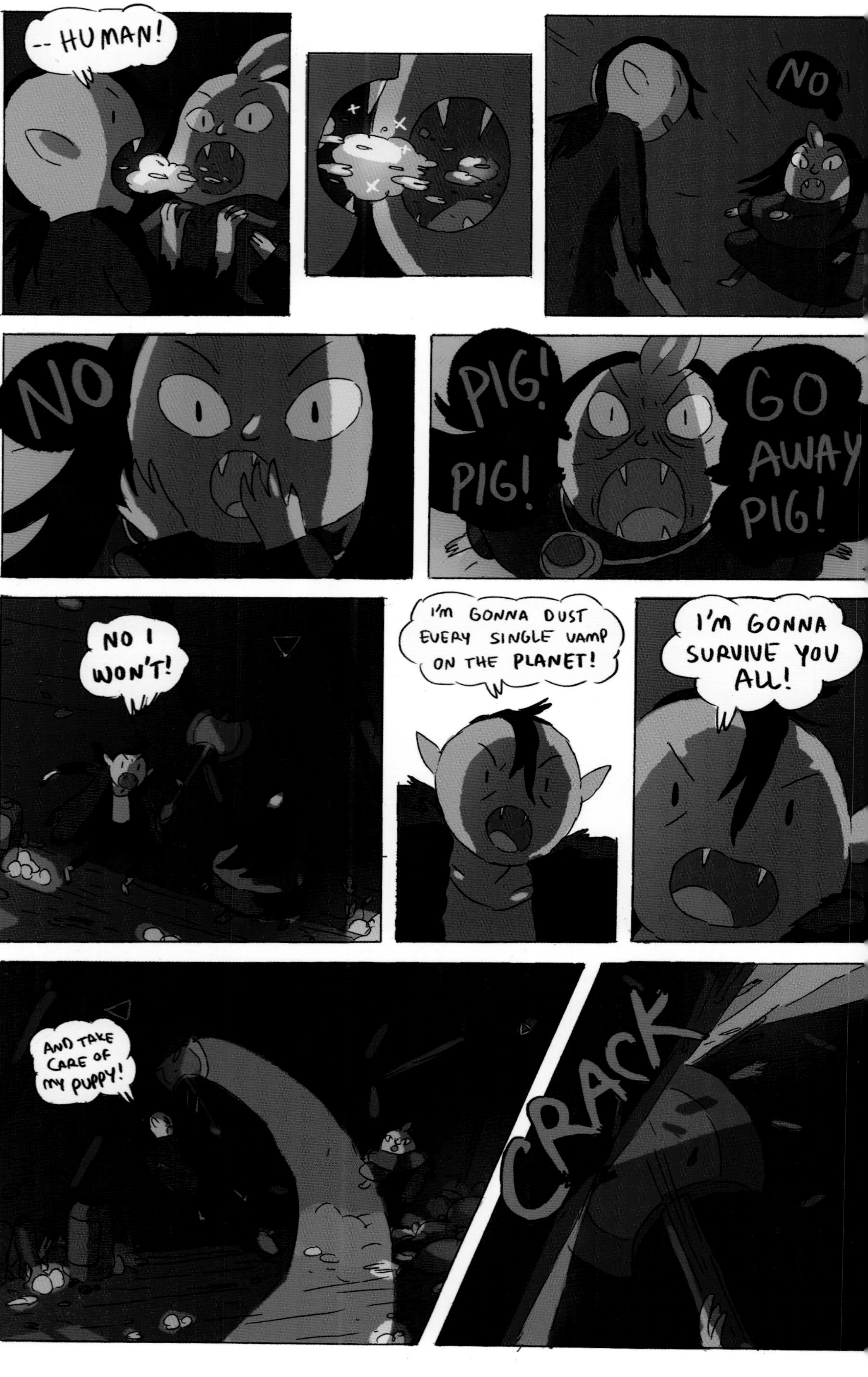
-- HUMAN!
NO
NO
PIG!
PIG!
GO AWAY PIG!
NO I WON'T!
I'M GONNA DUST EVERY SINGLE VAMP ON THE PLANET!
I'M GONNA SURVIVE YOU ALL!
AND TAKE CARE OF MY PUPPY!
CRACK

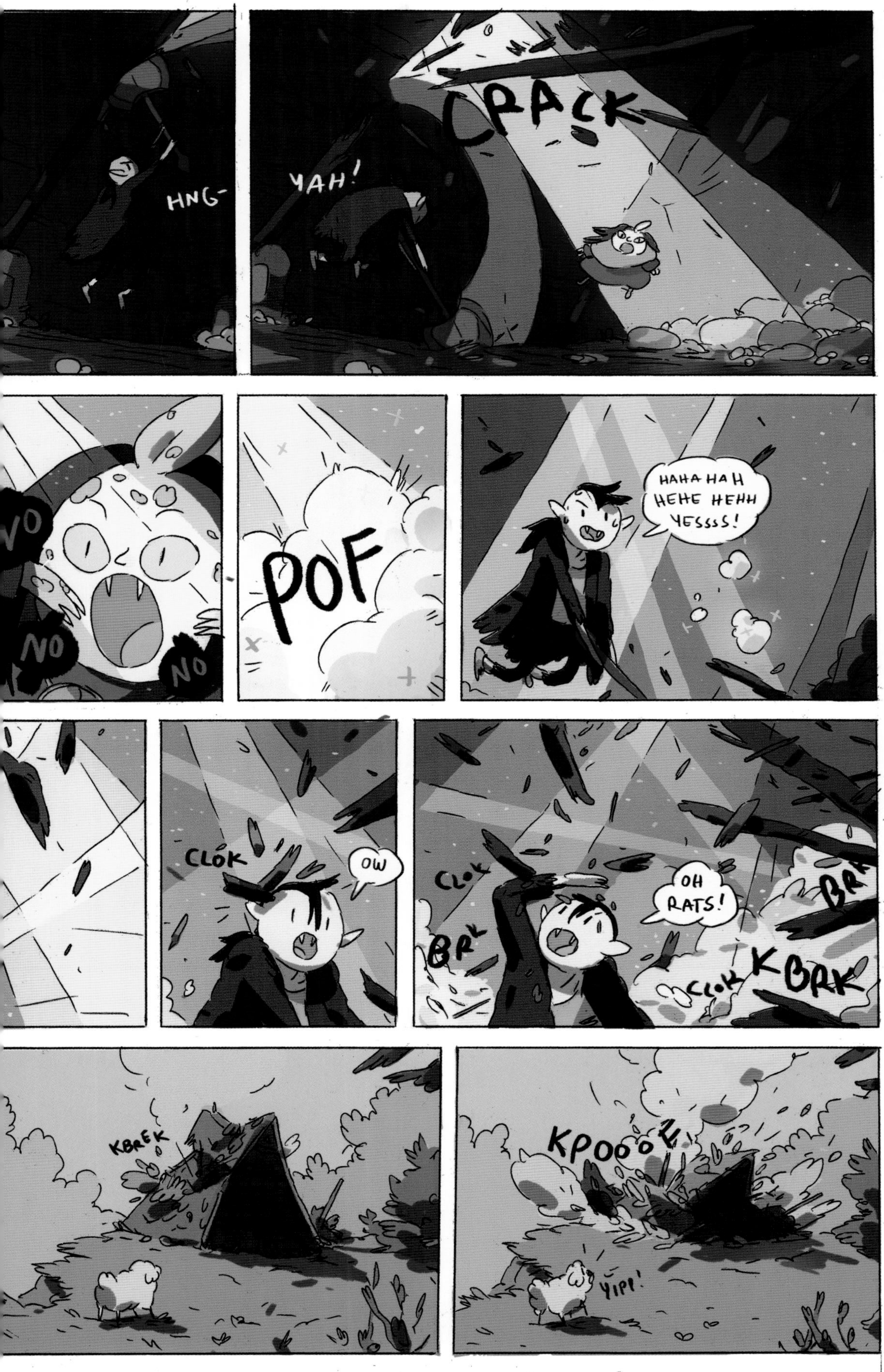

HNG-
YAH!
CRACK
NO
NO
NO
POF
HAHA HAH HEHE HEHH YESSSS!
CLOK
OW
CLOK
BRK
OH RATS!
BR
CLOK
KBRK
KBREK
KPOOOOE!
YIPI!

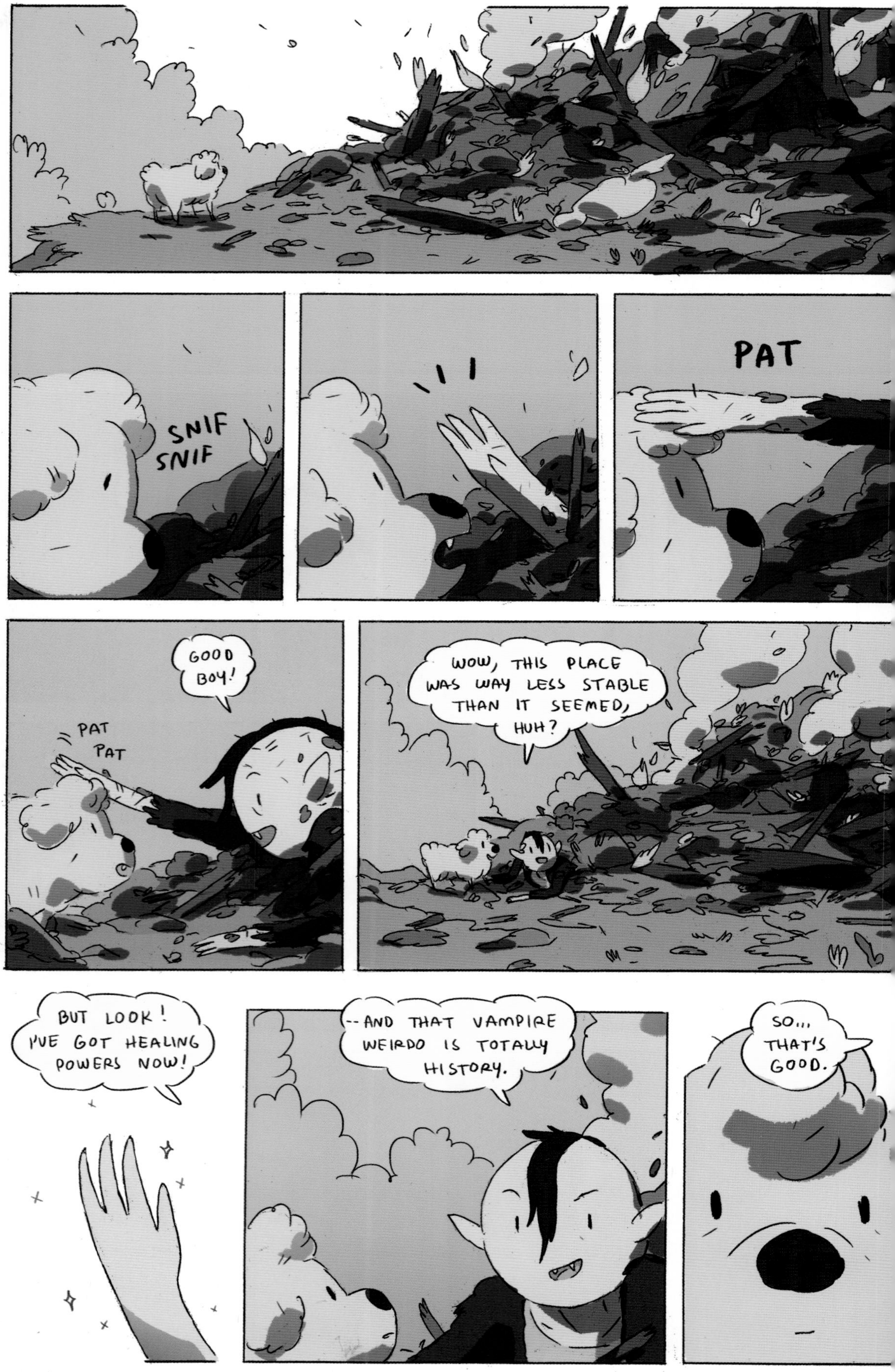
SNIF
SNIF
PAT
GOOD BOY!
PAT
PAT
WOW, THIS PLACE WAS WAY LESS STABLE THAN IT SEEMED, HUH?
BUT LOOK! I'VE GOT HEALING POWERS NOW!
--AND THAT VAMPIRE WEIRDO IS TOTALLY HISTORY.
SO... THAT'S GOOD.

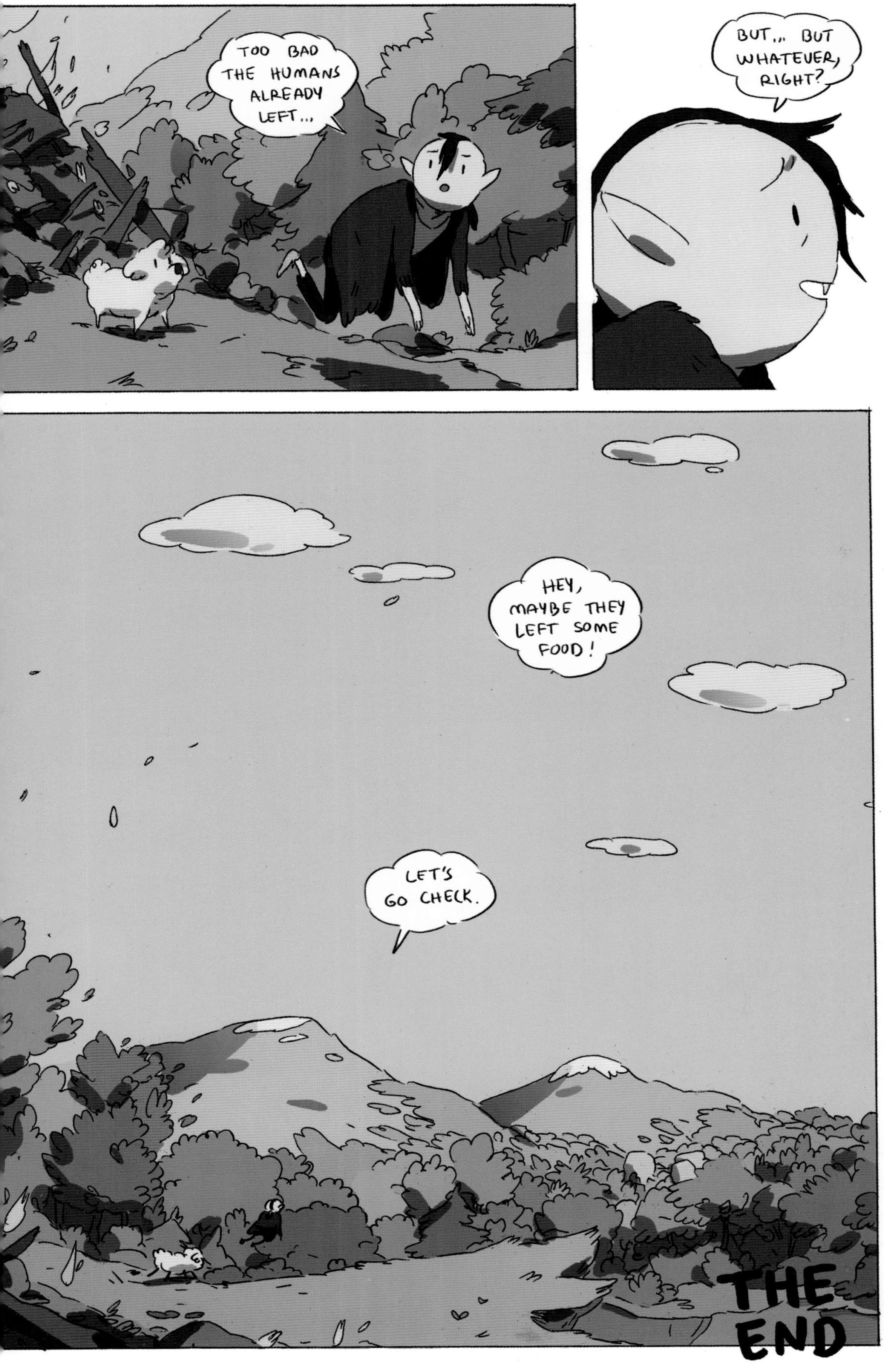
TOO BAD THE HUMANS ALREADY LEFT...
BUT... BUT WHATEVER, RIGHT?
HEY, MAYBE THEY LEFT SOME FOOD!
LET'S GO CHECK.
THE END

BMO AND FLAN

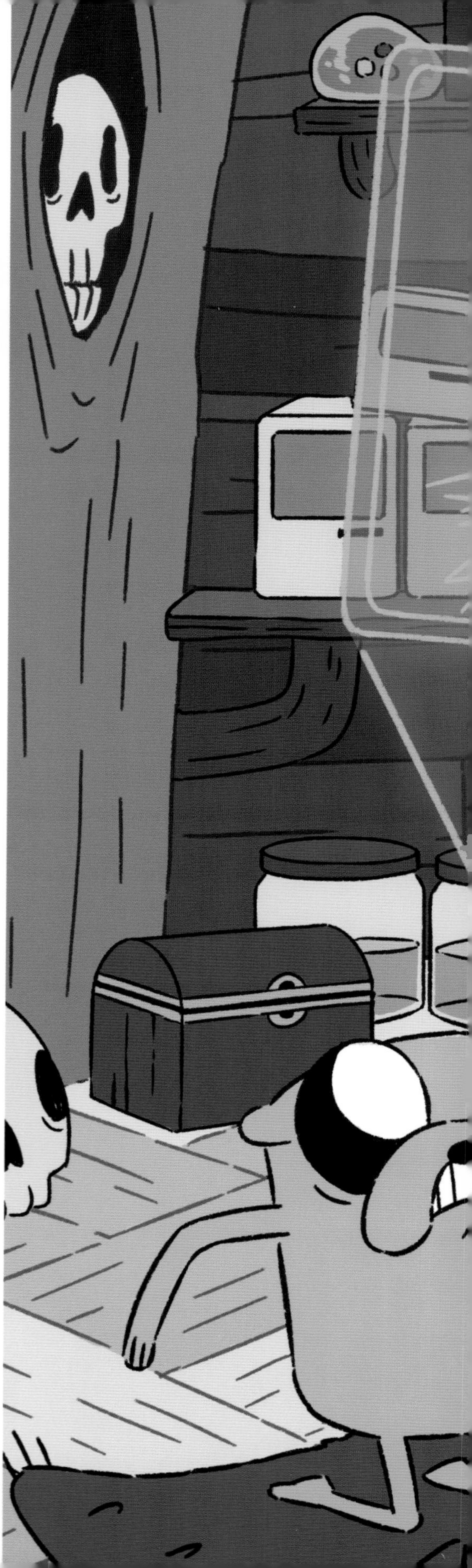

ADVENTURE TIME: GRAYBLES SCHMAYBLES COVER
STEPHANIE GONZAGA

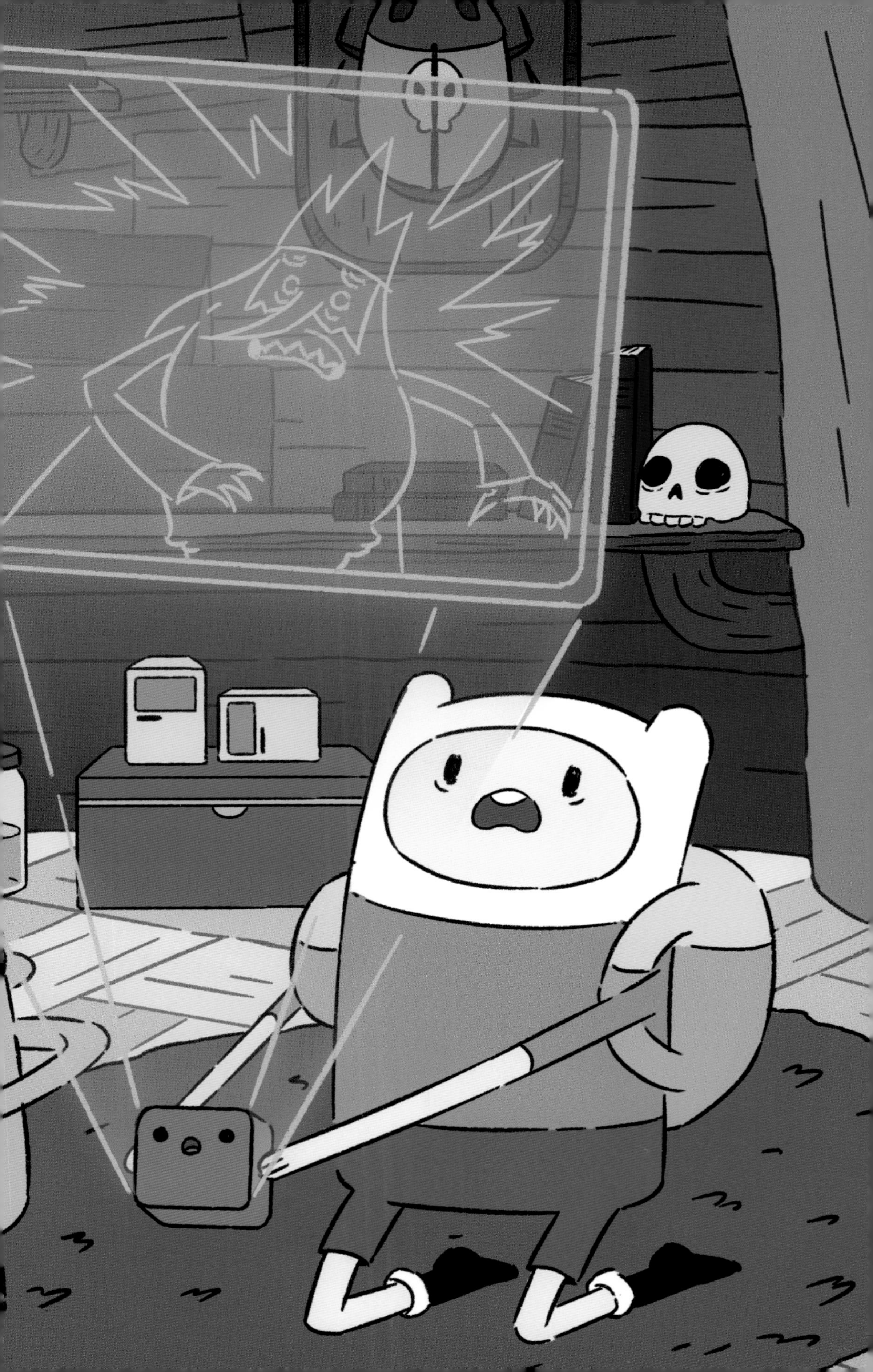

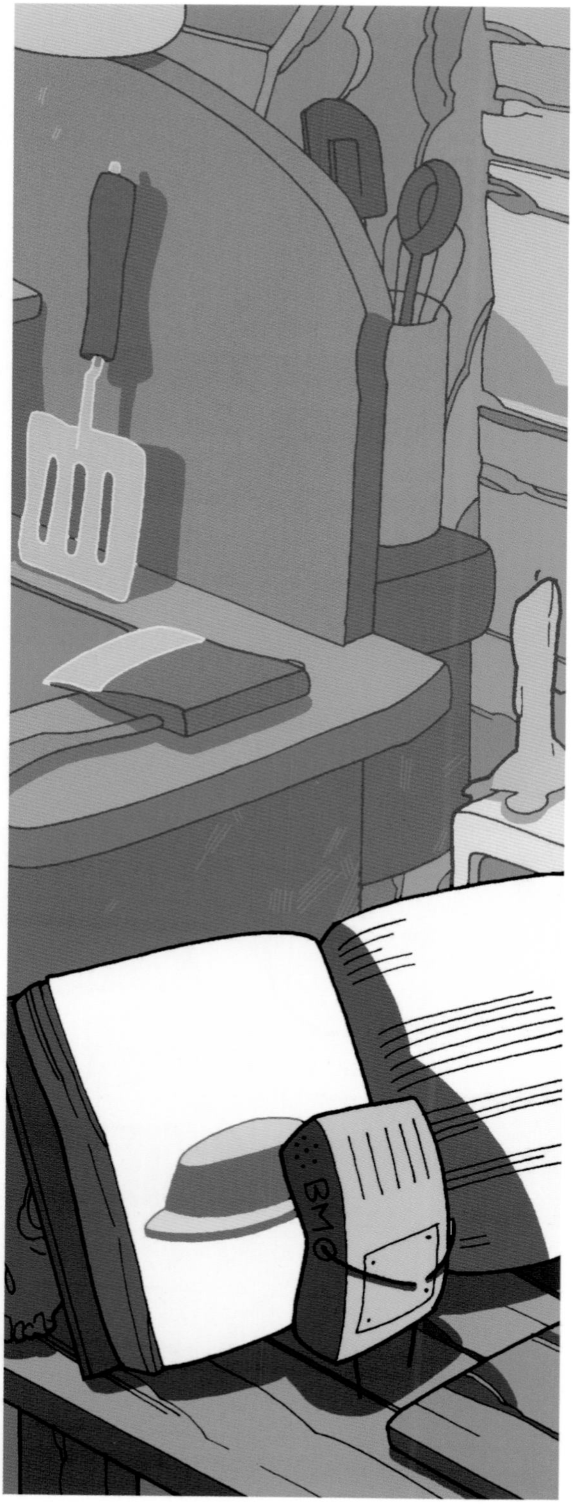
BMO

FLAN

MEREDITH MCCLAREN

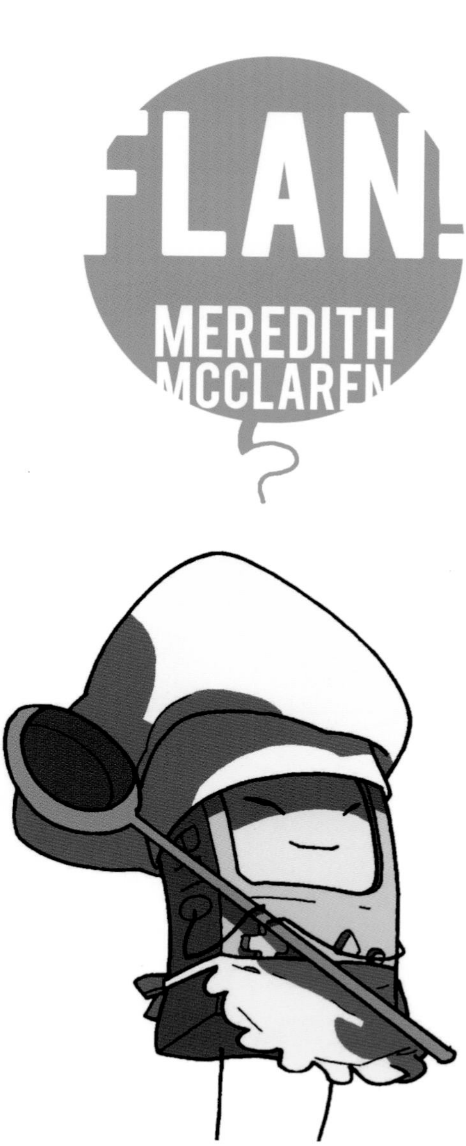

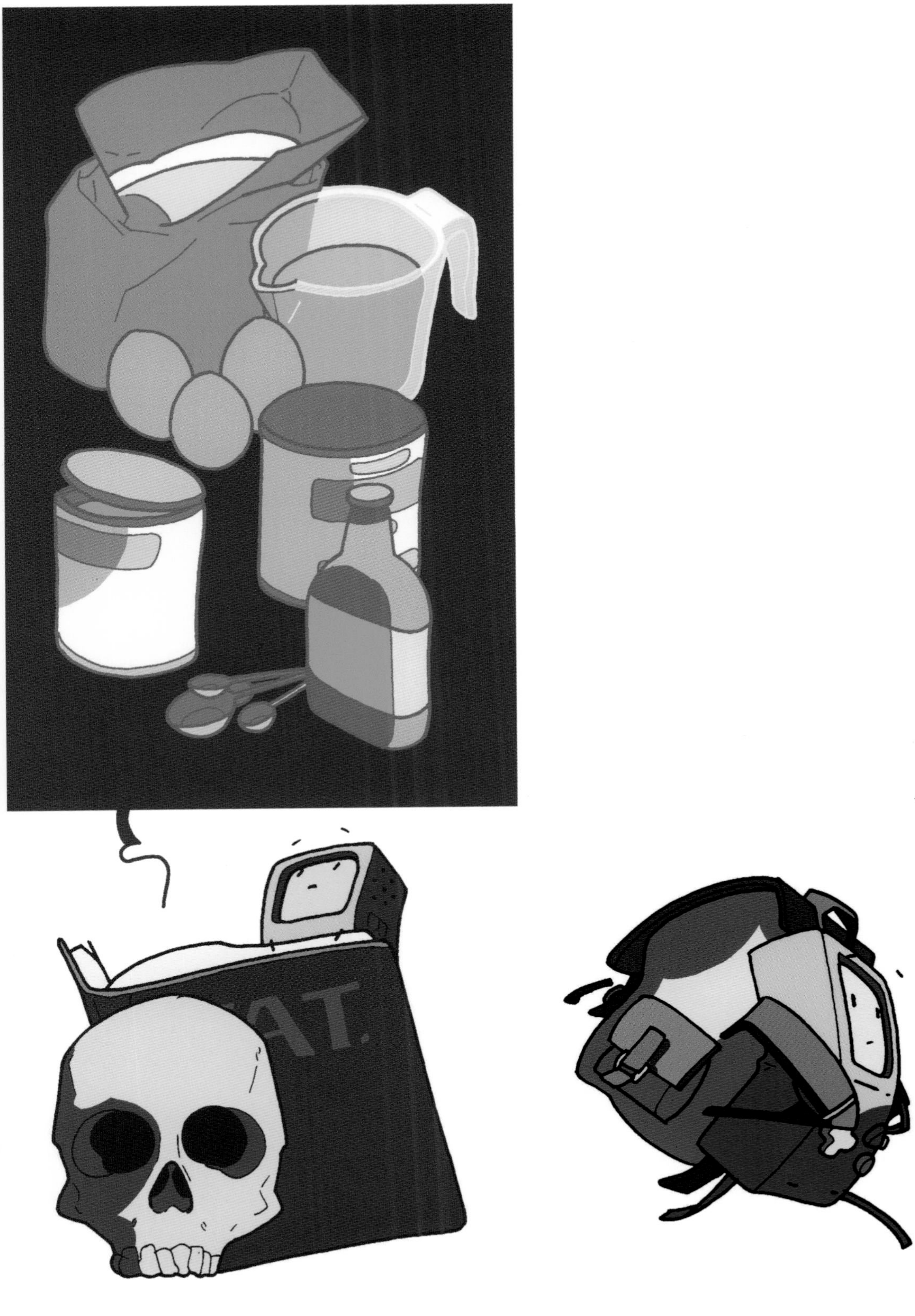

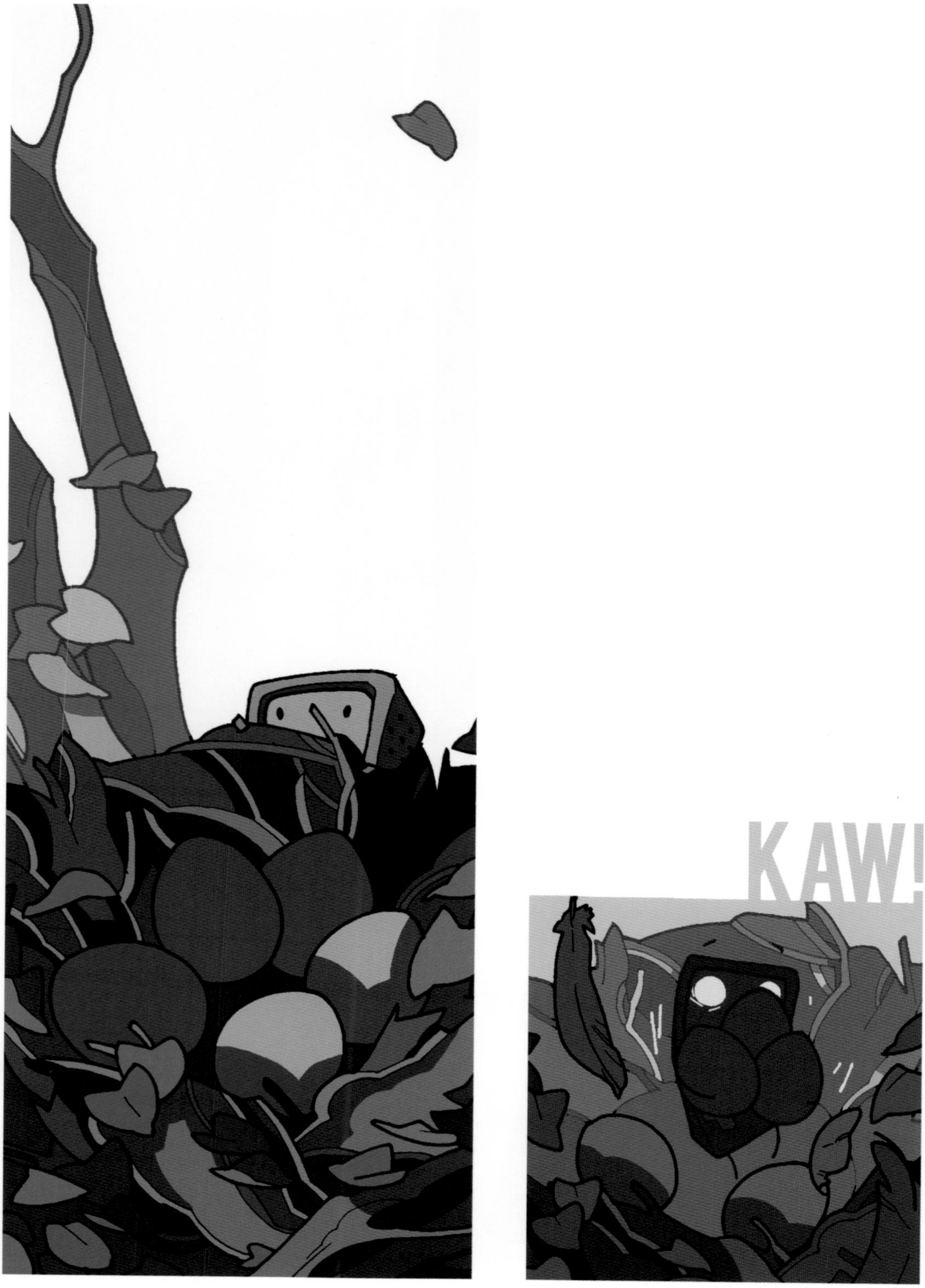
KAW!

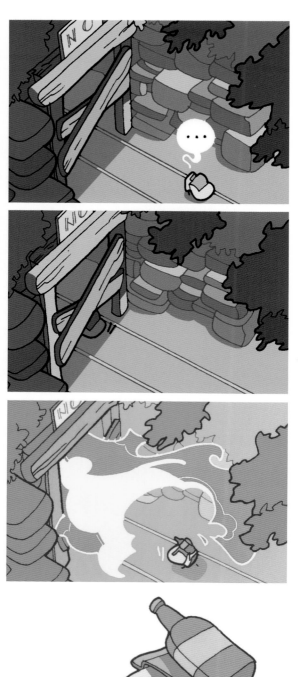

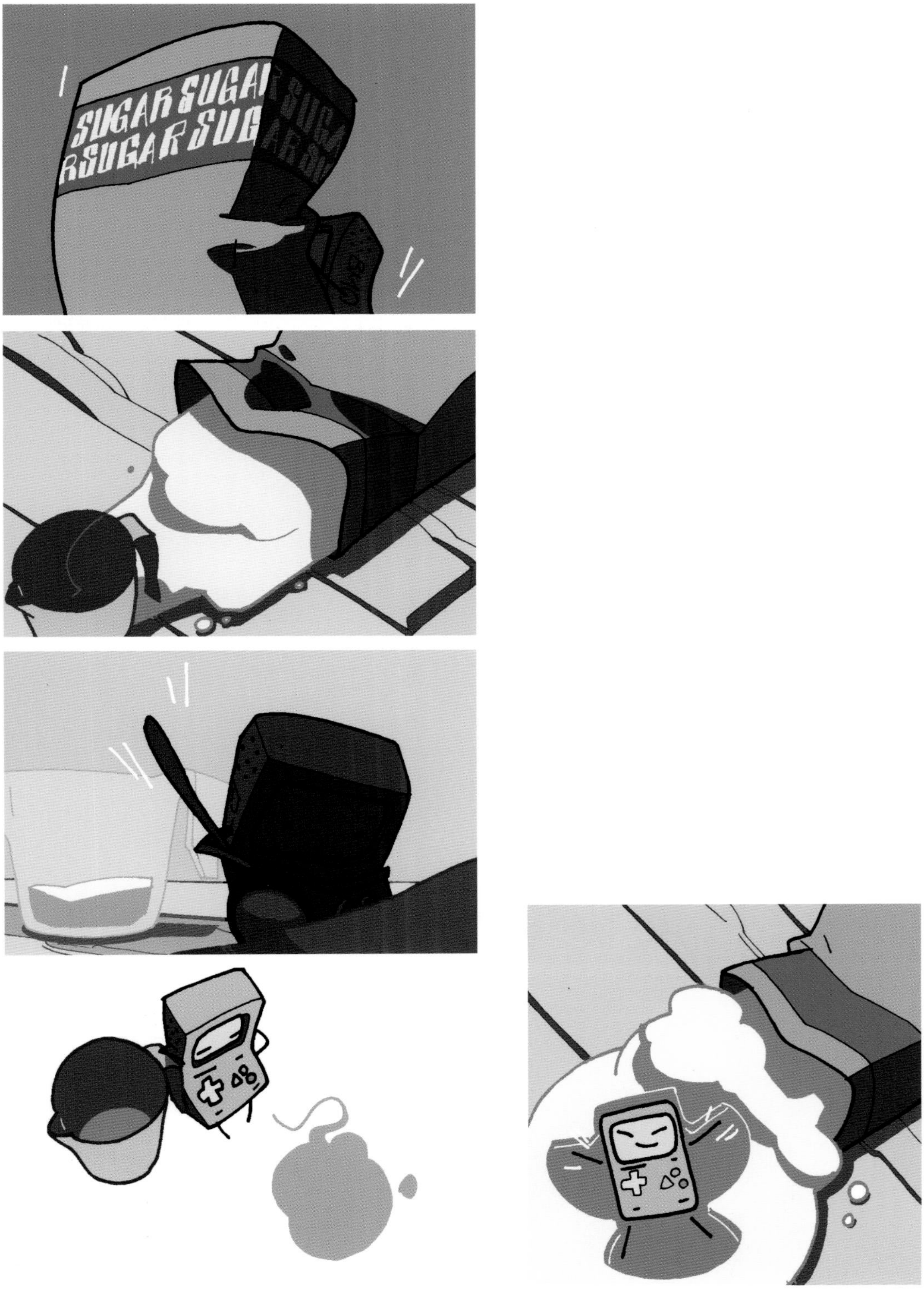
SUGAR SUGA
RSUGAR SUG

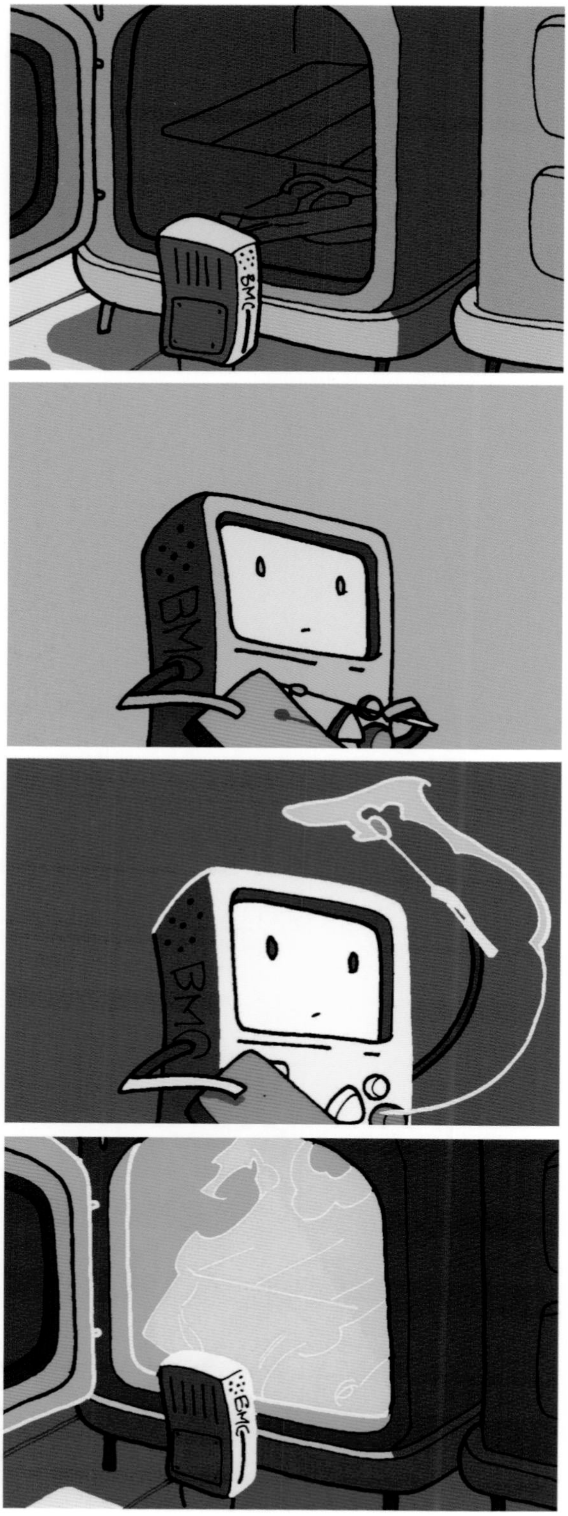
BMC
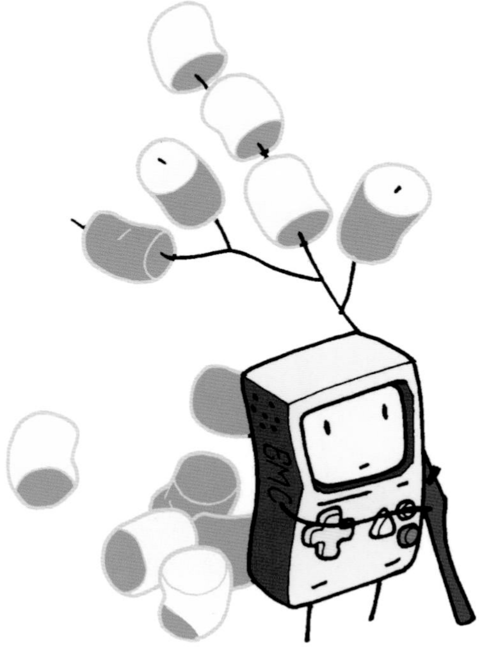
BMC

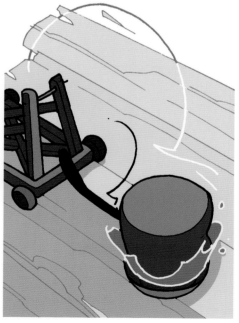

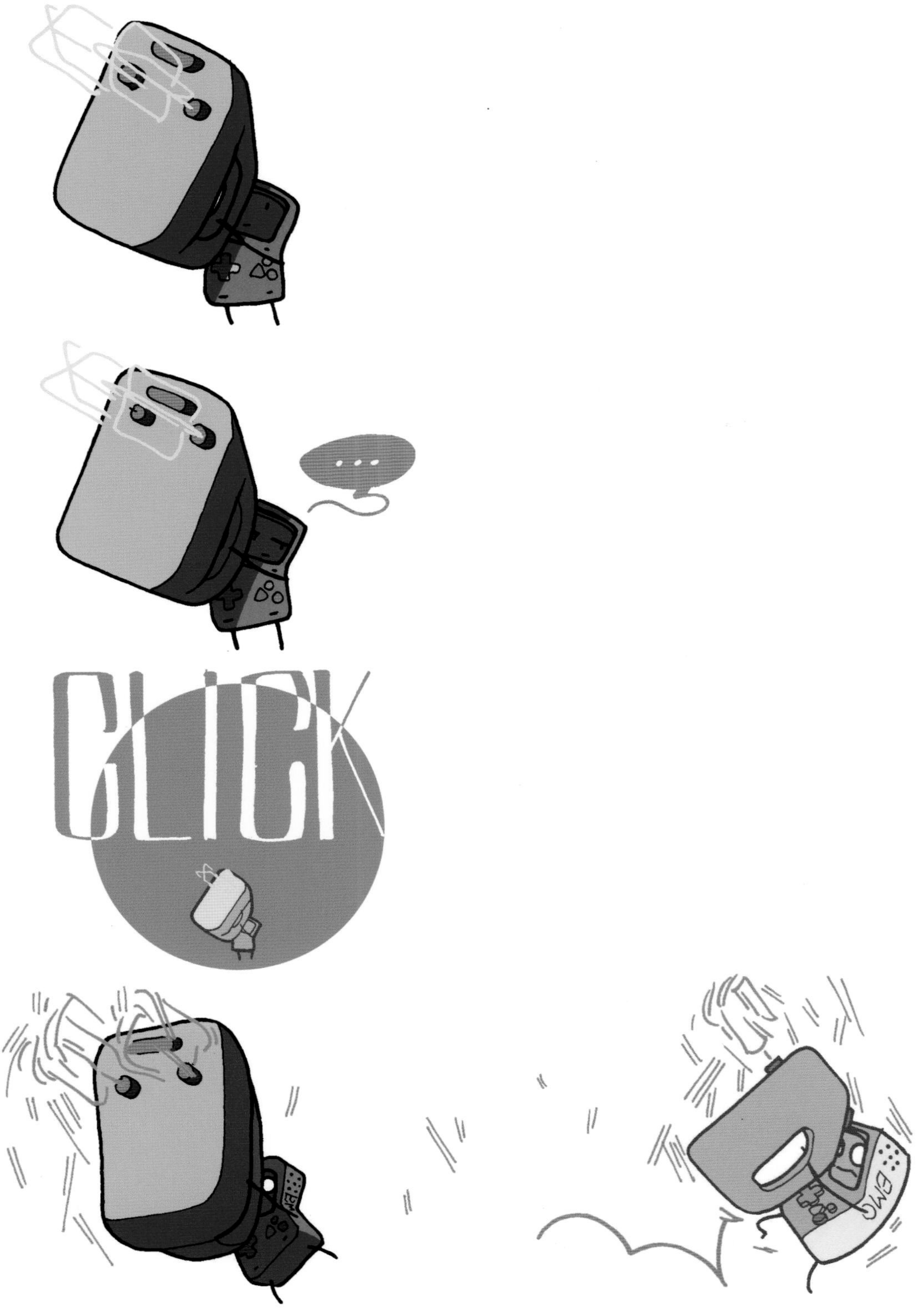
...
CLICK

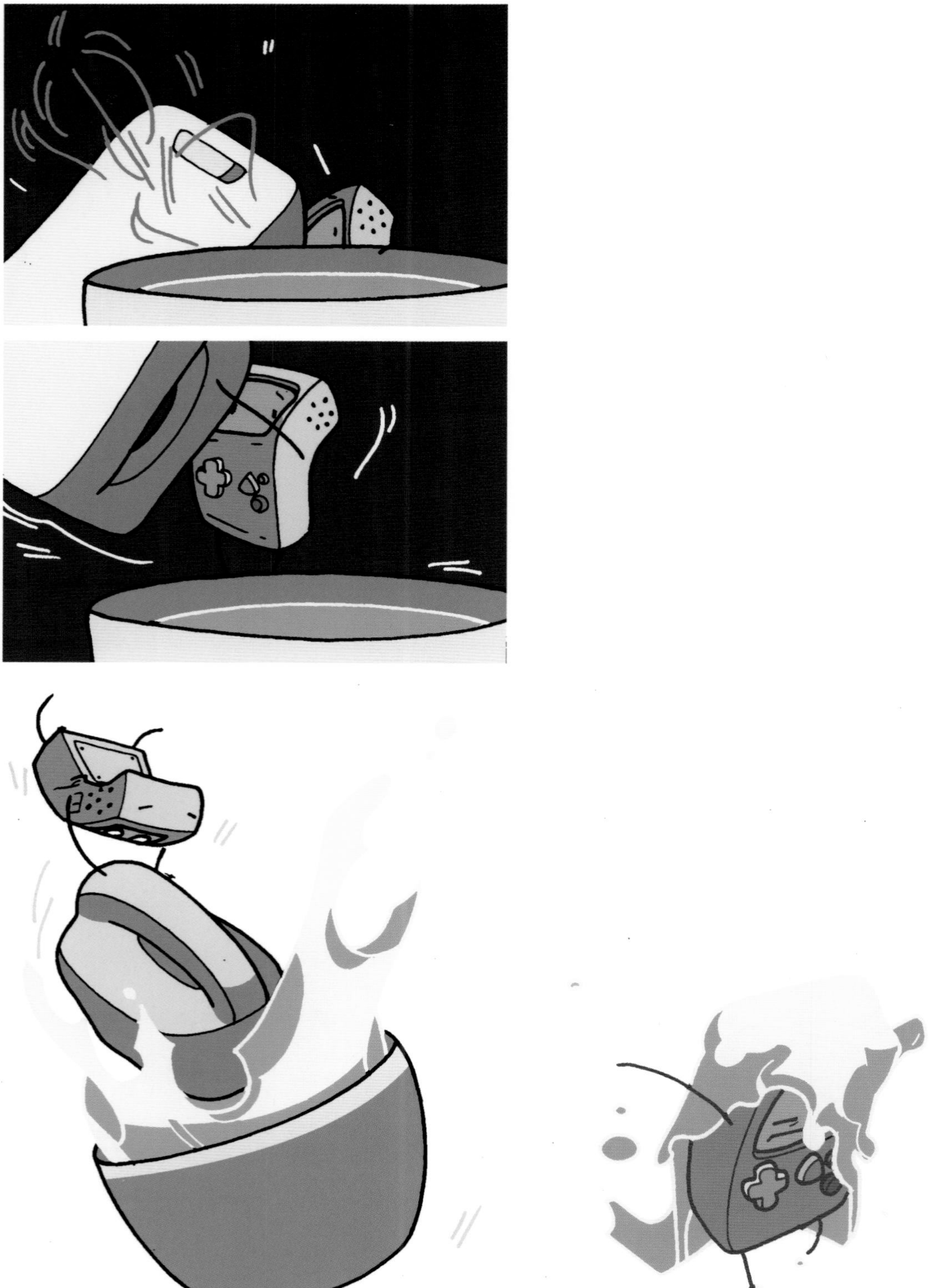

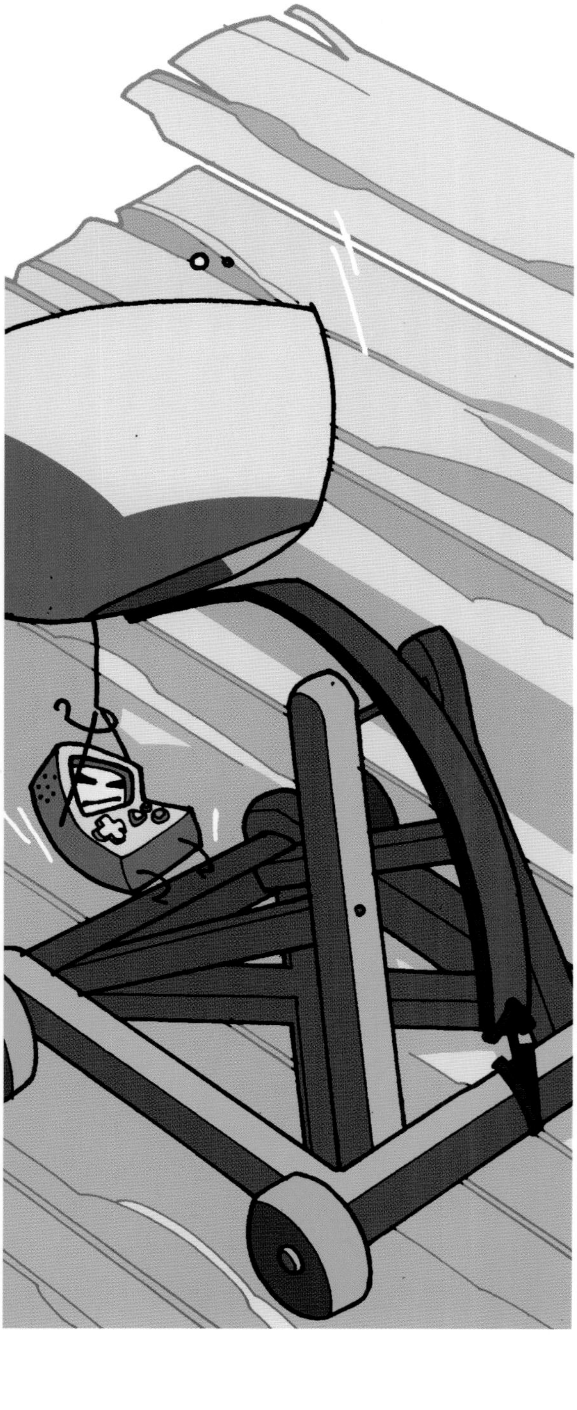
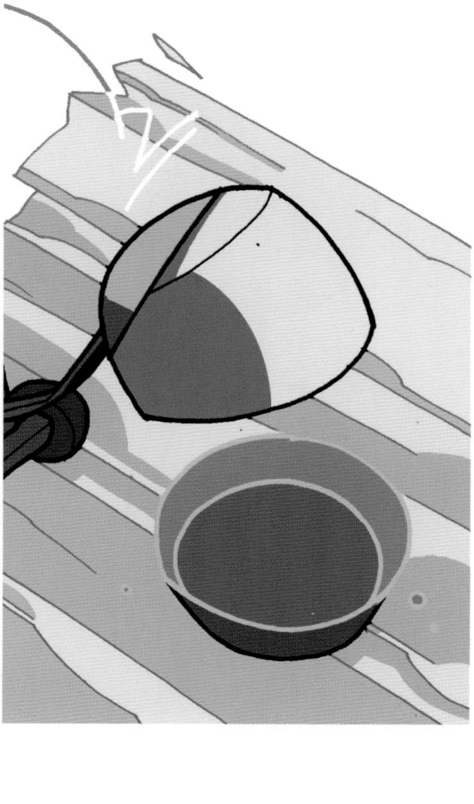

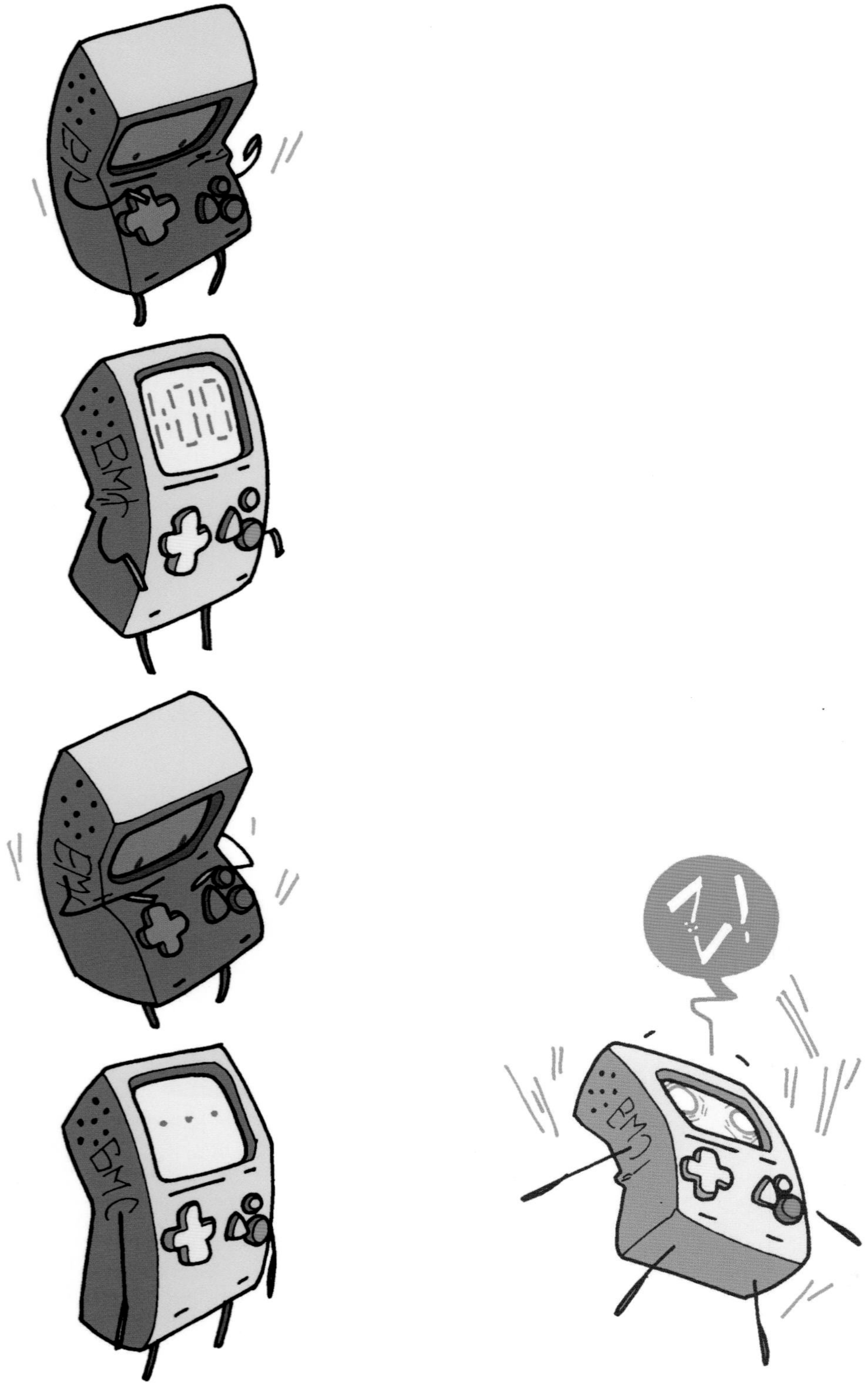
BMC

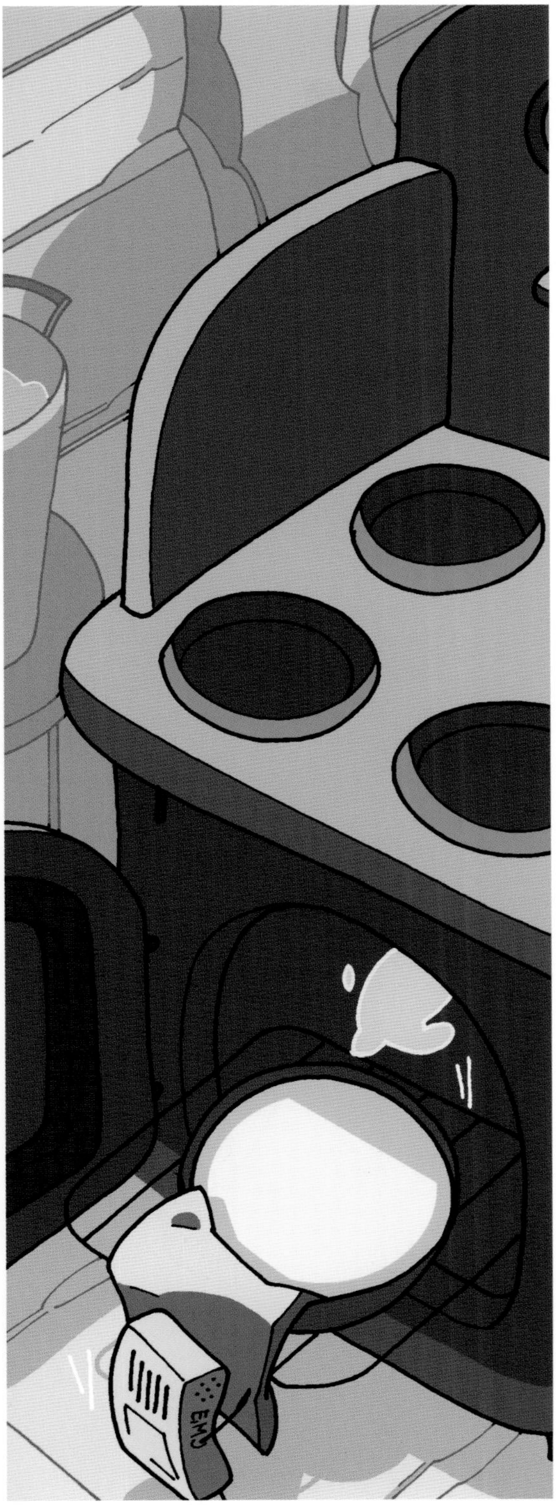
EMO

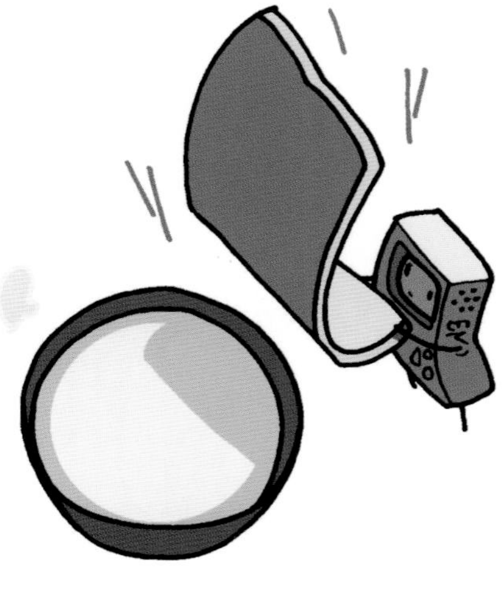
EMO

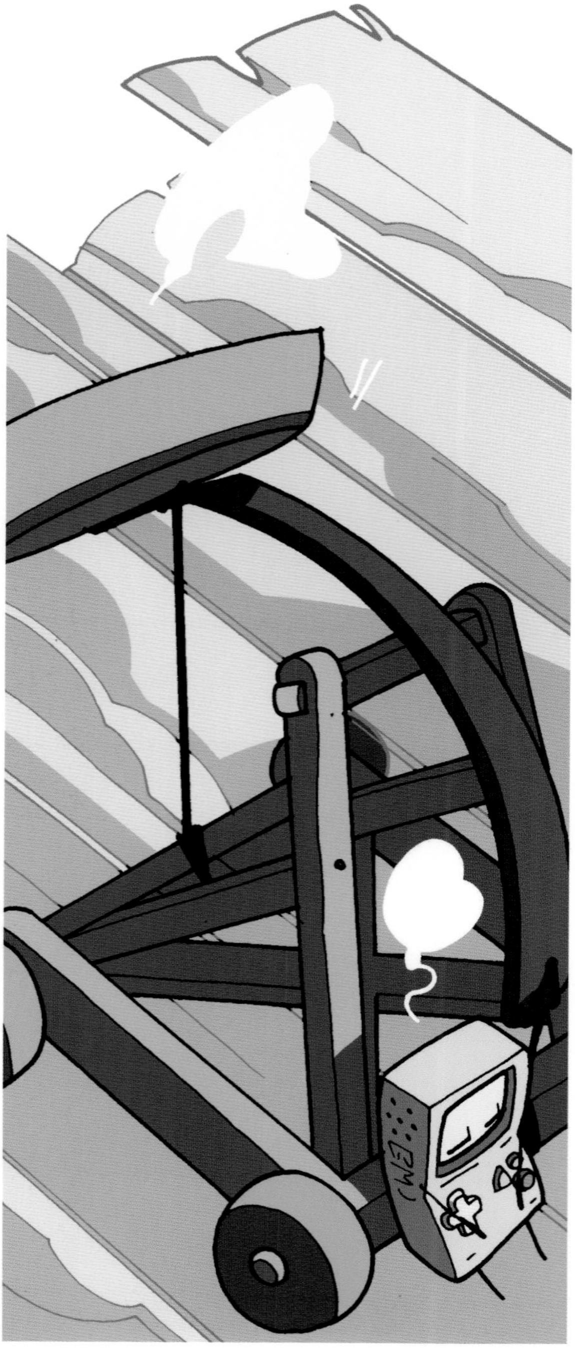

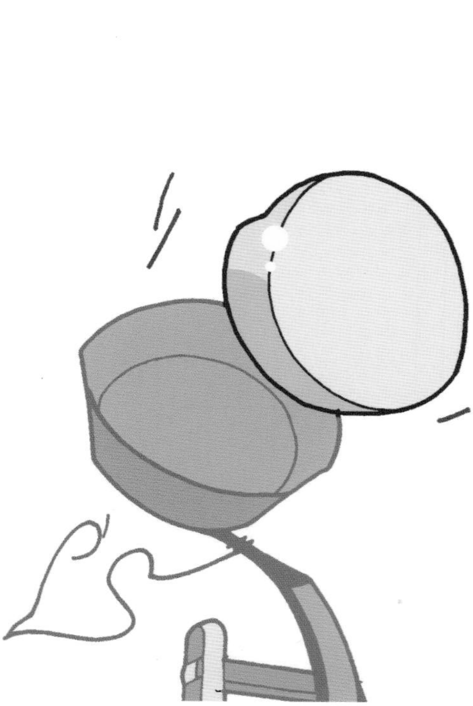

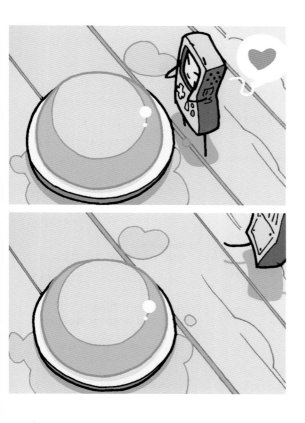

END.

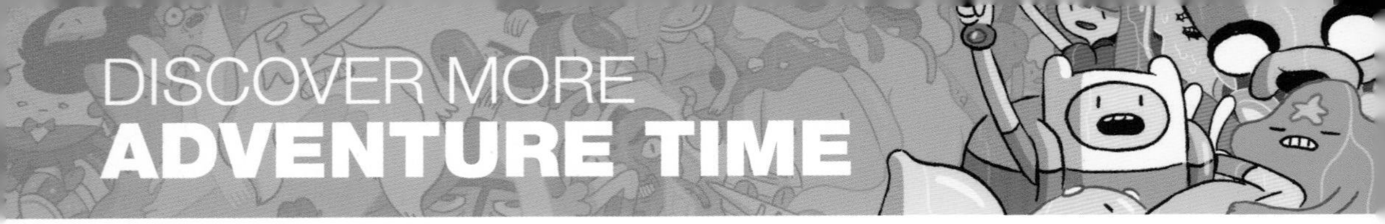
DISCOVER MORE
ADVENTURE TIME

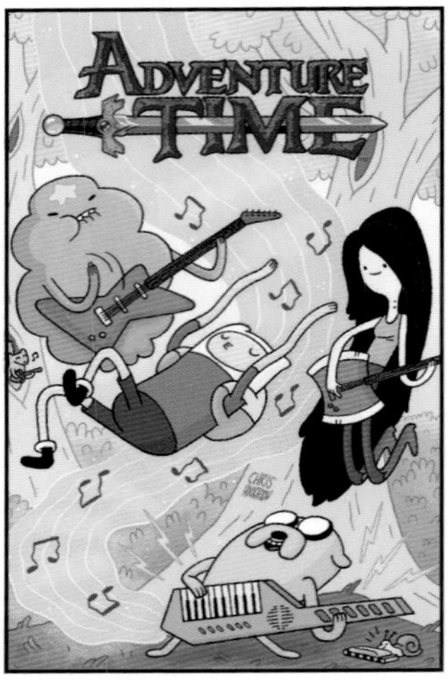
ADVENTURE TIME

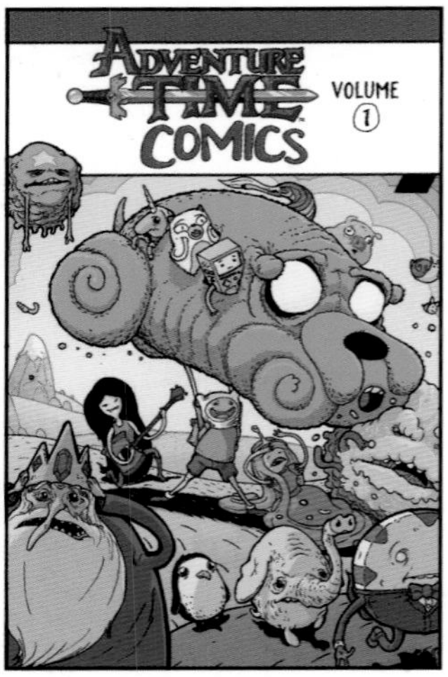
ADVENTURE TIME
COMICS
VOLUME 1

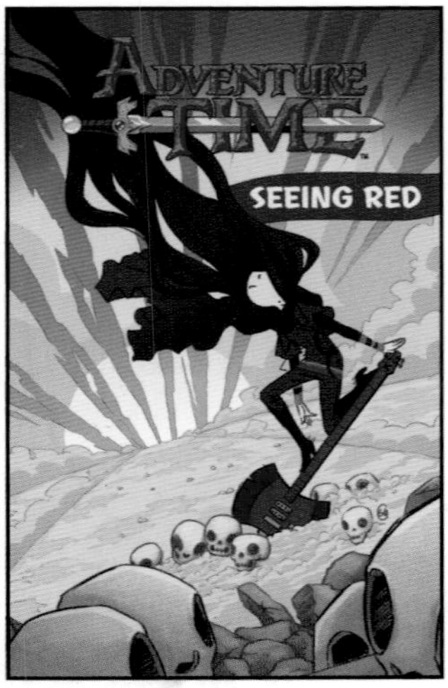
ADVENTURE TIME
SEEING RED

Adventure Time

Volume 1
ISBN: 978-1-60886-280-1 | $14.99 US

Volume 2
ISBN: 978-1-60886-323-5 | $14.99 US

Volume 3
ISBN: 978-1-60886-317-4 | $14.99

Volume 4
ISBN: 978-1-60886-351-8 | $14.99

Volume 5
ISBN: 978-1-60886-401-0 | $14.99

Volume 6
ISBN: 978-1-60886-482-9 | $14.99

Volume 7
ISBN: 978-1-60886-746-2 | $14.99

Volume 8
ISBN: 978-1-60886-795-0 | $14.99

Volume 9
ISBN: 978-1-60886-843-8 | $14.99

Volume 10
ISBN: 978-1-60886-909-1 | $14.99

Volume 11
ISBN: 978-1-60886-946-6 | $14.99

Volume 12
ISBN: 978-1-68415-005-2 | $14.99

Volume 13
ISBN: 978-1-68415-051-9 | $14.99

Volume 14
ISBN: 978-1-68415-144-8 | $14.99

Volume 15
ISBN: 978-1-68415-203-2 | $14.99

Volume 16
ISBN: 978-1-68415-272-8 | $14.99

Adventure Time Comics

Volume 1
ISBN: 978-1-60886-934-3 | $14.99

Volume 2
ISBN: 978-1-60886-984-8 | $14.99

Volume 3
ISBN: 978-1-68415-041-0 | $14.99

Volume 4
ISBN: 978-1-68415-133-2 | $14.99

Volume 5
ISBN: 978-1-68415-190-5 | $14.99

Volume 6
ISBN: 978-1-68415-258-2 | $14.99

Adventure Time Original Graphic Novels

Volume 1 Playing With Fire
ISBN: 978-1-60886-832-2 | $14.99

Volume 2 Pixel Princesses
ISBN: 978-1-60886-329-7 | $11.99

Volume 3 Seeing Red
ISBN: 978-1-60886-356-3 | $11.99

Volume 4 Bitter Sweets
ISBN: 978-1-60886-430-0 | $12.99

Volume 5 Graybles Schmaybles
ISBN: 978-1-60886-484-3 | $12.99

Volume 6 Masked Mayhem
ISBN: 978-160886-764-6 | $14.99

Volume 7 The Four Castles
ISBN: 978-160886-797-4 | $14.99

Volume 8 President Bubblegum
ISBN: 978-1-60886-846-9 | $14.99

Volume 9 The Brain Robbers
ISBN: 978-1-60886-875-9 | $14.99

Volume 10 The Orient Express
ISBN: 978-1-60886-995-4 | $14.99

Volume 11 Princess & Princess
ISBN: 978-1-68415-025-0 | $14.99

Volume 12 Thunder Road
ISBN: 978-1-68415-179-0 | $14.99

kaboom!™
A BOOM! Studios Imprint

AVAILABLE AT YOUR LOCAL COMICS SHOP AND BOOKSTORE

WWW.**BOOM-STUDIOS**.COM

CARTOON NETWORK

DISCOVER MORE
ADVENTURE TIME

Adventure Time: Islands OGN
ISBN: 978-1-60886-972-5 | $9.99

ADVENTURE TIME
ISLANDS

Adventure Time Sugary Shorts

ADVENTURE TIME
SUGARY SHORTS

Volume 1
ISBN: 978-1-60886-361-7 | $19.99

Volume 2
ISBN: 978-1-60886-774-5 | $19.99

Volume 3
ISBN: 978-1-68415-030-4 | $19.99

Volume 4
ISBN: 978-1-68415-122-6 | $19.99

Adventure Time: Marceline & the Scream Queens
ISBN: 978-1-60886-313-6 | $19.99

ADVENTURE TIME
PRESENTS
MARCELINE
AND THE SCREAM QUEENS

Adventure Time: Fionna & Cake
ISBN: 978-1-60886-338-9 | $19.99

ADVENTURE TIME
with FIONNA & CAKE

Adventure Time: Candy Capers
ISBN: 978-1-60886-365-5 | $19.99

Adventure Time: The Flip Side
ISBN: 978-1-60886-456-0 | $19.99

Adventure Time: Banana Guard Academy
ISBN: 978-1-60886-486-7 | $19.99

Adventure Time: Marceline Gone Adrift
ISBN: 978-1-60886-770-7 | $19.99

Adventure Time: Fionna & Cake Card Wars
ISBN: 978-1-60886-799-8 | $19.99

Adventure Time: Ice King
ISBN: 978-1-60886-920-6 | $19.99

ADVENTURE TIME
ICE KING

Adventure Time/Regular Show
ISBN: 978-1-68415-166-0 | $19.99

A CARTOON NETWORK ORIGINAL
ADVENTURE TIME
×
REGULAR SHOW

kaboom!™
A BOOM! Studios Imprint

AVAILABLE AT YOUR LOCAL COMICS SHOP AND BOOKSTORE

WWW.**BOOM-STUDIOS**.COM

CARTOON NETWORK.

OVER
LOSIVE NEW WORLDS

ADVENTURE TIME

Sam Sykes · Selina Espiritu · Sarah Stern
Brave Chef Brianna

KELLY THOMPSON BRIANNE DROUHARD M. VICTORIA ROBADO
MEGA PRINCESS

THE NOT-SO SECRET SOCIETY
DALEY · CRAFTS · CLARK · BRUNI

OVER THE GARDEN WALL

STEVEN UNIVERSE
VOLUME ONE

Adventure Time
Pendleton Ward and Others
Volume 1
ISBN: 978-1-60886-280-1 | $14.99 US
Volume 2
ISBN: 978-1-60886-323-5 | $14.99 US
Adventure Time: Islands
ISBN: 978-1-60886-972-5 | $9.99 US

The Amazing World of Gumball
Ben Bocquelet and Others
Volume 1
ISBN: 978-1-60886-488-1 | $14.99 US
Volume 2
ISBN: 978-1-60886-793-6 | $14.99 US

Brave Chef Brianna
Sam Sykes, Selina Espiritu
ISBN: 978-1-68415-050-2 | $14.99 US

Mega Princess
Kelly Thompson, Brianne Drouhard
ISBN: 978-1-68415-007-6 | $14.99 US

The Not-So Secret Society
Matthew Daley, Arlene Daley, Wook Jin Clark
ISBN: 978-1-60886-997-8 | $9.99 US

Over the Garden Wall
Patrick McHale, Jim Campbell and Others
Volume 1
ISBN: 978-1-60886-940-4 | $14.99 US
Volume 2
ISBN: 978-1-68415-006-9 | $14.99 US

Steven Universe
Rebecca Sugar and Others
Volume 1
ISBN: 978-1-60886-706-6 | $14.99 US
Volume 2
ISBN: 978-1-60886-796-7 | $14.99 US

Steven Universe & The Crystal Gems
ISBN: 978-1-60886-921-3 | $14.99 US

Steven Universe: Too Cool for School
ISBN: 978-1-60886-771-4 | $14.99 US

kaboom!™

AVAILABLE AT YOUR LOCAL COMICS SHOP AND BOOKSTORE
WWW.**BOOM-STUDIOS**.COM